The Author

ERNEST BUCKLER was born in Dalhousie West, Nova Scotia, in 1908. He took his B.A. (1929) in Mathematics from Dalhousie University and his M.A. (1930) in Philosophy from the University of Toronto. For five years he worked as an actuarial mathematician in Toronto. Ill health prompted him to return in 1936 to the family farm in the Annapolis Valley. There he embarked on a farming life and began his writing career.

In his first novel, *The Mountain and the Valley*, as in many of his short stories and essays, Buckler reveals an astonishing sensitivity to the rural landscape and the inhabitants of his native Annapolis Valley. He also wrote many book reviews, magazine articles, newspaper columns, and radio plays.

Among Buckler's many honours were the Canadian Centennial Medal "for valuable service to the nation," honorary degrees from Dalhousie University and the University of New Brunswick, and the Stephen Leacock Medal for Humour.

Ernest Buckler died in Bridgetown, Nova Scotia, in 1984.

ERNEST BUCKLER

The Mountain and
the Valley

With an Afterword by Robert Gibbs

Much alliteration and assonance.
Draws similarities in disparate ideas
through similar sounds.
→ Much like an epiphany finds
similarity amongst differences,
much like metaphors and
similes.

M&S

The following dedication appeared in the original edition:
To my family,
who did not model for this book,
but whose faith sustained it.

This book was first published by Clarke Irwin in 1952.

Library and Archives Canada Cataloguing in Publication

Buckler, Ernest, 1908–1984
The mountain and the valley

(New Canadian library)
Bibliography: p.
ISBN 0-7710-9952-5

I. Title. II. Series.

PS8503.U2M68 1989   c813'.54   c89-093678-1
PR9199.3.B82M68 1989

We acknowledge the financial support of the Government of
Canada through the Book Publishing Industry Development Program
for our publishing activities. We further acknowledge the support of the
Canada Council for the Arts and the Ontario Arts Council for our
publishing program.

Printed and bound in Canada

McClelland & Stewart Ltd.
The Canadian Publishers
481 University Avenue
Toronto, Ontario
M5G 2E9
www.mcclelland.com/NCL

7 8 9 10   07 06 05 04

Contents

PROLOGUE—THE RUG

CHAPTER I

DAVID CANAAN had lived in Entremont all his thirty years. As far back as childhood, whenever anger had dishevelled him, or confusion, or the tick, tick, tick, of emptiness like he felt today, he had sought the log road that went to the top of the mountain. As he moved along this road, somewhere the twist of anger would loosen; a shaft of clarity would strike through the scud of confusion; blood would creep back into the pulse and pallor of the emptiness. He would take happiness there, to be alone with it; as another child might keep hidden for a day a toy that wasn't his.

He stood at the kitchen window now, watching the highway.

The highway was irregularly noduled with whitewashed wooden houses. It cut through the Annapolis Valley; and on either side of it lay the flat frozen fields.

On the north side, the fields and orchards ran down to the big bend of the river, cut wide by the Fundy tides. Blocks of grimy, sun-eaten ice were piled up in Druidic formations on the river's banks, where the tides had tumbled them. The North Mountain rose sharply beyond the river. It was solid blue in the afternoon light of December that was pale and sharp as starlight, except for the milky ways of choppings where traces of the first snow never quite disappeared.

On the south side of the highway, beyond the barn and the pastures, the South Mountain rose. Solid blue too at the bottom where the dark spruces huddled close, but snow-grey higher up where the sudden steepness and the leafless hardwood began. At the peak the gaunt limbs of the maples could be seen like the bones of hands all along the lemon-coloured horizon.

The mountain slopes were less than a mile high at their topmost point but they shut the valley in completely.

The afternoon stillness simmered soundlessly in the kitchen. The soft flutter of flame in the stove, the heat-tick of the stove itself, and the gentle rocking of the tea kettle with its own steam, were quieter than silence. The mat hook which his grandmother held in her right hand made a steady staccato like the sounds of seconds dropping, as it punctured the meshes of the meal bag, to draw up loop after loop of the rag she held in her left hand beneath.

His head was physically heavy. An ache fountained somewhere above the scar that sickled, like a smile-scar, from the corner of his mouth to his left temple. It never rose to actual pain, but it seeped through his whole head like the penetration of a night fog that crept up from the marshes.

Occasionally he moved his head from side to side, as a deer does that tries to dislodge, by the flick of tongue to flank, the bullet wound that hurts and puzzles him. His breath came smoothly, but as if it beat back and forth between two weights; one blocking the limit of inhalation and one the limit of exhalation.

Rain had taken the first snow on the fields. Then the sudden cold had come. Islands of milk-ice speckled the brown fields where the withered aftergrass held the snow longest, and in the ploughed land gravel was frozen into the lips of the brown sod like stones in a setting. Sockets of rocks which the plough had dislodged were frozen smooth as moulds. Honeycombs of ice stood white in the valleys of adjacent rows. In the flat dead furrows the ice shone enamelled and colourless in the glance of the sun that slanted, without warmth, from the bruised lids of the sky. The twisted arms of the apple trees and the bushes along the line fence looked locked and separate, as if all their life had fled its own nakedness.

Detail came clearly enough to David's sight; but it was as if another glass, beyond the glass of the window pane, covered everything, made touch between any two things impossible. He saw the children skating on the flooded marshes, but the sound of their voices fell in the thin air before it reached the house. Their movements were like line drawings of movements. His eyes followed the peopled cars as they passed down the long straight stretch of road; yet when they disappeared around the corner there was no impression of severance.

He stood absolutely still. He was not quiet with thought or interest. It was simply that any impulse to movement receded before the compulsion of the emptiness: to suspend the moment and prolong it, exactly as it was, in a kind of spell.

At a first glance his face looked young. The tentative, blue-eyed look of a boy's face still shadowed it. A touch of sun still lingered in the quick blond hair. The eyes and mouth were sober, but a trigger-readiness to grin lurked in them. At a second glance his face seemed old. The flesh was firm over the broad bones (so much broader than the tall slender body seemed to call for; but it had the cast of a bad night's sleep. The longer you looked, the less you could be sure whether the face was young or old.

"What are you doing, David?" Ellen turned from the rug as

she spoke. The patience in his face was his father's; the quickness that disputed the patience his mother's. Its fine graining was hers.

He didn't reply. She scarcely noticed now, whether you answered or not.

"What are you looking at, child?" she asked again.

"Nothing," he said.

She turned back to the rug.

She was so old that her face no longer held any trace of how she had looked when she was young. Only her eyes had no dustiness of age about them. The years that had washed away their colour seemed to have disclosed an original brightness. Neat, bright, delicate: that pattern was repeated everywhere—in the white hair caught back into a tight bun; in her hands, her feet; even in the black dress she wore, with the white piping at the neck. Her clothes had always stayed neat and clean, even if she had been transplanting cabbage plants on a wet day. She was the sort of woman whose daughters, if she had any, are delicate like herself, but who bears incredibly sturdy sons.

The pattern of the rug was not intricate. It had a wide dark border, then a target pattern of circles radiating from the centre of the canvas. David had marked them for her. Her eyes could no longer trace the outlines of scrolls and flowers.

She selected each rag carefully for texture and colour.

Rags were scarce now. These were the last she could find. The bag they were in had been tied tightly at the top, inside a trunk. They were good rags. All the garments were whole. She had torn them into strips herself.

The coat she'd used for the border was of sturdier cloth than the rest, but it felt rich and soft to pass her fingers over. It had been at the very bottom of the bag. Whose coat was that?

She stopped and thought: There is Joseph, my son—he married Martha; and there are the three children: Christopher, David, and Anna. She might have been writing the facts down somewhere, for reference. Her own husband's name had been Richard. She didn't remember him today.

But she remembered Joseph. The grey in the first lap of circle next the border was a work shirt of Joseph's. She remembered Martha feeling it for texture the first day he tried it on, the day he went back to cut the keel. It still looked almost new. Where was Joseph?

The next ring of flowered gingham was an apron of Martha's. Martha had sat that night with this apron to her eyes, but what night had it been?

She drew the last garment from the bag. It was a dress. Her

9

fingers touched a bit of lace at the bottom of the sleeve. It must have been for a wrist no larger than mine, she thought. The wrist *was* mine. But when did I wear that dress? There was music. It wasn't here. It was some far-off place. She couldn't remember where. She felt cold.

"David," she said, "are you going to let the fire out?" There was a querulous note in her voice.

David caught his breath. He put a stick of wood from the oven, where it was drying, into the stove. Then he returned to the window.

"What are you doing, child?" she said.

"Nothing."

"Child"! He winced now, just to feel it coming. There was a minute or two of silence.

"You'd better fix the fire," Ellen said.

"I just fixed it."

"That's a good boy."

Brown. She tumbled the little knoll of rags, searching for a strip of brown. Yes, that was brown. That was the stocking cap Chris had worn the day Joseph tied a bag of straw on the trailsled for a seat and took him back to the woods for the first time. She could see the tiny hatchet clutched in Chris's own hand. He had been crying because they'd teased him about hauling Charlotte Gorman on her sled. She had spun that yarn herself, and knit it, and dyed it with alder bark. She could see the stain of brown on the kindling stick she'd stirred the salt into the dye with, to set it. Chris was two years older than David. Chris was ten. Is David only eight years old then? Where was Chris? David was there by the window, but where was Chris?

"What do you see, child?" she said.

"Nothing."

"Is someone coming?"

"No."

Herb Hennessey was coming up the road, but he wouldn't be coming here. He'd never gone into another house, as far back as when David was a child. He'd been the strangest creature in the world to the children.

There was music . . . Was it, "I'll take the high road, and you take the low road . . ."? No. It was before that. Quicker music. She began to hum, in a high quavery voice. "But me and my true love will never meet again . . ." David's fingers tightened against his palms. She hummed the tune over and over and over.

"Is someone coming?" she said.

"No."

Pink. That was Anna's. That was the hair ribbon Anna had

worn the Sunday afternoon she got lost trying to follow David's tracks back the log road. They had found the ribbon first, caught on the limb of a tree, and then they had found Anna.

"That sailor was here yesterday," she said. "The one Anna married."

Or was it the fugitive sailor she'd hidden in the hay loft once? But that wasn't yesterday . . . was it? Or was it the man she couldn't quite remember, the one who had worn that fine coat? She hadn't dared to tell him about the sailor, even when she slept by his side that night. No, it was Anna's sailor. They were married. But Anna was David's twin, and David wasn't married. Anna was only eight years old. She had on a flannel petticoat with red feather-stitching all around the hem. Where was Anna?

Red . . . Red . . .

Yes, that was red. That was a tablecloth. The neighbours had given it to Joseph and Martha, the night of the surprise party at the new house. It had tassels all around the edge. They used it only on Sundays. The blood stain was still there in the centre. They had laid David on the table that day they carried him into the house, without waiting to take off the cloth. No washing could ever get the stain out. They had all sat around the table yesterday—Joseph there, and Martha there, and Christopher and David and Anna, and the lamp in the centre by the sugar bowl. And was that other man there too, the one with the fine coat, the one she had danced with that time? Where were they all? Wasn't his name Richard?

"Have you fed the hens, David?" she said.

"It's only two o'clock," he said.

"It will soon be dark. If you don't feed them before dark, they won't fly down to eat."

"It's not dark yet." He said it as if he were repeating a lesson. He had said it yesterday and the day before and the day before that.

She filled the space between two circles with strips of the tablecloth, and clipped the loops close with her scissors. Blue . . . She searched for a strip of blue.

"Have you fed the hens, David?" she said.

He turned then, suddenly. His mouth twitched once, as if from a blow that can have no other response. In a single movement he took his cap from the row of hooks beside the window and put it on his head. He took his jacket from the next hook.

Ellen turned. "Where are you going, child, at this time of day?"

"Not very far," he said.

"Will you be warm enough? You're not half clad."

"Yes, yes, I'll be warm enough."

"Don't fall."

He put on his jacket and filled up the stove again. He hesitated. "The stove's all right till I get back," he said. He had to say *something*, because he had spoken to her sharply.

He opened the door and went quickly past the window, toward the road that went to the top of the mountain.

Blue . . . blue . . . Yes, that was blue. That was David's. That was the blanket they'd wrapped David and Anna in the night they were born. But David is not a baby. How . . . ?

She turned. "David," she began, "how . . . ?"

There was no one in the room. *David* was here. Where was David?

CHAPTER II

A CAUCUS of hens outside the window wakened David.

There was nothing repetitive about the mornings then. Each one was brand new, with a gift's private shine. Until the voices of late evening began to sound like voices over water. Then, quite suddenly, sleep discarded it entirely. You awoke again, all at once. The instant thought that another day had something ready for you made a really physical tickling in your heart.

David opened his eyes. April air plucked at the curtains like breath behind a veil. It held a hint of real warmth to come, but the linen chill of the night still sharpened it. Clean limb shadows palpitated with precision and immaculacy on the breathing ground outside. The whole morning glistened fresh as the flesh of an alder sapling when the bark was first peeled from it to make a whistle. It glinted bright as the split rock-maple, flashing for a minute in the sun as it was tossed onto the woodpile.

A ribbon of sunlight stained the softwood floor and made a warm-looking spot on the bedside rug his grandmother had hooked. It spotlit the cool white bureau. David narrowed his eyelids, distorting the furniture of the room into macabre patterns.

Then something jumped in his heart the way water flashed right through your bare-free body when you took the first plunge into the Baptizing Pool.

This was the very day!

This was the day his father had promised to take Chris and him fishing. The brook started beyond the crest of the mountain. And when it was dark, they wouldn't come home. They'd eat at the camp, and *sleep* there. He'd seen anything but the mouth of the dark log road before; but today they'd walk on it, farther and farther into the deep, safe, unfathomable, magically-sleeping woods. The voices from the houses would be soundless and far off. The only sound would be the soft undulant hush of darkness. He could feel the touch of the road in his feet, like a kind of dancing.

He could hardly wait to get started, to leave the house behind. It would try him to keep the slow pace of his father and

13

Chris. He'd want to run on ahead. Yet, somehow, having his father and Chris *with* him would make him more securely alone with his mind's shining population than ever.

A confirming glow flashed back from everything he looked at in the room. Most of all from the face of his brother sleeping beside him. I never noticed before, he thought : Chris has got a wonderful face!

"Chris!" he said. "Chris!"

"Unhh?" Chris said. "What?"

Chris and David didn't look like brothers, except with some trick of light or flicker of some transient thought. Even asleep, without the eyes imposing their definition on the other features, they had no feature alike. David's body was thin. His sun-faded hair was fine as corn tassel. Chris's hair was dark. Something like the lip-moistness of sleep seemed to cling in it, as it clung in his firm brown flesh. David's eyes were so clear a blue they gave his face the look of a face in too strong a light. Everything beneath it seemed ready to surface there instantly. Chris's eyes were blue too, but the blue was layered. They roiled, but they didn't expose.

When Chris slept, his lips fell apart a little. When David slept, his lips seemed to rest on a line of junction so fragile that even his breath must be careful not to rupture it.

Chris opened one eye. He stretched both arms over his head. He drew his muscles taut, then let them subside all at once. He lay perfectly still for a minute, then threw back the quilts and stepped out of bed. He yawned and pulled up the woollen shirt he'd slept in, scratching his hips. He reached for his clothes on the chair and began to dress.

David's clothes were in a tangle on the floor. His drawers were still inside his pants. His shirt sleeves were inside out. One of the garters that pinned to his waist was under the bed.

He ran to the window before he pulled on his drawers. To make sure the weather had declared itself to be fine all day. The others always had to be so certain about the weather before they'd let him go anywhere like this.

"I think I'll leave off this old woollen shirt," he said.

"What?" Chris said. "You don't know how cold it gits, back there at night."

"Cold!" It was a word that had no more real sense than the "meanings" in his speller.

"You'll see," Chris said.

David heard his mother and father talking downstairs. There was no special excitement in their voices. It was funny, they hardly seemed to know what was going on, sometimes.

14

"Is it fun back at the camp, Chris?" he asked. His face puckered up in a smile of excitement to hear the answer he was already certain of.

"Sure," Chris said.

"I dreamed about it last night," David said.

Chris's hand hesitated for a second on a button. His own dream came back to him. It made the room seem small and strange.

"I dreamed," David said, "you and Dad and me was on the log road, only it was funny"—he laughed—"all the trees was trimmed up like Christmas trees. And then it was like there was two of me. I was walkin with you, and still I was walkin by myself on this other road that *didn't* have any trees on it. I saw the camp on this other road and went and told us on the log road, but when we come back to the other road the camp was gone . . . and we walked and walked, and I guess that's all, we didn't get to the camp. Did you dream about the camp, Chris?"

"No," Chris said.

He couldn't tell David about his dream. There wasn't any story to it. It wasn't a crazy dream like David's.

He was walking down Gorman Hill. Halfway down you couldn't see any of the houses in the village at all, just the smoke from their chimneys. He was going swimming in the Baptizing Pool that was suddenly deep like a varicose rupture in the shallow vein of the brook. Some of the sweetish fresh-water smell of the meadow seemed to get into the dream. He met Bess Delahunt on the bridge, and she kissed him.

That was nothing new. Bess was always kissing young boys and squeezing them in her big warm arms. Only suddenly he didn't have any clothes on. And his body didn't feel small and scared, as it had in dreams of nakedness before. It didn't feel like being naked in front of his mother or any of the other women. Bess didn't seem to notice it at all. And there was something else today besides just the squirming minute of face-nearness and the woman-smell of Bess's black hair and the body-smell of her arms. Your own body seemed to swell in a dizzy clamorous way you could hardly stand it was so sweet. Every bit of it ran up to the spot where Bess's flesh touched you, and then drained back, and then ran up again, faster and faster.

That was all. The dream shifted. He was at the pool with the other boys, not remembering her at all. And yet he felt as if he'd been someplace new; where he'd seen what people were really like. He'd never noticed before how flesh-whiteness and flesh-moistness were like no other whiteness or moistness, to see or to touch. His own flesh seemed to have a new light inside it. He knew that whenever he saw Bess again now he'd feel awake (though why only with Bess, and not with any of the other women?), a shadow of the same thing he'd felt in the dream.

"David?" Martha called from the foot of the stairs.

Chris felt a sudden shame at the sound of his mother's voice. He started out of the room.

"Wait for *me*," David cried.

"I'm just goin downstairs!" Chris said.

"*Please* wait for me, Chris," David said. He couldn't bear for Chris to get started on the day first.

"Ohhhhh," Chris said.

He sat down on the bed and waited.

David's crazy whims never made any kind of sense to him, but he always gave in to them. He played more often with other boys than with David; but when the other boys had left and he'd see David's slight body coming toward home in the dusk, he liked Dave so much better than the other boys it almost made him cry.

He smiled. That crazy dream of Dave's. Yet that part about not getting there was kind of like his own dream, just the same. His flesh didn't seem to quite get there, either . . . would it ever? He looked at David's face. You could tell that David's flesh had never felt that way.

David saw him smile. God, he thought, Chris looks like Dad this morning! That's the way the older ones watched your kind of fun; just watched and smiled—the way you watched the kitten with a ball.

"Chris," he said, "what if the old Jersey gets her quim hot while we're gone? Hadn't we better leave a note for the bull?"

Chris laughed outright. He could always bring them close again, with what each one liked to laugh at, every time.

II

"I told you to wake me when you got up," David said to his mother.

"Well, I wanted to get the kitchen warm first," Martha said.

The thin spring sunshine reached through the window and latticed the boards of the kitchen floor with long still shadows of table and chair legs, and twisting shadows of the steam from the kettle and the rising breath of the breakfast food. It was the kitchen the sun seemed to seek out the year round. In the summer it basked there, bodily, like a cat; and even when the winter wind mourned outside, fingers of it reached through the frost-fur on the tiny panes and touched the handle of the stove lifter or the curve of a rocker or a hand.

The kitchen was the perimeter of Martha's whole life. She dressed it as carefully as she would a child. She had small wherewithal to make beauty with; but just as you could feather-stitch Anna's petticoat with bright thread, though it was only flannelette, so you could pleat the curtains instead of letting them hang flat. The kitchen was nearer to her than a voice. Her feet travelled there in the steep mornings and in the quick-declining afternoons. She thought there the slow thoughts that come and go silently when you are working alone, without speech. When she was outside it she felt strange. And for Joseph too, though he never thought of it consciously, it was like an anchor: the one small corner safe from the sweat of the fields and the fret of the seasons.

When the day's work was done and supper over, the kitchen seemed to smile. The other rooms seemed faceless beside it. Martha would sit near the lamp, sewing or mending, thinking quietly, but not clearly on anything at once, the way a woman does when she is tired and dark has come again. For a minute Joseph would sit motionless in the rocker after he'd pulled off his heavy boots, and curl his toes up and down in his woollen socks; he'd be tired from the plough or the axe, but the pattern of all the steps he'd taken outside that day would make a kind of far-off song in his blood. The children would still be busy, but the quick day-planning would be gone out of them; and Ellen would be young again, going back to her youth in the evening as the old do.

The kitchen's heart would seem to beat with a great peace then. The paths of the day which had been separate for each (patterned for the old, patternless for the young) melted together. The breath of them all seemed to lift in one single breath.

The kitchen had been witness to everything in their lives, and so was like one of them. If strangers, with different tread and different plans and other thoughts, should ever come to inhabit it, all the light would go out of its face.

Joseph had just finished milking. He was washing his hands at the sink. Martha gathered the muslin strainer over the lip of the milk pail.

Her features were each too generous to allow her prettiness. But she had soft light hair, and true light eyes, and whatever her face did it did all the way, in smiling or in sadness.

She enjoyed these morning chores: scalding the creamers,

brushing crumbs off the pitted face of the stove with a hawk wing, doing the chamber work—making the untidy waking face of the house orderly again. Most other women she knew found their morning work a burden and a waste. Their faces looked hot and ravelled as they worked about the stove. They didn't seem to come alive until they'd changed their dress after dinner and gone out to talk with another woman. But even when she was alone in her own house, her tasks were like a kind of conversation. The objects she touched had animacy. Even in the morning she wore a dress of bright print.

Ellen sat on the lounge. She was ripping old garments apart at the seams; then nicking each section with the scissors; then tearing them, with quick clean strokes, into rags for a rug.

Anna sat beside her. She kept picking out sections of the brightest coloured garments and holding them up to her as if she were testing dresses at a counter.

"Gosh, *that's* a pretty colour," David said. Everything seemed beautiful this morning.

"I don't know which I think is the prettiest," Anna said, "this one or that one. Which do you?"

"Oh, this one," he said. "Or . . . I don't know. Which do you?"

Anna had almost no look of the others. She was David's twin, but her hair and her eyes were dark. Her face had the delicacy of the child who is beautiful before its time: a tiny replica perfection that gave it a vulnerable look. She would always keep that trace of prettiness in that same soft childlike way.

"Well, if everyone's washed," Martha said.

The food had a ghostly taste to David, like food in a dream. It just took time. The fresh bread with the faint smell of milk and hands in it he swallowed almost without chewing. He couldn't touch his egg.

"Eat your egg," Martha said. "You'll be hungry."

"Aw, Mother, I won't be *hungry*!" Always that: Would you be hungry, or tired, or warm enough? If he could only make them see how meaningless the possibility of being hungry later on was.

"You'll see whether you're hungry or not," Chris said. "You never walked there before."

"Oh, I can walk as far as you can!" But he wasn't angry. He knew that if any argument really went against him, Chris would switch back to his side.

"Joseph," Martha said, "do you thing it's too far for David, way back there? You don't know how far it *is*, Dave."

"Let the child go." Ellen whispered it, but David heard. He loved her.

"*Yes*, Mother." He looked at his father. "Dad, you *said* I could." He was almost crying. It would be awful if this was one of the times when nothing could make his mother understand how full you were of never being tired or cold or hungry.

"What do you think, Dave?" Joseph said. "Think you kin walk that far?"

"Sure I can! Mother's always so *scared*."

"Oh, I don't know," Joseph said, "I guess maybe he kin go. We'll take it easy. What do you think, Martha?"

"Well," Martha said, "if he'd keep his jacket buttoned, and promised me to *tell* you if he starts to get tired."

His mother was suddenly wonderful when she began to waver like that. He promised her all these things, yes, yes, truly, from the bottom of his heart.

Joseph looked at David the way he always did when he let him have his way about some small thing. A slow humouring smile gathered in his eyes, although it wasn't quite overt in his lips.

Joseph's body wasn't heavy, but it was corded with muscles that rose everywhere at the slightest movement. He had a slow, handsome face: dark hair; dark sober eyes; and blood showed healthy beneath the beard shadow on his cheeks, even after shaving. As soon as they left youth behind, most of the men in Entremont got a cold-pinched look about the flesh in the hollows under their cheekbones, their hair was like lodged beach grass, their eyes like puddle water. But Joseph was without that cragginess. He could exchange clothes with a city man and you couldn't tell that those weren't the clothes he'd always worn (though the city man would look lost in Joseph's).

He was a slow man, but his life beat was no less varied than Martha's for being inarticulate. They said his nerve was strong enough to "cut off your head and put it back on again." (Once he had chopped a man's leg free from a jam between two logs, with a hand so steady the axe kept grazing the man's larrigan but never nicked it.) But he was a kind man, with no thought of the shame of being thought kind. He was not brittle anywhere, not spotted anywhere with softness; yet he was tender. It showed in the way he'd look at a new rug Ellen spread out before him, though he could find nothing to say; or the way he'd hold up the sweet pea vines Martha had planted in the vegetable rows, carefully from the hoe; or the way he'd look at the children sometimes, though he hesitated to touch them.

He almost never laughed aloud, but there was no severity whatever in him. His anger came seldom, but when it did—in loyalty to a friend, or at lies or meanness or pretence—it was fierce and deep.

His lack of fear (so utter it wasn't a matter of courage at all) and a kind of stubborn thoughtlessness to alter circumstances for his own ease were local legend. He'd work all day with an axe so dull any other man would have walked three miles to grind. When he came to a slough on his way to the woods, he wouldn't pick his steps around it, he'd walk straight through. He'd dive to the bottom of the cold stream for a saw they'd lost cutting ice, and finish the rest of the morning's work in his wet drawers. But he never thought of any of this as a thing that gave effect. He did it that way when he was alone. The other men joked about the things Joseph did, but they loved him as no other man in the place was loved.

"I'm goin," David whispered to Anna, pulsing with glee. Anna would know exactly how he felt. They didn't act alike, or think alike; but she watched him and listened to him as if he were the final reference for everything. He knew that she alone understood everything he told her, exactly.

"I asked Mother if I could go," Anna said, "but she said I couldn't."

David's mood brought up short. He felt as if he'd betrayed her. He'd never thought of Anna wanting to go. She didn't coax or tease, once she'd been told "no." She must have wanted to go terribly, to have asked at all.

"I tell you, Anna," he said, "don't you wait for me, you go see the fawn Syd's father caught, and get Grandmother to tell you a brand new story." He wanted to think of her doing something special without him, to make up for this thing he was doing that excluded her.

She nodded. He saw that she was almost crying.

"A girl couldn't go way back there, Anna," he said. Then it came to him how awful it was when the others said something reasonable like that to him, and Anna helpless to argue even, as he did.

"Listen, Anna," he said desperately. "I'll go today, see, so I'll know the way. Then someday I'll take you back. Just the two of us."

"All right." She smiled.

Suddenly, because she couldn't go, because she didn't know she looked as if she were almost crying. David loved her fiercer than he'd ever loved anything before.

20

"Anna," he said, "look at the way Chris's hair's stickin up. It looks like a scairt cat." She laughed, in spite of herself.

Anna watched them cross the road. Water sighed in the great holes of the road where the frost had collapsed. The mail team passed by. Fans of muddy water fell constantly from the spokes of the wheels. She watched them go across the field and over the pole-fence and across the pasture and out of sight. But she didn't call to them, and the tears didn't fall.

III

The sun was warm now, really warm. It came close enough not only to dry the dead leaves on the ground but to make a rustling among them. David could feel it through his jacket, and as he walked dampness gathered where his cap was tight in front. He pushed his cap back. The air felt cool and clean on his forehead. Joseph and Chris didn't loosen any of their clothing. They never seemed to feel the weight of their heavy garments, even in the hot summer.

I hope we won't meet anyone, David thought. Just us together. This was one of the few times when his father had given himself over entirely to a day of pleasure. No part of him was absent in thoughts of work. When he cut the alder for a fishing pole, he searched and searched until he spotted the perfectly straight one you couldn't see yourself. When he made the whistle, he didn't do it practically, like a job. He did it so carefully and so perfectly as you wanted it that you wondered how it was possible. You couldn't imagine him ever making a whistle for himself, when he was a child.

"Dad," David said, "can you see the camp quite a ways before you get there, or is it . . . ?"

"Oh I guess maybe you kin see it, a little ways," Joseph said.

David started to say, "Dad, will you let *me* build the fire in the camp stove tonight?" Then he hesitated.

He knew that his father could refuse him nothing. Yet why was it easier to ask his mother for things, even if he had to plead and argue?

When he was alone with his father, he didn't know what to say. The quick things in his mind sounded foolish even to himself. Not that Joseph would laugh at them. There'd be an anxiety in him almost, to listen and to understand. But somehow David would be struck shy when he started to talk; and then, when he didn't speak true to his thoughts, he'd feel as if he were keeping a secret from the person he could most trust.

Chris had no such trouble.

He could talk and talk, whether his father answered or not; or they could work in absolute silence without any constraint. All the time David worked alone with his father, he'd be afraid something would come up he couldn't do, something he couldn't lift. He knew his father wouldn't mention his clumsiness or weakness, but still he didn't want him to see. Chris never seemed to be afraid that anything would be beyond his strength. He didn't feel that way at all about his father seeing.

(The funny thing, when Chris asked his father for anything, Joseph would argue with him the way Martha argued with David.)

Sometimes when all three worked together, David would try to imitate their sober speech. He'd wish his thoughts could just move along with the pace of the day, as theirs did. But this morning he wouldn't part with his secret extra senses for anything.

As they came close to the mountain, it was so exciting David was almost afraid. He almost wished there was some way he could save it. The second time was never as good.

They came to the bridge at the end of the pasture. The brook started high-up, from a spring. It was shallow here because of damming above, so that logs could be driven down the mountain part of it. But it ran exultantly. Glinting and leap-frogging, in the sun. Cool and smooth, under the scooped-out banks. Twisting and tumbling over its own heels on its way to the river, and from the river to the sea.

Joseph and Chris stopped to urinate on the bridge. They used their whole hand, like a shield. David urinated into the brook, so that he could think of it going all the way out to the sea. He held his hand as they did. He was going up on the mountain.

"Do you want to fish here a while, Dave, and have dinner?" Joseph said. "Spell you a little before we strike the mountain."

"No," David said. How was it possible for his father to consider waiting and going on, and have the tug of both choices equal?

"Yeh, let's do that," Chris said.

David started to protest. Then he felt a twinge of the appetite he'd believed forever dead. He thought: Yes, let's wait till we eat. Then there'll be nothing—not hunger, not tired, not a thing—to spoil it. Let's wait. I can be near the mountain and save it at the same time.

He fished by himself, a little upstream; so he could hear the others, but not see them. He looked at the bubble-coins on the surface of the water and let his mind not-think. He seemed to be floating along with the brook. He felt the sun through his jacket, and waited for the tug on his line that would be firmer than the tug of the current. Whenever he looked at the mountain and made the sun-shiver in his mind into a conscious thought, he knew this was the best time he'd ever had.

Soon fire was catching in the little tent of dry sticks his father (who else could have?) discovered you couldn't imagine where. The brook water came to a boil in a sudden volcano. It spun the tea leaves round and round in the black boiling kettle, and a little of it hissed out on the flames. He sat on a sun-warmed rock, with his father's coat beneath him. The tea in the tin cups had a little taste of smoke in it. The egg slipped out of its shell smooth as glass. His teeth found layers of cold meat beautifully between the thick-buttered bread. It was like food had never been before.

He thought, we could do this every day! We will! We'll come back here and eat every day!

Joseph lit his pipe. He tightened the shoulder straps of his pack where they tied around the mouth of the meal bag and the potato pocketed in each bottom corner. They rinsed the tins in the brook and put them back inside the pack.

The food was warm in David and the sun was shining and no part of the day had begun to decline and they were crossing the bridge to start to climb the mountain, when they heard the voices.

CHAPTER III

ELLEN TOOK Anna to see the fawn. It darted its glances and twitched its ears and flesh as if its muscles moved by dainty triggers. Anna tried to make herself feel the wonder of being close enough to a living wild animal to touch it. But something in the circumstance's being actual robbed it of the excitement she'd expected.

"Why didn't the mother hide it?" she said.

"A hunter must have wounded her last fall," Ellen said, "and the snow was so deep. She was too weak to move. She had no milk."

The fawn looked suddenly at Anna; then its lost glance, unbounded by the coop, darted to the woods. Anna knew that even if she put her hands on its side she couldn't touch it really. She had a sick, shivery, feeling.

"Let's go," she said.

They walked aimlessly back across the fields, searching for

signs of new life in the earth. There was a feeling of lift and stir in the ground. The ploughed land was brown; but far off, around a house or wherever water trickled, the fields had a cast of green. The gun-metal buds of the apple trees were fattening. The row of sugar maples behind the barn had a faint salmon blush.

"I'll put my squash in the outside row, this year," Ellen said, "so they'll have more room to run." Any seed she touched seemed to prosper. Her hands were still white and delicate, despite their years with hack and hoe.

They stopped at the new church.

Joseph had given the site for it, as well as his share of lumber and time. Everyone in the place (Baptists and Catholics too) had driven a nail or laid a board or helped raise a rafter. Spurge Gorman had hewn the cross from the great mountain ash he'd looked out for axe handles; and Peter Delahunt had fixed the cross to the steeple. The bishop from Halifax had consecrated the new burial ground only last week.

(Martha's hands had stopped cold at her work whenever she'd thought of having him to dinner. She'd wanted to get their own dinner out of the way first, but Ellen said no, *not* to act in any way extraordinary, Joseph said, "Hell, he's only a man."

It was easy as could be once he was inside the house. He was a smiling man who made you feel like smiling too. His boots were skinned at the toe. He smoked a pipe. He ate heartily, and remarked about her carrot fern. She'd felt pride almost to tears to see his great Ring resting on David's head when he asked David what he wanted to be. She'd wished he could stay to supper.)

The church was cool inside. It had a stillness all of its own. Anna liked the organ-and-prayer-book smell, the smell of new paint and lumber. She liked the hollow sound of her voice and steps, echoing among the pews.

But for Ellen the mystery still dwelt in the old church four miles down the road. Her husband had helped build that one. Now he lay beside it. It too was a building made by human hands like any other building and that settlement was deserted now, but she felt that the mystery breathed there all by itself whether there was the sound of voices on the road or not.

They left the church. As they came close to the house, a fine rain gathered suddenly out of nowhere. The sun still shone. You could see where the skirt of the shower stopped; short of the mountain on one side and short of the river on the other. Who did that painting my father had in the big hall, Ellen thought, that looked like this? The rain silky and transparent in the air, but green on the grass and pink on the maples. His name began with a "C."

"Quickly," she said. "Run."

"Oh no," Anna said, "let's go in the barn." In the barn you could sit safe and dry and hear the rain on the roof.

The cows and oxen lurched to their feet. They stretched their whole length, languidly. Patch, the horse, threw up his head. His sleek skin rippled nervously. He stamped his sharp-shod feet heavily in the stall. Ellen let him sweep up a hand ful of oats from her hand with his cool leathery lips. The oat-dribble mixed with green bit-dribble at the corners of his mouth.

Anna was afraid of the horse. She drew her grandmother away, into the barn-floor. They sat on two feed boxes. The barn-floor was dark after the bright sunlight outside, and cool. There was the dusty smell of hay. Motes defined a ribbon of sunshine that came from the window above the scaffold. Every tiny knothole in the boards was a star of light. The rain made a plushy sound on the roof. Anna felt a fascinating shiver of secrecy.

"Tell me a story," she said. "Tell me when you were a little girl."

"I'm not sure I remember so long ago," Ellen said.

Anna sighed. Her grandmother would never talk to her about England. It must have something to do with things she'd overheard her father say. Ellen's parents had thought her husband wasn't good enough for her. He was older than she was. He was proud and stubborn. He'd never let her mention their names. He'd never let her write back home. Not a line.

If she insisted, Ellen would put her off. ("Did I ever tell you about the Governor of Annapolis—or Port Royal, then—who died on a voyage back from France? They put his body in the sea, but they brought his heart on and buried it. I'll take you to Annapolis sometime and show you the very spot." Or, "Did you know that the road to town—*it* used to be called LeCroix, so many trails branched there, before they changed it to New-bridge—was only a footpath when I came here?" Or, "Did I tell you about the dry summer when the fires were so thick around us? The sky was dark as evening all day and the cari-bous came right out to the edge of the fields. Even the men went to the church and prayed.")

Or she'd tell her again about the time a robber came into their house at night. He thought she was alone. Her husband identified him for the sheriff the next day by a bayonet cut he'd given him in the dark. It turned out to be a man he knew. Richard could eat no supper that night; but he said justice must be done. He was that kind of man.

Or about the two moose hunters with the gold snuffboxes. Joseph was playing in the yard when they stopped to ask directions. They poured his small hands so full of silver dollars that some spilled out on the ground. That was a hard year, but the silver dollars lay inside the clock all winter. Until Richard could find who the men were and return their money.

But if Anna said, "Where did you learn to waltz like *that?*" she'd only smile.

"Well, tell me about somewhere," Anna said now. "Not about here."

Ellen thought for a minute. She looked as if a frightening idea had come to her. One of those secret things you are suddenly tempted to tell no one else but a child.

"I could tell you about the places where they've never seen snow," she said.

"*Never?*"

Ellen seemed to be talking to herself.

"Or where the sea is blue as—what's the bluest thing you can think of?—and you can always smell spices."

"Where did *you* see them places?" Anna said.

Ellen hesitated. "Right here," she said.

"Right *here?*"

Ellen started to rise. "Hark," she said. "Is the rain over?"

"No," Anna pleaded. "No. Tell me that."

"If I told you something," Ellen said very softly, "would you promise not to . . . never?"

"Yes. Oh, yes!"

"Do you see that scaffold?" Ellen said. "I hid a man there once."

"Oh, this was wonderful. "Was he a bad man?"

"No, he was young."

"You too?"

"Yes."

Ellen smoothed her apron with her hands. She said, "One day . . ." Anna let all the questions curl up, cosy and delicious, inside her.

"One spring day"—Ellen spoke slowly, as if the facts she could remember, but some other part of it was hard to find again—"your grandfather and I were planting potatoes in the burntland. I came back to the house first, to kindle the fire for

26

supper. I went inside and there was a man standing there. He said, 'I *thought* you might come first.' He had on a sailor's middy."

"Did you screech?" Anna said.

"No," Ellen said. "I don't know why I wasn't afraid. The woods weren't cleared to the river then. I couldn't see Richard. But I wasn't afraid. I picked up the poker we had for the pigs' potatoes, but when he smiled, I saw he meant no harm. A sailor looks like a child when he smiles."

"Why?"

"I don't know." Ellen spoke as if she were trying to get the story straight for herself, not for Anna. "But something keeps their eyes new, like a child's eyes."

Anna didn't understand. This wasn't such a good story.

"What did Grandfather say?"

"I didn't tell him. It was wrong, but he wouldn't have understood. He'd have notified the authorities. If he'd been in the sailor's place, he'd have given him*self* up. So what could I do? The sailor kept saying, 'I was afraid you might be an *older* woman.' As if one young person couldn't think of betraying another. I'd never thought about what it was to be young, before, I was always with older people here. But I thought of it then. I felt sort of frightened. Someday my youth would be gone. I wouldn't even notice when. So I hid him. I only meant to hide him for one night."

She spoke as if she were trying to justify something to herself. She'd forgotten that she'd left out the facts of the story.

"But what did he have to hide for?" Anna said. "Did he steal?"

"Yes." Ellen smiled. "A peacock feather."

Anna giggled. This was a real story after all.

The sailor, Ellen said, had gone with the captain of the man-of-war on an errand to the governor's house in Halifax. He had waited outside. There was a peacock in the garden. It had fascinated him. He'd thought: If I just had one feather from its tail, to show the other sailors. The bird had screamed. The captain had rushed out and there he stood, with the feather in his hand.

He had run. He had travelled the road by night and the woods by day. Now he was here, and she must hide him until the ship sailed.

"What would the captain have done to him?" Anna said.

"He'd have been lashed."

Ellen spoke so intensely that Anna peered at her face. Her face didn't look like that when she told other stories. Older people's faces had a kind of covering. All the things that happened to them piled up there, one over another. But now her grandmother's face looked as if some kind of breeze had lifted the covering. What she was telling showed bare as on the day it had taken place.

"His flesh was strong enough," she said, "but young flesh is soft. They would have split it."

The breeze died and her face was old again. She straightened her apron. "Hark," she said again. "The rain has stopped."

Anna had forgotten to listen to the rain.

"But what happened?" she urged.

"He stayed a week," Ellen said. "I took food to him when your grandfather was in the fields. It was wrong, but . . ."

"Did *he* tell you about them places?"

"Yes. I couldn't help listening. There would be things to do in the house, but . . ."

Anna was enchanted. To think that stealthy words had been spoken about those far places, under these very boards.

"Where did he go?" she said.

"The night before he left," Ellen said, "he told me the sea was a lonesome thing. He meant it, but . . . I suppose he went back to the sea. Do you know what I think it's like when the sea's right in you?"

The breeze brushed her face again. Her face forgot itself like a face struck, at first waking, with the memory of the night's dream of some time when you were another person. You lie there, listening intently for a sound that you know will never come again.

"Sometimes when you hear a train whistle and everything turns quiet around you, like the way flowers lie on a grave after the mourners have all gone home, or sometimes in the fall when the hay is cut and it's moonlight and it seems as if everything is somewhere else—I think the sea is a little like that," she said. "When a thought of it comes across you, it's like thinking of some face that's lonesome for just you. All the faces around you turn strange. You know that the sea's face some one place, somewhere you've never been will be like your own. But child, why do I—?"

"Oh, I *know*," Anna said. She didn't, really. Yet this had a kind of meaning for her just the same.

The covering fell back on Ellen's face, more immobile than ever.

"Is that all?" Anna said.

"Yes. He told me, that night, he wanted to find work on land somewhere. He asked me to bring him some old clothes. I took the clothes the next morning, but he was gone. I called to him. I thought he might be sleeping. But he was gone."

Anna sighed. Partly the nice sigh when a story was over; partly a sigh because the ending to this one was frayed, somehow.

They brushed the hay dust off their clothes and went out into the sunlight.

"Your grandfather was a good man," Ellen said suddenly, almost fiercely. "I loved him."

A rainbow arched from mountain to mountain. It was almost faded over the valley, but bright-banded as a new hair ribbon at its roots.

This was the day that came once a year. It, and the day of its fulfilment, were never repeated. On the day of fulfilment the grass was burdened with its own freshness, and the fullness of its sudden growth made a carpet sound in the air. The blood-red leaves of the maples unfolded overnight on the dark limbs. The sun warmed the shadows and dusted the ploughed land. The smell everywhere was thick with green breathing and sun. But this day had only the shadow-cleanness of promise. The only smell in the air was of cool water.

"Grammie," Anna said, "I think I'll marry a sailor."

CHAPTER IV

IN THE house, Martha's hands darted about with quiet skill. She opened her kitchen door and placed the round varnished stone against it. She scalded the churn, and fetched the jug of cream from the cellar. As her arms moved rhythmically at the dash of the churn, spinning it simultaneously with each upward or downward thrust, her thought fed calmly, like an animal grazing.

It was pleasant to be alone in the house. There was no loneliness when the others were away, but not isolably away, each happy with his own things. It was pleasant to have all the tasks of a new year at the threshold, but none of them clamorous yet.

She bent to see if the butter had begun to gather. As she straightened, she caught a glimpse of someone's shadow pass the window. She felt the instant defocus an unidentified movement provokes. She glanced at the clock, almost frowning. There was a step on the porch, and Rachel Gorman came through the door.

Martha felt the morning sag. She put away the nice feeling of being alone. She didn't know why she always dreaded to see Rachel come. But somehow when Rachel had left it was hard to go back to the way you'd been thinking before she came. Somehow, though you couldn't trace it exactly to anything Rachel had said, you'd find yourself rankling about something.

She glanced at her apron to see if any cream had splashed on it. Rachel was always spotless.

"Come in, come in," she called. "Good morning."

"Good mornin."

Rachel's thin grey hair was drawn into a tight bun on the top of her head. The enormous black eyes in her skimpy face were deceptively canine-wistful. They could take complete charge of her other features in a second. Caution seemed to limit any smile as soon as it began.

"Isn't this some day?" Martha said. "It makes you feel like living. Set down."

Rachel sat by the window, where she could keep her eye on the road.

"Yes," she said. "But nothin'll start up if we don't git a rain. I thought we'd git a shower this mornin, but it didn't amount to nothin."

A picture of the land after a warm rain flashed through Martha's mind. The warm rain, and then the spilling green of the grass taking all the roughness from the fields. Feeling the freedom of no-coat when you stepped outside. The sun coming through the mist that lifted cleanly from the sides of the immaculate blue mountains, just before dark, and varnishing everything with yellow-green shadow.

"We'll likely git enough rain next month," Rachel said, "when it's plantin time. We'll git more'n we want then."

When Rachel spoke the picture changed. Martha saw the day of seeding. How often the rain *did* come then; steady at first, then sulking in the damp-breathing clouds, refusing to declare itself. Drops of it would chandelier the trees, hanging sullenly on every twig; and the sodden grass would be slovenly underfoot.

"Are you all alone?" Rachel said.

"Yes," Martha said. "Joseph took the boys back to the camp. I don't know just where Grammie and Anna are."

"That'll be a long tramp fer David," Rachel said. "I suppose I'm foolish"—she smiled her beginning-of-a-smile—"but I'd be worried sick, if I was you."

30

"I didn't want him to go," Martha said, "but Joseph seemed to think . . ."

"I know," Rachel said. "Men don't see any danger in anything."

It *is* too long a tramp for David, where he isn't strong, Martha thought. It was a crazy idea. She felt almost angry at Joseph.

"Did Spurge go on the drive?" she said.

"Yes," Rachel said. "Why he always hankers so to git away on that drive, I don't know. It leaves me all the milkin—and my hands so cramped up with rheumatism now!" she sighed. "But I suppose nothin could make em any worse. And maybe it's all right. Likely we'll have a wet spring, and he couldn't do nothin around the place anyway."

"And you have Charlotte," Martha said.

"Charlotte," Rachel sighed. "Bless her. She hardly leaves me alone a minute."

"Charlotte *is* a sensible girl," Martha said.

Rachel smiled. "Well, I always *tried* to bring her up right. None o' this gaddin around every night with *her*. I don't know what some women are thinkin about, the way they let their young girls run around. If anything happens, they only got themselves to blame. I never have anything like *that* to worry about."

Martha wondered what particular woman Rachel referred to.

"I often wonder," Rachel said, "if someday Charlotte and your Chris . . . they seem to like each other."

Oh no, Martha thought quickly. She didn't quite know why.

"She was goin around with that Effie Delahunt, but I soon put a stop to that."

"But do you think there's any harm in Effie?" Martha said. "Why, she's only a child, and I always thought, well, such a gentle one."

"No," Rachel said. "I don't say there's any harm in her. I wouldn't condemn *anyone*. But if she turns out bad, she comes rightly by it. Her mother before her. *You* know that, Martha. And I don't want Charlotte mixed up with either of em. If I had a young boy, I'd warn him too."

She must mean David, Martha thought. But that was ridiculous. Effie was such a child, even if she was thirteen; and David, though he was so smart he seemed twice his age sometimes, was really only eleven.

Rachel glanced out of the window. "Ain't that her now?" she said.

"Effie?"

"No. Her mother. Bess. Comin up the road. Is she comin here?"

Martha looked out of the window. "Yes, that's Bess. But I don't think she's coming here. She hardly ever comes here."

"I shouldn't think she'd feel like goin' anywhere," Rachel said, "if she had any shame at all. I don't know where Pete Delahunt's eyes are!"

For some reason Martha felt like taking Bess's side.

"Well now, Rachel," she said, "I don't know whether to believe all the stories you hear or not. I couldn't say I ever saw anything out of the way with Bess, myself. She's got that manner with her, I know, but I suppose she can't help it. She's offhand like that with everyone."

"Yes," Rachel said. "Well, as I say, I don't want to condemn anyone. But I don't think it's right to shield anyone, either."

Who's shielding anyone? Martha thought. Things she'd heard about Rachel's own husband and Bess came into her mind, and before she could stop herself she was doing it the way Rachel did.

"And you can't blame *her* altogether, if it *is* so," she said. "The men are as bad as she is. You'd be surprised if you knew which of them, too."

"Maybe," Rachel said patiently. "But she chins up to em, and what can they do? Did you see her chinnin up to Joseph after service the other night? And after shoutin the hymns louder'n anyone! I knew Joseph didn't *want* to have anything to do with her, but she kept chinnin up to him, he had to be civil, I suppose."

"Joseph don't want anything to do with her!"

"I know," Rachel said. "That's what I say."

There was a short bristling silence. Martha's morning was tarnished. She felt bitterness toward Bess for the first time. Maybe those things *were* true.

"I'll tell you what I run over fer," Rachel said quickly. "I was wonderin if you'd finished with the quiltin' frames."

"Why, didn't you get them back?" Martha said. "I let Esther Barnaby have them, and she said she'd send them back to you."

Rachel hesitated a minute. "Would she do a thing like that?" she said, in a small, wondering voice.

Would she do a thing like *what*, Martha thought irritably. Esther was her best friend.

"I saw them frames there," Rachel said, "and sez I, they're my frames. But she said, no, you didn't say anything about em being mine, she'd have to return em to you." She smiled. "I suppose she wasn't quite through with em."

"You must have misunderstood her, Rachel," Martha said, "I told her they was yours, plain as anything."

"Oh, I knew *you* wouldn't let her think they was yours," Rachel said quickly. "She musta made that out of whole cloth."

"She must have forgotten," Martha said.

"Maybe," Rachel said. "Oh, it doesn't matter. Only I just thought I'd mention it to you sometime." She hesitated. "They *say* she fibs, you know."

They did say she fibbed, Martha thought. But surely Esther wouldn't deliberately put her in the wrong like that. It gave her a bad feeling to think Esther might try to put her in the wrong.

"Well, I'll see that you get them, Rachel," she said. I'll go right over there today, she thought, and thrash this thing out.

Rachel rose. "What time's it gittin to be?" she said. "I told Charlotte I was just—Why, Martha," she exclaimed, "that looks like David. No, no, back there on Delahunt's road. See? And the men from the drive, ain't it? Suppose they's anything wrong?"

Martha's eyes collected David and Christopher quickly from the first group, but where was Joseph? She searched the next group frantically, frantically—ah, there was Joseph too. She relaxed. She thought, I didn't see any chinnin up to Joseph, Rachel always . . .

And then she thought, Bess Delahunt knows *better* than to show her nose in here, the brazen . . .

II

"Hark!" Joseph said, when he heard the voices.

They stopped and listened. There was absolute silence for a minute. Please make it not a voice, David prayed. The time Anna had fever he'd wake in the night to hear the cry and then the silence. He'd pray: please, she's going back to sleep . . . if it can only be quiet an instant longer. But she would cry again.

And now the voices came again, this time beyond doubt. They were men's voices, just around the bend of the dark road. But they were sober and spaced. They weren't like the ordinary voices of men walking and talking together in the morning. There was no laughter.

They didn't call any greeting when they came in sight.

"It's the men on the drive," Joseph said. "They only went back a Tuesday. What . . . ?"

The moment he saw the other men, the day changed. The

adult way came back to him, he wasn't the same man who had searched for the fishing pole. Somehow David knew they wouldn't be going back on the mountain today at all. Why did I ever say we would wait? he thought.

The men didn't speak until they came to the bridge.

"Joseph." Their heads dipped sidewise, the way they dipped their heads and spoke your name only, when they came into the kitchen just before a funeral began.

"What's wrong, fuhllas?" Joseph said.

Quickly, not to hear their answer, David ran a few steps along the mountain road. He had to touch it, anyway, before he knew indisputably that the day was over.

When he came to the bridge again, the men were in a group about Joseph. Their solemnity was shattered. Each one was telling over and over whatever part of it he himself had seen.

"I was standin be the still-water there, and . . ."

"I *heard* this shoutin, but thinks I, it's jist . . ."

"It couldn'ta bin five minutes before that I . . ."

They repeated again and again the things they'd said to each other along the road, asking each other over and over again for sanction.

"Spurge Gorman had no business on the drive, clumsy as he was. But the poor bugger always seemed so glad to git away."

"Pete's a good swimmer. Spurge musta drug him under, mustn't he?"

"There wasn't a goddam sign of em after they once went down, was they?"

"It couldn'ta bin over seven, eight, feet deep there, could it?"

"I suppose some'll always think they was somethin funny about it, but what would Pete want to drown hisself or Spurge Gorman fer?"

Joseph kept saying, "My God. Well, my God."

"What happened?" David whispered to Chris. Chris's face was the colour of wet paper.

"Charlotte's father fell off a log, as far as they know, and Pete Delahunt tried to save him and they drownded."

"Effie's father?"

Chris nodded.

They didn't speak any more. It was as though the day had burst and parts of it were striking all around them.

Joseph turned. "Boys," he said, "Spurge Gorman and Bess's man have been drowned, so I guess . . ."

David couldn't think straight at all. He was breaking off the end of his fishing pole without waiting to unwind the line. He was thinking crazily that the trout he'd caught would lay there in the damp moss until the moss dried and then its slippery soft-spotted skin would be tight and wrinkled as a dry pig's bladder.

The men walked homeward, bonded together by what had happened like chastened children.

The sunlight crackled clean in the lichens on the rocks. The brook sounds of the first birds struck clean-piercing through the fern-cool air, like the shiver of running water. The floor of the woods was brown; but boxberries, fruited before the leaf was green, speckled it with red, umbrella mosses with a hint of green, and star-flowers, blossoming before the leaf, shone as water-washed a white as the cable of a moist cobweb when the sun slid down it. The air widened with listening and the shadow-freshness of promise.

The air smelled of water. The damp-springing water of the pollywog pools. The water soaking in leaves and needles where the shade was thick. And the sun-whitened water of the running brook—that soaked into the lungs of Spurge and Peter as other men, farther behind, carried them home on their shoulders.

The men were mostly silent. But now and then they spoke about their work, the season, even a smirking joke that had to do with women. This had no relation to the shock that was basic in all their minds, but David didn't understand that. He didn't know that adult speech was merely an instrument of disguise. Their remarks seemed heartless to him. He didn't see how they could talk at all. He hadn't said a word, even to Chris.

He could think only of Effie's face—she loved her father. He felt an awful guilt, to be without suffering himself, to have his own father so wonderfully safe beside him. He wished that somehow he himself could be struck sick.

"To think Pete went all through the war, without a scratch," Seth Lachine said, "Wypress, Verdoon, and . . . and then right here."

"That's the way she goes," Joseph said.

Suddenly David wasn't with them at all.

There were different faces around him. They were lying on the ground and bullets were whining over their heads. And then he got up and ran toward the German trench with the invincible, invulnerable strength that comes after you are tired out; and when the others saw him charging so bravely they all got up and shouted and ran with him. And suddenly, like waking from a muddled dream, he knew exactly what he was going to be. He was going to be the greatest general in the whole world.

CHAPTER V

THE news ricocheted from house to house. Each listener, his own shock subsided to a kind of thought-trembling, himself became a messenger; anticipating the effect of his words in spite of himself: watching almost eagerly for the sudden wiped look on the face of a woman stirring the dinner on the stove, the instant focusing of time and place in the face of a man who glanced at the spade that went loose in his hands as if it were unreal.

Then when all the first shock had settled and the thing was at last really believed, the village seemed to fuse. Women found in other women, just to see them coming up the path to talk over this terrible thing, a glow as of reconciliation. Men who had been bad friends for years sidled next each other in the groups and took up each other's remarks, warming at the sound of their own voices.

In the evening a hiatus fell over the place. Spurge and Peter possessed everyone's mind with a curious kind of distinctiveness the living lacked—as if, by dying, they had achieved their first clear outline of identity.

Each told of the last time he had seen Spurge or Peter, as if something significant could be read out of what he was doing or wearing or saying at that time. "I remember the last time I saw Spurge, he was comin up from the barn with them old cut-down larrigans on. I remember what he said. He said, 'I guess it's about time I shed some o' these clothes, ain't it?' " Or, "The last time Pete was up here, he come to borrow my compass. I don't think he liked to ask for it. I can see him now. He always set in that chair be the woodbox, didn't he, Hattie?"

The houses where they lay took on a face of cataleptic awe, as if the dead had communicated to them alone their mystery. A woman, passing from the sink to the stove, would stop suddenly at the window and looking to one or other of the houses try, desperately for an instant, to read their illegible secret. A man, milking, would catch a glimpse of the sinking sun, striking but not surprising the truth from the enigmatic windows. He would let his hands drop for a minute and try to think, for the first time, what it was to be alive.

Then it all became ritual.

There were the visits of condolence: the limbs struck with

sudden awkwardness at the door, the entrance so clumsy as to be almost sly. As if at a signal, a gust of fresh sadness welled in visitor and mourner alike when they shook hands. There would be a nod of indication as the pie or the pan of rolls was slipped unobtrusively onto the pantry shelf, and a nod and the fabrication of a smile of acknowledgment. There were the tears and the surreptitious gauging of the widow's grief.

The visitors went into the front room as if the floor were perilous walking. There was the moment of willed solemnity, with the face of the visitor pretending to understand what he read, as he or she gazed at the enigmatic face. "He looks lovely, don't he?" the visitor murmured, as he turned away; while Bess touched protectively the hair of her tender exhibit, or Rachel stood by the window, pleating meticulously the hem of her handkerchief from border to border, as she waited to pull the blind down again.

In the kitchen again, they smiled at the children, Effie or Charlotte. Sometimes the children were proud at being singled out for pity. Sometimes they cried, of necessity or to follow example. Sometimes they sat forlorn, like children after punishment; feeling guilty for having forgotten to be continuously sad.

And when the visitors had left the house, there were the little stories that, in the telling, bound them together closer still. (Rachel and Bess, by reason of their greater sadness, were isolated.) "Grace said that when *she* went in, Bess, poor soul, was in the room, cryin, and mendin his shirt cuff where the frayin showed." Or, "Rachel won't eat a bite. I told her she had to eat to keep up her strength, but she won't touch a thing."

No one worked the afternoon of the double funeral. The children tried to play, but their games would not move. The day seemed to be waiting. Gathered outside the church, when the time was come, a woman would brush a speck from her husband's good suit (setting on him so gravely in the middle of a weekday afternoon); then recall herself to the occasion, as if habit had betrayed her. Smiles were begun, then stopped halfway, in the conflict between greeting and the observance of solemnity. The black hearse horses moved slowly through the sunlight. They seemed to trail a hush behind them, out of the houses and the fields and the eyes of all that watched.

Inside the church, the spring sunlight struck batedly through the windows, engraving the artificial flower on a mat, or a pulpit moulding or the wrinkle of a face. The leaves of the poplars outside touched the windows remotely. Between stolen scrutiny of the mourners the gaze of the people strayed to the fields. Outside sounds came like sounds over water, deflected by the church-hush inside. The houses and all the men's handiwork in the fields lay alien between the mountains, as if for this hour the men had no part in them.

Rachel and Charlotte sat in one front seat, Bess and Effie in the one opposite. Rachel's face was hidden by a long black veil; but Bess's was exposed. It looked washed out. Something seemed to strike it wherever her eyes fled. When Bess was hurt she was hurt everywhere at once, and all of it showed. The dishevelment of sadness lay almost comically on a face moulded so smooth with laughter and quick impulse.

The two children sat motionless. They were congested with the intensity of child-sadness that nothing can help—until the next hour, merely with coming, takes it entirely away.

Neither looked at all like her mother. Charlotte might have been Bess's child. There was promise of the same generosity in her body. She had the same lush fruiting in her high-coloured cheeks and heavy black hair. Only a timidity at the sound of her own laughter was different.

Effie was small. There was a fragile blondeness all about her. She shed a sort of light, like the light behind the parchment of a Japanese lantern. Even as a child that not-quite-penetrable mist about her made her thoughts and actions more illegible than a mask.

The people held up their faces meekly to the rain of solemn words. They heard only the sound, not the heart of them. It wasn't until the organ began, the one sound which chords with the watcher's feeling at the enigmatic language of death, that everyone wept.

David looked at Effie. Her face had a pleading, retching, look. He had never seen her cry before. The death-sadness that had blown against him like a breeze, all day long, suddenly sharpened. He felt somehow blameful that Effie cried more lonelily than he. He thought: I'll marry Effie, that's what I'll do. Then she'll know that whatever happens will happen to us both, and she'll never cry like that again.

The day stopped and listened at the grave . . . no more of touch between them after this minute, or sight or sound.

Then, as the handful of dust sprinkled the coffins, even before the heads rose, the day moved again. Swiftly as a breeze, Peter and Spurge passed from fact to memory. The cord with the living began to ravel. Now the grass was ordinary grass only. The fields became familiar weekday fields again. The men, moving away, felt restless in their good clothes and thought of catching up on the time they'd missed. "We need rain," they said. Or felt for their pipes. And now each woman was different to the others in the way she had been different before.

Rachel and Bess moved off among the groups, careful to keep more than speaking distance apart.

"Is there anything I can do?" the women said to Rachel.

She shook her head. "No. I was good to him. I give him a respectable funeral. There's nothin else anyone can do now. Only time can heal."

They passed on to Bess. "If there's anything I can do . . ."

They spoke a little furtively in spite of themselves. They were anxious to record their offer and move away. The constraint of never knowing on exactly what footing they stood with Bess was back, the parched feeling they always had sudden consciousness of in her presence.

"No, it must be God's will." Bess's face had a glow and a force even now, like when she sang in meeting. "I'll just have to keep busy, so I don't have time to *think*."

What would she think? they thought as they moved away. Was she a good woman or a bad one? Could anyone cry like that woman'd cried today, if there'd been other men? If you could just be sure.

CHAPTER VI

D AVID kept his eyes on Effie. He kept willing her to detach herself from the others' attention. Then, when she'd seem about to do so, he'd chill with the thought of speaking this message of his he was so ignorant of. At last he moved beside her. She was staring at a geranium blossom she had plucked from the wreath his mother had made. She thrust it into her pocket quickly. She smiled her light impenetrable smile.

He was tongue-tied. You planned how it would be with someone, seeing ahead how their part must go as certainly as your own. Then when the time came, they started off with an altogether different speech or mood, and your part became useless and wooden. She was smiling. It would sound abrupt and foolish to tell her she would never have to cry alone again.

"Have you learnt your piece for the concert?" he said.

She nodded.

"Mother made me a new dress," she said. "It's shot silk. It's blue and then it goes green." Her eyes were soft and bright, as if just to speak the word "silk" gave her the touch of it too. "Do you know yours?"

"Yes."

"Let's go somewhere and say them," she said.

"All right," he said.

They went down where the brook crossed the road and wound through the alder-circled meadow on its way to the river. Where they'd be all alone.

They began to speak the lines of the school play.

"Who are you?" she said.

"I came to play with you."

"I am rich and beautiful," she answered haughtily, "I'm not allowed to play with beggars." David was startled. She sounded as if she really was rich. She moved about as if she really had fine clothes on, without knowing it.

"Do you *always* play alone?"

"I like to play alone. No one takes my things, and I never have to laugh or cry unless I want to."

"I know," he said. "I play alone too."

"Are there no other beggars?" she said.

It was his turn to speak proudly. "I am a prince," he said. At the sound of the word "prince" he became tall and strange and wonderful. "I put on this disguise, to find out what it would be like to play with someone else. See my ring?"

He held out his hand. He could see the great emerald stone as plainly as if it were there; his fingers were long and fine.

"You *are* a prince," she said. "Oh yes, I see it now. I will ask my father if . . ." She stopped.

A spontaneous breeze swept the black alders low to the brook. A fresh, awful, gust of sadness came out of the word "father." The magic of the word "silk" was gone. Her face came through the mist of lightness, twisted like a precarious smile falling apart.

She sank down onto the meadow moss, as if she wanted to make herself small. She hid her face in her arms and sobbed.

David looked at her cheap cotton dress. Her crying seemed to endow it more with forlornness than her face. The word "prince" emptied out of him too. He sat down on the moss beside her and put an arm around her shoulders.

And they knew then what it was like for two people to cry together. The breeze of sadness blew outward now, not inward. Even children can never cry together equally: there is a sort of selfishness in the one whose hurt is the more immediate, a sort of desperation in the one who cannot share equally the burden of that immediacy. But they were crying together.

David found his message easy to say then. He said, "Effie, someday we'll be married, won't we?"

Her lips were trembling, but she nodded and nodded.

The word "marry" filled them both. It was like a *place*—a place waiting for you when you got older. It was like a house. You could go in and close the door. The lamp would not flicker in any breeze.

II

It was different with Chris and Charlotte. They maintained an air of having found themselves side by side by accident; though, edging through the groups, their eyes had been on each other, sidelong, all the time.

Just before the funeral Chris had slipped upstairs and looked at himself in the mirror. He smoothed back his dark heavy hair and straightened his tie. He put his face close to the mirror and passed a thumb over the dark silky shadow beginning on his upper lip. Then he tilted the mirror backward and, turning, watched the back of his coat draw tight across the muscles in his shoulders. His body felt smooth and full beneath it.

He listened. There was no one on the stairs. He stripped quickly to the waist and drew a deep breath, bunching the muscles in his arms and patting his chest. He smiled a lazy, knowing smile at his own eyes in the mirror, and stretched both arms over his head, watching the muscles rise up at his sides. He felt something new and secret. There seemed to be an extra voice inside him now, that he heard only when he was alone.

I'm almost a man, he thought. That was the way they looked: the men who came to the pool sometimes after a hot day's haying and took off their shirts, rubbing their hard-muscled chests slowly, then bending soberly to slip out of their pants. As they straightened up, their bodies came out with a thicker, harder, completeness than you'd have guessed from the slack bunching of their clothes. Before they walked into the water, they stood for a minute passing their hands almost in an act of modesty up and down over the suddenly thick crotch hair and the hairy thighs and the lazy, stupid-looking, horse-lip heaviness of the parts that hung beneath.

He listened again. Then he opened his own trousers and glanced inside. Yes. Already.

He had never looked in the mirror like that before. He'd never thought of wanting to have a room by himself. Now he wished the room was all his, so every night before he went to bed he could check the growth of his body, in the mirror, and have that wonderful secret feeling.

But when he spoke to Charlotte, only the parts of his body which were exposed felt large.

"You going up the road tonight?" he said.

"I don't know. If Mother don't want me to stay with her. You?"

"I guess. If you do."

"I imagine I kin," she said.

He nodded, and moved awkwardly away. Speech between them was always halting. It was as if they thought in one language but had to speak in another, choosing only those words their clumsy mastery of the second language could translate.

But when he was back with the other boys, he felt the nice firmness in his muscles again—to look at Charlotte without her knowing it and wish he could be walking alone with her after dark.

(That wouldn't happen, though. The girls always walked ahead, in groups, the boys behind. Their progress was clotted and slow. The boys whispered together, with one of them letting out a lewd "Wheeeee!" now and then; the girls whispered together and giggled constantly. Now and then one of the girls would shout something derisive to the boys, or one of the boys would shout something teasing to the girls. One of the girls might break ranks to clout one of the boys in mock indignation, but she'd race quickly back to her own group.

When they turned and came homeward again, the groups would lose one member after another, as this or that house was reached; but the remaining girls still stayed together and the remaining boys together. And if, finally, there was a single boy and a single girl left, they'd talk with sudden soberness about school or something as they walked purposefully home, the clowning struck out of them entirely.)

How can Rachel and Charlotte run that place now? Chris thought. Lottie'll have to get married.

What would it be like to be married? he thought. Mark Corbett was married, and he was only sixteen—only two years older than himself. But when they teased Mark at the woodsplitting frolics about his back getting weak, he didn't take it up like he used to when they kidded him about girls at the Baptizing Pool. He just smiled—like he'd found something that, once you'd found it, you didn't even have to talk about it any more.

Two more years. If you went into a room with a girl and she was your wife and she took off her things, even the very last

42

one, and there was nothing at all to have to guess through—he caught his breath—what would it be like? If you woke in the night and it wasn't David, but a girl, beside you. If you touched her and there was no dress over any of those places.

He wished he had a room of his own.

III

"What will we have for supper?" Charlotte said to her mother. The rocker Rachel sat in seemed to move by itself. She gazed out the window as if the level of her vision passed above anything that was to be seen. She kept pleating and unpleating the handkerchief she held in her lap.

"Supper?" The tone of her mother's voice made Charlotte feel guilty for having thought of eating. "You git what you like, dear. I don't want anything."

Charlotte got herself some bread and molasses and a cup of milk.

There was always food in the pantry, but never anything fancy: no boughten cookies, no frosting on the sponge cake, never an orange, except at Christmas. They didn't make toast in the morning. They never made the blueberries into a fungy, as Mrs Canaan did—they just stewed them. And in the summer they never fixed up potatoes *on* the lettuce as Mrs Canaan did; the lettuce was in a bowl by itself and the vinegar beside it. The plate of cheese when the minister came to supper was the only frivolous food they ever had.

Our house isn't like Canaan's house at all, Charlotte thought. The curtains didn't have ruffles, the kitchen had no mats on the floor, the organ was always closed so it wouldn't swell in the dampness, the banisters were just square wooden sticks. The only pictures they had on the wall were the enlarged ones of her grandfather and grandmother, the only book was the Bible on the centre-table in the front room. She didn't mean the Bible shouldn't be there (and once it was there, how could you replace it?); but she'd seen Mrs Canaan move theirs sometimes, to make room for a jar of daisies, and it didn't seem as if there was any sin in that.

She thought of Chris; and before she could help it, she felt a little inward touch at the way his pants slimmed down so smoothly over his haunches and the suggestion of a bulge in front which she'd glimpsed sometimes as he walked towards her.

"Kin I go up the road tonight, Mother?" she said.

"If you *feel* like it, child."

As her mother spoke, suddenly Charlotte didn't feel like it at all. She thought of Rachel sitting there, with the lamp not lit, folding and unfolding her handkerchief in the darkness. She felt traitorous for the way she'd thought of the Canaans. She almost hated them. She began to cry.

"No, I *don't* feel like it," she sobbed. "I feel awful."

"It's hard," Rachel said. "It's hard, child, ain't it?"

"I couldn't leave you alone, Mother," Charlotte cried. "Not now."

"I didn't think you would, dear," Rachel said. She shifted her gaze from the window and sighed. "If I had just a crust of bread, Lottie. I don't know, I might try . . ."

IV

After supper the sun shone lonesome in the church windows. The meadow hens trailed their lonesome cries as they flew upward from the swamps.

"I think I should take a run down to see Bess," Martha said to Joseph. "Poor soul, let her be what she is, I . . .".

"I don't see nothin wrong with the woman," Joseph said. "If some of these damned gospel-grinders'd keep their jaws shut."

David had never heard his father speak so short in the house.

It was the way he spoke outside, sometimes, when one of the men had kept at a joke until it became a malice. He judged so seldom that his fierce opinions on things you'd never have thought such a quiet man would have any feeling about, when they did come, came as a kind of shock. The men never tempted him further when he spoke like that. It was funny the way they'd drop a thing immediately, without resentment when Joseph snubbed it.

David glanced, alerted, at his mother's face.

Sometimes when his father spoke sharply, there'd be no open quarrel, but her face would look as if everything retreated behind her lips and eyes. For a day or two after that, his father's voice didn't seem to reach her at all.

But this was one of the times when the savagery of his father's expression struck her the alternate way. She looked a him with a kind of wondering indulgence in her smile; as if, if she let herself begin to laugh outright at what he'd said ("gospel-grinders"!), she'd be helpless to stop.

"You don't think *I'm* a gospel-grinder, do you?" she said.

"No," Jospeh said, "I didn't mean you."

He smiled too. He looked half-abashed, and lurkingly half-pleased that his remark had turned out to be a funny one. For an instant they seemed newly wonderful to each other.

44

"Bess shouldn't give them a *chance* to talk, though," Martha said, holding onto the thing a little yet.

Joseph didn't reply. He'd said what he had to say, and it was over.

"Better ask her how she's off for wood," he said. "Maybe we would git her up a frolic."

The spring-sad dusk echoed with irrevocability.

Walking down the road, Martha thought: How will they ever get along? Rachel could sell some timberland maybe. (Poor Spurge, she'd never let him sell a stick while he was alive. He had to go on working, whether he felt like it or not.) But what would Bess ever do? There'd be some way, she supposed. Things had happened to so many families in Entremont which made it impossible, really impossible, for them to get along; yet somehow they had. But how could you get along without your husband?

How would she ever get along without Joseph? Not to walk with him through the garden rows the first Sunday after planting and look for sprouts . . . not to wait to put the tea down at noon until she heard him scraping the dirt from his boots on the edge of the porch step . . . not there in the evenings, when everyone else was older than you or younger, unless you were the one who had travelled the same path . . . not there in bed beside her at night, more sheltering than sleep itself . . . "There must be strength given." She said the words aloud.

She was almost at Bess's gate. She glanced at her dooryard. Poor soul, there *was* no wood there. That was a good idea of Joseph's. Not right away, but as soon as Bess felt like giving the men their suppers.

Would the men be joking about Bess again (she knew they *did*) by that time? she thought. Would they tease Joseph if Bess's arm touched his neck when she reached over his shoulder to fill up his plate? Would Bess herself be laughing again by that time?

She walked slower. Then she stood still. Maybe Bess would rather be alone tonight, she said to herself.

She hesitated; then she turned and walked homeward. She stopped for a few minutes at Rachel's on the way.

V

While Martha was gone, Ellen sewed a meal bag into the mat frames with twine. Anna held the side pieces taut as she fixed them securely with the iron clamps. She rested the

45

frames on the tops of four chairs and marked in the border scrolls with Joseph's carpenter pencil, dipped in brown dye.

Anna chose the rags as she began to hook—so nearly the ones Ellen would have chosen herself that almost none had to be rejected. She told Anna some little thing about the garment from which each rag had come.

That was the skirt she'd worn the night of Joseph's saluting. Her feet had still moved so lightly they'd made her lead the Lancers and the Eights.

That was the dress that had come so like a gift to Martha. The catalogue dress she'd ordered had been out of stock and they'd substituted one for twice the price. She'd found the very dress on a coloured page. She had kept it good, for years.

That was the blouse David had worn the first time his father took him to town, but it had rained on the way home and all the colours had run.

That was the dress Anna herself was baptized in. The sunlight had fallen so brightly just where Joseph stood with her by the church window that she'd begun to laugh and try to catch it.

"Grammie," Anna said suddenly, "what is 'dead'?"

Ellen's hook went slack for a minute in the loop of a rag. I don't know. It isn't sound or silence. It isn't here or there; now or then. It isn't laughing or crying. Or sleeping or waking. It isn't any of the things we know or like any of them.

"I can't tell you, child," she said. It wasn't day or night. It wasn't health or sickness.

"Is it like old?"

No. They were wrong, it wasn't like old. You came nearer and nearer to it, but you could never touch it. It was as strange to the old as it was to the young.

"No, it isn't like 'old,'" she said.

"That man in the barn," Anna said. "Is he dead?"

"I think so," she said. "I think he must have died when he was very young." The picture of him had always gone blank whenever she tried to think of him as a man grown old.

"If he died when he was young, would it be like 'young' then?"

"Yes." Yes, she thought, with him, death would be like "young."

"It will be like young when my husband dies too," Anna said.

"Hush, child!" Ellen said. "Hush."

CHAPTER VII

IN THE country the day is the determinant. The work, the thoughts, the feelings, to match it, follow.

Some years use only a few variants of the day. That year had them all; so that it was a sort of lifetime. If all the possible kinds of day are present, then too are all the possible feelings; if not in shape, in some sort of shadow.

They would never need to see another spring than that, to know spring thoroughly. From the first day Martha left the kitchen door open, to dry the scrubbed floor . . . through all the days between : the day of the rushing sound in the dark spruce mountain (that husky, susurrant night Joseph looked down at his nakedness as he stood by the bed, and felt in one instant's edification everything there was in the feel of man and woman and of having children), the day of the wild roses on the stone wall . . . until the last one, when dust first dulled the ploughshare's moist gleam. That day the sun watermarked the red-ochred shop where Martha had hung out the hams. The children, coming home from school, carried their jackets like burdens. There was no hunger for food in them today; they were satiate with the heat returning, miraculously unchanged.

All of summer they knew : the day of the daisy-trembling in the still hynotic air (if the day had been enough otherwise to make the concatenations of the moment a hair's-breadth different, Anna wouldn't have seen a sudden undulance lick the grass and felt, in essence, all the things her heart would never actually find) : the day the mowing machine dribbled the shocked clover between its chattering teeth, and spongy sprouts of last year's potatoes, thrown behind the shop, grew sickly in the unwinking heat, almost to the eaves . . . until the day that was full of green to the last brimming : the white-green of the poplars and the oat field and the river : the storm-green of the orchard and the spruce mountain : the black-green of the potato tops : the green-green of the garden.

Joseph walked back to the woodlot that day and blazed a road for the fall chopping; but not quite yet was there any yellow in the umbrella ferns. When Martha dug the mess of potatoes for dinner, their skin still chafed off under her fingers and root tendrils still clung to them like quills. She parted the green crepe folds on an ear of corn; but the kernels were not quite yellow. And when the children came up the road from the Baptizing Pool, they thought for the first time of an apple. They went to the orchard. The apples *looked* like apples now, the way green apples didn't; but when they bit into one there was no yellow in the taste—not until tomorrow.

All of fall they would know that year. The first day the sun overslept, then cut faster than ever through the leftover coolness of the night; and a leaf drifted down from the chestnut tree before the house, as if undecided after it had left the twig. (As at a sign, Joseph mowed the first swath of oats for the cows, and Martha put sheets over the tomato vines that smelled sharply of harvest under the full moon, and even Chris opened his books after supper, without prompting.) The others followed: the day of the dug potatoes lying in the dusty sunshine like fruit in a mist-thin wine: the day of the frost-starched grass and the still yellow smell of the sweet fern or the huckleberry or anything your foot crushed: the day of the yellow apple on the yellow ground (If the day when David stood listening to the soundlessness of the pasture dying had not been exactly as it was, he wouldn't have looked up suddenly at the coloured stillness of the hardwood mountain and seen in the mountain all the things that were beyond it) . . . until the day when ice first needled across the water in the cows' tub.

That night Joseph built the first warm-smelling fire in the room stove when he came in at dusk with the partridges he'd shot dangling from his belt, and Martha shook the needled earth from the dahlia bulbs that were to go into the cellar, and the children touched the chestnuts in the quick dusk as if their chocolate shapes shining in the cold leaves held in them the smoothness of all the days that were gone. (The sun went under a cloud when Martha looked out and saw Joseph walking toward the house, so that he seemed to be walking in darkness almost and the supper she'd been waiting for him seemed later than it was. If it hadn't, she would never have glimpsed every feature of her love for him, in a single instant's focus.)

And that year had all the days of winter. The day when the ploughed land was honeycombed with frost and the first snow caught like feathers in the yellow aftergrass (when Joseph covered the strawberry bed and the rosebush with straw, and Martha creased the clothes she took off the line like cardboard to get them into the basket, and the bodies of the children looked larger and darker and they seemed to play closer together) . . . the day clammy-flaked snow and rain came together and larrigan toes were bleached grey (because arteries of rain broke up the reflection of Chris's face as he glimpsed it in the window just *then*, he knew the loneliness of them for whom loneliness of the flesh is never recognized for what it is) . . . the day when fine fierce frost blew in the air and everywhere a damp mitten touched a latch a coating of wool was drawn off, like raw flesh from bone.

There was the day snow, falling like sleep, piled up in the limb-cornices, and weighted birches over the log road like someone frozen in a perfect curtsy : the soft day after that, when shoulders of snow slumped off the black-boled trees like discarded garments, and the ground snow was stained urine-yellow with the peckings of steady twig-drip, and steam rose from the backs of the horses like their own manure steaming behind them in the stable : and the day after that, when the sun lay on the lava curves of drifts in the field like yellow silk on a woman's thighs and breasts. (Joseph warned out the men to break the roads, and the shadows of great cubes of snow, sliced out with one movement of the shovel and tumbled onto the high banks, angled with underwater refraction down the steep sides of the tunnel and out over the blindingly bright tracks of the sled runners. Martha shut the drafts on the stove and went down the road, to call, in the bright-beckoning, woman-cosy afternoon. The children played in a kind of time suspension, as if even suppertime had withdrawn its encroaching tendrils.) . . . To the day when the first trickle not of rain cut the feet from under the grey sandy snow on the side hills : the day when Ellen touched the softened stubble and felt her hands draw from things the meanings her mind could no longer surprise.

II

The school concert was postponed until Christmas. Rachel thought it wouldn't look right to have it in June. *Some* people might forget in two months, but you couldn't expect *her* child to feel much like . . .

All through the year the words of his part in the play kept flushing in and out of David's head like an exalting secret. From the time when Christmas was only a word, till the time when it became like some magic lamplight turned up, haloing the days and drawing them toward it.

The words were something no one else had. For that reason, everyone who was there when the thought of them came seemed revealedly wonderful, and somehow more fiercely loved, for being so pitiably, humdrumly, outside it.

He thought of them when Joseph thrust his fork slowly into the great cock of hay, lifting the whole thing except for a few scatterings that clung to the ground, above his head : settling it carefully into place on the side of the load and then walking patiently alongside the snail-slow oxen on the sun-parched stubble, hawing or geeing them to the next cock. He had a surging, binding, kind of pity for his father—so drugged with patience. His father wasn't drawn to the moment ahead, as he was, but pushed to it by the moment behind. He would try desperately to help him, with another fork. (Though, piercing more than he could lift to the load, the hay would break apart and fall about his shoulders.)

He'd feel the same binding pity for his mother, when her thoughts seemed to slip away from her and weave in and out of their own accord, like the knitting needles she watched in her hands as she rocked gently back and forth. Or for his grandmother, when she tore the map-shaped parts of clothing into rags for a rug, as if motion of her hands were the only kind of movement left to her.

He thought of them when Chris was dropping seed potatoes, aligning the odd one that tumbled out of place, with his foot; pressing it into the soft brooch-coils of manure automatically. He'd say, "It'll soon be time for swimmin, Chris"—so that Chris could break away a second from the steadiness of the furrow; so that he could think of his naked body in the water and have somewhere outside the moment to go, too.

He thought of them, with Effie; but the bond with her wasn't of pity : he knew she had the thought of her silk dress in the same way.

And to think of them, with Anna, was best of all. For Anna was like a second safety : a place he would still have—to go to, if his secret thoughts ever failed.

The words gave him a more selfish sort of safety when he was with the ones he *didn't* love.

Sunday afternoons, perhaps, when the men dropped in to see his father. They'd sit in the kitchen, slicing their apples with a jackknife and holding the slice between thumb and knife as they bit into it, talking and silent in seesaw pendulum. Their thoughts seemed to sprawl drowsily, like a cat asleep. Later they'd all stroll to the barn to look at Joseph's stock. They'd slide their hands lazily over the cows' flanks or feel the oxen's cods. They'd turn their backs to urinate against a manager, watching the operation meditatively and speaking over their shoulders; then make a slow motion of rump-withdrawal after the moment of finishing and, turning again, patiently manipulate their buttons. They'd take their final leave so haltingly it was like a rope fraying apart. They would seem, beside himself, like people tied.

Or when the women came to a quilting. So neat there seemed to be a little of Sunday in them; neat with their stitches, and as if their talk were quilted together too, with their needles; like *one person* over the tea . . . so terribly without private excitement like his.

Or, with the other children, when they gathered the slippery pollywogs in their hands; or dragged the two bottles behind them with miniature ox yokes on their necks; or when he met them drawing their sleds up the hill as his speed grew and grew, going down, till the Big Rock moved too, and it seemed as if the others were coasting in the dark.

The words were a kind of refuge when the moment was bare, stripped right down to time and place.

These were the days when the December freshet lay manure-water-yellow over the ice in the flats and grey vapour curled from the eaten snow into the sodden air. His woollen clothing had a urine smell about it, and his father might start to file the crosscut saw, or his mother might lay the pattern on her apron material, or he could hear Chris somewhere with a hammer, but it didn't seem to be the kind of day for keeping *at* anything. Or when the hot sickly marsh-smell came up out of the dry-brooked meadow, and the spongy moss roots stuck in the hay he raked out of his father's heel prints in the swath. He'd feel tired enough for noon, but it was nowhere near noon yet.

He thought of the words too, when the moment was already brimming.

That was when he'd hear the shiver of the sleighbells as the shafts were pulled out of their tugs at the horse's sides, and then his father came into the house with the one magic paper bag in the pocket of his bearskin coat that you could tell held something special. Or when one of the men referred to something his father had done, in a good-natured perplexity that Joseph could never be made to see anything extraordinary in it, himself: the time he'd climbed into the bull pen, without even a cudgel, to ring the cross bull's nose; or the time he'd clamped a scooped-out potato over the spurting head artery of the man who'd fallen on a ledge; or one of the times when his rare anger had had a comical effect, though no one dared laugh.

The men told these things about Joseph pridefully—as if they might be telling them about themselves. Maybe Joseph would half-smile and say, "Git me my tobacco, will ya, son?" The asking of this little favour and the granting of it seemed to make a gentle conspiracy between them. When he passed the tobacco to Joseph and touched the broad hairy hand that was like the way his father was with the men (his quiet face was like the way he was about the house), he'd think, "This is my father."

He'd think of the words in the play then, to make the moment really spill over.

He thought of them too, when his mother would give him her best stew kettle for the sap to drip in and say, "Now don't you lose it, mind" : and he'd almost burst with the fervid promise that he wouldn't lose it. Or when she'd come downstairs from changing her dress. Somehow her woman-softness made a lull in the afternoon so he could look at the pictures in a new book without seeming to borrow from the time that was for other things.

He thought of them in the magic moment when his grandmother said, "Did I ever tell you about the time . . .?" Or with Anna, when they were all playing hide-and-seek and it was almost dark and suddenly she looked frighteningly small as she stood against the house, with her arms across her eyes and her skirt drawn up so the red hemstitching on her flannelette petticoat showed, counting, "Five, ten, fifteen, twenty . . ." The others seemed to run so cruelly fast then and hide so securely that he'd hide close to her and almost exposed, so that he could feel her small, soft, searching, defenseless hand gladden desperately as it felt over his face, and it wouldn't matter to her then where the others were hiding at all.

He thought of them when he was all alone : when he put on the new sneakers with the black rubber soles so shining he could hardly bear to take the first step on the ground. Or when he took the brand new Reader in a room by himself and passed his fingers over the scooped-out lettering on the bright covers and there'd be a delicious guilt as he read the words in it, as if even reading might soil the wonderfully sleek pages.

They came to him when the teacher walked beside the desks meditating on whose work to place the (1), seeming to make up her mind and then change it again, and then finally he felt her arm coming over his shoulder. Or in the satin moment of waking . . . or in the woollen moment just before sleep.

He'd think of them then, and be *doubly* translated. It would seem as if he touched the very quick of the day.

They went through him shiveringly, like cold or heat. He felt his heart really get bigger. But they weren't like any other excitement.

52

Not like when you hit the ball and then ran to the tree and back, with your breath all gone and your side all shouting, just before the ball got back too; or when the calf you were leading suddenly began to caper and then run like the wind, you couldn't stop him, you could barely hang onto the chain, and then the laughing struck you, and as you bounced along, your feet barely touching the ground, the laughter gaining in you with each step, you seemed to be lifted right out of the bright daylight still. Nor like when you said, "Yeh, she gives twice as big a mess as that, but her mind wasn't on her *milk* today at all," or "Rachel's face looks as if she was settin on a pot all the time," and the *rest* of them laughed.

They weren't that kind of wonderful. They had a snugness about them.

They were more like in the haymow when the rain was on the roof; or under the tent he and Chris had made out of meal bags, when the last flap had been fastened on tight with shingle nails and the last bit of sunlight shut out; or the moment in bed at night when his body and Chris's next it made a puddle of warmth in the shockingly cold blankets, with the thoughts of the day (when he had been running and laughing) sinking away from his body as softly as bare toes in the warm dust.

They were still more like when his father took him with him to buy a pair of cattle, the horse trotting at first through the same stretch of woods and then slowing its pace, and Joseph holding the whip against the spokes of the turning wheel so that the hollow tick of it made a core of stillness as they crept so beautifully saving-the-time along. Or when the other men all came to help shoe the bad ox and he'd sit on the top beam of the haymow and watch them lash its flailing legs into the slings on the barn floor; in it, but above it and outside it at the same time. Or with Chris, walking by the churchyard at night, and thinking of walking by the churchyard alone.

Or were they most of all, he would think sometimes, like when Anna would fall asleep on the lounge before it was time for bed and he'd cover her up gently with a coat? Her breath would come so softly without any movement he could see, like the smell of a flower, that he'd think with a shimmer of the most beautiful sadness, because she wasn't: What if she were dead?

Or were they most of all like Christmas itself?

CHAPTER VIII

THERE were the three days : the day before Christmas, the day of Christmas, and the day after. Those three days lamplight spread with a different softness over the blue-cold snow. Faces were all unlocked; thought and feeling were open and warm to the touch. Even inanimate things came close, as if they had a blood of their own running through them.

On the afternoon of the first day the cold relaxed suddenly, like a frozen rag dipped in water. Distances seemed to shrink. The dark spruce mountain moved nearer, with the bodies of the trees dark as before rain.

Martha had done up all her housework before noon, and the afternoon had the feel of Saturday. It was a parenthesis in time—before the sharp expectancy began to build with the dusk and spark to its full brightness when the lamp was lit. There were so many places it was wonderful to be that afternoon that David was scarcely still a minute.

He went outside and made a snowman. The snow was so packy it left a track right down to the grass roots. It was a perfect day to be alone with, the only confidant of its mysteries. Yet it was equally nice to be with people. The claim of their ordinary work was suspended today, no one's busyness was any kind of pushing aside.

He went inside and sat close to his grandmother. He asked her a string of questions; not for information, but because he was young and she was old. To let her feel that she was helping him get things straight was the only way he knew to give her some of the splendid feeling he had so guiltily more of.

He went out again where Chris was sawing wood. How could Chris *stand* there like that, today . . . his shoulders moved so patiently, the saw sank with such maddening slowness. Yet because he did, he was somehow wonderful. When a block fell, David would thrust the stick ahead on the saw-horse with such a prodigal surge of helpfulness beyond what the weight of the wood asked for that Chris would have to push it back a little before he made the next cut.

He went back into the house and stood at the table where his mother was mixing doughnuts.

Everything was clean as sunshine. The yellow-shining mixing bowl in the centre of the smooth hardwood bread board; the circles of pure white where the sieve had stood; the measuring cup with the flour-white stain of milk and soda on its sides; and the flat yellow-white rings of the doughnuts themselves lying beside the open-mouthed jug that held the lard, drift-smooth at the centre and crinkled like pie crust along the sides. His mother carried the doughnuts to the stove, flat on her palm, and dropped them one by one into the hot fat. He followed her, watching. They'd sink to the bottom. Then, after a fascinating second of total disappearance, they'd loom dark below the surface, then float all at once, brown and hissing all over. It had never been like this, watching her make dough-nuts before.

He went into the pantry and smelled the fruit cakes that lay on the inverted pans they'd been cooked in. He opened the bag of nuts and rolled one in his palm; then put it back. He put his hand deep down into the bag and rolled all the nuts through his fingers: the smooth hazelnuts that the hammer would split so precisely: the crinkled walnuts with the lung-shaped kernels so fragile that if he got one out all in one piece he'd give it to Anna: the flat black butternuts whose meat clove so tightly to the shell that if you ever got one out whole you saved it to the very last.

Then he leaned over and smelled the bag of oranges. He didn't touch it. He closed his eyes and smelled it only. The sharp, sweet, reminding, fulfilling, smell of the oranges was so incarnate of tomorrow it was delight almost to sinfulness.

He went out and sat beside Anna. She was on her knees before the lounge, turning the pages of the catalogue. They played "Which Do You Like the Best?" with the coloured pages. Anna would point to the incredibly beaded silk dress that the girl wore standing in a great archway with the sunlight streaming across it, as her choice. He'd say, "Oh, I do, too." And as his hand touched Anna's small reaching hand and as he looked at her small reaching face, he almost cried with the knowing that some Christmas Day, when he had all that money he was going to have, he'd remember every single thing that Anna had liked the best. She'd find every one of them beneath the tree when she got up in the morning.

He went out where his father was preparing the base for the tree. All the work-distraction was gone from his father today, and David knew that even if so few pieces of board were to be found as to defeat anyone else, his father would still be able to fix something that was perfect.

Joseph lay one crosspiece in the groove of the other. He

55

said to David, "Think you could hold her just like that, son, till I drive the nails?"

"Oh yes," David said, "yes." He strove with such intense willingness to hold them so exactly that every bit of his strength and mind was soaked up. He touched the axe that would cut the tree. The bright cold touch of it shone straight through him.

He ran in to tell Anna it was almost time. He waited for her to button her gaiters. He was taut almost to pallor when Joseph stepped from the shop door, crooked the axe handle under one arm, and spat on the blade for one final touch of the whetstone.

"Chris," he called, "we're *goin!*"

"All right," Chris said. "You go on. I guess I'll finish the wood."

How *could* Chris stay here? How could anyone *wait* anywhere today? It was almost impossible to be still even in the place where the thing was going on.

Joseph walked straight toward the dark spruce mountain. David and Anna would fall behind, as they made imprints of their supine bodies in the snow; then run to catch up. They would rush ahead, to simulate rabbit tracks with their mittens —the palms for the parallel prints of the two back feet, the thumb the single print where the front feet struck together; then stand and wait. Their thoughts orbited the thought of the tree in the same way their bodies orbited Joseph's.

"Anna, if anyone walked right through the mountain, weeks and weeks, I wonder where he'd come out . . ."

"Dave, hold your eyes almost shut, it looks like water . . ."

"There's one, there's one . . ." But when they came to it the branches on the far side were uneven.

Joseph himself stopped to examine a tree.

"Father, the best ones are way back, ain't they?" David said quickly. This *was* a good tree, but it wouldn't be any fun if they found the perfect tree almost at once.

"There's one . . ." But it was a cat spruce.

"There's one . . ." But the spike at the top was crooked.

"There's one, Father . . ." But a squirrel's nest of brown growth spoiled the middle limbs.

Joseph found the perfect fir, just short of the mountain. The children had missed it, though their tracks were all about. He went to it from the road, straight as a die. The bottom limbs were ragged, but those could be cut off; and above them, the circlets of the upward-angling branches were perfect. The trunk was straight and round. The green of the needles was dark and rich, right to the soft-breathing tip.

"How about this one?" Joseph said.

The children said nothing, looking at the lower limbs.

"From here up," Joseph said. He nicked the bark with his axe.

"Yes, oh yes," they cried then. "That's the best tree anyone could find, ain't it, Father?" The ridiculous momentary doubt of their father's judgement made them more joyous than ever.

They fell silent as Joseph tramped the snow about the base of the tree, to chop it. David made out he was shaking snow from his mitten. He took off Anna's mitten too, pretending to see if there was any snow in hers. He stood there holding her mitten-warmed hand, not saying anything, and watched his father strike the first shivering blow.

The tree made a sort of sigh as it swept through the soft air and touched the soft snow. Then the moment broke. The children came close and touched the green limbs. They thrust their faces between them—into the dark green silence. They smelled the dark green, cosy, exciting smell of the whole day in the balsam blisters on the trunk.

Joseph stood and waited: the good kind of waiting, with no older-hurry in him. Then he lifted the tree to his shoulders, both arms spread out to steady it at either end.

The twins walked close behind him. They let the swaying branches touch their faces. They walked straight now, because the first cast of dusk had begun to spread from the mountain. The first dusk-stiffening of the snow and a shadow of the first night-wonder were beginning. Now the things of the day fell behind them; because all that part of the day which could be kept warm and near was in the tree, and they were taking the tree home, into the house, where all the warm things of after-dark belonged.

Anna whispered to David, "I got somethin for you, Dave."

And he whispered, "I got somethin for you, too."

"What?"

"Oh, I can't tell."

Then they guessed. Each guess was made deliberately small, so there'd be no chance that the other would be hurt by knowing that his present was less than the vision of it. Each of them felt that whatever they had for each other all their lives would have something of the magic, close-binding smell of the fir boughs somewhere in it, like the presents for each other of no other two people in the world.

Martha had huddled the furniture in the dining room together, to clear a corner for the tree.

"Aw, Mother," David said, "you said you'd wait!"

His mother laughed. "I just moved the sofa and mats a little," she said. "I didn't touch the trimmings. Do you think it's too late to put them up before supper?"

"No," David cried, "no. I'm not a bit hungry."

"I suppose if supper's late it'll make you late with your chores, won't it?" she said to Joseph.

"Well," Joseph said, "I suppose I *could* do em before supper." He hesitated. "Or do you want me to help you with the trimmin?"

"Oh, yes," David said. "Help us."

He wanted everyone to be in on it. Especially his father. It was wonderful when his father helped them with something that wasn't work, *inside* the house.

David fanned open the great accordion-folding bell (because of one little flaw his mother had got it—it didn't seem possible —for only a quarter). He tied the two smaller bells on the hooks of the blinds. Then he and his father and Chris took off their boots. They stood on chairs in their stocking feet and hung the hemlock garlands Ellen had made; around the casings and from the four ceiling corners of the room to a juncture at its centre, where the great bell was to be suspended.

Someone would say, "Pass the scissors?" and David would say, "*Sure,*" beating with gladness to do them any small favours. Martha would stand back and say, "A little lower on that side," and they'd say, "Like that? Like that? More still?" all full of that wonderful patience to make it perfect. Everyone would laugh when someone slipped off a chair. His father would say, "Why wouldn't some red berries look good in there?" and to hear his *father* say a thing like that filled the room with something really splendid. Sometimes he'd step on Anna's toe as they busied back and forth. He'd say, "Oh, Anna, did that hurt?" and she'd laugh and say, "No, it didn't hurt." He'd say, "Are you *sure?*" and just that would be wonderful.

The dusk thickened and the smell of the hemlock grew soft as lamplight in the room. The trimming was done and the pieces swept up and put into the stove.

Then Joseph brought in the tree, backward through the door so the limbs wouldn't break. No one spoke as he stood it in the space in the corner. It just came to the ceiling. It was perfect. Suddenly the room was whole. Its heart began to beat.

They ate in the dining room that night. David smelled the roast spare ribs that had been kept frozen in the shop. He felt now how hungry he'd been all the time.

The room was snug with the bunching of the furniture and the little splendour of eating there on a weekday. And when

Martha held the match to the lamp wick, all at once the yellow lamplight soft-shadowed their faces (with the blood running warm in them after being out in the cold) like a flood and gathered the room all in from outside the windows. It touched the tree and the hemlock and the great red bell with the flaw no one could even notice, like a soft breath added to the beating of the room's heart: went out and came back with a kind of smile. The smell of the tree grew suddenly and the memory of the smell of the oranges and the feel of the nuts. In that instant suddenly, ecstatically, burstingly, buoyantly, enclosingly, sharply, safely, stingingly, watchfully, batedly, mountingly, softly, ever so softly, it was Chistmas Eve.

The special Christmas Eve food lit their flesh like the lamplight lit the room. Even Christopher talked fast. Even the older ones spoke as if their thoughts had come down from the place where they circled, half-attentive, other nights.

David glanced out of the window. He saw "Old Herb Hennessey" walking down the road. When Herb went into his house tonight there'd be no fire in the stove, and after supper he'd sit and read the paper and it would be just like any other night.

David watched the blur of his heavy body move down the road in the almost-dark. It seemed as if no sound was coming from him anywhere, even if you were there where his feet were falling. He felt the funniest, scariest kind of pity for Herb. He felt the sweetest, safest sort of exaltation: that such a thing could be, however incredibly, but not ever for him. (He was to wonder, years later, if this now were some sort of justice for the unconscious cruelty in that thought.)

When he went to help his father with the chores, great-flaked Christmas snow began to fall against the sides of the yellow lantern. The barn smelled warm and cosy. He secretly poked in extra hay to the cows, because it was Christmas Eve. The torture of being outside the house was an exquisite one, because the tree was there to go back to.

All evening long, some things (the faces, the conversation) were open as never before. Other things (the packages somewhere in the closet, the sound of nuts tumbled into a bowl behind the closed pantry door) were bewitchingly secret. There were the last desperate entreaties of him and Anna on the stairs: to call each other in the morning and *please* not to go down first. His prayers were over so quickly they might have been read at a glance from some bright sheet in his mind. Then the blanket warmth and the tiredness in him stole out to meet each other.

He lay beside Chris and listened to the voices downstairs behind the closed doors, the footsteps, the rustlings. He tried to identify them at first: Would that be hanging oranges on the boughs? Would that be a sled for Chris? That sound of paper, were they unwrapping a doll for Anna? Would that be some swift gleaming thing like skates, for him?

Then the sounds began to wave and flicker through the candlelight of drowsiness and warmth.

He whispered to Chris, "Chris, when you learn to skate fast, is it the best fun of anything?" "Kind of," Chris said. He whispered, "Chris, someday let's go way back to the top of the mountain," and Chris said, "Maybe." He whispered, "Chris, how old is Herb Hennessey? Is he four times as old as us?" and Chris said, "I guess." The pauses between questions and reply got longer. He said, "Chris, are you asleep?" There was no answer at all. He thought, "How *could* Chris go to sleep?"

Then the sounds downstairs started to flow along a stream, and he floated alongside them. Then they drifted ahead of him and he began to sink. But the stream was of wool, so foldingly deep and closingly warm that he didn't try any more to reach out for the surface.

Ellen slept dreamlessly when the house was still.

Joseph dreamed that as he lifted the log onto the sled bench Martha and the children came running to help him, but suddenly he was powerless because the snow had disappeared. And Martha dreamed that it was morning and the children were all laughing as they opened their things, but she couldn't find Joseph anywhere in the house and suddenly all the needles of the tree began to fall. And Chris sighed in his sleep because he and Charlotte were on the bank of a moving stream, but as they knelt together to drink they couldn't seem to draw any water up into their mouths. And Anna dreamed that it was morning and some voice kept calling her to come see the tree. She said she had to wait for David, but she couldn't resist this voice; and when David came to the head of the stairs, there was water across the step, and she couldn't quite reach his hand across it.

David slept and he dreamed that they were all walking back the road that led to the top of the mountain. All the trees along the road were Christmas trees. They were shining with presents, but as he reached for something (for himself or for Anna) the thing would disappear, and Herb Hennessey would be there, cutting down the tree.

A train whistle carried through the soft air all the way from town. As the tree fell the sound of the train whistle crept into the dream, into the sound of the falling tree.

CHAPTER IX

D AVID awoke at five o'clock. The morning was
Christmas-still. He thought it must be night yet
until he heard the crackle of kindling in the
stove, and the voices of his father and mother in the kitchen.
They were day voices. Suddenly sleep past put a sharp edge of
clarity on everything. This was the morning that had had Tuesday and Wednesday before it, and then only Wednesday, and
now this was the morning itself.

He shook Chris. "Chris, Chris, it's morning!" He leaped out
of bed. "Anna, Anna," he called, "it's morning, the fire's made."

He and Anna waited, shivering in the hall, for Chris ("Chris,
Chris, hurry up"). They went down the stairs, shivering more
than cold had ever made them shiver. They went past the dining
room where the wonder waited, into the kitchen. Chris glanced
into the dining room as he passed, but David whispered to
Anna, "Don't look." Neither of them turned a head.

They stood by the kitchen stove. They said, "Merry Christmas"; but their voices were like the voices they recited with
when they'd forgotten the next line. They tried to stop shivering; but they couldn't, even by the stove. These were like
moments out of time altogether, because they were up and
going to do something splendid, but the lamp was still lit, the
day hadn't really begun.

Martha had warmed their clothes on the oven door. David
pulled his on in the porch. Anna took hers into the pantry.
Joseph came in from the barn with the milk, and Martha
strained the milk while he washed his hands. Not till then did
she pick up the lamp and say, "Come, Joseph." She led them
all through the dining room door.

The tree was there. So still. So Christmas-still. So proudly,
evenly full of its own mysterious bearing that even when
Martha turned up the wick of the lamp, no one rushed to touch
it. For a minute no one moved. This was the tree of hope: the
yellow globes of oranges hanging on the boughs, the perfectly
scalloped garlands of popcorn, the white tents of handkerchiefs
on the green limbs, and secretly between the branches, nearer
the trunk, the mesmeric presents themselves. They knew so
surely that everything they wanted would be there, they could
wait.

"Joseph," Ellen said, "do you remember the first little fir we . . .?" Then the children swarmed about the tree.

Joseph and Martha guided their explorations. They passed down what was beyond the reach of young arms; pointing at something that still remained for one or the other if that one had decided his allotment must be exhausted; holding one thing back for each of them, so that no one would run out of gifts first.

Chris's sled and larrigans were on the floor. But David's skates and Anna's doll were at the top of the tree. When Joseph reached for them they held their breath, as if somewhere on the way down the miracle might disappear before they had touched it once. David put one bright blade against his face. The cool touch of the bright, swift steel and the smell of the new leather mingled with the smell of the oranges and the tree. Anna touched gently the soft, fragile doll's face. There were scribblers and pencils and the jackets and the dress.

Then almost at the last, David found what Anna had got for him. It was a book. *Robinson Crusoe.* He opened it and saw the wonderful waiting words running over the starch-clean pages. He said, "Oh, Anna."

Then he told her, no, higher, a little higher, this side, *there,* until at last she saw the ring he'd got for her with soap-wrapper coupons. And when she laid down the doll itself and held the ring in her hand (forgetting to finish the smile she'd started, because the ring was so beautiful), that was better even than any of the things he had found for himself.

They thought it was all finished. But it wasn't.

"You didn't look *behind* the tree," Martha said.

There they found the miniature house, perfect right down to the tiny covers on the stove, for Anna; and the kaleidoscope for David.

"Chris got them out of his rabbit money," Joseph said.

They could hardly believe it. They'd never thought of Chris getting *anything* for them, and here he (Chris!) had thought of getting them things like that.

They had the funniest feeling. It was hurtful, but sweet for feeling it together: the shame that neither of them had thought of getting anything for Chris at all. He'd seemed like the older ones, who watched *their* having as if that were a gift itself. He'd seemed to have no special separate place in him that a special gift could match.

They exclaimed more about his presents then, than about their own. They said, "Chris, ain't that sled a beauty! It's the best thing of all, ain't it!"—because, though Chris's things did add up to more than theirs in a way, there was nothing amongst them just like the kaleidoscope or the little stove with the perfect covers.

The tree was delivered now of its mysteries and the plain having began. The lamp grew pale in the beginning sunlight. Martha remembered breakfast, and Joseph remembered the rest of his chores. David got a hammer and broke the first nut. He broke the skin of the first orange and felt the first incarnate taste of its sharp juice. And suddenly it was Christmas Day.

After breakfast Chris went to his snares. "Do you wanta go with me, Dave?" he said.

"Yeh, sure." To*day*? he thought—but Chris had thought of a present for him, and he hadn't thought of Chris at all.

"Are you going to try out your new jacket?" his mother said.

"I guess not now," he said. He couldn't bear to think of putting it on just yet and maybe getting it wet and wrinkled in the snow.

There were no rabbits in the snares. When they came to the last one, David said, "I guess I gotta squirt my pickle, if it won't take all the snow off yer rabbit roads."

Chris laughed, but he turned his back to fiddle with the snare pole. David tossed his mittens quickly under a tree.

Halfway home he said, "Chris, I musta laid my mittens down back there. You go ahead. I'll run get em."

He drew up all the snares as he went. He didn't blame Chris for catching rabbits. Chris wasn't cruel. If Chris stopped to *think* about hunting, like he did, he couldn't do it at all. But David couldn't bear—not tonight, especially not when he turned the glittering kaleidoscope—to think of the rabbits strangling somewhere in the moonlight.

After dinner (the Christmas dinner food was like food to satisfy hunger developed specially for it; the Christmas Eve food had been more like something for thirst than for hunger), the tree stood still with ripeness, its wonder safely fruited. It could be left. The children went to see Effie and Charlotte.

Effie had a tree. It was a small one, but there was the same feel in her house as in theirs : of this day brought snug into the room from other days. The same touch through the window of the sun that shadowed noon-lazy on the Christmas snow and on the Christmas-lazy walking of anyone on the road. Yet there *was* a difference, David thought. Their Christmas was like a natural garden, with the foliage as well as the blossoms. Effie's and Bess's had only the flowers, and those were planted. They had to feed them with their own closeness.

"Our tree ain't so very pretty," Bess said. "We couldn't lug a very big one."

She always spoke like that about anything of her own. The others seemed to think that nothing pretty should rightfully *belong* to her. Somehow, if she disparaged it first, she could prevent them from taking her custody of it away.

"Why didn't you ask Father?" David said. "He'd have got you a tree." Chris frowned at him. David didn't understand.

"We *wanted* a small tree," Effie said. "We could carry it all right, couldn't we, Mother?"

She seemed to put a fence around it. She too knew how her mother was deflected by the other women whenever their paths came close to touching. She resented beforehand any surprise that they could have special things like anyone else.

There wasn't much for Effie but the silk dress for the concert. Her silk dress and Anna's woollen one were like the plant and the flower again. They all touched the silk, Chris twice. It made David think of the play.

He whispered to Effie, "Do you know your part?"

She whispered, "Yes, do you?"

Something they shared then lifted their feet off the day. They seemed to forget for a minute where Chris and Anna were to be found. She withdrew her protectiveness from the tree. She stood looking at it *with* him; as if, if it *shouldn't* be beautiful there would be no hurt in accepting that judgement from him now. As if, if you both knew what beautiful *was*, it wouldn't matter what anything of yours looked like to the other.

"We better go," Chris said, "if we're goin to Charlotte's."

Bess slipped some candy into their pockets as they left. It wasn't a bit like the skimpy-tasting candy the women made for church socials. David wondered why his mother never said anything when he told her how wonderful Bess's candy tasted. When they came home from Bess's, she never said like she did when they came from another house: What did they have for supper? Was she cleaned up? Did she ask you what *I* was doing?

"*Dave*," Chris said, outside, "what made you say that about Father gettin em a tree?"

"Why?"

"Why, Chris?" Anna said.

"Ohhhh, never mind."

They went to Charlotte's. Charlotte had no tree. When they went into Rachel's kitchen, it was as if they'd gone in *out* of Christmas.

Rachel rocked by the window in the cushionless chair. On no day in their house did the moments move faster or slower. Time was something captive in that room always; something she wore away, bit by slow bit, with each movement of her rocker. There was no echo of the laugh of someone who'd just gone. No lingering of a sentence spoken in the day's work, when a thing was tried one way and then another ("What do *you* think?"); or of a hum in the day's planning. There was only a kind of smell of walls, of the doily under the Bible on the centre table, the bare kerosene smell of the lamp that stood on the mirrorless bureau beside the bed when time had finally been worn away till nine o'clock.

David could hardly sit still. It was like the long dry sermon when there was only a handful at church.

"What did you get, Lottie?" Anna said.

"I got these shoes," Charlotte said. She held out one foot.

"She needed em, so I give em to her last week," Rachel said. "There wasn't any sense keepin em."

Wouldn't that be awful, David and Anna both thought; but Charlotte didn't seem to mind.

"And I got some scribblers."

"We didn't make much fuss," Rachel said. "We didn't feel much like Christmas this year." She sighed. "I'll be glad when it's over."

"Was you down to Effie's?" Charlotte said.

"Yes."

"I shouldn't think Bess'd feel much like Christmas, either," Rachel said. She sighed again. "I should think remorse . . ."

David whispered to Anna, "Let's go."

He took a long breath outside. He looked toward their own house. There'd be the smell of oranges in it and the cosy, personal smell of the tree. There'd be a kind of resonance lingering still of all the teakettle-singing words his mother and father had spoken to each other while they were away.

Chris stayed. He said he'd bring in the night's wood for Charlotte.

It's funny about Chris and Charlotte, David thought. (For a minute Charlotte seemed to like Bess, except for Bess's great free laugh and something outward-moving about Bess like the spring in their pasture that found its own force amongst the driest rocks.) When Chris went near Charlotte, something in them both seemed to reach out for touch, then recoil. They'd both stand there for a second like two strangers who'd met in a path too narrow for passing.

He kept glancing down at his new jacket as he walked along

the road. Little wrinkles were already showing at the crook of his elbows. He walked on, with his arms held straight at his sides. When they went into the house, he took the jacket off and folded it again the way it had been on the tree. It didn't seem to him that he could ever take it for everyday and have the sharp creases of the sleeves become round and sloppy.

He took it off now, because he and Anna were going down to the meadow with the new skates (screwed right onto the boots, like the older boys'), and he might fall. He was going to try crossing one leg over the other, to make a proper smooth turn. He could never manage that with the old spring skates. If anyone was looking when he came to a corner, he just coasted around it or stopped to make out he was tying his bootlace.

He was glad now that Chris had stayed at Charlotte's. Somehow he wouldn't want Chris to see him, if he failed. Anna was the only one he could bear to have watch him try anything in which he might fail.

But he didn't fail.

They went down the long hill behind the church, in the soft Christmas-kindled air, to the meadow. Its ice shone blue and wide and smooth; so infinitely full of possible paths for the swift skates to take. The brook ran, open, through its middle. Lips of shell ice hung over the brook's edges. He stood on his skates. And Anna watched.

The skates felt stiff and strange at first. He could go fast enough on them, straight. But when he tried to turn, it was just as jerky as it had been on the old spring skates. He tried again and again. Once he almost got it, but the next time was no nearer than before.

Then just at dusk—just when there is that nice lonely feeling about the whole world as you stand below a cold hill at the edge of the trees and it is dusk in the wintertime—just when the dark spruces began to come in closer around the blue meadow ice and the blue ice seemed to stretch farther away toward the other side of the woods, hardening and booming with a far-off sound so it would bruise you if you fell on it and you were alone, but not now, because Anna was there with you, watching —just then, he did it.

He didn't know, in his head, how. But he knew the minute he felt the cool flight-smooth dip of it, that it was right. Now his legs knew it, to repeat it, whenever they liked. He was so sure of it now he knew he could do it slower, or faster, or horse it up, or do it any way he liked. He was so sure of it now he knew he wouldn't even have to test it again. He knew he would be the best skater in the whole world.

"I did it!" he said to Anna.

"I know!" she said. "I saw you!" That was the best part of all.

And then his skates were off, and he was walking back up the hill in his larrigans. The funny feel of them as they touched the ground was almost as treacherous after the swift skates as the skates had been when he'd first put them on.

He was tired. The little lonely feel of dusk in the wintertime (like dying, when the dying is over and only the stillness is left) was in the wheels of the wagon that stood at the top of the hill with a little fine snow drifting through the spokes, and in the windows of the church, and, looking back, in the meadow they had left. But Anna was with him. That made it all the nicer for being that way. You would know it was Christmas night no matter where you were and if you had no idea of the date at all.

They were too tired to play that night. They left their things beneath the tree. They only looked at them or touched them. Outside, Christmas moonlight latticed the snow with shadows that grew out longer and longer from the dark roots of the trees. And when David went to bed, sleep covered him at once like an extra blanket drawn up.

11

A shuddering of the bed awakened David as sleep wore thin with the thinning of the dark. Then he heard the mourning wind. It lashed the house, hard and lost. The house seemed caught inside one great mouth. The wind tried to swallow it, then rushed moaning across the fields like something out of its mind, gathering up the helpless snow, and returning again and again to knock itself out against the windows.

David pulled the clothes up tight. He lay with his eyes shut, exquisitely listening. He knew the house would hold. He knew the sad, driven, crazy teeth of the wind would break when they bit into the friendly wool of the scarves and extra sweaters.

When he went downstairs, Joseph was coming in from the barn. The wind plucked up waves of milk from the pail, like fans of cow urine. It slammed the storm door back and reached inside, sifting a fine layer of snow onto the porch floor. Joseph's frost-creaking boots skidded and he almost lost his feet. The snow was embedded in his clothes and encrusted his eyebrows.

"Boy, this is a snifter!" he said.

The windowpanes were furred over with frost, except for little parabolas of drift in the sash corners. David thawed out a peephole with his breath. The trees weaved in the wind. They looked almost too tired and distracted to stand. When the wind sucked back from the house and broke in a sudden explosion before the barn, the barn disappeared. The wind spun a bluster of light snow on top of the drifts, lifting it, dropping it, baffling it. The drifts themselves, scooped out on the underside in the shape of a scythe, looked hard as bone; and here and there a patch of ice, swept smooth as a hand, shone blue and mournful.

Joseph warned out the men to break the roads; but before the frost-whiskered oxen had gone the length of a sled runner, the vicious snow had filled in their tracks. When Chris and David went to water the cows, the wind sucked their breath from them as if it were a loose hat on their heads. The bite of the cold went right down to their lungs. They had to shout to make themselves heard. The cows shied their heads into the biting wind and tested the water again and again with their teeth before gathering up a great frosty ball of it and rolling it down their long throats. The nails in the clapboards of the barn were drawn out and furred with the frost. The barn's timbers creaked as if with the next gust they must surely split. When Chris and David came back to the house, the only way they could hold their breath at all was to walk back-to.

Now there was no *night* between him and the lines of the play, David's heart caught when he thought of them, like in falling. But around noon the teacher came to say that the concert was postponed on account of the storm (how warmingly funny the man's pants she wore looked when he heard her say that!), and the afternoon was perfect.

The afternoon was totally safe, because the storm kept them all in the house together. Nothing could get at them from outside. Nothing could leave. Even his father, shed of his own outdoors part, was together with them in the close house-safeness.

Joseph drowsed on the couch in the kitchen, Ellen tore rags, and Martha knitted. Their talk made a sound like the flutter of wood in the stove or the stewing of the kettle—almost a no-sound. It was as if the cable of time had been broken and they were all magically marooned until its strands were spliced together again.

Chris plaited strips of moosehide into a snowshoe bow on the dining room floor, and Martha let Anna drape blankets over the clothes rack to make a house for herself and her doll. (There were no rules this afternoon about the appropriate place to do anything.) David curled up on the dining room sofa, near enough the tree to smell it and the oranges constantly. He read his new book with an ecstatic caution, as if even reading might soil its pages.

Each one seemed to have a sheltered moment for his own thing. Yet the silence amongst them was itself like a kind of visiting, one with the other.

Sometimes David found the spell of the story so strong he must somehow break it and prolong it. He'd go out to the kitchen and ask his father what was the very highest drift he'd ever seen, or ask his mother if she didn't want him to hold the skein of yarn over his arms, or help his grandmother tear a few rags. He'd come back and watch Chris's weaving, silently, as if it were a spellbinding thing that no one else could do; and look inside Anna's tent of blankets, smiling only, as if to bestow his blessing on her good time without breaking into it.

Then he'd go back to the sofa and rejoin Friday on the hot, mysterious island. And then he'd go to the window and look through the breath holes in the pane at the fans of snow howling against the sash. You'd freeze, outside, if you were naked like Friday; but inside, the wood was sighing under the covers of both stoves. He prayed that the storm would last all night.

It did. When the wood boxes were full and the water in and you knew no one would have to go outdoors any more, the storm mourned, more lost than ever, at the pane. At suppertime they pulled the kitchen table closer to the stove. Joseph covered up the potatoes in the cellar with the bearskin laprobe from the sleigh, and Martha brought her ferns out into the kitchen so they wouldn't chill. She said they'd have to stay up late and keep the fires. She got them a lunch at twelve o'clock. He'd never seen midnight before.

The wind was still cold and lost outside, but the lamplight and the wood warmth and the slow-cosy talk melted them all together. And with this the latest he'd ever stayed up in his whole life (the tree was still awake and shining), there had never been anything like it.

Martha wrapped up a hot stick of wood for his bed. When his feet touched it, it was like touching sleep itself.

There was still a long safe night between him and the words of the play.

CHAPTER X

THE next night was the night of the concert. David's head felt light. The words of the play kept up an uncontrollable chatter in his mind. Supper made a taste in his mouth like the taste after running.

"Why won't you let us *hear* your piece, Dave?" his mother said.

He couldn't tell her why not. She wouldn't understand about the curtain and the spell. He felt as if his refusing was betrayal—but he could only speak the lines aloud *there*, or when he was by himself. Or with Effie and Anna.

He was saying them to himself as he poked hay in to the cows. He didn't hear his father's footsteps behind him.

"That sounds all right," Joseph said.

But they sounded silly to David then. He stopped short. He tried to imitate his father's voice in the barn. "Git yer head *back* there, you damn . . ." he shouted at the black cow.

As the time came closer still, the words touched his mind with the chill of bedclothes touching his flesh times he'd had a fever. His arms were trembling so when his mother made last-minute alterations in the sleeve lengths of his new suit that he could hardly hold them straight at his sides. He almost wished he'd refused to take a piece at all, like Chris had. Chris never had to do anything but *listen*.

A wire was stretched across the platform of the schoolhouse. Bedsheets were looped over it for a curtain. Behind this curtain a small corner of the stage had been screened off for a dressing room. Here the teacher and the children were clotted.

The children whispered frenziedly. They fussed continuously with their costumes. They ran to the teacher with bright, terrible confidences: "Miss Speakman, Tim can't find his star!" "Miss Speakman, the oil's almost below the wick." "Miss Speakman, it looks like the curtain's caught—right there, see?"

Miss Speakman fixed the lamp and the curtain. She made Tim another tinsel star. She told Cora, through the pins in her mouth, for heaven's sake to keep her head still. She said, "Danny, don't you dare to laugh tonight and spoil *everything*."

Some of the children got out the scribbler pages their pieces were written on. The pages were worn furry at the creases. They read them over desperately, as if to catch the words before they rushed off the lines. Some whispered them out loud in a solemn voice. Some moved their lips and said them over only in their heads. Some of them peeked through the curtain.

The audience had straggled up the road with their lanterns, in groups of two and four, talking around the edge of things as they always did when they went together to something after dark. Now they were cramped awkwardly into the desk seats.

Once they had sat there as children themselves. They had had the thought ahead of no more school shiver in them like a different breath. But now they waited, patiently, for their own children to come out and say their pieces. These children seemed younger than they had ever been. They seemed older than these children would ever be.

The children peeked and giggled.

"I saw Mother, but she didn't see *me*."

"Old Herb Hennessey's there!"

"Miss Speakman? I gotta go out!"

("Oh Lord! Well, slip out the side door. Now don't get snow on that crepe paper.")

"Miss Speakman, what time is it?"

"What time is it, Miss Speakman?"

"How much longer?"

("Oh, please be quiet. Why can't you act like David there? He isn't making a sound.")

He couldn't. He was absolutely still inside. The moment when he must say the first lines of the play had started to move toward him.

There was no comfort in anyone near. It was worse than being sick. Then the other faces were outside your pain, but when they smiled at you the pain softened. Now he was absolutely alone. Even Anna's smile was the smile of a photograph, a smile of some other time. The people outside the curtain seemed to have a cruel strangeness about them. He felt as if nakedness had spread his face and body wide and unmanageable. The words of the play were frozen. They had no feeling at all.

He tried to think of tomorrow. Somehow, tomorrow must come.

"Shhhhhh . . ." The moment stopped moving. The curtain was pulled back.

"Ladies and gentlemen . . ."

David listened to Anna's opening recitation. She said her piece better than the others—almost as if it were something she'd thought up herself; only hesitant for trying to say it exactly the way he'd told her to.

(For some reason Martha felt a little catch in her throat when Anna bowed—the rosette on her shoulder wasn't quite straight. She wished she could adjust it. And Joseph felt a kind of incredulity that his own Anna had been carrying around all those heavy words, all that time, behind her small soft face.)

The others said their pieces doggedly, as if they were reading the words off their mind. The spring of their nervousness kept jerking the words out one by one until the spring finally ran down. They said the funny parts in the dialogue as they read the words in a lesson they weren't quite sure how to pronounce. David wondered why the audience laughed. You could see they weren't speaking to each *other*; it was just the lines of the book talking back and forth. When they came back to the dressing room their excitement was only because it was over; not because for a minute they had made themselves into someone else.

The tableau came next. The teacher had planned this as a stunning surprise. The children had been pledged not to breathe a word of it beforehand.

Anna and Charlotte stood on two chairs. Effie stood, between and above them, on a step ladder. Everything was swathed first in sheets, then in billows of cheesecloth. The three figures were supposed to come out of a cloud. Their hair was combed out loose about their shoulders: Anna's a soft brown; Charlotte's coal black; and Effie's a light thin gold. Each had a silver crown—of stiff cardboard covered with pressed-out tea lead. Each had across her breast a wide band of flour bag dyed scarlet; with cut-out lettering so that a legend showed in white from the cheesecloth beneath.

Anna's was FAITH; Charlotte's HOPE; and Effie's LOVE.

"Now don't move," the teacher whispered.

The audience was as immobile as the girls. It was like a spell. It was as if some beautiful flower that grew only in warm climates had suddenly sprung up in their own fields. They didn't see where the cheescloth gaped behind the ladder, or the little cracks in Effie's crown where the tea lead was joined or the tiny trembling of Anna's hand or Charlotte's black shoes that she had seen before Christmas.

(Bess was so startled she almost cried out. It was like a vision. So much like the picture of Effie she'd had sometimes

in thought. She prayed, "Don't move, oh, please don't move."
No woman her own age was sitting near her—they had located
where she was sitting their first glance through the door, then
sat somewhere else. But she didn't care. Effie was the loveliest
thing anyone had ever seen and she was hers. Even if no one
said so to her, they needn't, it was true . . . if Effie could just
hold it that way.

The curtain closed. Martha leaned ahead and whispered to
Bess, "Wasn't they beautiful? What in the world held Effie *up*
there?"

The defiance wilted. She could scarcely answer for tears:
Martha had spoken to her about their two children being
beautiful in the same way; she had added a little joke.

"I don't know," Bess said, "but she never moved, did she?"

The teacher disentangled the cheesecloth both hastily and
with caution not to tear it. It would be cut up and distributed
for table throws. The older boys, Chris amongst them, came
back to set up the castle for the play.

The castle was a cardboard front; crenelated at the top like
a geography castle, and nailed to uprights of two-by-four.

David wished desperately that he was Chris. Whatever
Chris had to do was always so simple. It was like lifting. The
weight was there and the muscles were there. You just put
them together.

Effie was a princess, so she kept on her crown. She had a
ruby necklace of wild rosebush seed-sacs. She had a brooch of
Ellen's at the neck of her silk dress (though it had a real diamond, it didn't shine near so brightly as the rhinestone brooch
her mother had bought her in town), and she wore a beaded
and tasseled sash that Martha had come across in the attic.
Her slippers came from an old trunk of Ellen's. They were too
large, but they had high heels and were made not of leather
but of some brocaded material almost like dress stuff.

David wore only his plain corduroy suit at first. At the very
end he'd step behind the castle and come out in the crimson
cape, with a piece of snow-white rabbit fur sewn on the collar.
They had copied it from a picture of the little Plantagenets in
his history book

"And now, ladies and gentlemen . . ."

"Come on, Dave," Anna said.

She took his hand, as if for a minute she were the older one
because it was he who must go. She could go no farther with
him than the edge of the curtain. David stepped out on the
stage.

It was like the time they'd taken Anna to the doctor's

office. When they were almost there everything had become hostile and unfamiliar with the thought of Anna going in; but they had walked up the street just the same, because there was no way to jump out of the relentless minute now.

A searching light seemed to come from every face in the audience and focus on him.

"I came to play with you." The words might have been pebbles lying in his mouth.

They dropped through the surface of the silence and disappeared. But when the silence closed over them again it had a different quality. When the chipyard was so awry you didn't know where to begin cleaning it up but picked up a random object anyway, as soon as you did, the total plan sprang up instantly. The next words came like the notes of a tune on the organ your fingers went to without watching, as if they were the only notes there. He couldn't remember *learning* them at all. Faster and faster he came to the princess and the castle, actually. In the routeless movement of light or thought.

"Do you *always* play alone?"

He commanded the silence now, surely, masterfully. Now they all listened as if to someone who had come home from glory in a far place—not in envy, but endowed with some of the glory themselves, because that one's knowledge of his own wonder before them had no pride in it.

He thought, not proudly, but with gratitude toward them: oh, I'm glad I'm not like the others now. He knew how they were looking at him. They'd looked at him that way the day he calculated a rafter's length down to the fraction of an inch, by right-angled triangles. They hadn't believed he could find that out with just a pencil, but they'd taken a chance on cutting it as he said and it fitted exactly.

"I play alone too."

Oh, it was perfect now. He was creating something out of nothing. He was creating exactly the person the words in the play were meant for. He had the whole world of make-believe to go to. They had only the actual, the one that *came* to them.

How much better this was than saying the words to himself had been! The kind of better you could never imagine, until you were into it. (You thought you'd rather sit in the corner and listen to the fiddle music, but they made you fill up the set even if you were small; and then when you polkaed out they all clapped, they all laughed so warmly because where did you ever learn to dance like that? And then, oh then, when you all joined hands in the Big Ring!)

This was better than the cosiness of doing anything alone.

He'd never do anything alone again. He'd take them with him always, in their watching. Closer somehow *because* they followed. It would be like the burning loyalty to his father (somehow suddenly to his father's mended socks drying on the oven door), when he spelled the long hard words in the evening lesson exactly right. Oh, this was perfect. There was a bated wonder coming from their faces: to know that this was David, but a David with the shine on him (they'd never suspected!) of understanding and showing them how everything was.

The first scene was over, and the curtains were drawn together for a minute.

One time the whole family had tried a thousand dollar contest. The object was to total correctly the myriad numbers that made up the shape of a huge elephant. They had traced the numbers one by one with dye, and he had added as they went. They had checked and rechecked until they were tired out. But when the total was sealed in the envelope, ready to go, a shine went out over everything. They had a lunch, and whenever two would reach for the sugar at the same time they'd both laugh and say, "No, no, you go on." All the next day he'd think suddenly of someone: "She's pretty, ain't she!" or "He's awfully strong." If anyone made a joke he laughed right out loud it seemed so funny. If he read a story that was sad he'd almost cry, because he'd never noticed the sadness in it like that before. If he looked over any work he'd done in his scribblers it seemed as if he'd done it far better than he'd known at the time. If any man spoke to him on the road, after he'd gone by, he'd think: "Gee, he's about as good a man as there is *around* here."

A shine like that went out over everything now.

None of all this was consecutive and time-taking like thought. It was glimpsed instantaneously, like the figures of space. And orchestrated in the subliminal key of memory: cold water reaching to the roots of his tongue when thirst in the haymow was like meal in his mouth . . . the touch of the crisp dollar bill he had changed his dented pennies for at the bank in town . . . the light on the water curling white over the dam when his line first came alive with the dark, secret sweep of the trout . . . the cut clover breathing through his open window just before summer sleep . . . the sound of his father's sleighbells the night of the day he'd sent for the fountain pen . . . the date of the Battle of Flodden looked up tremblingly in the book and found to be exactly the same as the one he'd put down, uncertainly, in the examination . . . the doctor com-

ing out of the room and saying that Anna would be all right
. . . his own name in printed letters on the envelope from the
city . . . the moment in the dream when he climbed to the top
of the mountain and looked down . . .

The curtains parted again for the last scene.

"But I am a prince . . ."

(He *is* some kind of prince, Martha thought. And Joseph
watched as if he were touching a garment he was proud to
own, but which he could never wear, because its texture was
so much finer than his skin's.)

"I am a prince . . ."

When all the stray scraps in the door yard had been gathered
into one pile, the flame roared through them, melting and
levelling them, gathering up all their separate piecefulness into
one great uniform consummation.

He thought, I will be the greatest actor in the whole world.

He stepped through the door of the castle for his cloak. He
thought: When I go out, I'll kiss her. That wasn't in the play,
but that's how it would really be.

He kissed Effie so precipitately that she was startled. Her
head went back. Her crown came off and rolled across the
floor.

Jud Spinney was lounging in a group of young men at the
back of the room. He shouted gleefully, "That's it, Dave. Slap
em *to* her!"

Once a sudden blow of sickness had struck the pit of his
stomach when he smoked a moss cigarette. It sheared away
everything but the shape and movements of the other boys
watching him turn grey. This moment now was shorn of all
its dimensions as suddenly as that one. He saw the raw edges
of the flimsy cardboard and the verdigris on the clasp weldings
of Effie's rhinestone brooch. He saw the parched underskin
of the rabbit's fur on this foolish damn cloak. They were like
the flame of a lamp that has burned on into the daylight.

Once he'd been trying to imitate the smile of a Zane Grey
hero in the mirror and he'd turned and Chris was standing in
the door. He felt the shame of having spoken the foolish
words in this goddam foolish play as he'd felt shame then.

Shame struck first; then anger. His breath trembled. His
lips puckered over his teeth. The anger gave him a rough
physical shove. He threw the cape on the floor, as one smashes
a mirror that reminds of some hateful scar. Tripping over it,
he stumbled from the stage.

CHAPTER XI

THE TEACHER cried, "Dave . . ." She tried to close the curtain quickly. "Dave . . ." Anna cried. He paid no attention. He grabbed his coat and rubbers. His cap was buried in the pile of other caps. He ran out the side door in his bare head.

He ran toward home, not because home or any other place was a place of escape, but in the blind way he'd pulled on his rubbers outside the door because they'd happened to be in his hand. He didn't feel the cold on his head or, missing the path, the weight of the drifts he plunged into. The anger hummed inside him louder than any information of feeling.

The shameful anger at that goddam foolish . . . that goddam treacherous play. The furious hatred of himself, of everyone, of everything. One rubber came off in the drifts. His new suit became sodden. He didn't notice. He despised, as if it were another person, the foolish treacherous part of himself that listened to books. That was the only part of him anyone saw . . . they thought that's what he was *like*. It was like some damn fool that kept telling people he was your brother.

He *knew* who yelled at him, the ignorant know-nothin. Oh, he'd fix him, when he got older. He'd never forget. The damn thing would say something smart and wait for the rest to laugh and then he'd just stare at him until he felt that even his face was funny-looking, and then he wouldn't hit him—oh, no—he'd just take him by the collar and turn him around and kick his ass and walk away.

He hated the others almost equally, as if their hearing the guffaw had made them accomplices. When he grew up they'd *see* what he was like. A great surge went through him to leap ahead into time, into the strength that was coming.

Oh, they'd be surprised when they found out what he'd been like all the time. They thought he wasn't like his father. They'd see. A surge of identification with his father flooded him stronger than the grinding twist of the anger: his father's toughness which was to the toughness of the others as blood to dye. If the jeezless bastards had sense enough to know that. *Them* laughing at *him*. Oh, when he grew up he wouldn't make any account of the logs being jammed or his feet being wet or his axe being dull. When they knocked the snow off the bushes ahead of them in the log road, he'd come along behind them and walk right through the bushes and say, "For God's sake, what'r'ye doin?" Caution, caution—they'd see what he thought of that, they'd feel pretty goddarn small.

He said over all the oaths he knew in a harsh grinding pride. They thought it was kind of smart when they swore themselves. But they were kind of scared too. They laughed when he swore. They didn't know how he could swear. They didn't know how to swear at all. He'd swear so it scared them.

He said over all the words of sex he knew. They teased him about girls. They fooled around girls, but when it got right down to hard, meaning stuff they were kind of scared about that too. They'd feel pretty small when he showed them. He'd ride girls the minute he come up to them, whether anyone was looking or not. They wouldn't tease him then. They'd look kind of sober and foolish because not one of them would dare to go *that* far.

He'd go 'way from this goddam place so fast and make so much money . . . and when he come back he'd drive down the road in a big car and pick up Bess (yes, Bess was the only one . . .) and when he passed any of them he'd nod at them as if he couldn't *quite* place them. He'd have to speak to them as long as he was here, but he'd never laugh with them again. He'd never have anything to say to them when he or they were in any kind of doubt or trouble, not as long as he lived.

"Dave . . . Dave . . ." He heard his father's voice. It was loud and deep, but shaken with calling as he ran.

He heard his mother's voice too, fainter, yet with more asking, "Dave . . . David . . ."

But the anger (which always bit itself more bitterly inside him when someone else tried to save something for him which because it was imperfect in any part he had to destroy totally) glowed fresh again. If they say anything to me when I get home, if they just open their mouth to me . . .

The running was hot in his throat now. His hands curled inward, flopping at his sides. He forced himself to run faster still. You couldn't escape this minute, everywhere you ran it was there. But you had to get home as soon as possible.

Ellen was still up. She stared at him.

"David!" she exclaimed. "Where's your cap? You'll catch your death of cold. Where's . . .?"

"I don't care," he shouted. It was not an answer to her, but to his own tumbling thoughts. "I'm all right. I don't care what you say."

He ran upstairs and into his room. He closed the door and

began to tear off his clothes. The orange he'd taken from the tree, to eat after the concert, was lying on the bureau. He didn't touch it. Its skin was beginning to shrivel.

He heard his mother and father, then Chris and Anna, come in. He heard the nervous jumble of their first words with Ellen.

Martha came to the bottom of the stairs and called, "Dave." She put her foot on the first step.

"Shut up!" he screamed. "Leave me alone!"

Martha hesitated. Then she went back toward the kitchen.

It was no use. When the other children hurt themselves or were sick, she'd hold them and look into their faces. Strangely enough then, despite the pity or the fear, she'd feel how awful it must be for people who had no children at all. But with David, those were the only times when she seemed to lose him.

She hung up his cap which she'd been carrying. And looking at it on the nail, she felt the most hopeless kind of wretchedness. She didn't know why, or just what it was; but there was something about David's clothes when he wasn't inside them that made her think of all the times when his feet might have been cold, or he might have been hungry somewhere and not wanted to ask anyone for anything to eat, or he might have been frightened, without knowing it, and no one else there.

Joseph said nothing. How could he? Even when David was *willing* to talk he couldn't seem to find any words that fitted what he meant to say back.

David lay with his eyes closed when Chris came into the room and undressed.

Chris didn't speak; but after he was in bed a while he let one arm fall across David's shoulder as if it might have been a movement in his sleep. The only way of reaching out that Chris knew was touch. David was like a stranger when something was wrong. But somehow when Dave was in trouble like this he seemed more like his own brother than ever.

David twisted away from Chris's arm and moved over to the very edge of the bed. He heard Anna come upstairs. She stopped a minute outside his door. Then he heard her go into her own room.

It wasn't until the house was completely still that the anger began to settle. It settled bit by bit, building up a sore quiet lump physically in his heart. He thought of the way he had sworn and bla'guarded. He said over his prayers in fear and pleading.

Then he thought of the door, closed tight. (Chris, who humoured David's wishes even when they puzzled him, had left it as he'd found it.) He thought of Anna standing there outside the door, but not intruding as much as a word. Of the time his mother had worked at the cost of a new wallpaper all evening and after she'd gone to bed he'd come across her clumsy figures and seen that the multiplication was wrong and she could never afford the wallpaper now. Of the time in town his father had bought him the expensive suit instead of the durable one, because another boy in the store was trying on only the expensive ones. He thought of all the times any of them had surprised him with something they thought he'd always wanted, and then tried not to let him see that they could see it wasn't what he'd wanted at all. Fiercely, and guiltily now, he thought of all the times in town when they'd fallen back from the counter as better-dressed people approached and he'd separated himself from them a little. (Oh, if it could only happen again.)

He wished the door could blow open, but it wouldn't. He wished he could make out he wanted a drink and go downstairs and leave the door open when he came up again, but he couldn't. He wished he could put Chris's arm back over his shoulder, but he couldn't. He wished he could open the door and go in and say something to Anna—not about this, just anything—but he couldn't.

He pulled the quilts over his head. He began to sob. "Anna ... Anna ..."

The next morning he went to look for the rubber he'd lost. As he came near Jud's place he kept watching the house, as if it might suddenly move toward the road. He wasn't afraid, but he'd desperately not know what attitude to take if Jud himself came out. The anger was no longer there to instruct him.

The snow had drifted over his tracks. Chris found the rubber in the spring, but he said nothing about it.

CHAPTER XII

"AVERAGE: 96·8." That braided up all the straggle of last term's school. (David had gone as far as he could in school here, two grades almost every year.) The wet feet in the swamp and the limb scratches where the crotched fence ran through a thicket were forgotten, now the fence had been gone all around. Close up, the potato rows were ragged. Sometimes the plough, dragged on its side to cover the seed, had lurched, and sometimes the shaggy feet of the horse had plunged into the row itself. But from the house the rows looked perfectly straight and smooth. David was thirteen now; yet the day they went to fix the graves in the old cemetery had still its shut-in magic for him.

The buckboard was broken, so this year they would take two single wagons. Joseph would go ahead with Martha and Ellen, and Chris could bring the other horse, with David and Anna.

"Chris, go see if you can borrow Rachel's wagon," Joseph said.

When Chris came back, he said, "Lottie wants to know if she can go too."

"Oh," David said. "What's *she* want to go for?"

"Why, the child can go if she wants to," Martha said. "Go call to her, Chris."

"Ohhhhh . . ." David muttered. He didn't want Charlotte to go. When anyone else was there you had to watch what you said. You had to remember to talk to them, and see they had a good time. This was one of the days when he wanted least to break hands and take an outsider into their ring. The day they fixed the graves was one of the days when the family was indivisible.

"She said she'd be ready when I come fer the wagon," Chris said.

"You musta asked her then," David said accusingly.

"Oh, don't git so big!" Chris said. "You ain't runnin everything around here." His eyes narrowed with the touch of anger. It was something new for Chris to be quick like that with David.

David didn't say anything. He inhaled his anger. The instant fascination of hating someone he loved caught him. Later in the day, he thought, when Chris had forgotten these words and maybe would say, "Let's go around the cove fer a swim where the girls can't see," he'd say, "No, I don't think, you go if you like." Not as if he were sore, but as if swimming with Chris were a little tiresome. Chris's face would look as if he'd run into something in the dark. And when Chris saw that through all the years, never, never again . . .

All four rode in the seat. David and Anna couldn't stand on behind, as they did in the buckboard. That space was now filled with bags of hay for the horse. Charlotte sat on Chris's knee.

She sat way ahead at first, as if touch had suddenly made her and Chris strangers. But each time Chris leaned forward to touch up the horse's flank with the alder switch, she relaxed a little. Then as Chris cradled his knees, with one foot up on the whip socket, she was resting in his lap and the circle of one arm. When he leaned ahead now his cheek touched her hair sometimes. His hand that held the reins through the thumb and forefinger lay lightly against her thigh.

They hardly spoke. But just the slight synchronous sway of their bodies as the wagon moved slowly through the clean June-growing air seemed to soak up their presences, one in the other, like the steady night feeding of animals in a pasture.

Charlotte didn't block the flow of things this morning as David had feared. It wasn't as if they were in a *room*: making ice cream in a kettle whirled round inside the dishpan full of ice, or paring winter apples and stringing their quarters in long garlands to dry behind the stove. The minute you'd hear a strange step on the porch then, everything was spoiled. You could go on with what you were doing, but the presence of the outsider glanced about inside the four walls of the room. It seemed to split the single bee-sucking mood of them all over one thing, into fragments.

In the wide-warm June space, it was different. Your thoughts could slide past Charlotte and circle in a groove all by themselves.

They drove along and David felt the old magic. Of the road still there, but no one now to walk it. Of June finding it even in the silence with the green-breathing leaves full as fruit, and nearer the ground, where the shadows hung, the mothlike velvet on the uncurling canes of fern and on the low bushes. He could hear the echo of the voices and the movements which had once made this old place young—hear them with no matching chord of sadness but with simple fascination, because he was so generously young and echoless himself.

He saw exactly the spot on the log road where Effie's great-great-grandmother had been murdered by a drunken Indian. He'd torn the earrings from her pierced ears; they'd found one in his pocket. The rock maple that her arms had clasped and bent as she prayed had grown tall and rigid now, but the fact was still there in it and in the flat stone beneath that someone had nicked with a sledge hammer to mark the place. The stain of whatever had happened in any place always remained for him there, however long afterward he came to it.

He saw exactly the spot in the road (exactly, because he had remembered the crooked tree that day, to mark it) where he and his father had met Enoch Holland taking his daughter away. She was laughing and waving incessantly; and worse somehow than her look of not knowing that her hair and arms and clothes were parts of her person was the fact that her dress had shirring all about the red sash at her waist. They said she had put on her best dress the night before and danced and danced and danced, all through the house. They could do nothing but stand and watch her because she had the lamp in her hand. The frightful fact was still shiveringly there, in the dust of the road.

He saw the cellar of the old house where his grandparents first lived. Lord Rothesay had once spent the night with them there, on a hunting trip. The Rothesays down the road, who were descendants of the same name and blood as he, wore moose shanks with the hair still on them; but in the morning this one had given his grandfather a gold powderhorn that had come all the way from Austria. The autumn-pulsant stain of that fact marked off the spot exactly from the rest of the field.

And then they rounded a sharp bend and there suddenly the road was freed from the trees. The graveyard sloped upward on one side, and on the other the lake lapped softly in the sun, like the breathing of someone asleep.

David couldn't wait for Chris to tie the horse. He and Anna raced up the slope to join the others.

The older ones had stood silently, when they first came, willing a minute's tribute of intimate recall. Now they were at work. "I wonder if they know we're here. I like to think so," Martha said, as she stooped to pluck the first weed.

Joseph had laid his coat over a tombstone and rolled up his shirt sleeves, inward, to the elbow. He was mowing the tall grass from the grave sods. He swung the scythe wide and smooth where the swath was free, and curbed it near the markers with the precision of a knife. Martha had a black stocking drawn like a gaiter over each arm, to protect her from the poison ivy. She was chopping plantain and kootch grass out of the gravel lanes between the graves with the point of a hoe.

The three graves in their plot held Joseph's father; his brother whose name was also Richard (the one who had died of "brain fever," the one in the tintype they always said David resembled so much); and another brother, Philip. Philip had fallen in the well when he was only a child. There had never been any picture taken of him. There was none, even in any-one's mind, now. The graves, one full length, two half length, lay against the unused extension of the plot like notches on a ruler.

Most of the tombstones in the rest of the cemetery were awry. The tall cubical ones (bearing on top a sculpted lamb or urn or open book, and beneath, in copybook script, "Blessed Are They That Sleep In The Lord") teetered on their founda-tions. Some of the chalk-white slabs had fallen and split across the lettering. Grass grew through the cracks, and moss lined the grooves of the name. The great black granite stone of an old English general was still satin-smooth, but bird droppings defaced its flat top. Pickle jars or tin cans burrowed into the sand of other graves. They were rusted with fall rains and held only the skeletons of last year's flowers.

Yet there was no gloom about the place; only a gentle steep-ing together of the quiet and the sun and the lake. The black granite stone was warm as flesh to the touch.

Ellen knelt where someday she would lie, smoothing out white lake sand on the surface of her husband's grave. She felt no sadness. Not even the watered sadness of memory. No pictures sprang into her mind, as they did when she tore rags for a rug. This was the one sure spot, the spot where her husband lay. All of him with her was gathered here, unchange-ably ended, nothing to be added now or taken away. It was like a focus of light she stood in so that all the separate images dis-appeared. The quiet warnings on the tombstones about her—Aged 23 years, Aged 51 years—had no message of urgency or fear. Those were places she had passed. Now years were no longer footholds in the treacherous cliff going up. She had reached the plain. She knelt by her husband's grave in this focus of peace. She felt nothing but the peace of her hands moving in the warm white sand.

Joseph and Martha thought as they worked.

But their thoughts had an echo quality too, like the sounds of their voices hollowing in the sigh of the pines and the lapping of the lake. The pictures of memory played and faded against their minds as pictures play and fade against the mind as you read. They were on the cliffs still. All around them was the record (Aged 43 years, Aged 46 years) that the place where each stood could be a place of danger. But the fact had no insistence for them. As always when they worked together, their thoughts fed quietly in small circles, keeping the perimeter of each other's presence always in sight. They felt that bondage so much freer than freedom that neither wandered far enough to tauten the cord. They were on the cliff, but the cord between them was like the cord between climbers, so that neither thought of falling.

David and Anna gathered up the grass Joseph mowed and threw it across the fence. When that was done they darted about, reading the tombstones.

Sometimes David stood beside a grave and willed himself to know just what it was to be standing at the spot where someone lay no longer alive. But the thing had no language for him. The inaccessible mystery itself, coming physically from the ground, kept brushing away the thought that was seeking to touch it.

He calculated from the tombstones how long ago each of the dead had been born. 105 . . . 129 . . . 200 years ago, exactly! Maybe that man had had parts of England or France in his eyes once. Maybe he had run into the forest and hidden—beside that old tree maybe, or that one—when they sighted the overpowering enemy fleet sailing into Annapolis Basin. Where was all that now? The lake lapped gently, and all the stain of the word "ago" was suddenly in that spot. It made a rushing stillness that spoke to some other sense than hearing.

He kept calling to his father or mother : Who was this one, and how did that one die?

They were farmers, they told him, or blacksmiths, or brick-makers, or coopers, or woodsmen, or soldiers; or they made harnesses, or had grist mills or carding mills, or . . .

"I know, but wasn't there something else about them?"

It was Ellen who told him that.

Daniel Worthylake had shaved shingles all day long, the year round; Ambrose Fowler had made boots and butter moulds and coffins. This one, whose name was Gregoria Ramona Antonia, the Duke of Wellington had brought to England from Spain. He had tired of her and married her off to a sergeant bound for Annapolis. She had diamond bracelets, but the sergeant couldn't understand a word she spoke; and that one, Valentine Robichaud (Anna giggled), was four axe handles tall and his wife, Diadam, no bigger than Anna. Nathan Hardwick was an odd one—when Lord Rothesay offered him a cigar he said, "Never touch the cursed stuff," and Oliver Delacey always took off his cap when he ate outdoors, even in a blizzard.

"And did you know that the Goldsmiths there . . . did you know that Peter Goldsmith's great-great-great-uncle, I guess it would be, wrote that poem in your Reader?"

"'The Deserted Village'?" David exclaimed. "Gosh, I bet Pete don't know that, or he'd learn to recite it better."

And Delia Holland had "warnings"—she was forever seeing people coming up the road who had never stepped from home. And one day Lydia Comeau took the priest from Halifax into the front room to show him her collection of tree punks and there was her husband, cutting his thick toenail. Caleb Tyler was too bashful to pass a woman in the road, he'd hide in the bushes, and the Swift man there was of the same family as Dean Swift, a famous writer (how could there be no mark of that on Aaron Swift now, David thought, to reduce the townspeople who were proud of such empty things themselves, when he hauled wood into their back yards?), and Matthew Larrimore had a long overcoat exactly the colour of his sorrel horse. Phoebe Brewer used to tell them to lock their doors nights when they went to bed, because sometimes something came over her so she didn't know what she might do. She went down to the mill one day and held her wrists against the saw.

And they died of consumption and black diphtheria (three to a family) and scratches that didn't heal. This one died because the doctor was drunk and didn't scald the handsaw he took his crushed leg off with, and that one had to be laid out under an apple tree because her tissues were so swollen with fluid they dripped constantly. These three Elcorn brothers were always kept home so they wouldn't catch anything; but they all died within a week, of some strange disease that no one else who took food and helped at the house while they were sick ever came down with.

And some of them died in bed suddenly of age or childbirth; and some of them suddenly outdoors, from the stroke of an axe or the falling of a tree or the terror of a horse. And Barney Starratt there died because he didn't rest on the big rock in the centre of the lake, as his companion did, the Sunday morning they both started to swim across.

David touched his tombstone. "Aged 17 years." These were the graves where David felt the strangest spell of all. How could it happen to the young? They couldn't have been *watching*.

The stain of young flesh was in those spots almost reachably, then more unreachably than any. Their faces seemed clarified by this great stubborn mistake: their always-mobile faces and then the great incongruous error of quiet. He felt almost a jealousy of them. It seemed as if they had done some bright extra thing. They had made the stain brightest of all by their very unconsciousness of having put together the shiveringly matchless words "died" and "young." He, the watcher, though he felt that, could only stand there and grow still. He felt a little loneliness for never having known them. He felt a little loneliness because he knew that, conscious of knowing what it *was* to share a careless thing, he never would.

He looked at Anna's face and thought, if one of them were she! This thought he struck himself with brought him so near tears, because it was *not* she, that a sudden sun-shiver on the lake seemed to pass right through his body.

Charlotte was helping Chris. Sometimes when they reached for the same tuft of weed his hand would touch hers or they'd catch a scent of each other's sweat. Their thought then, the first conscious one so far, would be more like a sigh.

Why did the pines they ate under at noon (so thick that only island-shaped patches of the white lake could be seen through them) have anything to do with the food? Why, because it was outdoors and here, did the basket his mother brought from the wagon, with the immaculate napkin tucked over the top, have that quality of excitement, though he knew everything it contained: and why did she bring a lump to his throat, almost, because she carried it? The way his father moved the boiling kettle on the end of the crotched stick up and down in the flame was only an ordinary motion; why did he watch it as if his father were making some sort of miracle for him? Why, when the milk was discovered in a self-sealer or the butter in a jar or the pepper and salt, mixed together, in a twist of newspaper, did they have a brand-new texture, like a thing of Christmas? And why, when dinner was over, did the pines seem as if they had the little torpor of noonday food in them too?

There was no work for the children in the afternoon. They stayed by the lake a while.

There was no constraint between any two of them, to make a fifth presence. The group was fluid. And yet it was as if, if the day were suddenly split by an instant of hydrolysis, David and Anna would be at one pole and (though there was hardly ever any direct communication between them) Chris and Charlotte at the other.

It was the nice resting part of the day, before the day began to go. Anna looked across the lake. Its soft tongues licked the shore and then drew gently back. She seemed to be sucked out with it, floating and bodiless. The mountain across the lake looked like the far-off furniture of a dream. David looked across the lake. The day seemed concentrated in this one spot. The mountain looked to him as if, with one great leap, he could touch it.

The sun began to be afternoon-hot now. Some of its warmth, slipping heavy from its grip, fell of its own weight onto the ground.

"I'm thirsty," Charlotte said. "Was there any water left?"

Chris alerted. "That's warm," he said. "Let's go down to the spring and git some fresh."

CHAPTER XIII

CHRIS and Charlotte took the pail and started down the road to the spring.

"It's hot," he said, "ain't it?"

"Yes," she said, "it's real hot."

Now they were alone, question and answer perched awkwardly on each other.

"Got any garden seeds in yet?" he said.

"No," she said, "have you?"

"No. I mean, *yes*, we got all ours in. Have you?"

"No. We have to wait till we can get a team to help us."

"I'll help you," he said.

"Oh, that'll be fine."

"Sure, I'll help ya. We got ours all done."

Silence was between them again, like the road dust settling after tiny whirlwinds had spun it for a second. They walked along with half the road between them.

"Are you going to the pie social?" Chris said.

"I imagine. Are you?"

"I imagine."

"I bet I know what kind of a pie you're goin to take."

"I bet you don't."

"Will you tell me if I guess right?"

"I can't."

Charlotte stepped around a pock in the road and walked closer to him.

"You're gittin burnt," Chris said.

"Where?" she said.

"Turn around."

She stopped and turned. He stood close behind her and put his hand on her neck.

"All along there," he said. He ran his fingers along the neck-rim of her dress and beneath it. She bent her head forward. "Sore?" he said. He touched her neck here and there.

"No."

She turned again. She adjusted the neck of her dress as if she had just pulled it over her head and were shaking herself into it straight.

"You're burnt too," she said. She ran her fingers along the brown bulge of muscle above his elbow.

"Oh, that ain't sore now," he said.

The pail swung against her thigh. He shifted it to his other hand.

"Boy, I got burnt all over swimmin down here last year," he said.

"You did?"

"Do you burn when you go swimmin?" he said.

"I can't swim."

"I know, but when you just go in, down to the brook."

"Mother won't let me go down to the brook. She says I'll git sores."

An emperor butterfly fastened itself to a spot in the warm road. It moved its black-and-gold mosaic wings up and down idly, like the chest movements of breathing. A devil's darn-needle held itself motionless in the warm air. Its long parchment wings blurred almost to invisibility with their swift beat.

"Was it hot in your room last night?" Chris said.

"A little."

"Where do you sleep?"

"Over the ell."

"It was hot enough in *our* room last night. We never had a stitch on us."

There was a long silence.

"That time the doctor tested your lungs—" Chris stopped. "Did . . . did he say you was all right?"

Charlotte looked confused. "Why yes," she said. "That was almost a year ago. I'm all right."

He thought, almost agonizingly : to be a doctor . . . to be that bunch of alders by the Baptizing Pool when the girls went in swimming . . . to be the mirror in Charlotte's bureau . . .

He laughed. "Boy," he said, with such a great show of amusement as might eat up the silence all at once, "you shoulda seen Bess yesterday. She got caught crawlin through that barb-wire fence be the short cut. She couldn't budge one way or the other."

"Did she tear her dress?"

"No," he said. "Oh, a little, but she just had to stand there, all humped over, till I got her loose."

"I'd liked to heard her," Charlotte said. "I bet she made some kind of a time."

They both laughed, but their laughter was too loud. It stopped too suddenly.

"It's hot," she said, "ain't it."

"*Yes*, sir," he said, "it's hot."

He held back the bushes so they wouldn't switch in her face as he walked before her going down the path. She watched the movement of his smooth solid hips. Their circumference was no larger than that of the circle where his shirt was tucked in tight at his firm round waist. She stole privy glances at the small patch of bare skin showing where his shirt was torn inside the angle of his braces. It was a whiter, more flesh-coloured, sample than his face, of the skin beneath his clothes.

Chris felt the haymow woods-secrecy, the June-softness, the crackling warmth, and the shadowed light on the dried leaves of last year. It spread, physically, in his body. There was a kind of pleasant, fever-moist weight about his groin.

The spring extended in a dark pocket beneath the root of a fallen tree, so that the bank made a little ledge over it. It was never dry, but now it was shallow. You could dip out one pailful only, in a quick scoop, before it roiled.

They sat down a minute on the bank. The heat sighed gently in the leaves. It was too nice to move.

"Do you want a drink before we dip into it?" he said.

"You drink first," she said.

Chris lay down flat on the ground. The support of the earth didn't relieve the weight in his groin. It made it more tantalizing still.

The peak of his cap touched the water. He tossed the cap aside. His face showed in the dark pool: the dark hair falling forward: and silkier, like wet chest hair, on his dark-pale water-smooth face the shadow of the beard beginning at the corner of his lips. When he touched his lips to the water, the pattern of his face wobbled like the patterns he and David used to make of their faces in the curved surface of the copper tea-kettle.

He finished drinking and rolled over on his side, but he didn't rise.

"Lottie," he said, "look at your face in the water."

"What for?"

"Well, just look."

Charlotte lay down cautiously and bent over the pool. Her face showed in it like a ripe fruit.

"I don't see anythin," she said.

"When you drink . . ."

She began to drink. Concentric circles distorted the image. Chris leaned over and pressed her face down to the water so that her nose touched it.

"Chris," she squealed, "I knew . . . darn *you*."

She put one hand in the small of his back to push herself up to her knees. She felt the hard, twisting trunk-smoothness that the clothes hid. She could have got up all the way, but she hesitated a minute. Then she made a move as if to push *his* head into the water.

They wrestled and laughed. And then they were wrestling, but they weren't laughing. They moved only slightly, and silently. Neither's grip relaxed, even when it might have, either in victory or defeat. They clung to each other as if the arms might be willing to let go, but as if there were a kind of suction in each other's flesh.

They didn't speak, because they knew what they were doing now. They knew the ducking had no part in it. Their faces were fixed, like the face of someone holding back an expression of pain. They didn't speak. By not naming it, by making the motions of resisting it, it would come as a thing that just happened and there would be no blame of having willed it.

"No!" Charlotte said at last. "Chris! No . . ."

But the miracle of discovering each other was too accessible. Their physical secrecies had had a distance about them before, different from the distance of space. Now these secrecies were as near as the overalls he slipped down every day and the dress that Charlotte pulled over her head every night before she went to bed. Their clothes were no heavier to lift than clothes off the line; and he and Charlotte were both there.

For an instant, the rawness of the flesh-look of first discovery was in them both, and the adjustment of imagination to fact in each particular of it. She was taken off guard by the whiteness, all at once, of his buttocks, and the little hammock of cords in the back of his bent knees. He was surprised by the little hollow, like a breath-cup, between her startling breasts and the fleshier girl-flesh of her thighs. None of it was beautiful like a leaf or a flower or the soft smell of the breeze. All of it had that flesh-raw stupid look; but all of it the moist, drawing, tantalizing shock. Seen now by the so simple disclosure of lifted clothing, there was no more now of mystery and wonder about it. It made each of them more immediately and consumingly knowledgeable of the other than the face, for all its expression, ever could.

The first shock to him was that her part was of no outward intimacy. It had a name, and because of that he'd expected a thing of some (he didn't know just what) features. But because it was negative and hidden, he felt the inundation in his own flesh gaining a life and a rush like water as it is forced into a small channel. It was crowded the more distillingly sharp by its own pinpoint contraction, and drawn the more swimmingly and rivingly to this bud-pink focus both of infinite secrecy and of total information.

The shock to her was the dark, outward grossness of his part: the flesh-dumb, vein-blind weight. Its terrible purplish urgency, its eyeless olderness, marked it off from any other part of his body.

"No," she said again. "Chris . . . no . . ." But she didn't move.

The swift, spilling search was sharp and clear and then over, like the note of a bird. But it wasn't as Chris had known it, alone: the mounting wash of sensation, oscillating between dismemberment and fusion; then the exquisite draining of all his limbs and the sweet-crucifying blast of forgetfulness; then the drum of it hollow and hollower echoing. Now the drum of it was soft and proudly contained, the voice of it was kept.

Only he had the moment of complete forgetting. But it was he who, even as he conquered, was by the very conquering made naked. It was she who owned all his defenseless secrecies now.

Charlotte sat up and picked the pieces of crushed fern off her thigh. Chris touched gently the imprint of them on her flesh. He felt pride and shame together for having put it there. She moved away a little. The separateness came back quicker to her. She stood up and straightened her clothing. He smiled at her, shyly, but taking her all in. Before they could speak of it and heighten it, the day began to return to them both.

They didn't mention it; but walking back the path, Chris felt all the pendulous itch gone from his flesh. The heat fell shadowed through the trees that bore their miniature samples of leaves like bright green flowers, and through the chalk-white blossoms of the wild pear and the bursting dye-purple of the sheep kill. He tipped his cap on the back of his head. He felt a jaunty strength throughout his whole body. It wasn't like any other strength, even of muscles. He had found the one place to go that took in all the others, as near as Charlotte and as often as they were together. He had discovered the one transcendent appetite (so wonderfully because almost by chance, and as if no one else had ever done so) and the food for it at the same time. All of it possible now, directly, without having to touch just the edges of it, making out you were doing something else. He gave Charlotte a slap on the rump.

They walked side by side down the road. There was a kind of steaming closeness between them. The tantalizing flesh-secret, discovered together, was deposited safe beyond the need of watchfulness now, one in the other.

"Chris," Charlotte said, "what will Mother say?"

"She won't say nothin. She won't know."

"What if anyone should find out?"

"Oh, who *gives* a goddam!" he said.

"Chris Canaan," she said, "you stop your swearin!"

"All right," he said softly. With this jaunty new mastery he found it wonderful to be tenderly penitent to her.

He set the pail down in the road.

"Kee-*roust*, ain't it hot!" he said.

"Chris," she said, "now you *stop* that, do you hear?"

He ducked his cap ahead over one eye. He caught her and reached down the back of her neck, to tickle her. She disengaged herself—not angrily, just indifferently. She walked on ahead. He picked up the pail again.

"Listen," he said, "I forgot about the swearin. Honest."

Charlotte smiled. She knew there'd be no more swearing today.

It was almost time to go home. Joseph was carrying the tools down from the graveyard. Chris began the before-departure check of odds and ends. This was an adult concern he'd always left to his father before. Charlotte stayed apart. She didn't busy herself collecting the baskets as you were supposed to do when you'd been taken on a picnic with others. She was afraid there was something about her another woman would notice, just to be near.

"Chris," David said, "are we goin for a swim?"

"It's too late," Chris said.

"Oh, it ain't too *late*. They'll wait for us."

"It's too late," Chris said. "We're goin home, *ain't* we, Charlotte."

Anna sat on David's knee again going home, but Charlotte squeezed into the seat between him and Chris.

"You can drive better without me stuck up in front," she said to Chris. "There's lotsa room this way."

"Do you want to drive?" Chris said.

"I can't," she said.

"Go on," he said. He passed her the reins. "Just hold em tight goin down the hills so the horse don't stumble, that's all they are to it." It felt good to humour her, to let her try a man's thing, a thing that was his.

The horse broke wind, in an endless series of staccato puffs.

"Speak up, speak up—don't stutter," David wanted to say. But he didn't. Charlotte wouldn't laugh. She only laughed at things that fell into a *pattern* of what was supposed to be funny. She didn't understand the patternless fun *they* had when they were alone together at all. Damn her, he thought, she had to come this special day and spoil the whole thing. It could have been just us, together.

He looked back once at the graveyard and the lake.

The near-evening sun seemed to thicken the grass and varnish it with the bright yellow-green before thunder. It varnished the poles of the wooden fence with a thin bone-white shining. The lake shone in it too, but drawn out thin and intense like the shadow of moonlight. And yet it seemed as if (recoiling from a shaft of loneliness so bright it struck at the very quick) the whole place had drawn all its life back within itself. It was like a house you've always lived in, at the moment of leaving. It would never bring its life out for them again, just for them alone.

"That Starratt boy was only seventeen years old when he drowned," David said.

Never to have done it once, Chris thought, maybe not once.

When they were undressing that night, David noticed that Chris's fly was buttoned up crooked.

"What happened, Chris?" he said, kidding, "did you get a crack at her old mus'ntouchit up to the spring?"

"Don't you tell anyone!" Chris said.

It was like a slap.

David felt small and strange. He felt like when you'd been helping the men, working as equals, and then they went in to the keg in the woodshed and when they came out they didn't notice you were there at all. He felt betrayed. He felt almost a sudden hatred of Chris.

He'd been able to do it, himself, for a month now. He'd *thought* about what it would be like, but he'd never really thought about *doing* it. It was like getting married or having children or going away to work. You knew you'd be doing it sometime for sure, but it was among those things that went with "older"—it seemed like something not quite real.

94

He'd do it now all right, he thought, lying in bed. He'd get even with Chris.

He planned it feverishly, lying there. He planned Effie's part as well as his own, the way he always planned the other's too when the other wasn't present. He made it as real as fact.

They'd be walking up the mountain and he'd say, "Are you hot?" She'd say, "Anybody'd be hot today." He'd say, "I'm not. I'm frozen stiff." "Dave," she'd say, laughing. "you're foolish." "All right," he'd say (giving her a teasing, devilish, enigmatic smile), "wanta bet?" "What'll I bet?" she'd say. "That new skirt?" he'd say (with another smile). "I guess," she'd say. And then he'd show her where he was frozen.

He thought of the whole lost month he might have been doing it, with irremediable anguish. But he'd make up for that. He'd show them whether he was a kid or not. He'd do it so many more times than Chris, so many more times than *anyone* else . . .

"I'm through with school, that's one thing," Chris thought, lying there. "Athens is the capital of Greece. England exports cutlery. The earth revolves every twenty-four hours because .. Balls!"

CHAPTER XIV

THE SUMMER David was fourteen had every day like August. The sky was so purely blue from morning till night it had a kind of ringing, like the heat-hum of the locusts. Joseph no more than glanced at it for possible rain before he cut the clover or stripped the shop roof. Martha could wash any day she chose. There was no wasteful mosaic in the sunset even, to disturb Ellen with a haunting uneasiness over memories that were inexpressible. The children ceased to look at the window, first thing when they awoke, to see if rain had blotched the pane or webbed the intertices of the screen.

The sunlight was so clear when it touched the ash-white shingles on the barn in the morning it seemed more unsubstantial than space itself; and at the same time so equable as it explored the green leaves in the afternoon as to seem almost tangible. There was something almost audible about it. It might have been a transmutation of the tick of the flying grasshoppers that swivelled, as if on axles, in the dusty road.

Yet nothing parched. Other summers of drought the edges

of the potato leaves crumbled to the touch like a flake of burnt paper; the hummocks in the pasture which the cows had grazed short browned like a weathered knuckle. This summer each night's dew was reviving as sleep. Little hairnets of it clung to the glistening grass in the early mornings when Joseph went to the barn. His feet left tracks in it. It shone like drops of mercury on the cabbage leaves until almost noon. When Martha went to the garden to pluck a cucumber for dinner off the crisp furry vines, the dew was still releasing, like a crushing between the fingers, the sharp smell of the tomato stalks. It lingered in the rhomboid shadows of the buildings until, as at a signal for the full symphony of heat to begin, the first locust sounded its brass.

The swamps cracked open like a buttermilk pie. Bugs tented in the alders and gauzed their leaves. The cow path to the brook (through the pines dropping their immaculately scalloped cones, the poplars rattling their leaves like silver coins, the red pyramids of bunchberries, the lush green ferns patterned like snow crystals, and the sudden storms of small white butterflies) was firm as stone. But the brook itself ran cool and clear over its white sandy bottom. Waterbugs twinkled across it on their lightning pontoons like the sun glint on its surface split into sudden arrows by the rubbery lips of the cows in the hot-ringing afternoons.

In the afternoons a steady heat, like Sunday hush, seemed to bring the mountains closer. It gave them a dreamy light-greenness. They looked like *pictures* of mountains. The clear blue heat outlined everything with stereoscopic immaculacy. The repleteness in the air, as if the thirst of growing were forever slaked, gave it an almost churchy texture. Even in the stifling backhouse, where a dead fly forever lay imprisoned in an abandoned cobweb, David would feel it. In the stuporous, trancelike afternoons the tools of planting—the spade against the wall or the harrow with the earth of spring caked on its comma-like teeth—lay as if their work would never have to be repeated.

Then in the blue evenings the dew began to make a clamminess in the hay while it was still dusk. Scarves of haze blued and exiled the mountains. Later, the breath of the whole blue night was bated with the pulsating hum of insects.

11

The water was low where the brook ran under the bridge. The boys undressed on the bridge in the hot blue afternoon. They loitered there, clowning in a sudden exuberance the first moment of bare-free nakedness released. They walked the rail. They cut their initials in it or rude diamond shapes supposed to represent that part of a girl known to them in imagination only. They aimed corkscrews of urine at the shrill-green piss frogs that sat on the singed moss of rocks protruding above the shallow current. They dropped an alder branch into the brook on one side of the bridge; then raced to the other side, with stones in their hands, to see which one could hit first the white broomed-up end of it, as it came in sight again no one knew where.

Then, suddenly, David started to run. He crippled, with toes curled inward, over the harsh gravel in the road, till he came to the path. The path led across the meadow and past the saw-dust heap where rotted timbers of an old up-and-down mill stood, to the deep Baptizing Pool. When his feet struck the soft yielding moss, his running smoothed out into ecstatic speed.

The others swarmed after him. They shouted questions that neither asked nor waited for answer. They laughed at anything, everything. At the strawberry mark on Howie's buttock, at Snook's wrestling with the cobweb that smeared his face when he ducked under an overhanging alder, at the ravelling of blouse cotton that clung to the back of Manley's head like a queue. David braked suddenly and toppled the whole column behind him, like a bunch of dominoes. It convulsed them. They saw a tuft of grey moss hanging from a dead spruce the beavers' flooding had killed. It reminded them in spasmic, convulsing recognition (though they had never seen one), of an old witch's crotch. They laughed at the bobbing of their own appendages as they ran, at the sun, at the water, at the afternoon, at just the feeling (never dreaming what it was) of being young. Summer impregnated their flesh like the flesh of Early Transparents.

David was in the thick of it at the pool.

With another boy alone, he was always conscious of there being nothing but his own company to feed the other's attention. Their moods would never quite dovetail. He'd have to keep trimming and adapting the way he really felt. But in a group, his private part was sucked suddenly inward, like rags of smoke by a draft. None of it showed, to make a strangeness with the others. It didn't nag him for release. He could be with them then, immediately, more immediately than any two of *them* could be together by themselves. He could spark any plan of theirs into a shape which they could see was much more exactly what they'd really had in mind.

Because of that, they all liked him in a special way. There

was a kind of waiting to respond to him, like the smile kept half-ready in the presence of someone who may be depended on to come out with something funny. It wasn't brotherly liking, but a kind of narcissism. He seemed forever, by the twist of essentiality he gave to whatever they said or did, to be disclosing and illuminating a part of themselves they'd never recognized before. They weren't envious of him or jealous to be his special friend. It was a proprietary liking: though (and yet because) they were duller than he, self-warmingly protective.

He belonged, equally, with the youngest and the oldest.

He swarmed with the youngest ones first. Their absorption was complete with nothing beyond incessant movement. ("Look, fuhllas, I'm gonna do a belly-flapper, look . . .)" They shouted. ("Listen, fuhllas, listen, let's all . . .") They concentrated intently on one tiny plan after another: to stalk a devil's darnneedle ("Stay back, stay *back* . . . Dave's got an idea"): to see who could stay under water the longest ("I did . . . You didn't . . . Did . . . Didn't . . . Did, did, did . . ."): to make a dam across the narrowest part of the current ("Quick—gimme some moss. Hear what Dave said, fuhllas? Says we oughta shave Bess Delahunt, we'd git some moss").

Then he lay on the bank with the big boys.

He was a full member in the subtle conclave of their older-ness. They teased him. ("I guess Dave's been eatin eggs, the way he's bin shinin around Effie lately"), and he teased back ("Yeah? Well, tell em about the time you struck a double yolk and you know *who* got her petticoat slit from asshole to appetite"). It wasn't like the tantalizing way they teased the other kids at all. He was inside the subtle line where encroach-ment by the younger kids stopped. The physical sign of older-ness on their bodies strutted so surely in them that sometimes they didn't have to talk big at all. It was ungainly in them when they were with grownups, whose mere presence forced it into conscious secrecy; but when they were with each other, con-spiratorially tacit in them with a moist, heady lolling.

They lay on the bank and let the pattern of August stamp itself on them as on young wandering animals. It wasn't like the parent-pattern of summer at all, tied to the day's tasks. They heard only the language of water against flesh, the conversation of sun and nakedness. They felt only the smooth slide of muscle and the stirring of their own seed. It wasn't really overt, but there, like the sedimentation of some deliciously accomplished memory.

The drowsy anaesthetic of after swimming was in their bodies when Effie came in sight at the top of the hill. She had a lard kettle in her hand. She was going blueberrying in the barrens along the mountain road. Mike Benson spied her first.

"Effie," he called, "come on down. Dave's got something *for* ya."

"Don't!" David said. If it had been any other girl, he'd have thought up some crazy antic himself. But he didn't like it being Effie.

"Aw, shit, she can't hear," Mike said.

"What would ya do if she did come down, Dave?" Steve Sproul said.

"What do you think?" David said, in spite of himself. "What would *you* do?"

"Onnnhhhhhh." Steve made a nasty sound through his nose. He wriggled his naked body against the moss.

Howie grabbed David's wrist and pushed him out into the open. "Effie," he called, in a high clowning voice. "Oh, Effie."

"Aw, don't," David said; but laughing and only half-protesting. He knew they were only acting brave because the girl was a safe distance away.

"What's the matter, Dave?" Howie kidded him, "are ya scared?"

Even as he answered, he felt the hurting stab of betrayal, but he had to say what he did. "I bet I wasn't as scared as you'd be," he said.

Howie was put off his thought so suddenly it was almost comical. He stared at David with wavering half-belief.

"You never did. Dave, did you ever, honest, what?"

David didn't say a word. He just looked wise.

"Dave, you old *bugger!*" Steve said. He poked him in the shoulder. "When, David? Come on, tell us."

"You sly old *bastard!*" Snook said. They all gathered round him.

"G'way. G'way," David said. He shooed them off with his hands.

He just looked wise; he didn't commit himself one way or the other. He acted the way the boys who had really done it, did: except for that curiously teasing smile, you'd think they'd just as soon no one knew. The boys looked at him with a half-grudging, half-exalting, "you-old-bugger" grin. It made him feel wonderful.

Steve began to have trouble with his body. "Look at Steve," they screamed delightedly. Steve plunged into the water. They all rushed in after him, trying to drag him out. David sat on the bank. He just looked wise. They wrestled in the water.

"I guess I'll go now, fuhllas," David said.

The wrestling stopped. Grasp fell from grasp with comical suddenness.

"Aw, Dave, for God's *sake*," they said, "why? We just gut here."

"I know," he said. "But I guess I'll go."

"We was goin down to let the beaver dam out," they said. (Was he crazy, to have forgotten that?) "We was goin down the road to hunt porkypines in the old orchards."

"You don't have to leave," he said. "You can stay."

"Yeah, but—aw, fer God's sake, Dave, whatta ya gonna *go* fer? Where'ya goin?"

"I dunno," he said. "I guess I'll go."

He got up and started toward the bridge.

He was halfway up the path before the implication he'd baited for them sprung. He heard them whispering and giggling. They called to him then, in a chorus of mincing, teasingly knowing voices: "Oh *Da*-ave, where are you *go*-ing?" He just dismissed them with a flap of his hands.

What he was letting them think about Effie struck clear in his head. He felt like that day he'd actually cuffed Anna for trying to follow him to the store. A woman he hadn't known was watching laughed a siding-in-with-him laugh and he'd turned and seen Anna trudging back home, small with rejection. But he had to keep on with it now.

They called to him while he dressed. "Oh Da-ave, don't fall i-in."

"You're crazy," he called back.

"Oh, Da-ave, watch out fer the bri-ars."

"I don't know what you're talkin about."

He dressed and walked up the road. The other boys went back into their fun again.

CHAPTER XV

H E WAS alone now in this thing he'd got himself into.

He had the cold sensation he always felt when the time was now for a thing (no matter how pleasant) which had hitherto been left to lie in the comfortable realm of the any-moment-he-chose possible. The bushes and the long hill struck in his mind with an exacting emergence from background. He thought, with overwhelming clarity, how wonderful it would have been dawdling down the road with the other boys in the safe-hot afternoon, nothing clamorous in any of them.

He tried to breast the minutes before the act by skipping thought of the act itself. He thought of how it would be afterwards: the doing of it would be proudly and safely in him forever, for the other boys to see: he'd never have to face it again for the first time. Or if he did think of the act itself, he thought of Effie providing it, but not really *in* it. That's the way he thought of it nights in bed, or in the haymow, or beneath a tree whose branches almost touched the ground.

The girl he'd called up then wouldn't be anyone quite actual. It would be a girl, or (very often) a woman, he'd seen in a magazine or heard about in a story. Or a girl he made up in his mind. She'd have no actual features; except the hot, coarse, feature of wanting to do it with him matching the way he wanted to do it with her. His body would respond instantly then.

If *then* he thought of any girl he did know (she also shorn of features, in the secrecy and in the photography-without-depth of memory), he knew he could be free and confident with her, too. Yet with that girl the next day, actually—now a girl who had said this or that, or done this or that, or whom he remembered having seen one time looking as if she wanted to cry—the suddenly added dimension of her presence would expose and cripple his desire.

He wished he could do it with Effie as if somehow she wasn't there.

He saw the back of Effie's head over a cradle hill.

He crept up behind her. He felt that funny guilt and power you feel, watching someone for whom you have a plan; while he or she, unaware, seems to steep in the formless thoughts that come and go when the hands are busy and one is alone.

"Oh Dave," Effie said. "You scared me."

She smiled the afteralarm smile. The breeze-lightness came back to her soft marigold face and her soft light body. It seemed as fragilely attached to her as the grey puff of stamens to dandelion stalks in the fall. She trusted him so utterly that the thought of *dis*trust was never there even to deny. David felt like a friend turned enemy without the other's knowledge.

"Thick?" he said.

"Not very."

He saw that the bottom of her kettle was barely covered she picked so slowly, not to get in any leaves or green ones.

He wished somehow that her kettle had been full. He wanted to sit down and help her fill it. The sound of a mowing machine would come to them faintly, but they themselves would be working at something that didn't drive or tire. There'd be the clean afterswimming feel of his clothes on his body, and the shine of the blueberries inching up the clean, shining inside of the kettle, and the clean girl-smell of Effie's hair when they'd both bend over the same brush sometimes.

"Let's go back the road a ways," he said.

"There's none back there," she said.

"I got somethin to show you," he said.

"What?"

"I can't tell."

"Is it far back?"

"Not very far."

"Will I take my kittle?" she said.

"No," he said. "We can find it agin."

She put her kettle on top of the cradle hill, and broke off two alder branches to mark the place. Something about her doing that stabbed him again with the sense of betrayal.

They walked along the road. He felt the secrecy of the woods and the genital-consciousness it always gave him. He kept glancing about for a spot that was completely screened.

But the spruce that seemed at first to tent the ground beneath had a branch missing, like a window. A finger of sun reached nakedly through the cluster of pines he'd thought opaque. A stripping eye of light everywhere came between the urgency and the act.

He put on a bold, roguish insinuation, as you would a coat. But it didn't feel right. It was like it used to be when they'd be playing hopscotch. They'd both be absorbed in it on exactly the same plane of enjoyment. Then an older boy would come along and he'd begin to clown. He'd toss the stone into the squares without taking aim. He'd hop in a squat—as if the only way you could be bothered with such a simple game was to poke fun at it. Effie would still play it seriously, and after the other boy had gone he would play it seriously again too; but it wouldn't be quite the same.

He tried to steer the talk as he had planned it, alone. It wouldn't seem to go that way at all. The only feature about Effie then had been one of receptivity. The answers he put in her mouth seemed the only ones possible if he said so and so. Now she replied differently altogether.

"It's hot, ain't it?" he began.

"Mmmmm," she said. "But I like it." She put her face up against the sunshine.

"I'm frozen stiff," he said.

"Silly."

"Yeah? Well, I'll bet you your skirt I am."

She just laughed. She was rubbing the soft knobs of a squaw-weed blossom against her chin.

"Dave," she said, "what does it feel like? Feel it."

He felt the blossom. "Moths?" he said.

"Yes," she cried. "Moths—it does, doesn't it?"

They always felt an instant closeness when both saw the same likeness of something else in what to others was never more than just the thing it was. David couldn't go back to the "frozen" business now. It was used up.

But he put on the clumsy roguishness again. And now Effie began to notice that something was wrong between them. She noticed that something, apart from the turn of the talk between them, was steering his mind. She walked along, quieter, waiting for it to wear itself out.

"I wonder if I got burnt today,". David said foolishly. He unbuttoned his shirt at the waist. He wanted her to think of him being naked.

"Dave," she said, "what did you have to show me?"

"I can't tell you."

It began to feel late. This part of the road they knew seemed to have left itself and followed the road beyond.

"Dave," she said, "is it much further? I gotta fill my kittle."

"It's right here," he said.

Miraculously, it was. A little patch of ground the tree limbs hid completely.

They crawled beneath the low-hanging branches.

"It's like a little house," Effie said. "Was that it, Dave? Was that all it was?"

"Set down," he said. They sat down.

Their bodies touched, but he sensed Effie's sensing of his own strangeness today.

"Effie . . ." His breath came short and shaken. "Effie . . ." he said, *"let's . . ."*

He'd mentioned it, the moment was really now. His consciousness emptied of everything save the fact of him and Effie sitting there, exactly as they did. It was like a single surging sound.

She looked at him, not understanding. "Let's what?"

"*You* know," he said. He didn't look at her.

She understood then.

He waited for her to pretend anger (like the girls did when you yelled "mad dog backwards" at them). Maybe she'd slap him or get up and run away. He needn't run fast enough to catch her. She didn't move.

"I can't," she said.

She wasn't angry. She looked at him as if she wished, the first time he'd asked her for anything, why did it have to be this?

"Why can't you?"

A real boldness sprang up. She was resisting. They would wrestle a little. He could tell himself he wouldn't want to hurt her, and let her go.

"I couldn't," she said. Her look still asked him please to understand that if it were *any*thing else . . .

He put his arm around her. Now the surface of the moment was broken, now she knew, a flow was coming back.

"Come on, Effie," he said, "*let's* . . ."

He wasn't ready for what happened then.

"All right, Dave," she said, "with you . . ."

She spoke with a kind of awful docility. As if, if it was something he *had* to do. As if, if anything denied him would make a quarrel between them. As if . . .

" 'Effie loves David.' " The silly chant other kids had mocked them with sometimes suddenly into his head.

"Love" had been only a word before. Like "sickness" or "death." Now, all at once, it was like a page that had had only the blind side turned to you. When you picked it up and turned it over, there was the meaning, written plain and alive. It lay warm in your hand. " 'Effie loves David.' " He could see her gathering up the discard of his every action and keeping it inside her, pitiably secret. He felt as if he had stepped into a strange place of light. Everywhere he looked mirrors threw back and complicated his image.

It made him feel big and spreading; and it made him feel lost. It made him feel like the times there had been presents for him he couldn't believe were his; and it made him feel like, when getting well, you looked back to the time when, with the sickness, everything had been so deliciously contained. It made him feel like the time he'd overheard them saying he had such an open little face they could hug him and he'd never thought of his face at all, as a thing for anyone to notice; and it made him feel like the sad-sweet look back at the lonely passed-over road when you first came in sight of the houses.

It made him feel rich; and it made him feel destitute. There was no room anywhere inside him now where he could keep the things that sprang to life only at his turning of the lock. She too had a key.

She was still looking at him that funny way. He looked at her and spoke earnestly for the first time.

"You don't have to, Effie," he said.

But she stood up and began to undo the hooks and eyes on her made-over skirt. She lay it across a limb. Then she moved it to the ground, so the pleats wouldn't muss and she wouldn't get any balsam on it. *I never knew she was so small underneath,* he thought. *She looked like Anna did, when Anna was a child, taking off her clothes at night, dead tired. She looked like a child undressing for bed.*

He saw the secret, drawing, flesh-look exposed. Then the fact that it was Effie was suddenly no more in the way. His body responded as instantly as a heartbeat to fear. Thought went out, as if from a blow. It quickened so fast there was no following it. The core of all searching met with the focus of all receptivity in a swoon of helplessness. Sensation peeled back, like tight-packed leaves, to layer, to deeper layer, to the convolute essence of hot, moist desire.

The almost instant climax stung like a throbbing of wires all through him. It exquisitely contracted and scattered him at the same time. When Effie moved toward him, of herself, he tried to fix her in his thought (not even then completely swamped), like someone trying desperately to see through the clamour of sudden blindness. He tried to absorb every bit of her in a kind of swallowing.

And then when he lay relaxed, he couldn't tell if everything had come inside him, or if everything had been lost. Or was this simply the most complete weariness he had ever known?

A squirrel set up a shrill complaining chatter on the limb above. The moment splintered. The secrecy was all gone.

And right then, he heard the dry limb snap and the conspiratorial "Shhhhhh . . ." The boys must have sneaked up on them! The soft pelt of sensation turned inside out, like fur pelts on his father's stretchers exposing their lardy underside smeared with burst capillaries of blood.

"Quick!" he said.

He tried to help Effie fasten the hooks and eyes on her skirt. The inhibiting mystery of her clothes was gone now. He had a new feeling for them. He touched them now as if they were a pitiably helpless part of her, like a limb that had lost its locomotion. His very sense of possession gave an almost total clumsiness to his hands.

They began to run. The boys located them exactly with the sound of their running. They began to laugh and shout.

"*Waaaaa-hoooo*," Steve called.

"Shut your goddam mouth!" David shouted.

His voice split with anger. He'd like to kill every one of them, coldly, inexorably. They'd beg for mercy and plead that it was only a joke—unable to believe till the very last that he could do it to them, remembering who they were—but he'd be merciless and unreachable as a stranger. The pride he was to have felt before them never came into his head.

They circled toward the meeting house lot, where cover was thickest. He couldn't take time to hold back the branches for Effie. She followed, stumbling, behind him. The limb of a dead fir made a triangular tear in her skirt. A wild-rose bush scraped her leg so the blood came.

"My kittle," she whispered.

David thought of her kettle. It wasn't even half full of berries. He saw the tear in her skirt and the branch of blood scabbing on her leg. He wished the boys would fall and break their necks. He wished a sharp limb would go straight through them.

They circled toward the road again. The others were almost in sight behind them.

"Lie down," he said. "Hide."

They hid in a tight clump of pasture spruce. They pressed tight together, but there was no feeling between them now except the impossible need of contraction to physical invisibility. They almost burst with holding their breath after running.

"Listen," he heard Howie say, almost upon them. "I don't hear em. They must be on the road."

The boys circled away then.

David saw them looking up and down the road. He could see hat with it under their feet the whole chase suddenly didn't matter much. They walked along the road, half-relieved, he could tell: if he and Effie *had* been in the road they didn't have anything prepared, to do or to say. They'd just have felt foolish. He knew they hadn't really seen anything. He almost forgave them.

Then one of them spotted Effie's kettle. Most of the boys went on. The thing was entirely finished for them. But a last flicker of interest fanned up in Howie and Steve—they thought it would be a good joke to hide the kettle.

David's anger flashed back as if his face had been struck. Boy, he thought, if I could just come up behind them with a whip . . . I'd slash them . . . I would, I would . . . I'd slash their goddam fingers right open. Handling Effie's kettle, and giggling so smart! He felt about her kettle now as he'd felt about her skirt; as he felt about everything that belonged to her. Somehow he seemed to have exposed it in a pitifully vulnerable light. He seemed to have a responsibility now for everything her hands had ever touched.

The boys didn't make much of hiding Effie's kettle. It was only a halfhearted gesture, like the last turnip thrown on Hallowe'en after the feeling of going-home had set in. They moved along the road and disappeared over the top of the hill. David and Effie were finally alone.

He turned to her as a man turns to a woman at night in the kitchen when callers have just gone home. She is setting things to rights again, smoothing out this interruption mirrored in the posture of the empty chairs and the insides of the apple peelings browning alongside the whole apples in the bowl. He turns to say something to her. She is the one place always to come back to.

Effie didn't look up. She kept smoothing the lip of the tear in her skirt back into place. She aligned the blue and red and green threads of the plaid, so that as long as she didn't move the skirt looked intact.

She kept her head bent and turned away from him. He saw that she was crying. She wasn't crying for anyone to see; but as if she'd be all right, as if it wasn't anyone's fault; as if, if you didn't talk to her, she could keep it quiet.

David had never had a girl cry because of him before. He was helpless.

"I won't tell, Effie," was all he could think of to say. "I won't tell a *soul*, honest I won't."

They went to search for the kettle. He watched her small arms part the bushes, when her back was toward him. And knowing that she loved him, David felt as if all the furniture of his mind and feeling would never stand dark and alone again, but in a lamplight; and he felt a kind of loss. She was like a part of himself that had slipped away where he could never again be able to watch it all the time. It might be hurt without his knowing it—beyond the cure of being brought back inside and thoroughly apprehended. He thought how he'd been going to marry the loveliest or richest or most famous woman in the world. That seemed like a different time.

He looked at the feather-stitching on Effie's skirt. It was neat even under the hem. He thought of how the only beautiful things she'd ever had were her flesh and her hair: the things her own body had given her. What could he *bring* her, he thought? What was the perfect thing she had always wanted?

They searched and searched for the kettle. They couldn't find it anywhere.

CHAPTER XVI

ANNA STOOD at the long pane inside the church. Dead flies lay parchment-dry on the sill and the safe, cloistered, paint-and-hymn-book smell was all about her. She was watching for David's head to come over the top of the hill. At last it came in sight and she ran out to meet him and Effie.

It was the first time that David, looking up and seeing Anna come toward him, had seen her as a stranger. The olderness of the thing he and Effie had done left her behind.

"Hi, Effie," Anna called. And then, immediately, "Dave, there's a letter for you at the house!"

A letter! A letter lying there on the table . . . with his name on it . . . with its message to be devoured privately, uncomplicated by the exactions of the writer's face.

Effie and Anna suddenly shifted places in his mind. Anna was let in again, and Effie left out.

Sometimes he had foolish but compelling intimations. Something would tell him that if he didn't pick up that particular stone and place it on top of that other, disaster would strike before the day was through. His eye would catch a particular tree along the horizon, and he'd think: That tree will be chopped down in exactly two years and fifteen days.

One flashed through his mind now: If I pass that letter from my right hand to my left before I open it, Anna will be safe all her life.

He didn't know why, but the complex magic a letter held for him erased the simple magic of what he'd done with Effie almost utterly. She had that sudden anaemia of meaning a puzzle he'd been putting together would have, or the supper dishes, or a sock his mother had partly knit, when he opened the door and saw them again, after the Magic Lantern show in the schoolhouse.

Effie felt him leave. She kept pace beside him; but as if she could never catch up, no matter how many quick steps she took to his one.

"Did you open it?" he said to Anna.

"No," she said. "It's from Halifax."

"You could have opened it." She could have. Anyone else opening it would spoil the whole thing, but Anna could have.

He had sent his name in to a correspondence club in the newspaper. This letter must be from a city boy or girl he had never seen. What could a city boy or girl be like?

The handwriting ran free across the page. Where there had been a mistake in spelling, the word was crossed out, not erased. The message ended where the page ended. Not as if it had exhausted itself; but as if, what was the sense of digging out more paper, to prolong it?

It said:

I saw your name. I wonder what it's like to live on a farm. Can I come see you sometime? I am fifteen years old. Yesterday I was on a big ship in the harbour. I like to swim. I haven't any brothers or sisters. Have you any brothers or sisters?—Toby Richmond.

David read it over and over. It baffled him. He could find almost no message in it—where then did he get the feeling that this was some kind of turning point in his life?

While Joseph, that afternoon, felt how the clover was drying just right in the perfect balance of sun and breeze. The summer-pulsing strength of his body was like an only sound in the soundless day. None of it was word-shaped and clear, but he felt the earth he owned contained in the touch of his feet. The buildings and the mountains he looked at were contained in his eyes. And contained in him also, safely as the lull of the August-blue sky, were the children (though they were by themselves at play), and Martha (though he could not see her in the house).

He went to the house, pretending he was thirsty, to tell Martha of his sudden plan. Always before a plan was something that only came, slowly, of an evening.

Martha's Saturday work was done. The lamp chimneys were shined, the floor scrubbed, her body bathed and clad in the gingham dress with the ironing creases still uncrumpled. The smell of fresh bread was clean in the sunny kitchen where it lay on the bread board to cool.

Seeing Joseph come toward the house, she felt, without word-shaped thought, the same containment as he. As if it were a garden they had planted together. Now the hard days of weeding and hoeing were over; yet such straggling fret at the time was absorbed, as a necessary part of the completeness, in the fullness of the growing. It was safe at last for her and Joseph to be spectators at their own peace. Depending for variety on the news brought in that such and such a thing had happened to someone else. Hearing, and interested to hear, of change; but feeling only of containment.

Joseph turned from the pump, his hand still on the dipper of well water.

"Martha," he said, "I bin thinkin. I think I'll git some logs out this winter and build you a new house."

That was the night of the social. While the others were dressing, David got out the dictionary and the box of writing paper. He composed his reply to the city boy excitedly. He wrote it out first on a scribbler page, then copied it very carefully.

I am fourteen years of age. I enjoy living on a farm, although it is often (he looked in the dictionary) quite somnolent here. Ha. The ship must have been exciting. What was its destination? I like to read and dance and go for walks up the South Mountain. I have a brother Christopher, and a sister. My sister's name is Anna . . .

Somehow he shied away from mentioning the visit.

The schoolhouse window was raised. Chris and Charlotte, waiting their turn to polka out, rested their elbows on the sill. They gazed out into the sensuous August dark. The sting of the fiddle music and the drinks he'd had made an urgent spilling in Chris's flesh. Even the bold swing of the dancing couldn't drain it away.

He whispered to Charlotte, "Let's go fer a walk after this one, and cool off."

She protested. "Chris Canaan," she said, "you've been drinkin! I can smell it on your breath."

But she went.

They went behind the boulder where the "Hunters" used to hide when the school kids played "Moose."

On their way back they had their first quarrel. Charlotte said she'd promised her mother she'd come home as soon as the pies were sold. She was bound he'd leave too. Go home before it was done? When it was ended so soon, anyway? My God, when you saw Seth bending to put his fiddle in the case and Jim reaching for the cover of his harp . . .

That was the first night that what he got from Charlotte hadn't seemed to Chris like the single miraculous thing, to be found in a single place. Maybe there was lots of it. Maybe he could find it better somewhere else—without this dinging at him that seemed to come up every time, with her.

Martha joked Joseph about his elaborate caution with her pie on the way to the schoolhouse. Its paper wrapping was drawn up into a tent and caught with a safety pin at the top, so the frosting wouldn't muss.

But she didn't laugh when her pie went cheap and Joseph paid three dollars for Bess's. She didn't join in the laughter when Bess took the wreath of artificial flowers from her pie and draped it about Joseph's neck. (Though how could Joseph do anything else but leave it there while they ate?)

When she had gathered her own plates and forks together, to go, she went up to him. He was chatting with the other men. "Are you goin home tonight?" she said. She carried the empty plates home herself.

And that night in bed, she said, "You *knew* her pie."

She put the words into her own mouth, to be denied; then when she heard them spoken, some dreadful fascination forced her to act as if they were believed.

She was impotent against the fascination of the silence she sickened herself with for the next two days. She watched Joseph stumbling against it, bewildered; but she was helpless to break it. Until a pain more riving than any before struck through her chest and, when it was spent, released them both into the most trusting peace they had ever known. Nothing could have made her believe that the silence was to come back on her, again, and again.

That was the summer that had almost every day like August. That was the night the weather broke.

Ellen awakened, late in the night, at the sound of the rain. She put out a hand to touch her husband. "Richard," she said. He wasn't there. For the first time in her life her mind wouldn't obey her. She couldn't make it focus, to tell her what had happened or where she was.

CHAPTER XVII

THIS WAS the day of evocative light: the thin October light of after-ripeness. It put everything just beyond touch, beckoned the thought to where the substance had fled.

The mountain was haloed with it, as with the dusty gossamer rain of light a painting sometimes sheds. In the fields the grass was brown. Piles of potato stalks were withered and black. The goldenrod rusted toward dust, and the squawweed was lint-grey. But the albino light, simmering patiently in the aspic air like a sound after the ear for it is gone, lacquered them like the shells of the pumpkins piled before the shop. It hung clearly and expandingly between the branches of the chestnut tree before the house, bare now as a tree a child draws. The bones of the tree seemed to have a luminosity of their own. It diamonded the bits of glass on the ground, prodigally and sadly, because it would not come again. It furred a strand of the wire fence with light distilled pure and memoryless from the light of summer. It steeped in the shingles. It hung hazy, and most nearly tangible, over the river. There it was like the face-light of someone forgotten, and remembered again on awaking from a dream.

The pasture decayed gently, lingering after sentience, and lacquered after death with the wistful fall-stain: the burning red of the hardhacks, the blood-red of the wild-rose berries, and the age-brown of the wafered alder leaves. The mud of the mountain road flaked like pie crust. But wherever a puddle remained in the ruts from last night's rain the yellow light sought it as a mirror. It looked for its own face but made no image but the bright reflection of its own transparency. Farther along, where the trees met over the road, the road was plated with the crisp coins of light. They showered through the spaces between the leaves; and beneath the leaves themselves, a dark aqueous filament of shadow trembled.

Further still, in the mountain proper, the light seemed to emanate from the trees. Jets and sprays of it from the red-burning maples hushed the dark spruces and soaked through the white-shining bones of twigs on the ground and through the crumbling bones of the crust-brown ferns. In the clearings, the fronded sea of ferns repeated it suddenly and threw it back like an exhalation. And at the very top of the mountain against the moted lemon sky, the cidery yellow-green leaves of the birches and poplars shed it with their ceaseless movement like the shiver of waves under the sun. They refracted it like leaves of glass; spilled it like a pool of yellow lint onto the freckling of fallen leaves that glinted with it on the ground beneath.

This was the day when, all sentience fled, all things of the country shed the last light of after-memory. Its unwithheld entirety stained as quietly as a shadow. It claimed, by its drawing stillness, that you know it perfectly and so possess it; as you could not. It beckoned you, by its very undemanding, to touch what was unreachable. It asked you, because it had no heart or tongue, to feel you knew not what and to find words for what was inexpressible.

In the afternoon, two people might sit, close together and silent, on a windfall. They would break twigs and drop them one after another onto the ground. The aqueous warmth and the musing yellow light would bask at their temples. They would look away, from mountain to mountain. They would have the feeling of floating that you get when you stare too steadily at the sea. Each of them would sense the same tug of the October light asking them to feel something they had never sensed before. But even in the same feeling of failure to do this, their separate thoughts couldn't quite touch.

This was the October day in Entremont when, at dusk, the spilling yellow light, imperfectly known and so unpossessed, retreated into the bones of the trees. Into the unyielding olive sky. The gleaming bones of the trees stamped their dark shapes immaculately against the exiled horizon.

As the light retreated, the silence sprang up with the same shivering stain the light had had. The feeding silence of the bluejay's dark sweep across the road . . . the partridge whirr . . . the straight flight of the dark crow against the deepening sky . . . the caution of the deer mincing out toward the orchard's edge . . . the caution of the hunter's foot on the dry leaf. And then the silence of the moment when the first faint urine smell of rotted leaves came from the earth, and the memory-smell of apples lain too long on the ground, and the sudden camphor-breath that came from any shade stepped into, the moment the gun barrel first felt cooler than the gun's stock on the palm. The breath-suspending silence of the gun sight in the second of perfect steadiness, and then the spreading silence of the gun's bark, and then the silence of the bird not flying away . . .

Ellen could see the mountain from both kitchen windows of the new house. She was binding the edges of a meal bag for rug canvas.

The new house was nearer the road. Nothing in it was skimped. All rooms save the attic had square walls. Its novelties were the talk of everyone: the banisters carved in the shape of hourglasses, a built-in china closet for the cheese dish, the cut-glass vinegar cruet, the maple leaf cake plate, the good cups and saucers.

The other women would walk through the house with Martha, of an afternoon. They shared this new thing of hers in the sisterly way they shared a death, or a birth, or a judgement passed upon any absent one who had set herself apart from them by some unconventional act. They'd say, "*My* old house looks so shabby when I go back home." Then Martha would feel a glow: not of pride, but of feeling that if it *were* of pride they wouldn't be saying those things.

It was the same with the men. The fashioning of any new structure (if it were only a tongue for a truck wagon or the hewing of a sill) was a thing of engrossing liveliness in the strolling pace of their day's work. They'd look up at the new house with Joseph and say, "By God, Joe, you built her big and high while you was at it, didn't you?" Joseph would say, "Yeh, I guess she oughta last me out." And he too would feel a curious humbleness for having the largest house in the village; one he wouldn't have felt at all if his house had been the smallest.

Martha rearranged the furniture from the old house every day at first. It had to be spaced so thinly to go around that the pieces seemed to lose touch with each other. The walls yawned backward from them. The tables and chairs had a bare and helpless look.

But when Ellen's rugs were laid on the floors they brought a contractual warmth into each room. Then the new window curtains lidded the impersonal daylight with the same contractual friendliness. They changed the spaces that had stood like extra furniture between the separate chairs to a kind of conversation link.

Martha went to the door of each room each night before she went to bed. Sometimes Joseph would stand in the door beside her; inarticulate, but somehow made complete by her pride in his gift. One thing only Martha couldn't confess to him. (There were so many things they *needed*.) No matter how often she alternated the wicker rocker with the Morris chair

114

in the southwest corner of the parlour, all she could see when she looked in that corner was the piano that wasn't there.

The children each had a room now.

David had chosen the attic. He couldn't explain to them why. From the attic windows he could see everywhere. He could see all the houses and all the fields and all the roads, right to the horizon. When he closed the door behind him, there was the exciting feeling of being unreachably alone. It wasn't the isolation of real severance (that was intolerable), but a cosy isolation of his own making. The sounds that came up to him were blurred beyond insistence by the height. They were just loud enough to remind him that company was to be had whenever he chose it.

To the others the new house held the excitement of novelty. But not to Ellen. She still found her sorcery in the unalterables she had brought with her from the old house: the tintype of her husband . . . her pictures of the Virgin . . . the locket with the sailor's picture inside . . . the remnants of cloth each still permeated with the wearer's presence . . . the waxberry bush she had dug up and transplanted, and (though they said it would rot the shingles) the old hop vine . .

She still found enchantment in the day itself. The days of the year did not change. (The day was always an added one, in whatever company; it shaped the climate of the mind as surely as a word or a smile or a touch.) The day of this year, coming again, was no older than it had been in a year gone by. Of all the company who had been there then, only the day could return exactly as before; and so bring word of them.

This October day made the climate of remembrance in her thoughts. She missed the face of the old kitchen.

The cloth she bound the rug with was the lining of a black coat. It was the coat she had bought for the day she and Richard followed the span of hearse horses that bore their first son so slowly to the churchyard. She alone of the family had known the death of a part of you which lived in another. She caught her breath. But the memory of her tears that day was like the October light. It beckoned where the quick couldn't be touched. She hadn't cried fresh tears for so long.

She sewed the bag into the wooden frames with darn-needle and twine.

Richard had made these frames from the slats of a corded bed. He had broken the point of the awl, she remembered. She remembered that cold chilling anger of his when clumsiness with a tool would thwart him. She had shivered then. She smiled now. She had seen that look since, though without the chill, on Joseph's face—when the obstinacy of cattle would resist all direction, or when his bafflement at Martha's unaccountable silences would pass over from stumbling patience, to appeasement, to a seething general rage.

It was queer, she thought, how each of them carried hidden in his face the look of all the others. It flashed out suddenly sometimes though none of the physical features altered.

She had seen Martha's face as Joseph changed to another partner in a figure of the polka quadrille take on the look of Anna's when Anna couldn't restrain the new kitten in her lap, no matter how tenderly she stroked it. She had seen Christopher's face, when the answer to an arithmetic problem remained stubbornly different from any his calculations arrived at, dissolve into Joseph's when Joseph looked out the window the morning he planned to haul the hay he'd got almost made so many times and the rain was beginning again.

More often she'd seen the look of some one of the others fleetingly on David's flesh.

How like his father's face (coming in wet to the skin from extricating the oxen from an air hole in the lake ice, beating his snowy cap against the woodbox, drawing the icicles from his eyebrows and moustache, scraping the sleet from his pants legs with a case knife, but not asking Martha for dry clothes till after supper) was David's, when David had walked all the way home from school with the gash in his foot. He wouldn't let any woman in any house he passed by put a rag on it. He hadn't wanted anyone to ask him if it hurt, though his face was white as chalk when they poured in the creolin. She had seen his mother's face, when Martha would test a strip of new wallpaper against the parlour wall, in his, when he'd look away from the book he was reading and she'd know that he'd recognized the likeness there of someone he would someday be. She had seen Christopher's face when Christopher would say, "Let's go look fer some spruce gum, Dave" (after the other boys had gone by on their way swimming without calling to either of them), mirrored in David's when David would show Christopher an easy way to solve the fractions problem he was apt to have in the examination tomorrow. She'd seen Anna's face whenever Anna cried, in his, the few times she had ever seen him cry.

She supposed her own face echoed in theirs sometimes too. She couldn't tell. You had no way of seeing your own face in the moments when it might be like another's. But she hoped it did show sometimes in David's. She loved the children equally.

Any moment she caught herself preferring any one of them she automatically loved the *other* two more intensely. But most assaultingly of all, David seemed to have no face of his own.

She explored the mound of rags in the centre of the canvas. That had been Joseph's good suit once. He'd torn it beyond repair, wrestling with Maynard Spruin one election day. He'd caught Maynard peeking through a window in the section of dining room screened off for a polling booth. Maynard was on the opposite side of politics.

You wouldn't know Joseph on election day, she thought. That one day, he was expansive with all the men on his own side. Just exchanging "Good morning" with one of them made a glow all through him. And though at no other time did he make any show of his physical strength, that day he was cocked for instant fight if anyone of the other side piped up anything against anyone on his. She remembered what he'd said about Maynard. It was so outrageously funny, coming from *Joseph*. "That thing snoopin around and then spillin his guts . . . with them damn piss-burnt pants on."

This was brand new.

This was the pair of pants with the braided anchors around the waist that David had started to coax for the minute he saw them in the new summer catalogue. The first time he put them on he walked like a cat in mud, the feeling of long pants over his legs was so strange. But his face shone when he looked down at them. He was going to Sunday school.

Jud Spinney, the tease, was there. "Are you gonna take up the ministry, Dave," he said, ". . . or d'ya lay out to follow the sea?"

David had gone white as a sheet. He had rushed upstairs and trampled the trousers on the floor so it was impossible to send them back. He could never be persuaded to put them on again.

That was Anna's.

That was the first silk dress any of them had ever possessed. (Except for the one with the lace on the cuffs, which she had brought from England. That one lay in the bureau drawer until it cracked at the folds.) She could see Joseph and Martha now, the day they bought it. She had been with them.

They went into the store to buy gingham for a dress for Anna, and this dress lay on the counter. Martha asked the girl how much it was. When the girl told her, she asked to see some gingham quickly. The girl went back shop to get the gingham. Martha stepped over and held up the dress. Joseph came and stood beside her.

"It is Anna's size?" he said.

"Oh, I don't *know*," Martha said, as if she'd never dreamed of it in connection with Anna. "It's some price."

She put the dress down and went back to her place at the counter. The girl showed her the gingham. Martha put her hand beneath it, testing its quality.

"How much did you say that other dress was?" she said. The girl told her again. "Oh yes," she said. "Well, I think I'll take about three yards of this."

Joseph was still looking at the dress. He came over now and whispered to Martha. "If you want that other one, I kin let you have some money."

"Shhh . . ." Martha said.

She opened her purse and looked inside. The girl measured off the gingham, ready to tear it across.

"How much did you say that other dress was?" Martha said . . .

Anna had kept smiling nervously when she first saw it, as if it frightened her a little. But that night (and each night for the next week) she slipped it on for a few minutes, then off again, when she undressed for bed.

She had kept it like new until that Sunday afternoon she saw David going back the mountain road for lady slippers. Martha had urged her to take it off. She called to David, and David called back that he would wait. But Anna was scared he would stroll ahead, out of sight. And if she only walked in the clear spaces, what could happen to it? She turned her ankle, running to catch up with him. The rock she fell against grated an unmendable hole in the skirt.

When Ellen remembered this little extravagance for Anna, she smiled.

She thought of the tea canister on the top of the pantry shelf where Joseph and Martha kept their money. She thought of how many times when Martha had gone to it (to pay the school rates, or settle with the storekeeper, or maybe just to buy a sweet-grass basket from an Indian at the door) she had had to tilt the canister from end to end, picking out the last bits of silver from the pennies, to make up the count.

Yet it was never altogether empty. Somehow that would be the very night Joseph would come in, sorting out some crumpled bills from the twine and matches in his pocket. He'd have money for a calf he'd sold, or the returns from his saw logs, or repayment of a loan he'd made (and forgotten about) to a neighbour.

Ellen didn't know how it was they always managed to have a little spare cash.

The money for butter and eggs was taken up in trade. The pig and most of the vegetables went into the cellar. If Joseph worked for a neighbour he was paid *back* in work. Yet, somehow, they were never caught helpless by any need that barter couldn't arrange for.

They didn't sell off land to make ends meet, as some did. One piece of timber, yes (and that night the lid of the canister would scarcely close, and all the neighbours came in to see the hundred-dollar bill); but all that money had gone into the new house. When Joseph came home from the drive there were ten-dollar bills amongst the one's—but those all went for the country rates ,the tote-load of flour and feed, things like that. There was often two hundred dollars upstairs in the box which held the marriage certificates and the deed and the locks of children's hair; but that was "cattle money." It might be borrowed from but must be repaid, against the time when Joseph bought another pair.

They made over and they made do. But they never watched the cent. At a pie social or a tea meeting they spent as freely as if the money were easy-come town-people's money. The bills were never folded in the canister; nor the denominations separate. There didn't seem to be any system of balance whatever.

And yet, wherever it came from (she shook her head silently and smiled), there always seemed to be enough for their needs and a little extra. Enough extra for anything, though it had a touch of luxury, that any one of them really had his heart on. A set of portieres for Martha. A shot gun for Chris. A book for David. The silk dress for Anna.

Joseph himself had no private wants; but he unquestioningly accepted the whims of the others as, for them, true necessity.

She could see him and Martha now. They were on their knees, picking up potatoes in the acre field. Soundless with distance, they looked as if they were praying.

CHAPTER XVIII

JOSEPH and Martha knelt facing each other across the double rows. A line of potatoes soaked in the dusty steeping light. They had two baskets. One was for good potatoes; one for the pig's potatoes—small ones, or scabby ones, or overgrown ones with a hollow heart. Martha's hands were rough as Joseph's with brushing the warm dusty earth off each potato she picked up.

They scarcely spoke. Except to check each other, smilingly, when one or the other would confuse the baskets; or to utter an exclamation when the lip of the meal bag which she was holding open would slip, and the potatoes from the basket he was emptying rolled down the side. But their thoughts seemed to hum together in the cidery light, like a bee over clover. Speech broke, rather than forged, the quiet contact between them. The silences between speech spliced it together again.

This was the time of day of the day of the year that Martha loved best. This the place and the work. Her thoughts were alert, but without comment. They moved, but without images, melting through each other like the configurations of clouds. This was like a recess from thought: the still remembering light, the hypnotic movement of her hands and Joseph's in the gathering.

And though he had no conscious notice of it, even Joseph's strength burned softer in him, to match Martha's, like a light turned down. Unity was so in them that any other person who came into their thoughts, even one of the children, was like a second person, not a third.

There was the sudden bark of a gun, far off in the mountain.

"Listen!" Martha said. She didn't let go of the potato she'd been about to drop in the basket. There was only stillness.

"That's the way they went," Joseph said. "I'd laugh if they got one."

"There'd be more shots if they was firin at a deer," Martha said. "Listen." There were no more shots.

"Wouldn't old Dave be tickled if they ever got a deer!" Joseph said.

Martha dropped the potato into the basket. "Joseph," she said, "you don't suppose anything happened, do you? Dave gets so excited."

120

"*Chris* had the gun," Joseph said. "Likely the deer was runnin . . ."

"Chris never fired at a deer before," Martha said. "You don't know what might happen if they got excited . . ."

"Now start worryin," Joseph said, grinning. "*They're* all right."

"Don't you ever worry?"

"What's the good a worryin?"

"It's all right to talk, but if you can't help it . . ."

She said no more, but the spell of the afternoon was broken. A little ant of fear began to crawl through her mind.

They ran out of bags.

"I'll git some in the barn," Joseph said.

"Don't be long," Martha said.

There was a hurry in the work now. The afternoon began suddenly to go. The light began to retreat into the hard olive sky.

The potatoes that had lain so easily to be finished in the rows now lay heavily. They weighted against the time left before dusk. She felt chilly. She got the sweater she'd thrown across the fence. She began to scrabble up the potatoes, without stopping to dust them clean. She glanced up the row, trying to split the potatoes up into basketfuls and make the row look short. Then she kept her eye on the ground, because when she did glance up, her work seemed to have made no impression at all.

Both baskets were full and Joseph hadn't come with the bags. She heaped them, though she knew the crown would fall off when the baskets were lifted for dumping. Then she went along the row, separating good ones from poor ones in little mounds on the ground. Still he didn't come. She got up and went to the top of the patch to see what was keeping him.

She saw him, with the bags under his arm. He was talking at the gate to a strange man with a strange team. They seemed to be talking leisurely. The man tapped the dashboard with his whip and Joseph moved a small stone with his foot. Joseph would straighten up to move away and the man would draw up the reins, and she'd think suddenly: it won't take long, with the two of us . . . But Joseph would put his foot up on a wheel spoke and they'd talk some more.

His back was to the field. He didn't turn, to wave to her that he'd be right along.

And then it came over her.

Sometimes it would take no more than that: the sight of Joseph completely taken up in conversation with another man;

forgetting that she was waiting or, remembering, making no account of it.

She caught her breath and started back to the baskets. But it was faster than movement. Movement couldn't lose or shake the wind of exile. It sprang up from nowhere, and she was helpless, once she had felt it, not to feed it. It was like the blue dusk light of August exiling the mountains; or the cold horizon light of winter exiling the skeletons of the prayer-fingered apple trees; or the retreating October light draining the fields.

She felt it stiffen her lips and creep cold-lip-blue into her thoughts. She felt the gathering wind of it blow everything inward. She felt her body shell over it—the heavy sore-ringing knot of it, blown inaccessibly inward. Even her hands, sorting the potatoes in separate piles, moved only with the numb direction of habit. She felt her breath shoulder again the breath-crushing burden of all the other times Joseph had . . . These times were instantly shorn of their former dissolution, instantly reaccumulated.

Joseph walked back, leisurely, to the field. He spaced the bags down the row. He dumped the baskets, each in a single expert motion. Martha didn't stand up to help.

He didn't mention the stranger. He never communicated even exciting news right away. Coming into the house with it, he'd take off his cap and coat first. Then, beginning with only a hint, he'd wait for Martha to draw it from him with questions.

Martha was silent.

"That was the new doctor," he said at last. "Doctor Engles, his name is." He spoke awkwardly. To volunteer even that much was difficult for him.

"What did *he* want?" The words formed in Martha's mind, but something stopped them on her tongue. Now the moment for reply had been let slip, retreat was sealed.

Joseph glanced at her face. His thoughts turned white. A heaviness sagged suddenly in his muscles, as if a cloud had passed over them. Her hand moved toward the basket as he reached for the handle, to dump it. He waited, but she drew her hand back. He picked up the basket and dumped it, snubbing a sigh. This was the bafflement, before the still-burning anger at something he couldn't get his hands on set in.

What had he done wrong this time? He didn't know.

But even when he did, there was never anything he could do. If he said he was sorry, or showed extra thoughtfulness toward her, or tried to make a joke of it, she wouldn't resist; but she would be patient with his advances, as if they were false. She wouldn't smile. His words would seem to grow louder and louder in the silence. His advances, rejected, would leave him stung and ashamed for making them.

There was nothing to do but wait. Until the minutes dropping on it, one by one, finally wore it out. Or until some little thing (he never knew just what, or why) flushed through her silence like a drop of dye. Wait . . . wait . . . wait . . . With their silence chaining them together, but as if, if their bodies touched they would make a sudden nightmare sound.

This thing that had come up with the stranger wasn't like manoeuvring a log onto the trail sled. This wasn't like the physics of turning a straight furrow, or judging his circuit through a jagged field so that no cock of hay would be hauled farther than necessary and he would wind up nearest the barn. There he was on sure ground. This was something he was helpless to decide, without Martha.

He set the basket down. He *forced* himself to speak again.

"He says he's out so much nights. He said someone told him maybe he could git Anna to come stay with his wife and go to school in town."

"*Anna?*"

As the word broke from Martha's lips the silence unclasped as if a tourniquet had been cut. (As it would rupture instantly if Rachel should say, "You oughta make Joseph lug that water fer ya . . . but I guess all men are alike" . . . or when he'd be going to town to get the oxen shod and she'd notice a button off his good suit coat she'd think, because she had nothing cooked in the house, of him eating just the bread and butter in his lunch, uncomplaining even in thought, though the other men in the livery stable would probably have cookies and pie . . . or when he'd say, as she turned the pages of the catalogue silently, compulsively, though he never said anything like that any other time, "What do you want for Christmas?" . . .)

Anna? The thought of Anna amongst strangers . . . the thought of Joseph confused about it . . . the thought of Joseph confused in any way by strangers, by town men, endowed his very features for her with a fierce cleaving.

"Who mentioned *Anna* to him?" she said. Her voice almost angry.

"He didn't say. I suppose they meant all right. It'd be a good chance for her to git an education."

"She's never been away from home," Martha said. Anna too polite to let her lonesomeness show, the first night at a strange table . . . her dress hanging in the closet the first morning she went away . . . the things she might be doing or saying if she were home . . .

"Of course it ain't like she was goin fur," Joseph said.

"I know," Martha said, "but she's only sixteen. She won't be sixteen till August. The fourth," she added. She was almost talking to herself. Was it so long the time had been so safe? Why had she never thought about it until the time for separation came?

"He said she wouldn't have to do no work," Joseph said. "Just go to school."

"She'd have to have all new clothes." The picture of Anna's small face looking around for another girl to walk home from school with, who had a dress that was made over too . . .

"I guess we could git her some new things," Joseph said.

"Joseph," Martha said, "do you think we ought to let her go?"

She saw his thoughts stumble when she put the decision up to him. He had put forth argument in fairness to the case for Anna's good, while she was arguing for both of them their feelings' contradiction. But she saw these reasons of his topple, now they stood alone.

"Do you?" he said.

She didn't answer. "Joe," she said, "reach me the basket, will you?"

"Now, don't cry," he said. "Don't cry, Martha . . . no one's makin her go if she don't want to go. She don't have to go if you don't want her to."

"I know," she said. But they both knew Anna would have to go.

She held the bag open for him. "Oh, Joseph . . ." she said. Her face crumpled completely.

She cried for Anna, because, with Anna ignorant of all this that concerned her, it seemed as if they were plotting against her. And for Joseph. In a sudden rush of hurting closeness, she saw that he and she had come to the end of moving forward; in any of the break and change from now on, they were the ones who would always be left.

The children came through the door in a rush. David and Anna were dancing up and down. Chris was quiet, but his eyes, too, were bounding.

"We got one!" David cried.

"We got a deer!" Anna said.

"Chris got him with one shot!" they said, over and over. They kept looking at Chris. They felt themselves exalted in the act of exalting him.

"This buck was standin there in the little swale where you

come round the turn in the log road—you know that turn in the log road?" they said. They repeated it over and over, as they had on the way home. They started at the beginning again as soon as the story was finished.

"Father," they cried, exalting their father, "you'll come with us and dress it up after you finish the chores, won't you? We'll help with the chores. We'll take the lantern back to the woods. We know right where it is . . ."

Oh, how gladly they would help him with the chores. Oh how directly they could take him right to the very spot. They were completely fused by this thing they had done together. It was a thing for such adult respect, because deer were scarce then and wary: and a thing of such chill wonder. They had gone up and put their hands on the deer's very head; and where was the timidity now that would take it leaping away at the mere glimpse of a human?

"We got a deer, we got a deer . . ." David sang. He put his arms around Anna and Chris and danced them around the room. Chris's steps were clumsy, but even he didn't resist.

They were almost ready to go dress the deer when Martha said, "Anna, how would you like to go to school in town?"

"Why?" Anna said.

Martha told her what had happened.

It was like one day they were all set to start making ice cream. A stranger had come to the door and offered Joseph a fancy price for the woodlot if he'd seal the bargain right now . . . and while they were talking, in indecision, the ice melted in the pail.

"What did that goddam thing have to come *today* for?" David said.

"David!" Martha said.

He ran, speechless, into the dining room. Anna followed him.

"Why don't *you* go, Dave?" she whispered. "You're so far ahead of me. I know you got Grade 12 all by yourself, but you could take more languages or something, for when you go to college . . ."

"No," David said, "that ain't what . . ." (He couldn't explain to her how he'd have the best education in the world anyway. His *certainty* of that glossed over the contradiction between going away to get it and the unalterable feature of staying here; but that wasn't a thing he could make plain.)

"I ain't goin," Anna said. But they both knew she must.

"Comin, Dave?" Joseph called.

"No," David shouted. There was nothing to the deer now

but the raw blood-smell, the coarse-hair feeling, the sick-sweetish spilling of the steaming intestines when the knife slipped . . .

"Are *you* comin, Anna?" Joseph called.

"Not if Dave ain't," Anna said.

That evening Anna was amongst them more tenderly than ever before, but more separately. She was like the one who is threatened with sickness, amongst the ashamedly well. For the first time the faces of leaving and of staying were in the kitchen. They made between quickened touch and quickened response a helpless excommunication. And the thin October light retreated and slept warily in whatever place it was where the glinting caution from the deer's gelid eyes had fled.

And somehow they knew that, though Anna came back within a month, no amount of willing on anyone's part could make it quite the same again.

CHAPTER XIX

DAVID put on his sport shirt and the brand new white sneakers right after dinner. He stood at the attic window now, watching. The pendant afternoon warmth of late June weighted the air, but he put on his new cap too when the mail team came in sight. His hand shook as he pulled the crown of it jauntily sidewise before the mirror. He ran downstairs.

"Are they comin?" Martha said.

"Yes," David said. "I'm goin down to the post office to meet them."

As near as Newbridge was, this was the first time Anna had been home since she went away to school. And Toby Richmond was coming too, for a week's visit. Anna was to meet him at the train and show him where the mailman could be found.

David wished his mother would take off her apron. But if he asked her to, she'd look hurt if she understood why he asked. If she took it off docilely, without understanding, he'd feel more ashamed still.

He saw Steve sauntering up the road. Damn it, they'd meet exactly at the gate. He stooped to make out he was tying up his laces. He wanted to be alone when he met Toby and Anna. But Steve waited for him.

He straightened the crown of his cap before he got to the gate. Steve glanced covertly at his new sport shirt and white sneakers. He didn't say anything, but it was the glance you give a friend in company with someone you've both been ridiculing before. David felt the shirt and sneakers like some foolish and betraying feature. They'd been smooth as breath on him when he'd looked at himself in the mirror. Now, with Steve so shielded himself in ordinary clothes, he was conscious of their very outline; grown enormous on him; something to be lifted each time he moved.

"I got the *white* sneakers," he said, "because they're so cool. Jazzus, Steve, this shirt's cool too."

"Yeah?"

David felt silly again. His explanation had been *too* eager to fool anyone. He felt half angered at himself for this compulsion to cut the whims of his privacy to pieces, before the other boys. He felt half angered at them because their own way seemed so snug inside them. They just looked out *over* it at everyone else. They never had to say anything at all.

He hoped Steve would move along when they got to the post office; but he didn't. He stood there awkwardly, yet with that maddening self-containment. He's taking everything in, David thought.

He had planned to take smooth charge of the greeting. But with Steve there, the things he'd had ready to say ("Welcome to the wilds" . . . "Isn't this a corking day?") felt shallow in his mouth. Treacherous, somehow.

"Hi, Dave," Anna called.

"Hi, Anna."

The wagon stopped. She sprang out and ran toward him. There was a moment of indecision in each of them : did the other expect to kiss or not? They didn't kiss. Only their hands met in a clumsy rush.

"Hi, Toby," David said.

"Hi, Dave."

"Ain't it hot!" David said. He couldn't bring out "isn't," with Steve standing there.

"Hi, Steve," Anna said, "how are you?"

She didn't speak as if Steve were among the things wonderful to find still here when she came back, he was just something on the periphery of the moment of arriving. Though he'd felt that Steve was in the way, himself, David wished her greeting had had more rush about it.

"Is this your bag?" Toby said to Anna.

"Bag"! Steve's eye asked David's to join in a smirk. David looked away.

Anna turned quickly to Toby. "No," she said. "*Oh*, yes, that's mine."

In that instant of Anna's deflected interest, David had a sense of loss. He felt the having-travelled-together of the other two; the stupid, static, sense of the one who waits. When Anna turned and gathered him up once more in the smile of arriving, he felt it sharper still. It seemed as if now Anna would never come home by herself. She'd always bring with her something a little strange; if only the having-been-away, the travel-muss in her clothes. He had lost all control of the greeting. He felt the spying rigidity of the one who waits, before the mobile freedom of the one who comes.

Toby picked up Anna's suitcase. David picked up Toby's. They started up the road.

"Dave," the mailman called, "tell yer mother I'll settle with her fer them berries."

"All right."

"Tell her I couldn't git only five cents a quart . . ."

"All right, all right." Oh, why couldn't he shut up about those old berries, in front of Toby!

Steve was fishing out the mailbag from the back seat.

"So long, Steve," David called. It sounded silly, but he had to say something to Steve. He felt, somehow, as if he had betrayed him.

David and Toby scarcely exchanged remarks. Each was thinking of the letters he'd written to the other. Each felt a crippling embarrassment in the consciousness that the other was secretly comparing him with the self-portrait of his own words.

Yet it wasn't the awkwardness between strangers. Even then it was the self-consciousness of two people, either of whom in the presence of the other, by reason of some affinity, feels himself on a stage. Alert for the other's reaction, he can't quite let his behaviour fall where it may. They communicated through Anna. Even then, it was as if the three of them were a unit.

"How long did it take to come out?" David said, looking at Anna.

"Oh, about four hours. Wasn't it, Toby?"

"Just about," Toby said.

He glanced at his wrist watch. David had never known a boy who owned a wrist watch. I'll save every cent I get, for a wrist watch, he thought.

"How about the fellow in the ox cart?" Toby said to Anna.

"Oh, yes!" Anna exclaimed. "We met Angus—you know how his team's always right in the middle of the road—laying back on a sack of straw." ("Sack"? He felt the little thrust of loss again. They'd always called it "bag." Pronouncing all her "ings" now too.) "He jumped up so quick his pipe fell right out of his mouth onto the straw. It was the funniest thing . . ."

"Did the sack catch?" David said.

"It almost," Anna said. "It looked so darn funny."

"He certainly thumped that old sack," Toby said. They both laughed as if it were happening all over again.

David stiffened. He had the sense of the one who is never there, who is told only. He felt the inhibition you feel when someone whose laughter has always been conspiratorial with you alone, tells you of laughing with another.

But when he saw that Toby's glance at him was tentative (he'd never dreamed that anyone from the city could be tentative like himself), the stiffness melted. It was as if Toby and Anna would never be quite sure they'd been right about the way a thing had struck them until they'd told him and he'd confirmed it. They both looked relieved when he laughed too.

David and Toby were the same height, but they couldn't have looked less alike. The bones of David's face were already squaring. They weighted it with the subtle cast of man-heaviness. But it would always be a face you could recognize from its snapshot as a child. His eyes would slip the leash of adult slowness all at once. There was a tic of uncertainty at his mouth when something snubbed a smile. He had nervous blond hair. He seemed to bear his clothes, rather than fill them. Toby's hair was black. Its contrast with his arrestingly light blue eyes (waiting without impatience, but with constant readiness, for something good to light them up) gave his skin a kind of sensual pallor. His smooth body was coordinated with his clothes. His suit looked as if there had never been a first time for putting it on. His shoes, his *hat*, had the look of experience.

Yet there was a curious identification between the two boys. It was different from David's identification with the boys here. The part of him which he must withhold from them was released now. It was like a second language come full-worded to him, without any learning. He was like this city boy too. He pictured himself in Toby's clothes. They'd look like a part of him too, even when they lay over a chair.

And Toby was shy! He felt his own shyness vanish.

"I hope Mother's got the trapeza all set," he said.

"Dave," Anna said, "what are you trying to get through you?"

"Got the table set for supper, I mean. I'm studying some Greek books I got from Mr Kendall."

"Oh," Anna said. "Mr Kendall's the minister from New-bridge," she explained to Toby.

"He went to Oxford," David said to Anna. "He said he knew where Grandmother's people's estate was."

"Did he?" There was no prompting in Anna's question. She'd seen through what he was doing. He wasn't telling *her* —she'd heard Mr Kendall say that herself. He'd tried too soon to make it sound as if they weren't really country people, as if finding themselves in the country was just a quirk of circumstance.

"Do you like that old language stuff?" Toby said. "I hate it."

"I like it all right," David said, suddenly crestfallen.

"I guess you have to be really clever . . ." Toby said, as quickly conciliatory.

"Dr Engles said you must be some smart to pass the provincial exams for Grade 12, just studying home," Anna said.

"Ohhhh . . ." David said, twisting with embarrassment.

"Did David?" Toby exclaimed. "Is that *right?*"

"Ohhhh, Anna," David said. "What makes you . . .?"

"How's Mother?" Anna said quickly, "and Father? . . . and Chris . . .?"

Even then she kept watching David and Toby, keeping the balance between them. She was always to do that when the three of them were together. Switching the discussion when it had got to a point where, if it went any farther, something might happen to it. Shifting to Toby's side when his quick enthusiasms, racing beyond reason (as she could see, herself) were vulnerable (though, strangely, David was the more imaginative of the two) to the penetration of David's common sense. Adding to David when Toby's unconsciously shattering frankness subtracted from David in the place where it hurt her most to see David reduced: his imagination. Even then, she knew that Toby would be her husband, as certainly as she knew that David was her brother.

A slow smile crinkled in David's eyes.

"Did the old horse have any trouble with his drawstring today?" he said.

He could level his seriousness all at once, with a foolery slanted just right for whomever he might be with; so that, remembering his seriousness other times, their feeling for him was intensified by a gentle incredulity. Toby's eyes flicked into alignment with his.

"David!" Anna said.

"It'd make a good horn," Toby said. He glanced exclusively at David, in such a way as to excuse Anna from listening.

"Yeah," David said. "Maybe Angus could hitch a kazoo up

to it." It was his way of leading up the other's suggestion, step by step, to its consummant statement.

"David!" Anna said again.

"I didn't say anything," he said innocently.

"He didn't say anything," Toby said.

That was the way they'd always join in a gentle teasing she wasn't entirely unwilling to submit to. They were a unit. It wasn't at all like when Charlotte was the extra one with him and Chris.

"There's Mother," Anna said. "Hi, Mother . . ."

Martha was waiting in the doorway. She didn't come out to the gate, because of Toby. Joseph and Chris stood in the doorway behind her. Anna ran ahead.

David and Toby were left behind. The suitcases were suddenly burdensome. It was as if the three of them had been keeping a ball in the air and now it had fallen to the ground.

"Did you get my letter?" David said awkwardly. "I didn't know if you'd want to come or not."

"Sure, I wanted to come," Toby said. "Did you get mine?"

"Yeah," David said.

"It's hot, isn't it?" David said.

"It sure is."

Anna was home again.

She couldn't seem to stay still. She'd start with a dish from the pantry to the dining room, helping her mother get supper, and then, forgetting the dish in her hand, walk into the hall and look around the parlour, or walk to one of the windows and look out over the fields. She'd go down cellar for a bottle of preserves and call up, "What's this big barrel with the tub over it?" She'd come back without the preserves.

Martha whispered to her to sit down and entertain Toby. But she couldn't sit down. She'd say a few words to Toby, then she'd be getting a drink at the pump and glancing into the mirror over the sink, or lifting the stove cover, or slipping a pickle into her mouth from the pickle dish. She'd open the sideboard drawer to get the good knives and she'd say, "Where did this picture come from?" She'd look at the picture and forget all about the knives. She'd say to her father, "Have you cut any hay yet?" or to Chris (for the second or third time), "How are you, Chris?" She'd smile all the way at them as she spoke, but turn before they had time to answer, and trace the pattern of the new kitchen tablecloth with her finger.

She was home again, but her hair was flattened with the ring of her hatband, and she had on her good dress in the afternoon. All the familiar things seemed to slant away from her in a funny perspective, as if she were getting used to new glasses.

David was restless in a different way.

It was wonderful to have Anna home again. It was fine to have Toby too. But somehow the excitement of having them both together wasn't quite the total of having them separately. One seemed to take away from the other. And there was the ineptitude of his family with strangers. His grandmother, who could have guided things so smoothly, was visiting in Annapolis.

He couldn't help wishing his father and Chris would make some remark right after the introduction. The clumsiness of shaking Toby's hand seemed to hang in the air. He couldn't help the sense of contraction, as if to stop his hearing, when his mother said, "Pleased to meet you" instead of "How do you do?" He couldn't help wishing that if Chris had been going to change his clothes at all, he'd put on his good shirt and good shoes too, not just his good coat. It seemed only to accent his country look. Why couldn't his mother have waited till they were alone to ask, "Did Horace say anything about the berries?" Why did his father have to turn to Chris so soon and say, "That grass's showin brown in the acre field, did ya notice it? We oughta strike that tomorrow"? It sounded private and intrusive. And they knew how to speak grammatically: they noticed when anyone else made mistakes just because he didn't know any better. Why could they never take the trouble to show it?

Excepting Anna, he felt a curious responsibility for his family's behaviour. He was some sort of interpreter between them and Toby. He had to keep his finger firmly on the conversation. Guiding it this way or that. Shearing off quickly, by some interjection of his own, a question or an answer which he knew would be wrong.

But whenever he stepped out of the room, the whole thing would fall apart. Toby and Chris and his father would sit there speechless.

And the others didn't take away the directness between him and Toby, as Anna did. He could feel that funny segregating attention between him and Toby. Each caught what the other reflected, like following mirrors.

He wished his mother wouldn't beckon to Anna in the pantry and whisper, "Give him that china cup, won't you." He had to talk loud to cover it, and even then wasn't sure that Toby didn't hear.

And when they sat down to supper, he wished his mother

132

hadn't put on the butter knife. Anyone could see that Chris and his father weren't taking any butter for fear they'd fumble it. He wished she *hadn't* made such an obvious thing of straining the tea in the pantry; that she *hadn't* given Toby the one linen napkin.

He put one elbow on the table casually, and twisted the salt cellar about. He tried to say something light and laughable. But nothing relaxed them. They didn't take half what they wanted of any special thing like the sweet pumpkin pickle when it was passed. He wished they'd let the finish of the meal die out gradually—but they pushed their chairs all back at once when the last bite was swallowed, as if at a signal. His mother stacked the cups and saucers nearest her, for carrying back to the pantry. He wished she would wait until they were out of the room.

"Where's the toilet?" Toby whispered to David in the evening.

"Outside," David said. "I'll show you."

(That damned old backhouse! The walls and even the box that held the catalogue were papered with parlour paper, twenty-cent border and all, but . . .)

Chris got up too. "I'm just showin Toby the toilet," David whispered. (He felt embarrassed, somehow, using the word "toilet" with Chris.) But Chris followed them.

They stepped off the platform.

"I guess I'll drain my potatoes too," Chris said. He moved off a step and began to urinate, meditatively, on the grass. He tried to make it men-together amongst them.

Toby seemed to hesitate about urinating there.

"It's the second door on the shop," David said, "with the button on it. Take a coarse sight, and curb your trajectory." He spoke as if he were really a visitor in this place himself, *denying* any part of its crudity except as the basis for a joke.

Toby laughed. David glanced around to see if Chris had caught what he said. He felt sheepish to have Chris hear him talk like that.

"He must be scairt he'll git cold in it," Chris said, when Toby had closed the door. He came close to David, assuming common ground with him in smirking at a stranger's unorthodoxy. It was a convention in the country that men never used an outhouse. They went behind it, and urinated against the wall; or used the shovel in the barn.

But David felt suddenly defensive for Toby. It might have been Chris who was the stranger.

"Well, that's what it's for, ain't it?" he said. "It ain't a parlour."

For a minute Chris seemed to have the same stupid indrawn spying as Steve.

CHAPTER XX

TOBY slept in the attic with David. It was the first time David had ever shared that room. Toby stood naked over the suitcase, fishing out pajamas. (The boys here had a shyness about their bodies anywhere except swimming. They'd slip down their pants and sidle in under the sheets almost secretly.) David stripped down to his shirt. He wished he had pajamas. He'd get pajamas before Toby came again. And a wrist watch.

In bed, talk sprouted with a new ease. Their words seemed to rise straight up from their mouths and, when their force was spent, fall into each other's mind and germinate leisurely.

Toby's watch had a luminous dial. "Is that your watch shining?" David said.

"Yeah," Toby said, "it shows in the dark. See?" He waved his arm about. "Look," he said, with his instant generosity, "do you want to wear it while I'm here?"

"Oh, I might break it," David said.

"You can't hurt it," Toby said. He was already undoing the fastener.

David put it on. The defining feel of the strap on his wrist seemed to crystallize all his wavering edges into one clean core. It transported him beyond this room like a magic talisman.

They talked with an interplay of affinity and divergence. It would always be there, in the way one led and the other followed, by turns.

Toby chuckled when David told him about the things of the country. But even then David knew that Toby's interest was in their novelty only. He had to transmute them in the telling. He had to make them discardable as anything but a basis for fun. He knew that if Toby found himself alone in the country, it would have no language for him at all. Toby would never understand how the country spoke to him strongest when no one else was there. He had to hide that.

Toby told him about the things of the city. He never doubted they were the only real ones. He wasn't bragging. He was giving them to David too. ("Dave, you've got to come visit *me*. I'll show you . . .") David listened eagerly and with identification. He found it more wonderful than anything before to have this boy from the city recognize in him the first person who'd ever understood anything he described, exactly. He felt the most exquisite flattery in the halt of Toby's enthusiasms when his own lagged.

For even then Toby's quick enthusiasms failed to distinguish (as David could) between the rich and the scant, just because both were bustling or new. He'd feel, before he'd gone far, David's halt; and deferring to David even then, his own enthusiasm would crumple.

"I'll take you to see the shows . . . Sometimes besides the moving picture they have jugglers and dancers and . . ."

"Yeah, I'd like to," David said.

(He, David, came out on the stage. He clowned first, so they almost burst, laughing. Then he began to sing. It was a sad song. It got so quiet he could hear someone sob, and afterwards they clapped and clapped. They couldn't believe it . . .)

"We'll go down to the docks. I'll take you on some of the big ships. There's ships in Halifax, you know, from all over the world."

"*There* is?"

(The ship glided softly into the harbour, spending exactly its own momentum. He waved to the people on the pier. He felt an exquisite twist of sadness and safety mixed. He was sad because so soon these same faces would be getting smaller and smaller as they waved to him when his ship was going somewhere else. Yet he was safe, because there were so many places in the world to go. There would always be some new place that he had never seen . . .)

"You better come vacation time, Dave. Then we can swim and play tennis and—can you play tennis?"

"No."

(Who is that new boy? He swam right across the Arm. It's the same one was playing tennis. He's got some way he hits the ball so you can't possibly get it back . . .)

"Oh yes, and don't let me forget to take you down where the trains go under the Arm bridge. We try to throw apple cores down the smoke stack. First one does, the rest have to buy him a banana split."

Toby felt David halt. That was thin. He halted too. They lay silent for a while.

"What are you going to do?" Toby said.

"Do?"

"Yeah. Be?"

"I don't know," David said. "What are you?"

"I'm going to be an explorer," Toby said. "Dave," he said eagerly, "let's both be explorers. We'll have more fun than anyone."

"All right," David said.

(Now they were swinging up the streets of all the strange places together. They were the only two people in the world who had the same beckon of somewhere else in them.) I have a friend, he thought. This is what it's like to have a friend. It's like the kitchen fire on your hands when you come in from pulling turnips in November. It's like the time I had three mugs of Ave's beer. (Someone tried to throw him out the night they were both roaring drunk in the saloon, but Toby sobered up that hot minute and knocked the bastard flat. The time a cutthroat came after Toby with a knife he rushed between them and knocked the tough flat. He was so strong then he could have knocked *any*one down . . .)

"I guess explorers see some funny sights down around the Equator there," Toby said.

In the subtle communication that was always between them, David knew that Toby meant girls. It was funny: he and Steve could come right out coarse about girls, but it wasn't half as stimulating as he and Toby just hinting at it.

"I guess they kind of skimp on the petticoats," David said.

Toby chuckled. "I wonder what they do in a gale."

"I wonder," David said. "I guess you'd have to keep your eyes shut—or else put a muzzle on it."

They didn't say any more. They just lay there, silently. They were like two people who have sensed in each other the same amusement with a serious speaker, but cannot commit themselves to any further conspiracy, right there, than a wink. They thought about each other thinking about girls.

David was tempted to tell Toby about him and Effie. But somehow he hesitated. Just Toby's *thinking* of doing it with a girl seemed to endow him with the getting-it-prowess more securely than his own actual deed.

He looked at the wrist watch gleaming outside the quilt.

"Toby," he said, "did you wind it?" He wouldn't dare, himself.

But Toby was asleep. He could always drop thought for sleep like that: in that instant abandonment of the now for the next.

David lay awake, thinking: I have a friend. What he'd been missing all his life had been a reflection of himself anywhere. Now he had discovered it at last.

But why, when the house was quiet with the sound the silence makes to the only one awake, why did he think of the others—his mother and father and Chris? He pictured their faces. Defenceless in sleep, somehow they bore marks on them (which only he could see) of the way he'd felt toward them throughout the afternoon and evening. Why did he feel that he couldn't wait till morning to talk to them, in front of Toby, about something Toby couldn't share? Why did he want to creep downstairs and awaken them, pretending he'd heard someone call, making them assure him over and over, until they began to laugh about it, that they were all right?

CHAPTER XXI

THERE were marks that stayed on David himself from Toby's visit. They soon scarred over; but so thinly, that even a duplication of the same shade of weather that had been there then would rupture them.

There was the moment of stepping back into the kitchen after Toby and Anna had left, with the voice of the room itself packed and gone: that first moment, after the illusion, when you have to go back to what you really are.

And the moment at the Baptizing Pool.

The other boys acted so queer with Toby. You'd think he had an invisible circle around him, bounding a limit of trespass. When he said, "Eh?" or "Shucks," they looked down at the ground. They kept horsing with each other, louder and foolisher when he was there than they ever did: it was obviously for his benefit. But the minute he *spoke* to one of them, they'd drop it. Their faces would turn serious all at once, like someone half deaf.

Toby folded his pants before he hung them on the bridge rail. He told them he collected stamps. Why couldn't they see there wasn't anything soft about that? Why did they look as if they were waiting for something to pass over? (When Toby could swim faster than *any* of them, and was hung like a stud horse.) Why couldn't they see that the slant way Toby talked about girls was twice as lusty as the way they sang, "My name is Jim Bowser, My rod is a rouser . . ."?

That day at the Baptizing Pool when Toby asked if anyone had a piece of paper in his pockets, they didn't ask him what was wrong with grass. They just looked at the ground in their foolish sanctimonious way. But later, when he called to David,

"Don't you think it's about time to quit?" Art giggled outright. ("Quit"!) They all looked at David. They actually invited him to snicker.

His glance caromed past theirs, to Toby's. "It's immaterial to me," he called back.

It was never quite the same with the other boys after that moment. Not ever.

He would always remember too the moment when he and Toby and Anna turned back on their way to the top of the mountain.

The day they started to walk up the mountain, a single tatter of cloud coasted across the bright blue sky. A film of thick sunshine covered the shapes of the spruces and the rocks and the moss as if they were wet with it. Chris was hoeing.

"Where ya goin?" he said.

"Just for a walk," David said.

Chris looked up and down the rows. "If I thought I could finish these Monday," he said, "I'd go *with* you."

David remembered the rare times his father would give them an opening like that. It was his way of letting them know he might be persuaded to drop his work. They always jumped at it with incredible gladness. He knew that Chris was waiting for just such persuasion now.

"Oh, we may just go as far as the bridge," he said.

Everyone has one place that seems like his own, one place he wants to take his friend. With David, it was the mountain. Somehow it *had* to be just him and Toby and Anna.

He glanced back before they went over the crown of the hill. Chris was leaning on his hoe, watching them.

Halfway up, past the pole bridge, the road turned and ran crosswise across the ridge before curving sharply upward again. He started to eulogize the mountain, for Toby.

"You can see the whole valley up a ways farther," he said. "You can't hear a sound, but you can see the whole thing."

"You can't see it as plain as you can when you're in there, can you?" Toby said, with his sudden devastating frankness.

"Well, no," David said, "but . . ."

Toby laughed his puzzled, whim-destroying laugh. "Is that all there is to it, Dave?" he said. "Is *that* all we're going way up there for?"

"I guess," David said.

"It isn't like it was a *real* mountain," Toby said. "What makes you think it's so wonderful?"

David didn't reply. The thought of the mountain went as lint-grey as the toes of his larrigans in November slush.

He remembered the time Chris had persuaded his mother to let him, David, go to the pung races on the lake too; though it was the one spot where the older boys liked best to swarm around together, without any kids tagging along. How when he couldn't keep up with the big boys when they started off on a race of their own, alongside the horses, Chris pretended a stitch in his side so they'd *both* have an excuse to drop behind. He thought: After the way I put him off today, Chris will never ask to go anywhere with me again.

"Let's go back, if Toby doesn't want to go any farther," Anna said quickly. "You and I can go some other time, Dave."

"I didn't say I didn't want to go," Toby said. "I bet it's great up there, honest."

But David was already turning. "I guess we won't bother going up today," he said.

He saw how the suddenness of Toby's veering off, just when they were surest of him, would always be able to desiccate their most vulnerable fancies. And (in Toby's overconciliation, at Anna's "You and I, Dave . . .") he knew how they could always make Toby suffer for it. He couldn't stand isolation. They had that exquisite power which only the lonely have (because they can bear their part of the isolation, from habit), of inflicting it on him.

Yes, and he would always remember the night before Toby went away.

They were walking up the road just after the rain. They met Effie coming from the store. She had a kerosene can in her hand. A potato was stuck on the spout to keep the oil from spilling. Her face was a small white blur in the near-darkness.

"Hi, Effie," David said.

"Hi, Dave."

"This is Toby Richmond, Effie," he said.

"Hello," she said.

"Hi," Toby said.

She angled out awkwardly, to pass.

"Wait a minute," David said. "What's your rush?"

"I got a cold," she said. "I got to go home."

Suddenly he had to do what he did. He had to show Toby he went all the way with girls. But he was glad it wasn't daylight. He was glad he didn't have to see the look on Effie's face: part shyness, part hurt; but worst of all, forbearance.

"Got a flannel on your chest?" he said. "Let's see . . ."

"Dave," she said, "stop."

"You said you had a cold, didn't you?" he said. Very reasonable. Very serious. "I gotta see if you got a flannel on, haven't I?"

He held her and tickled her under the arms. She had to laugh, but it was only physical reaction. He could feel her shrinking from the sound of her own laughter. He knew she was wishing herself away from here, terribly, because this stranger was watching.

"Dave," she said, "I gotta go home. Mother's waitin for the oil. She's settin in the dark."

"I'll go with you."

"You don't have to."

"*I* know, *I* know," he said, "but I guess I better. Let's cut across the field."

"I got a cold," Effie said. "The field's wet."

"Aw, it's not wet enough to *hurt*." He laughed meaningfully. "I kinda like the field after dark, don't you?"

He whispered to Toby, "Wait here. It doesn't take me long."

There was no pleasure in it, in the field. The spasm was as flat as the whirring of a clock just before it strikes the hour. He hated himself, thinking of the ruining look on Effie's face: the look of trying to accept, without knowing what it was, his reason for shaming her.

They upset the oilcan. The potato came off the spout and the oil soaked one side of Effie's skirt.

"Dave," she said, "it's all over my skirt. What'll I do?"

"It'll evaporate," he said.

"Are you sure?"

"Sure," he said. "It won't show."

"You don't have to walk home with me," she said.

"Sure?"

"No, I ain't scared."

"You're *sure?*"

"Yes," she said. "Goodnight, Dave."

"Well . . . goodnight, then," he said.

He ran back to the road. "That feels better now," he said to Toby.

"It does, eh?" Toby said. His voice was smiling; but with no more special smiling than it might have had for anything else amusing.

And in that moment David knew he could never outdistance Toby in anything he thought Toby would envy, however he might be willing to betray himself trying. Toby would always remain ahead, by not having to make the effort at all.

He thought of the little white patch in the darkness that Effie's damp handkerchief had made. She'd kept it clutched in her small palm the whole time.

CHAPTER XXII

THAT was Wednesday night. On Thursday Bess had the doctor for Effie.

The neighbours all stuck by their windows in a kind of suspension while the doctor's horse was tied at the gate. When the horse was gone, David ran down the road.

"What did he say?" he asked Bess.

Bess was beaming. The doctor had been there. He had left medicine. Now everything would be all right.

"Oh, he used some big word," she said. "I didn't like to ask him over. But I guess she just wasn't careful with her cold. Now I look back on it, Dave, you know she hasn't been well for a long time."

"He said she'd be all right, didn't he?"

"Sure. I mean, he didn't say, exactly, but—" (her face fell) "Dave, it wouldn't be anything serious, would it?"

"What did he say?"

"Well, he just said, 'Give her that medicine and I'll come back again Monday.' It couldn't be anything serious or he'd a . . ."

She hadn't really questioned the doctor at all. Her awe of him, her consciousness of the room's shabbiness in spite of the scrubbing she'd given it from top to bottom, her anxiousness to be alone with Effie (with the awful dread of the doctor coming, turned to the wonderful feeling of the doctor having come and gone) had been so in her that she couldn't.

"Would you like to see her?" she said to David.

"Yeah, while I'm here . . ."

"How do you feel?" he said to Effie.

"I'm better, I think," she said. "The doctor left me some medicine. Taste it. It tastes like peppermint."

He tasted it. "It does, don't it?" he said.

That's about all the conversation they had. He tried to think of some way to seek absolution for last night, he could think of nothing else; but with Bess standing there, there was nothing he could say.

The rest of it happened within a week.

Saturday, about the time when the afternoon is first shadowed with Sunday coming, he met Howie in the road.

"My God, Dave," Howie said, "I was just comin up to tell ya. Did ya know Effie's dead?"

It was as if Howie had thrown a rock inside his head. "Dead"? "Dead"? "Dead"? . . . The word whirled about in his brain like a crazy deafening stone. It came to rest right where he drew his breath and where his heart beat.

He thought of the way Howie had called to Effie that day on the meadow. He let him have it with his fist. Right in the mouth.

Sunday night the women came to Bess's once more with the pies and rolls. They said, "I don't know, she was such a *sweet* child. I remember one day . . ." They asked what Effie's favourite hymns were. Bess lit the lamp before dark; her face had a look of subtle dismemberment.

Monday morning, early, the men went to the graveyard, by way of the pasture, so that Bess wouldn't see them and the shovels they carried. And Monday afternoon neighbours carried in the extra chairs just before three o'clock.

When the last chord of the last hymn had died away, there was a moment of dreadful hush before the scrape of chairs on the floor as people moved again. They looked out the window, away from Bess—at fragments of the brand new sheet Bess had torn up so Effie would have clean handkerchiefs when the doctor came, flapping on the line. The carriers straddled their fingers, to draw the grey cotton gloves taut. They lifted Effie with an awkward tenderness: as if it were some sort of guilt that their strength found the burden so light.

In bed, Monday night, David tried to hide from the unremittent now. He tried to pretend that, by sheer will, he could reach back through the transparent (but so maddeningly impenetrable) partition of time, to switch the course of their actions at some place or other. It would have been so easy . . .

(Bess turned her head away from Effie when she sneezed. Or the first time Effie coughed, Bess made her go to bed, and tomorrow she'll say, "Oh, I *did* have a little cold, but Mother put me to bed and put some raccoon oil on my chest. I'm all right now." And now she still had the fields in her eyes . . . the parts of her body still sent messages to each other . . . her hand reached up to check the breeze in her hair . . .

Or—God, *God* yes— when Toby and I met her in the road I

142

whispered to him, "I bet you wish she was your girl." She heard me. It made her feel bashful, but in a good way. I whispered to her, "He's going away tomorrow. If your cold's better, we'll go raspberryin, I know where they're just hangin . . ." She said, "My cold'll be all right tomorrow." I kissed her, as if I had to do it even if Toby *did* see. She said, "You'll get my cold." I said, "I don't care." She knew I didn't care. The grass wasn't wet [it wasn't, it wasn't], and I didn't breathe a word of what we did, to Toby. And now she was asleep, with her breath floating her along from one minute to the next.)

Then a sudden gust of fact would bare the pretence, without warning. The stillness in Effie's face like a loneliness so intense it gives to the face an effect of smiling. Her hair parted on the wrong side. Her locket turned inward on her neck forever; though he'd seen her straighten it on the chain, time and time again, so that the garnet showed. The lightness in her body like the look of a child that has cried itself to sleep—like Anna's the day he'd conquered one of her rare tempers in the presence of someone else and later he had looked at her, with all her little stubbornnesses gathered inside her, so pitifully more exposed than she thought, in the protectiveness of sleep; and he couldn't waken her, to put the thing she had wanted back into her hand.

The summer night made a moted stillness outside the window. The stillness in the picture of Effie's face gave it a fugitive cast. He couldn't quite reach it even with crying. He buried his face in the pillow. But the crush of "never" got in behind everything, like a light that shows red even if you clasp your fingers over it. The spring sunset when the slush was chilling again in the road, but the doorstep had dried off white and clean, and you turned toward her house before you thought . . . the day in Ocober when the leaves sifted down from the twigs like sleepwalkers, but Effie not there . . . and dusk in winter when the sun burned red as fire in the church windows, but if you went and touched them they would be as cold as the sky . . .

There was nowhere in the world he could run where it wouldn't be true. Effie was dead. He couldn't tell her anything. He hadn't even caught her cold.

He could not remember, afterwards, just when the crippling disease of death-sadness first shaded off into something more like an inoculation against it.

The first few days his mind was sore all over and without appetite.

Then there was the day when taste for the present crept back without notice.

There was the day Steve said Herb Hennessey looked like "somethin that was sent fer and couldn't come," and he laughed. The thought of Effie followed almost instantly, and the sudden stitch in his heart was baring and bending as ever. But it didn't last.

And then (how long after that?) there was the day when he thought of Effie as he planned the camp he would build at the top of the mountain and write a book in, and the stitch didn't come at all. It didn't come with waiting. Then he *tried* to bring it back. He felt a wash of stillness, but it was echo, not voice; he had begun to *remember* her.

He looked toward the graveyard. But the stitch was still filmed over, unreachable. He felt a kind of panic.

It was just dusk. He went down the road and up the path to her house. There, surely, he could recapture it.

Bess was sitting close to the lamp, spelling out the news in the paper.

"Dave!" she cried. "It's so good to see someone."

The women didn't drop into Bess's so often now. Or stay so long. If they had bread in the oven, or soft soap to watch in the leach barrel, they might say, "I don't know, maybe Bess'd rather be *alone*." When she brought back their dishes, clean as wax, they didn't "fill up" the minute she came through the door. If she seemed to come oftener to any one woman's house than to any other's, that woman wouldn't press her to stay. They said now, "The poor thing *seemed* to feel bad . . ."

"I just thought I'd . . ." David said.

"Ain't I glad you did! No, this chair here, I never liked the back in that one." She moved the chair out *for* him, with the overanxious hospitality of one who never has callers unless they come on some mission.

David looked about the kitchen. He could see Effie's scribblers on the mantelpiece, with the fixity there now of whatever mistakes in multiplication she had made. He saw the table her elbows rested on nights he'd be passing along the road and glimpse her through the window; when the vulnerable look she always had whenever he watched her sitting back-to would assault him so. He saw the toes of her moccasin slippers, aligned exactly at the foot of the couch. But even here he couldn't bring the stitch back. He felt desperate.

"Oh Dave"—Bess's thought that had lacked audience so long burst out into speech—"it's so lonesome I'm just about . . . I had

144

to change her room around today. I couldn't stand lookin at it just like she . . . Come see."

They went into Effie's room.

"See? I moved the bed over there be the closet. There's all her dresses, bless her heart. I told the women they could have em, anyone could use em . . . I told em they could come git anything they wanted fer a keepsake, bless her." She half sighed. "They never have. Dave, ain't they somethin *you'd* like, to remember her by? Wouldn't you like that bracelet she wore in the concert? Bless her heart, she stood so still, didn't she, Dave? Do you remember?"

"Yes, I remember," he said. "Yes, Bess, I would."

He slipped the bracelet into his pocket. But the film was still there. He wished he'd never come. He wished Bess would stop talking that awful singsong about it.

"I don't know . . ." Bess shook her head back and forth. "If the dear Lord didn't give anyone strength . . . I guess he fits the back to the burden. But it's hard . . ."

"I know," David said stupidly. "But you have to keep up."

"She always thought so much of you, Dave. Bless her heart, she always thought so much of *you*."

David felt a sting in his throat at that. He could cry—but he could keep from crying, too.

Suddenly Bess began to sob. "Oh Dave, I'll never see her agin." She threw her arms about his neck and leaned against him. He put his arms on her shoulders, to steady her.

And then, because he couldn't bring it back at the sight of Effie's clothes, a sort of fury possessed him. A sullen self-biting fury because the only thing he could feel, clearly, was the stirring wash of Bess's so-softly-capacious body against him and the drowning smell of her black hair and the faint burdening scent of her armpits. He felt only Bess's gusty sensuality. It wouldn't cramp and confuse you as Effie's gentleness had done.

He had a savage urge to do it with Bess, in this very room. To stoke his frustration (as always) with bitter and bitterer self-destruction. To shock back the immediacy of the death-sadness by the very shame of defiling it.

It wasn't in any forgetting of Effie that Bess did it with him. She could attend to only one thing at a time—the thing that was strongest in her at the moment. She justified her own desire with the persuasion (invented, then truly believed) that the Lord would *want* her to help this poor forlorn boy.

Afterwards David cried; but the film was still there.

That was the rainy summer. The grass thrived, lush and lolling. By fall it had covered Effie's grave completely.

You could take a short cut through the graveyard to the acre field. One day that fall, David came across Bess clipping grass off the sods.

They didn't greet each other immediately, as they would have done, meeting anywhere else. But the minute's duty silence was no longer the automatic stitch that two people who have borne identical suffering feel at sight of each other. It was a thing of will. The line their hearts had drawn around this piece of ground was gone. Now the only thing separating it from the rest of the field was the visible border of sod.

David's sense of guilt about Effie's cold and the wet grass was mistaken. The big word the doctor had used, the one Bess couldn't remember, was "leukemia." But David never knew that.

The guilt soon passed from voice to echo. But it was the first thing he could tell *no* one. It taught him that secrecy about anything (even a hateful thing like this) made it a possession of curious inviolability, and tempted him to collect more. The essence of childhood is that the past is never thought of as something that might have been different. He was never, even for a moment, all child again.

CHAPTER XXIII

MARTHA was papering a bedroom. She was completely happy. She hummed a hymn with unconscious repetition. For years she had agreed with the other women that it would be a shame to cover up the new plaster. But the walls had always seemed faceless.

Now, with the crisp slice of the scissors edging the roll, the old feeling of secret indulgence was back. She felt excited, matching the roses in adjacent strips where the paper would cut with least waste, or when she found amongst the odd pieces a bit which would fit exactly under a window or over a door. The pattern grew steadily along the blind walls until, when the streamer of border closed its circuit, a bloom struck suddenly into the room. The smell of flour paste, and of springtime the first morning you could hoist the upstairs window and shake the mats against the side of the house where shingle flies swarmed in the first warmth, was better even than the smell of cotton you nicked and then tore the length of the weave, or of geranium leaves, or of nutmeg.

Housecleaning made the other women peevish. Martha loved it: airing disuse from clothes; turning the dejected fillings of straw ticks onto the trash pile (there was a curious satisfaction in watching flame level the house's excrescence of the past year); and then, when the ticks were swollen enormous again with fresh straw, sewing up their gaping stomachs.

She read again the clippings of weddings or deaths she came across tucked away in a closet; and when she came across a child's garment that had been kept out of sentiment, she'd shake it out and put it away once more. The little heart-sprain these things gave her was almost pleasant.

She liked the crackle of the paste drying out as she lay in bed, and the smell of moist woodwork in the cavernous-echoing rooms. Tomorrow they'd have their curtain ruffles crisp as shavings again, and their bureau scarves renewed and chaste as communion clothes. She delighted in the sweep of the floorcloth softening the cling of paper fragments or specks of whitewash on the floor. Even the grime on the side of the pail as she poured the gritty water down the sink pleased her, knowing that the grime was no longer on the woodwork. It was as if the house were a living thing. As she refreshed it she renewed her own flesh.

And each year there'd be at least one thing totally new.

This year there was the wallpaper, and a mirror for David's room. Small things, if you considered all the evening's calculations on the back of a calendar that had gone into them; but new, just the same. And maybe next year, or some year, the piano . . .

She looked toward the acre field. She could see Joseph and David clearing rock. She had the perfect contentment of a woman happy in her own work and watching her men work at something beyond her strength

Ellen's mat had a landscape pattern. Each year, in her mats, the house reabsorbed its own residue of discarded clothing. She sorted out her colours.

Brown, for the earth. That would do. That was the first Christmas present they'd ever got for Joseph; a boughten sweater. It was merely something he needed; but you could see he was pleased that they had wrapped it and kept it secret from him until the very day.

Pink, for the sky. She could see Martha fluffing that scarf out at her neck now. It was the only piece of silk she'd ever worn. Joseph had searched for it with the lantern a whole hour the night it blew off the line, but he hadn't come across it until the next spring. It was bleached and torn where the winter winds had fretted it against the wild-rose bush.

All the brighter colours were dyed, but she had no trouble to remember the cloth.

Dark green, for the stalk : that was an Indian suit of Christopher's. Lighter green, for the leaf : that was part of the same suit. It had been David's, after Christopher outgrew it. Though it was no fault of Martha's needle, she could never seem to make over Christopher's clothes that they didn't look burdensome on David. And after a while he wouldn't wear them at all. Even now, if he got on a sock of Christopher's or his father's he'd change it the minute he discovered his mistake.

Blue, for the flower. That was the dress Anna wore the day she went to work in Halifax. It was the one on the cover of the catalogue. It didn't look as if she'd worn it after she got there. Maybe the other girls in the office wore different clothes. Maybe the boy she mentioned so often in her letters—Toby, was that his name?—hadn't liked it.

Was it one year, or two, that Anna had been in Halifax?

Sometimes there'd be a sudden confusion about the years

lately. She'd feel as if she were waking from an overlong daytime sleep, and for a second not knowing if it were morning
or evening or in what room she lay. The years were like a ribbon
she was in the act of pleating. The far end of it stretched out
flat; but in the part her hand held, two creases were almost
indistinguishable from one.

Halifax . . . that's where the sailor had come from that time.
I wonder where he went, she thought. I wonder if he is dead . . .

She looked at Joseph and David (why was there no clear
memory of one's own strength, when it was gone?) lifting the
heavy rocks onto the wagon. That was the first field Richard
cleared; flat as your hand, when the clover had made sod. But
with the years of ploughing, rocks showed up again. There were
always more rocks beneath.

CHAPTER XXIV

JOSEPH and David were working alone in the field.
Ed Goucher had come for Chris to help on the
woodsaw.

They never ask to hire me, David thought. They bring me
their damned old letters to answer or their papers to fill out,
but they never offer me a day's work. Just because I'm studying languages . . . they think it has something to do with weakness. He picked up one of the rocks Joseph had left for the two
of them to handle together. A surge of petulance strengthened
him beyond any summonable physical power.

"Wait, Dave . . ." Joseph sprang to help him.

But David broke the rock's leaden root to the ground. A
dizzying rush of blood strained against his eyeballs as he threw
it into the cart body. It smashed against the upright plank on
the far side and tipped the plank into the air. Joseph brushed
the small rocks that tumbled beneath the plank. He braced it in
place with another stone.

Dave is tired, he thought, and he's fighting it. You can't do
that. You have to let it come and go, quietly, and remembering
it after supper, it's sort of like a nice soft tune in your muscles.

This was one of the days when David felt as if the wick
inside him were damp. There was a sludge in his feelings. His
thoughts smouldered like green wood with all the drafts closed.
He felt pulpy, his face the colour of paper in a puddle. It seemed
as if the work, rather than his breathing, dragged him along the

minutes. He felt the doggedness (though he wasn't tired) of afterexhaustion.

All day long his mind had grated against the peevish enmity of trifles. The cow tossed her head just as he was about to fasten her chain and struck him with her horn. There wasn't a match to be found in any pocket when his cigarette was rolled. The water seeped clammy into his woollen sock through the crack in his boot. A stone dropped on his toe. His face was splashed with muck when a rock they were pushing against slipped back into its muddy socket. It gave him something like grinding pleasure to let the damn rock *fall* on his toe if it wanted to, *not* to wring out his dripping mittens. *not* to wipe the dirty water off his face . . .

Other days like this, he could escape in thought. He'd think of a stubborn problem in binomials, and maybe it would fall apart all at once. Every step toward the solution would be clear as a path. He'd think of a letter maybe being posted to him somewhere this very minute. Or just some aspect of the day— the faint bronze water wash of spring sunshine on the bare limbs, or the fan of water that roiled mesmerically behind the wheel as it turned in a rut—would glint for an instant like the microcosm of some blinding truth. It would release him.

Today there was no leaven in any thought he could summon.

They didn't talk as they picked up the rocks and threw them into the cart. But Joseph didn't notice anything wrong at first. They seldom did talk when they worked together, and he had started the day with his own spirits high.

He was a quiet man. But that didn't mean that the things of the day passed through him unaffecting; any more than that food was less transmuted by the chemistry of his body than by that of another, in a way particular to him. His feelings weren't word-shaped, like David's. There was no page in his mind or heart where their tracery was legible to himself. But they made a tune in him just the same. He couldn't write the notes that made it up, if he tried. But whether he could translate them into words or not, the notes were there :

This is my own land. This is a child of my own flesh helping me clear it. This is the smart one. I love them all alike, but this is the one I am proudest of. But he's not ashamed of me. He's not smart just for himself, he's smart for all of us. He's not above us. It doesn't take him away.

Anna is pretty and Chris is strong. But Anna is pretty and Chris is strong for all of us. I am their father. We are all together.

Martha is papering a room, and the smoke goes up straight

and peaceful from the chimney. Martha is my wife. When we were married, it was like having my own hay in the barn and watching the others still mowing and wondering if the rain would come. She watches for me when it nears suppertime, and when she sees me scraping the mud off my boots in the chip-yard, she puts the tea down. Whenever I go amongst strangers she leaves her work until I've got into my good clothes, as if it were a sad or a dangerous mission. She speaks my name in her mind whenever she is faced with a decision. We are together.

The night we moved into the new house all the neighbours came and it was like between brothers with all of us. We are all together here. I stroll across the field any time of the day I like. I go see how Willis is getting along with his wagon shed; but the time I lose doesn't make any gap in my work. This is my land. It is there when I come home from town. In town their faces go stiff, hurrying after their eyes. They plant a shrub in their back yard, trying to make space of it. They lift up things in the stores and ask the price. The house-smell clings to the women-faced men and to whatever they do. My land fits me loose and easy, like my old clothes. That rock there is one my father rolled out, and my son's sons will look at these rocks I am rolling out today. Someone of my own name will always live in my house.

My life tastes like fresh bread. The days roll down the week like a wheel. Then it is Sunday and the wheel is still and we walk through the garden and try a hill of new potatoes, or go to the back pasture to see how much the steers have grown. All the time of Sunday is free and unallotted, like visiting time. I start summer and winter rolling down the year with my sled runners and the whetting of my mower blade. When one sea-son tires, there's another; fresh and freshening, from its year's rest.

The notes of things gone by added their faint counterpoint like the dying echoes of a bell : the pulling of the weed next the plant in the sprouting rows; the first clean "slythhhhh" of the scythe in the swath after the scythe had been ground; the sound of the cowbell in the cool deep swamp where the tender grass started the milk; Martha dividing the raspberries evenly and then heaping the children's dishes from the tops of his and hers; all of them going to the barn together to see the new calf; the rainy day or the blustery one coming just when you *felt* like a rest . . .

Dave is tired, he thought. He's quick, when something goes wrong with his work on the farm. But he's quick like you're quick with your own child: it's not like a stranger being quick with your child. This land is his, too. We are together.'

Joseph hummed a fiddle tune.

David winced. When he worked with his father, there was no constraint between them so long as their relationship, whether of harmony or dissonance, was tacit. But if any of it showed openly, in word or act, he was as embarrassed as when his mother tried the toilet door and he was inside. The expansiveness of his father's today—especially his embellishment of the tune with little variations (meant to be tripping, but clumsy)—gritted against his feelings like sandpaper.

Joseph eased the oxen into a gentle start, pressing downward on their horns. He cracked the whip over their backs, without actually striking them. "Haw, Bright, Brown . . . Easy, boys, *easy* . . ." The muscles sucked in at their necks and flanks. The heavy load crept forward.

David followed, behind the cart. He had to curb his stride to keep pace with the oxen. They rolled their docile bodies from side to side, depositing their hoofs with great cautiousness on the ground. The pace of an ox, he thought! He looked at them with hatred almost. For a minute it seemed as if the oxen were responsible for the draftless, unfocused resentment in him.

He would grow old here, he thought, like his father. That's what it would be like: the pace of an ox. Lifting their feet with such horrible patience. No revolt in them against the gall of the yoke straps, even when Joseph braced his knee against their noses and yanked the straps tighter still. They held their heads down, drawing the heavy rocks. Their eyes saw only the ground. He built up the picture and the dismay of himself being old here. It gave him the same self-biting pleasure he'd felt when he let the muddy water stiffen on his face.

Joseph manoeuvred the cart close to the stone wall. He lay the whip across the oxen's horns and scratched their foreheads briefly, under the straps, for having hauled such a good load.

"Is your end all right, Dave?" he said.

"I guess so," David said.

They began to unload.

"Look, Dave," Joseph said, "I think I kin swing your end in closer there. No need to carry em."

David didn't say anything. He waited with elaborate patience while the wagon moved. "Hufe, boys," Joseph said, "Hufe . . ." He backed the oxen, tapping gently on their noses with the butt of the whip.

"There," Joseph said. "Ain't that a little better?"

"It's all right," David said.

He unloaded a few more from the ground. Then he got up on the cart. He threw them onto a spot which would have been nearer as the cart sat first.

When the cart was almost empty, Joseph lifted the side plank. A rock tumbled down and struck David's hand.

"Ouch!" he said. "Jesus!"

"God," Joseph said, "did it ketch ya? Did it hurt ya, Dave?"

"No," David said. He didn't take off his mitten to look at the bruise.

"I never saw your *hand* there," Joseph said. "Didn't it hurt?"

"No . . . No . . ." He scraped the rest of the rocks off onto the ground.

Joseph lay the side planks of the cart flat and hitched his rump up, backwards, onto the body. "We might as well ride," he said. "Haw . . ." But David walked behind, back to the field.

They loaded the piles of small rocks then, working from opposite sides of the cart.

At the fourth stop there were two piles on David's side. One a little way from the cart, but they'd never be any closer to it again. Joseph didn't notice it. When the piles next the cart had been loaded, he moved on. David didn't say anything. He just stood there until the cart stopped. Then he began to carry the rocks ahead.

"Hell," Joseph said. "Was they another one there? Why didn't you sing out? Don't carry em! I'll hufe up."

David dropped the rock he had in his hand and waited.

"Hufe," Joseph said to the oxen, "hufe *up* . . ." He didn't speak so gently to them. He tapped their noses a little harder with the whip handle. He'd stopped humming.

The big boulder was left to the last.

Joseph's father had ploughed around it, and moved around it, all his life. Joseph thought this team could haul it away. The other men had always told him no team on earth could budge it, but he had thought, secretly: Some damp day the drag will slip good, if we can manage to load it, I'll show them what my boys can do. He'd thought, secretly, of showing them this rock someday on the stone wall. He'd thought of hearing them exclaim, "Well, I'll be goddammed!"

He'd dug around it with the grub hoe. He lacked David's physics to tell him where its centre of gravity was, but he knew exactly where to put the bunk hook of the chain so that the strain would come just right.

He took the oxen off the wagon and put them on the drag. He hauled the drag into place: just far enough off so the rock would topple onto it, but not bind against the edge and slide the drag too. David watched him silently. He didn't say, "Just an inch farther . . . easy . . . easy . . . whoa!"

Joseph tried the boulder with a long two-by-four pry. It moved slightly. "Ahhhhhhh?" he said. "Git me a couple rocks fer a bite, Dave."

David got two rocks.

"No," Joseph said, "them's no good."

"Well, which ones do you want then?" David said.

"What's them two over there be the fence?"

You could see, when you got up to them, that these rocks were no good. David brought them back just the same. He threw them down.

"No . . ." Joseph said. "Where's them two you brought first? I didn't notice they had a flat side."

Joseph tilted up the pry. David placed the rocks, one on top of the other, beneath it, next the boulder.

"Back a mite," Joseph said. "Jist a hair."

"All right," David said, "you do it."

Joseph fixed the rocks. Then they both pressed down on the far end of the pry. They took the strain as gradually as possible so that the pry wouldn't slip from the crevice in the boulder, or the bite tumble. The boulder moved a couple of inches out of its socket. "Ahhhhhhh?" Joseph said. The boulder moved up a few inches more.

"I'll hold her," Joseph said. "You git another rock and chuck underneath. We wanta save what we got, she's riz some. Then we'll take a higher bite."

"You get it," David said. He took the strain of the boulder. Joseph went to search for a chocking stone.

"Does it hold hard?" he called to David.

"No."

The muscles of his arms were trembling. The relentless weight of the boulder threatened from second to quivering second to split him from consciousness almost. His father seemed to take his time. He held on doggedly.

Joseph returned with a rock. When he tossed it underneath, it struck and collapsed the bite. The whole structure went limp. The pry fell useless to the ground. The boulder sank back into its socket.

"Well, hell . . ." Joseph said.

David said nothing. He set about placing the pry again as if he'd expected this to happen. They raised the boulder once more. Just as Joseph went to chock it this time, the oxen started.

154

"Whoa," Joseph roared, right under David's ear, "Goddam it, whoa!"

He went around and took the oxen off the drag. "Gimme a hand, Dave," he said. "We'll have to pull the drag back into place."

"What am I going to do with this pry?" David said. "Let it go?"

"Oh," Joseph said. "Well, all right . . ."

He tugged the drag back into position himself. David's muscles trembled so he was afraid they'd shake the pry loose. Joseph came back and threw the rock under the boulder. Two more hoists and the boulder was enough out of the ground to try the chain on it.

Joseph took the chain off the drag and hitched the grab hook through the ox yoke. David might have held the loose end up off the ground while the oxen turned, so they wouldn't step over it. He didn't move. Joseph had to thread the chain back between their bellies.

He placed the bunk hook for David to hold, then he circled the chain around the boulder so the tension would come in the right spot. He gave the chain a sharp yank to make sure the bunk wouldn't slip. It pinned David's mitten against the side of the rock.

"For . . ." David said. "Can't you wait till I get my hand out?"

The bunk seemed to be firm. Joseph went ahead of the oxen and eased them forward gently. The first pull, the chain sprang into the air, loose and flaccid. But the second time it held taut. The boulder tilted upright. For a minute it seemed to hold its breath. Then it tipped onto the drag.

"Whoa!" Joseph said.

But the oxen didn't stop quite short. The boulder slid on off the other side of the drag.

"WHOA!" Joseph roared. "You're hellish anxious all of a sudden, ain'tcha!" He leaned over the oxen's horns and gave them several sharp blows with the whip. They started again, with the sting of the lash, dragging the boulder still farther. It settled to rest on its flattest side.

David knew his father's temper was a reflection of his own mood; yet he felt a sudden flare of his own temper, as if justly, in return. "*Jeeeee*sus . . . *Jeeeee*sus . . ." he muttered under his breath.

"Take the chain off the rock, Dave," Joseph said. "We'll have to haul the drag around on this side agin."

David unhooked the bunk. He gave a savage yank at the chain.

"You can't get it off *now*," he said. When Joseph had struck the oxen, the second roll of the boulder had pinned the chain to the earth.

"Well, git me the one I dropped off up there be the fence," Joseph said.

David walked back to the fence. "Where is it?" he called. "I don't see any chain."

"No," Joseph called, "over this way. Ta yer left. Yer *left*."

"*I* see it. *I* see it."

The very first try, the boulder swivelled perfectly onto the drag and lay steady on its base. They chinked it with small stones so it wouldn't teeter off when the drag was in motion.

"Are you going to saw that beech?" David said.

"Well . . ." Joseph said, "if you ain't too tired. If yer hand don't hurt too much."

"I didn't say my hand hurt," David said.

He turned and walked away, toward the dooryard.

Joseph let the oxen take their wind every rod or so. He boosted the drag with a crowbar at each new start, and they just managed it to the stone wall. He manoeuvred the drag to the brink of a slight decline and kicked out the chinking.

*Un*loading was no trouble whatever. A single lunge with the crowbar sent the boulder toppling downward of its own weight. He sighed.

But it wasn't the kind of sigh he'd anticipated whenever he'd pictured the boulder leaving the drag. (He'd even fancied the words he or David might say: "Roll, damn ya. Roll wherever ya like now.") He could see the stripes of raised-up hair where the lash had struck the oxen's backs and David hadn't even turned, to watch this crowning moment of their connivance and victory.

"Haw, Bright," he said. The hammers that struck the notes of his feelings were padded and damp. "Haw . . ."

David was really tired now. A tired cord stretched between his temples. Blood throbbed heavy in his throat. The fatigue tuned his thoughts to a sharp feverish resonance.

Anyone to spend their youth in this God-forsaken hole instead of the city . . . the same damn talk . . . the same damn faces, every day and every day . . . the same damn coop of trees to look at . . . walking over and over your own tracks, like a damned ox. In the city there'd be movement, and something to feed your mind all the time. Your mind wouldn't spin empty and clacking, like the rollers of the thresher when the feeder got behind with the grain.

What was the good of learning here? All they thought about was liftin' and luggin'. They thought if anyone was smart it was like being half foolish. You had to cripple every damn thought you had, every damn thing you did, so they wouldn't look at you funny. In the city . . .

A sudden breaker swept over him (as it would sometimes when a woman's face, seen in a magazine, would invite his body in an instant flash and it would seem as if he could step right into the page and touch her anywhere). He thought of all the women in the city. Whether you knew them or not, just to look at them and think of it . . . Bess . . . always the same, even if he did believe her that he'd been the only one except her husband . . .

The breaker drained back. It sucked the voice out of the fields. Last fall's aftergrass lay withered and matted on the ground. Muddy water runnelled down the frost holes in the road. A dribble of excrement stained the white tall feathers of the Leghorns scratching in the wet sawdust of the dooryard. The boards of the barn were bleached grey. The sense of touch seemed to leave him completely. It was like a rainy day when he'd read everything in the house and whenever he moved his arms or legs he could catch the stale smell of sweat in his woollen underwear. The day had the sickly smell of scalded chicken feathers.

I'd like to get out of this place so damn quick, he thought . . . I'd like to go so damn far . . .

We won't saw the whole log, Joseph thought. We'll just saw a couple of cuts. Then Dave can do whatever he likes.

(With uneasiness inside, the notes of the outside day struck in him sharper still: the well brimming clear and cool again, the floating ring of ice to be lifted out in one piece now and shattered . . . the cows locking their horns languidly, at the lee side of the barn . . . the first dry spot in the road presaging dust . . . the green grass springing up already in the rake tracks where he'd scraped the chips inward around the edge of the dooryard . . . the trees bare as the face of someone sleeping, but something soft in the air already brushing against their winter's trance . . .)

I'll make out I have to do something else, Joseph thought, after the first cut or so. Dave is young. I suppose this work does get tiresome sometimes.

But that was reason, not understanding. He used to get weary here when *he* was young, but he was never fretful. There was no monotony in it. Matching the strength to the task had always been tiring; but never tiresome.

The great beech drag-log was a dead weight. They rolled it up on the saw horses with their peavies. One clinched and rolled it, then held it for the other to clinch and roll. When it was high enough, David braced it with his body. Joseph drove the Z-shaped iron dogs, one point into the log, the other into the saw horse.

David's muscles began to tremble again.

"Kin ya hold her?" Joseph said.

"I guess so."

"She won't roll on ya?"

"I got it, I got it."

They began to saw, watching the saw's descent with a kind of mesmeric intentness. It seemed to David as if he and his father and the log were bound together in an inescapable circuit. The saw sank quickly through the crown of the log, but when its upper edge disappeared into the log's wide heart, the groove deepened with maddening slowness.

David's muscles caught their breath between pulls; but the next instant (would it be really impossible this time?) it was necessary to pull again.

It got so he was pulling with the pit of his stomach, not his arms. The log was like a menacing concentration of all the weight in the world. He turned his face sidewise, to hide its uncontrollable twitching. He knew it was the colour of slush It got so he was suspended somewhere by his arms. The weight of his body was intolerable, but he was unable to touch ground with his feet. It got so his whole body was full of ashes. It got so his will trembled as uncontrollably as his arms.

"Don't press on her quite so *hard*, Dave," Joseph said. "It cuts better, and it makes it easier fer ya."

David let the saw go so limp it buckled.

"Oh, I don't mean let her go loose altogether," Joseph said David rode it then with every bit of strength left in him.

"I wonder . . ." Joseph said. He stopped, and lifted the saw clear.

"What are you doing now?" David said.

"We better see how she's comin out." He nicked off block lengths all along the log. There was an odd length left at the end.

"That block's too short, Dave," he said. "We better shift her over a few inches so she'll come out even."

"Well, Jesus!" David said.

All that grind wasted! A sudden puff of exasperation over

158

rode the embarrassment that always stifled any exchange of sharp words between him and his father. The fatigue flared up and focused his random anger. He was struck, for a second, by the dusty look in his father's eyes. The lines in his father's face grooved paler than the day-old beard—his father was tired too. But he couldn't stop. His anger slipped fluent into his own language.

"We exhaust ourselves and then when we're halfway through you decide the goddam block's too short! If you could ever decide anything in advance . . ." His voice was high and trembly. His glance rushed about. His feet trod nervously on the ground.

"Now don't git high," Joseph said.

He felt struck, sick. Not by David's anger, but by the words he'd used. He'd known that David possessed words like that; but he'd thought they were Sunday things, like the gold watch fob of his own that lay in the drawer. He thought now : They really belong to him. He's using them against me. He's not just tired, or quick. This place is no kin to him at all, the way it is to me.

"Who's gettin high?" David said. "Anybody with any intelligence could see that . . ."

"All right, all right," Joseph said. He picked up the saw, to put it away.

"Oh, go to hell!" David shouted. It didn't make sense. But those were the only words left in his head.

The fuse of Joseph's own anger was suddenly touched.

"Don't you want killin," he said, "you . . . you goddam snot." His hand shot across the log and clouted David across the mouth. "Don't you tell *me* to go to hell . . ."

David's first savage reflex was to strike back, to annihilate. And then the fascinating whisper told him not to move . . . to let the blow dry on his face like the muddy water. It was more grindingly sweet than anything he'd ever known. He didn't move. Oh, he'd never wipe *that* blow off his face . . . They made out they thought he was so smart. Then they called him a goddam snot. Oh, he'd never wipe that off either . . .

"I'd like to go so far away from this goddam hole . . ." he said.

"Well, go then," Joseph said.

"I *will* go." He turned and ran toward the house. I'll go so goddam far . . .

Joseph put the saw in the new cut. He began to saw alone. He watched the sawdust follow the teeth of the saw as before; but a vibration inside him seemed to sever senses from object. A single note sounded in his feelings : I struck my son! I struck *David*. Oh, David . . . David . . . David . . .

CHAPTER XXV

DAVID ran past Ellen in the kitchen, and upstairs. His mother heard him tearing up to the attic. "David," she called, "did you clean off your boots?"

He didn't answer.

His dishevelled face showed in the new mirror. It was as shockingly bright as a face feeding on a forbidden book. He tore off his old clothes. He put on his new suit and got his twenty dollars from the matchbox in the bureau drawer. He didn't take anything else. The lettering on his calculus text caught in his eyes like something dead lying there with its face uncovered. He didn't look back as he went out the door.

"David," Martha called again as she heard him coming down, "now look at that mud. And I just scrubbed them stairs!" He didn't answer.

He didn't feel his fatigue as he ran down the road. He ran down the long hill, and along the spring-cool road to town. The propulsion of the anger transcended the physical process of tiring. He had one complete thought amongst the tumbling phrases of feeling: I'm going to Halifax, where Toby and Anna are. The things he passed had no familiar voice. They were like objects seen from a train window.

He stopped running, to wash his face and hands in the brook. When he started on again he walked.

And then time stopped running with him and settled back into its own pace. The clamour of the anger began to drop too, and its suspension of all other voices. The trees and the road settled back into their familiar places, as the earth becomes familiar again, and solid, after stepping off a boat. The water-weakness in his knees crept back, stealthily, as if it had been waiting its chance.

The clauses of his thoughts tumbled slower in his mind, like the final revolutions of the barrel churn after the foot had been taken from the pedal. The fragments that belonged together joined, as kernels of butter precipitate and gather: It was sixteen miles to town. It was four o'clock. There would be no train until tomorrow. Where would he stay tonight? He had nothing but his good suit and twenty dollars. What would he tell Anna? It would be hard to tell Anna he was never going to write home. It would be hard to ask her never to mention his name to them again . . .

The anger settled slowly in his limbs. It felt quiet and sore.

He kept walking ahead, but doggedly. His legs had to depend on their own power. The familiarity of each tree seemed to obstruct his forward movement. It was like walking through a thicket of cobwebs. Determination, not the self-fuelling anger, was the only impulse now. He kept on now because, having started, there was nothing else to do. His mouth looked like the mouth of a child who doesn't dare to cry.

He didn't hear the car until the horn blew, right behind him. He started. The glance of the strange faces seemed to precipitate his own face suddenly, reassemble it. It was the final touch of invalidation to the dying anger.

"Can you tell us how far we are from Newbridge?" the woman said.

"About sixteen miles," he said.

"Thank you."

He knew from the way she smiled and spoke that they were city people. She smiled as if it were an *outside* gesture, like a movement of hands or feet. This was a bigger car than any of the town cars. These were the people the town people tried to imitate. They had that immunity from surprise the town people could never quite catch. That automatic ease. These were city people. They looked as if they didn't *know* they were in a fine car, as if they didn't *know* they were dressed up. Their eyes were like a dog's eyes in the heat. They took little bites out of whatever they looked at, lazily, without tasting.

"Sixteen more miles of this road, dear," she said to the man. "Of our short cut!" She didn't look at him directly.

"Sixteen, eh?" the man said.

He knew they were city people the way they spoke to each other. There was no question-and-answer about it; no word louder for meaning's sake than any other. The speaker didn't glance at the silent one to see if his silence meant disinterest or anything wrong. The man didn't look silly (or any way at all) when she called him "dear." She said the word as if it might be his name.

He knew how they did it, because he could do it exactly the same way.

The man stepped on the starter.

"Are you going far?" the woman said.

The musical languor of her voice made her questions all sound like statements. She kept speaking for the man, as his mother would never have done for his father; though it was plain that for the man she was only an annexation. These were city people. They didn't seem to permeate each other all the time, like his mother and father did. They were merely sitting there side by side.

"I'm going to Newbridge," David said.

"Well come *along* then," she said.

"Thank you very much," David said.

He wiped his feet carefully before getting into the back seat. He thought: I am wiping off my feet. I left mud all over Mother's stairs. She had just scrubbed them. He almost hated these people.

When the car was in motion again, the woman swung sidewise in her seat. She cuddled her legs as if she were in a chair. Her smile came again, automatically with the movement of her body.

"Do you live here?" she said.

"Yes," he said.

I mean, I *did* live here, he thought. He had never seen so clearly how the field sloped up behind the barn. You could lie in the grass and, squinting your eyes, make the mountain come as small and close as you liked. He had never felt so plainly the arching of his bare toes on the hay stubble . . . or heard so sharply his father's voice that night they were all lost. . . .

The trees were moving again now. He felt as if he were in a train, being carried beyond his destination.

"Do you work in Newbridge?" the woman said.

The trees fled by. "I am going to Halifax," he said.

"Oh, *are* you?" she said.

He could see her glancing at his father in the dooryard as she passed, commenting casually to the man beside her and then selecting, as if the landscape were on a tray, something else to look at. He saw the fraying of his father's sweater at the cuffs.

She faced front again. She had established, with a few words, his being there in the back seat; that circumstance could lie relaxed now, without further attention.

"If Alex is going to be there, darling," she said to the man, "I don't see why you have to go too. I don't see why you couldn't just write . . ."

"You can't put anything into a letter," he said. "And you know Alex!"

"But two days on that appalling train," she said.

"I know, I know."

David didn't know what they were talking about. He felt cramped, trying not to listen. He felt stung, having them discuss something personal before him as if he weren't there.

The trees went by. "Excuse me," David said, "but around that next turn is usually a bit of a morass."

The woman looked at him suddenly. She might have mistaken him all along for someone else. Then she glanced directly at her husband.

The man glanced back over his shoulder for the first time. "What education have you got?" he said abruptly.

"Matriculation," David said, "and some college texts I've studied myself."

"Really!" the woman said. "What are you going to do in Halifax? Where are you going to stay?"

"I have a sister there," David said.

"Oh?" She spoke as if Anna were irrelevant. (He thought of Anna as a child. Anna will go wherever *I* go, he thought fiercely.)

"Has your family *always* lived here?" the man said.

"Yes," he said. "My grandfather came out first with the governor's party, when he was quite young . . . and then, heaven knows why, came back later and took up a grant of land." He didn't thrust out the implication that they weren't quite the ordinary people they might seem. He planted it, as they would, under a light cover of amusement.

"*Did* he!" the woman said. "I think that's very interesting."

"Why don't you look us up in Halifax?" the man said. "I might have something for you in the office."

"We live in Halifax," the woman said. "We have a son about your age. He's taller than Ted, isn't he, darling, but really they look a little *alike*, don't you think?"

Now they weren't feeding on him with desultory questions, without stirring outside themselves. They were *communicating* with him. They were all talking together as if they were all alike. He talked to them their way. There was nothing angular about their speech. They laughed as if they *decided* how much anything should amuse them. It was like the knack of a fluid dance that came to him without practice.

He talked with them as they talked . . . with a bright chording soreness in his heart. It was like the time he'd broken the bobsled his father had made him, coasting. He'd said things to make the other boys laugh harder than he'd ever been able to make them laugh before, as he finished smashing it, deliberately and utterly, on the Big Rock.

"Now look us up, won't you?" the man said again. "Write down the address, Clare. There's a pad in the side pocket."

"Thank you," David said. "I certainly shall."

The woman was writing down the address. The trees sped by.

He thought of having used words like "shall" against his father, who had none of his own to match them or to defend himself with.

"Oh," he said suddenly. "I'm terribly sorry . . . but could you let me out? I forgot something. I have to go back."

"Oh," the woman said. "Stop, dear. What a *shame*."

The man glanced at his wrist watch. He looked up and down the road. There was no place to turn.

"We could wait," he said, "fifteen, twenty minutes . . ."

"No, please don't," David said. "Thank you very much." He was opening the door.

"But if you're going to Halifax," the woman said, "how will you get back to Newbridge? Will you have to walk?"

"I'll manage it somehow," David said.

He was outside the car now. He wished they would stop talking and let him go. It was like times he'd been sick to his stomach: if the others would only just leave him alone, so he could go off by himself where they wouldn't see.

"Now, aren't we stupid?" the woman exclaimed. "You could drive right to Halifax *with* us. Of course we'll wait."

"No, please don't," David said. "It might take me quite a while. Thank you very much, though."

He watched them out of sight. He looked toward home. He felt as if he were in a no man's land. He felt as if time had turned into space, and was crushing against him. He felt as if he must leap somewhere out of the now, but everywhere it was now.

He thought of the woman's idling glance at his father sawing alone, and he thought of the time in town he'd wished his father would put on his coat so the sweat marks beneath his braces wouldn't show. He thought of the time the men had laughed when he crouched back from the ox and his father had said, "Dave ain't scared of him, *are* ya, Dave. Pat him" . . . taking his hand though, first. He thought of the woman's hands as she wrote out the address so smoothly, and he thought of his mother's hands calculating so clumsily the cost of linoleum for a room. He thought of her, tired, scrubbing the stair steps all over again. He thought of the woman cataloguing Anna as just anybody, and he thought of him and Anna going there sometime maybe, and Anna behaving almost the right way but not quite. He remembered thinking he wouldn't volunteer any information about his awkward brother, and he thought of the time someone had called Chris "stupid" and Chris had said, "Well, I bet I *am* right. You ask Dave . . ." He thought of his grandmother, and he thought how often he'd made plans for his future in her presence, for years when she knew she couldn't possibly still be there.

He saw all their faces cameo-clear as remembered faces of the newly dead.

He looked both ways up and down the road. Then he turned and began to walk toward home. It was like the time in school when he'd made the page of 5's perfect beyond possible repetition—and then spilt ink all over the page. He'd begun again on a new page; but each figure he formed he drew his lips tight as he pressed on the pencil. Its imprint was on his very quick.

He came to the bridge. He could see the house again. The ash of the quarrel, of blows given and felt, was tamped down physically into his flesh. The soreness was drawn out wire-thin, pendant at the corners of his lips. Suddenly he put his head into the only place left to hide: the crook of his elbow along the rail of the bridge. He began to sob. He sobbed because he could neither leave nor stay. He sobbed because he was neither one thing nor the other.

He stole up the back stairs and changed his clothes. His face looked as if he had slept in it. It felt exposed and babbling when he walked through the kitchen again. He kept his head bent forward under his cap. He thought if anyone knew what had happened or mentioned it, he would die.

But no one did. "Dave," his mother said, "what are you runnin in and out about?" She was smiling.

He went out into the chipyard. He glanced at his father's face, he couldn't help it. For the first time an old man's eyes seemed to look out from behind the windows of his father's own.

He placed a block of wood in the hollow that carrying-through blows of the axe had hacked in the splitting-rest. He struck the block with the axe. It didn't divide. Only a crack twisted through its sinews.

"Stand it up on its end, Dave," Joseph said. "Sometimes you can git them tough ones that way."

"Like this?" David said. He stood the block upright and struck it again.

The axe clove the block this time, clean through to the ground. Never in his life had he felt such a crying-warm surge of release.

"Did you get a good chore done today?" Martha said at the supper table.

"We hauled the big rock," Joseph said. He didn't look David's way. There was a steady current between them. Each body seemed to reach for the other's magnetic field, but with contact set up a disorganizing confusion.

"Not the *big* rock?" Martha said. "How did you ever . . . ?"

"Dave and I landed her," Joseph said.

"Ya never!" Chris exclaimed.

Ellen said nothing.

The lamp in her room was still lit when David went to bed. She came to the doorway. She held out something in her hand. "Take it," she whispered. "I want you to have it."

"But what . . . ?" he said. It was a tiny locket.

"Shhhhhh."

He turned the locket over in his hand when he got to the attic. It didn't look as if anyone had ever worn it. He opened the catch and looked inside. There was an old-fashioned picture beneath the oval glass. The face of a sailor about his own age. It was one of those pictures where the eyes always follow you. He frowned. What an odd keepsake for her to give him. *Tonight* . . . And so secretly . . .

He closed the locket again and put it in the matchbox. But the restless eyes still seemed to follow and tantalize him. The face was familiar. He'd seen it somewhere before.

And then suddenly he knew where he'd seen a face like that. He was looking at it right there in the mirror. This locket had something to do with what had happened today. She'd sensed somehow what had happened. She'd sensed it because she too knew what it was like when the moonlight was on the fields when the hay was first cut and you stepped outside and it was lovely, but like a mocking . . . like everything was somewhere else.

He went to sleep at once, though. He was eighteen.

CHAPTER XXVI

EACH year marks the tree with another ring, the cow's horn with another wrinkle. But until you were twenty, you were not marked. If one day was lost, the others closed over it so quickly that, looking back, there was a continuous surface. Everything was this side of the future.

It was only when you thought back to the way you'd done the same thing you were doing now, in another year, that you could see any change in yourself.

You lifted a cock of hay in one forkful when you were sixteen, and remembered your enormous pride in doing that at fifteen. The argument of your feeling then was completely undecipherable now. You walked down the road when you were seventeen. You still clowned with the other boys; but if you listened to the boys of sixteen now, the particular horsing of that year seemed childish. Swimming seemed the same at eighteen as at seventeen; but if you thought of the way you swam then—not because it was a hot day, not because anything, just swimming till it began to get late—why, you thought, had you felt nothing vacuous about it? You still blushed when you polkaed out at nineteen. But if you thought about polkaing out last year, wanting them to think you were wriggling against the girl, that you were drunk, you felt silly for yourself at eighteen (now you could be with Bess whenever you liked, now you'd actually *been* drunk) as you'd feel silly for a stranger.

Your thoughts were more varied when you were nineteen than when you were eighteen; but less smoky, less involuntary, less assaulting. Now they stiffened a little, just on examination. You reined them like a colt you'd taught to take the bit. You could put them back, if you wanted, when they started to come out. Some things hurt you, coming into your mind of themselves maybe only a month ago. You couldn't *make* the same things hurt you now.

There was a kind of insolence in your flesh and thoughts when you were nineteen. Each day you felt the attainment, the security, of being as you really were, for the first time. (Remembering another day when that had seemed equally true, but in the light of today could be seen as false, didn't shake that security.) It could be tripped up. A joke you took the literal letter of, instead of the harmless intent, could do it; or a stab of child-anger or child-fear; or finding yourself in a situation in any way strange. But it could be established again instantly, as soon as you were alone. You felt as old as anyone then—but with the knowledge, so certain as to be undefiant, that you would always be young.

Yet the conduit to childhood wasn't entirely sealed over. A child's visionary enthusiasms still surprised you at times, trapped you into delight without judgement.

David's heart leapt the moment Joseph spoke that morning. "Dave," Joseph said, "what do ya say we go back to the top of the mountain and see if that keel-piece is sound, and look out some knees?"

They were building vessels in Annapolis that year. The only tree in the village tall and large and straight enough to be hewn

167

for a keel was on Joseph's land. It had stood as a landmark in the woods since his father's time. Knees were solid right angles of bole and root.

David's excitement was mixed of the thoughts of the mountain (though he was nineteen he'd never been to the very top yet) and the thought of their own timber going across the seas to far parts of the world. It was the childish excitement all over again that had always orbited any extraordinary job: setting off in the ox wagon to pick Snow apples in the township orchard, where bear tracks could be seen at the very door of the tumbling old house: shoeing the nervous horse: rocking up a new well. He'd always found a strange thrill in watching, without responsibility, his father's strength and sureness in the accomplishment of these things.

"We should all go," Martha said. She said it in a joking way but David knew she was throwing it out half seriously.

"Come on!" he said eagerly. He'd never thought of making a picnic of it—that was a wonderful idea. "You will, won't you? You'll go too, won't you, Chris?"

"Sure," Chris said, "I guess so."

"I haven't done my chamber work," Martha said.

"Ohhhhh, let it go," David said.

"I suppose we could have an early dinner," she said.

"Let's *take* our dinner," David said.

"I suppose I could do the work after I come home," she said

"The work'll keep," Joseph said.

"I'm not ready," she said. But she was putting forth denial without conviction. She used to do that with David, when he knew she intended to indulge him all the time.

"Come on, Mother," he said. "Please come with us."

"We'll wait for you," Joseph said.

"Well . . . Oh no, I couldn't!"

"You can . . . you can so . . ."

Waiting for her to pack the lunch was as exciting as it had been waiting for the older ones to take them some place special when they were children.

Martha was just working the nutmeg tin of tea down the side of the basket when a car drove in the yard. Its horn tooted in code fashion. Brakes snubbed it to a reckless stop, within a foot of the porch.

"There's a car!" she said. "It's strangers—and *look* at me.'

"Oh, god*dam* them!"

"David!" Ellen said.

Then Martha's voice boomed. "It's Anna," she cried, "and Toby."

"Oh good!" David shouted. He felt a touch of Christmas.

They crowded out the doorway. Exclamations and promiscuous greeting flared up like kerosine thrown on the kitchen fire in the morning. Then these died down. Each began to greet the other individualy, *attending* to question and answer.

And then David felt the strange toppling that always came at the sight of Toby. The instant resolve that before they met *next* time he must build himself up somehow, to equality. When Toby had come and gone, the way of the village grooved back into David like a more stubborn grain; but the instant Toby appeared again he was the one point of orient.

The smooth way Toby was dressed seemed to expose a sudden deceit in his own clothes. He felt defensive. He was compelled to snub him with unresponsiveness.

"What do you think of her?" Toby said to David. He swept the car with his eye, the way Joseph ran his hand along an ox's rump.

"She's quite a boat," David said.

Toby immediately yanked up the hood and began detailing her features to David. He forgot the others, isolated Anna even. David had no interest in cars except in their appearance. But Toby assumed one without question. He had the same old unwitholding grin.

"We were just getting ready to go back for the keel," David said casually.

Toby looked baffled. He put down the hood.

Anna looked at them then. "What's the matter, Dave?" she said, laughing. "Aren't you glad to see us?"

He felt ashamed. Her suggestion was so patently ridiculous she could speak it as a joke, but he felt more ashamed than if she were voicing any real doubt.

Anna looked about the fields, checking them with her memory of them. The look on her face made her stand suddenly alone. Then she ran into the house. The silk stockings encased her insteps so like a natural skin that it didn't seem possible her feet had ever gone bare. The trim brown suit fraternized with her body as smoothly as Toby's clothes did with his. But her face wasn't metallic and unsurprisable, as other city faces were. It was still soft and discovering.

"Were you really going somewhere?" Anna said when she saw the lunch basket.

"We was goin back to the top of the mountain," Chris said.

David frowned at him. This wasn't the time to say that, bluntly, without motive.

"Oh, that's a shame," Anna said. "But go ahead . . . now don't let us stop you."

"I'll bet we will!" Martha said. "Unless you'd come with us."

"We couldn't," Anna said, "really. We have to get back this afternoon."

"You ain't drivin all the way back to Halifax tonight?" Joseph said.

"Sure," Toby said. David wished his father hadn't shown such incredulity at the idea of a trip from Halifax and back in one day.

"You go ahead just the same," Toby said. "We'll stay here with Dave. You weren't going, were you, Dave?"

"Well . . ."

" 'Well . . .' " Anna mimicked good-naturedly. "You *planned* to go, now didn't you, Dave?"

"It doesn't matter," he said.

When Toby singled him out from the others as his and Anna's special company, he felt his allegiance slip back to the spirit of the trip. He had a sudden feeling of hurt at the thought of the others going off alone. The picnic mood which he could always infuse in them would fall apart without him.

"*I* know," Toby said. "Why don't we take the car and all go?"

"We couldn't take the car, dear," Anna said. Quietly, indulgently. "It's only a log road."

"What's wrong with that?" Toby said. "It's a good log road, *isn't* it, Dave. We could strike it from that road below the hill there."

"Oh, we couldn't take the car," Martha said. "*Could* we, Joseph."

"I don't think so," Joseph said.

"Where would you turn?" Chris said.

Toby looked crestfallen. David felt a shift to Toby's side. The others had the rights of it; but why did they always have to come out with so many sensible, indisputable reasons against anything a little foolhardy? Toby would think he had the same pinching caution as they had.

"It's no use, Toby . . ." he said.

"One of us would have to stay home anyway," Martha said. "There wouldn't be room for us all."

"We really couldn't take the car, Toby," Anna said. Almost whispering. She wished too, though she knew they were right, that they'd let him try it.

"Okay," Toby said. David knew he'd accept whatever they

decided, but that he still couldn't see why they couldn't take the car.

"*I'll* stay home," Ellen spoke up suddenly. "I'll keep the fire. There are only one, two, three . . . six of you . . ."

"What do you say, Mr. Canaan?" Toby said. With an unexpected ally in Ellen, he was all eagerness again.

"Well . . ." Joseph said, "I don't know. Whatever the rest *think* . . ."

"Okay," Toby said. He spoke as if it were all settled. "Anna, you and I and Dave get in front, and your mother and father and Chris in the back . . . eh?"

Just before they were ready to start, Toby winked at David and nodded toward the shop. He went to the shop. David followed.

"Would you like a little snort?" Toby said.

"Sure," David said.

He took a huge drink from Toby's flask, but without Toby's roguish attitude. To take a drink offered, to launch the rawest remark of all, to be the first to grasp the wild heifer by the horn, to bear a sudden blow or sudden pain incuriously and without pose . . . whatever the less imaginative did hesitantly, with a wink or cramped by thought: these were the things he did naturally, with no cramp of imagination at all.

Toby hummed "Some of These Days" as they drove down the hill below the church. He clowned and slapped the wheel with his palms, stealing an absorbent glance now and then at Anna. She sat gently satiate beside him and forbearingly amused. He seemed born to a car, as wings to air. He had a wonderfully clear voice. There wasn't a mote in either the high notes or the low. David too sat relaxed, except for *knowing* that he was happy. He *knew* it was the good-news-shine of the gin that, lifting, tingling, stripped things of their limiting corporeality.

"Why don't you sing too, Dave?" Anna said.

"Me sing?" But he *was* singing. He was saying the words in his head silently, taking the sound of Toby's voice for his own.

Sometimes Toby and Anna would say something to each other in a more matter-of-fact voice than they used when their remarks were general. There'd be something about it curiously contractural of the space between them. Then he'd think of this being Anna, who had never talked to anyone but him like that. He'd feel a sudden definition of his own body, as if he were riding in the front seat alone. But when Toby would clown a little for his benefit; or when Anna would watch the rapport between him and Toby, regulating it, catalyzing it; or when they'd glance at him for reaction, as if nothing they'd ever shared were quite ratified without the sanction of his under-standing, it was perfect.

The three in back didn't seem to share in this flow. They sat forward in the seat, as if the car were about to slow down and let them out. They couldn't quite seem to surrender inertia to the motion of the car. Their conversation wasn't free from awareness of motion. They spoke only of things their eyes picked out of the landscape, in passing. When one in front would turn to include them in a remark they'd lean ahead too quickly, then relax too quickly, as if they had grasped at a line and lost it. There seemed to be a partition between the back seat and the front.

If David had been going to the top of the mountain with his family alone, their bond would have been the trip and the morning. It would have sheared away all separateness amongst them. Or going with Toby and Anna alone, he could have shared *Toby's* excitement: not that they were going to the top of the mountain, but that they were taking the *car*. Now, with all of them there together and the gin wearing off, he had to keep up a kind of balancing. He talked a little louder to cover any remark he felt coming from the back about the wisdom of taking the car; he wished that Toby wouldn't talk so exclusively to him and Anna.

"How's the study coming, Dave?" Anna asked.

"Oh, I don't do much nowadays," he said.

He wished she hadn't brought that up. He felt sheepish. Study seemed a stifling thing, with Toby there; something that would reclassify him in Toby's eyes.

"I wish you could go to college *this* year," Anna said. "I don't suppose there's any chance, is there, even with the scholarship?"

"Are you going to college?" Toby asked.

"I dunno," he said. He'd known he was going to college, since he was ten.

"What do you want to go to college for, Dave?" Toby said. Indulgently, but as if all that were needed was a little guidance, to put David straight. "Why don't you come to Halifax and get a job with me? I left school, did you know? I couldn't stick that old stuff."

David felt the surge of defensiveness again. He'd go to college all right. He'd be a . . . a doctor, he thought suddenly. The best one in Halifax. Maybe the best one in Canada.

"Yeah?" he said to Toby. He spoke tolerantly, as if Toby's comment didn't merit serious attention. He turned to his father.

"Why didn't you bring the axe, Father?" he said. "You and I could have stayed and *cut* the keel."

Toby's face fell. David felt the old hurting power. He could inflict retreat on him by witholding responsiveness where un responsiveness was least expected.

He didn't look at Anna. She'd sense what was behind his break with Toby, though Toby didn't. Her face would look as if it had lost its footing. (Once the teacher had interrupted praise of her writing to scold him for laughing with Steve. When she'd turned to Anna again, Anna hadn't known what face to put on.) She couldn't bear it when he and Toby were at odds.

They were nicely onto the mountain road when the car struck a soft spot. The wheels began to spin.

"Are we stuck?" Martha said at once. "Are we stuck?"

"What's the trouble?" Chris said.

(Oh, if they'd only keep quiet, David thought.)

"Do you want us to git out and give you a push?" Joseph said.

"Naw," Toby said, "she'll go through that all right."

But the wheels buried themselves deeper and deeper.

"We'll have to get out, dear," Anna whispered.

"All right," Toby said, sighing.

They got out. Joseph broke an armful of brush and packed it tight around the wheels. He went for another. Toby insisted they didn't need any more. He raced the motor, but the rut went deeper and deeper. The others pushed, but the car wouldn't budge. Anna put her small hand against the back of the car and pushed too.

"Don't you get in the mud, Anna," Martha said, "with your good clothes on."

Toby got out.

"We shouldn't have brought the car," Martha whispered to Anna.

Anna didn't reply. She edged off toward Toby.

Toby looked the thing over. "Ain't that *somethin!*" he said to Dave. He gave him a tentatively-including grin. "I thought she'd go through that all right."

"She's in quite deep," David said. His tone was one of pure statement.

"Joseph, you better go get the oxen," Martha said.

"No, no," Toby said. "We'll work her out somehow—eh Dave?"

"We better let Dad get the oxen, dear," Anna said.

He hesitated. "Okay then," he said. "All right." He was still

173

unconvinced; but made concession to the sensible, as he always did, without rancour.

The sun was directly overhead.

"We might as well eat before you go, Joseph," Martha said, "means we got the lunch with us."

"Yes," Anna said, "let's."

It was Joseph who located the clearing. In a manner of minutes he had a fire going just sufficient to boil the kettle.

David watched his chance to catch Anna alone. He'd planned to tell her about the quarrel with his father. He wanted to give her the locket which he'd thrust into his pocket that morning.

When they'd eaten, Toby stretched out in the clearing, to absorb the sun. Anna wandered off to look for woods flowers. David followed her.

He'd thought it would be easy, as soon as Anna sensed that he had something on his mind, to break into confidence. He waited, but she gave no sign of knowing he had anything to tell her. This was so unusual it put him off.

"Father and I hauled off the big rock one day," he said at last.

"You did!" Anna said.

"I guess we were both tired out and cranky, and—"

"Oh Lord!" she exclaimed. "There goes my brand new stocking." She smiled. "What did you say, Dave?"

He couldn't go on. For a minute it seemed suddenly darker under the trees. He knew that time and separation had sealed them off from each other a little. Nothing like it did with others, but even with them, a little.

He pulled out the locket and passed it to her abruptly.

"Grandmother gave me this," he said. "It's no good to me."

"What is it?" Anna said.

"A locket, that's all I know. She was all sort of secret about it. There's a picture inside."

Anna opened the locket. She knew whose picture it must be. She started to tell David about Ellen and the sailor, but when she looked at him to speak, he said, "Did you ruin your stocking?" She didn't sense that steady listening which had always been between them. She felt the sudden little darkness under the trees too.

"It looks like Toby," was all she said.

Toby? David thought. It looks like me. Toby's face and mine are entirely different: how could we both look like someone else?

They were standing silent when Toby appeared.

"What's the secret?" he said. He gave David the unwithholding smile, trying, transparently to everyone but himself, to assault David's withdrawal by sheer ingratiation.

"Did you have a sleep?" David said.

He might have been instigating conversation to accommodate a stranger. He saw a kind of pallor strike in Toby's eyes. Their blue seemed to fluctuate with his feelings like the blue of water from depth to depth.

They heard the tinkle of bells then. Joseph and Chris had gone to fetch the oxen. Chris didn't return.

When Joseph arrived, he prepared to hitch the log chain to the back of the car.

"No," Toby said, "the front bumper. We're going on, aren't we?"

"Oh, Toby," Anna said, "do you think . . . ?"

"Let's not try it any further," Martha said. "Please. It makes me so nervous . . ."

(Ohhhhhhhhhh, David thought.)

"There's nothing to be nervous about, Mrs. Canaan," Toby said. "There aren't any more soft spots, are there, Dave?"

"I don't know," David said.

He didn't look at Anna. He knew she'd look as if she'd counted on *him*, anyway, not having to be so inexorably sensible with Toby's whims.

"All right," Toby said. "Hitch them on behind then." He moved to pick up the chain.

"You'll go over your shoes," David said. "Let me."

He took the chain himself. His old clothes gave him a sudden superiority then. Toby's seemed futile and finicky.

For all David's physics and Toby's mastery of the engine as long as the going was smooth, it was Joseph who knew exactly where to place the bunk hook; exactly how to *extricate* the car from the rut.

On solid ground again, Toby turned the car with incredible dexterity. He was smiling again now, unreservedly. Having turned the car in the impossibly narrow road was the thing now.

"All aboard," he called. "You going to sit in the middle again, Anna?"

"I guess I'll come along with Father and the oxen," David said.

Toby's smile dropped down.

"Oh, Dave . . ." Anna said. "What for?"

"Oh, I dunno," David said. "I guess I'll come along with him."

"You'll wait at the house for supper, won't you?" Martha said.

"No," Anna said, "I don't think we have time, Mum, really. You're coming with us in the car, aren't you?"

"I can't dear," Martha said. "Honest. It makes me so nervous in the car on this road."

"Well, it looks like we have to go alone, Toby," Anna said. She made a last effort to resolve all their divergent moods with a single smile at them—a smile humouring everybody.

"Don't forget to come again soon, eh, Toby?" David said. He made the words sound as if he were *trying* to make them sound genuine.

"Sure," Toby said. "I mean, we will. Sure."

Anna hesitated. Then she kissed them all around.

The actual moment of departure had set in. David felt the satisfaction of his deliberate offishness crumble all at once, because it had been in no way rebuked except by the involuntary look on their faces. He felt an awful penitence—as if somehow they must start the day all over again. He accused him*self* now for all that hadn't gone quite right.

He started to say, "I guess I *will* go with you and Toby." He looked at Toby. Toby was completely himself again. The going away was the thing with him now, exclusively.

"Good-bye, Anna," David said.

Then the car was moving down the mountain and Toby was tooting the horn and Anna was waving her small hand. She was ignorant of his surge to be with them, irretrievable by his penitence. The sheen of the leaves had been fresh as waking that morning. Now they were like the leaves in the old orchard that were seen only when you went there hunting. When it was time to go, they retreated into another time.

"Well, Dave," Joseph said, "we'll have to try her agin tomorrow."

But the next day it rained. The day, much much later, when Joseph cut the keel, there was no one with him at all.

PART FIVE—THE SCAR

CHAPTER XXVII

SOMETIMES WHEN the draining headache bled pallid everything he looked at, David would try to recapture the physical feel of that morning in 1935: the last morning he'd been unconscious of his flesh. Nothing would come clear except the weather and the circumstance. It must have been November, though he couldn't remember the date. There was a feathery snow on the ground. The pig had left a dark stain of blood when they dragged it to the barn floor for scalding. It must have been late November, so the meat could be kept fresh for Christmas. But not so late that the men couldn't scrape the bristles and riddle the fat from the intestines without their freezing.

Long after the incident of that day had ceased to be active in anyone elses mind, he'd think: If Chris had been standing where Steve was standing, I mightn't have heard him . . . If Chris himself had gone for the apple . . .

They didn't really need David. Joseph had engaged Steve to help them, the night before. And when David went to borrow Ben Fancy's .22, Ben offered to give them a hand also.

Ben was a spry stubby man, with a geniality you never spotted calculation in until afterwards. If he offered to help you with a casual job like this and you gave him a day's ploughing in return, he had a way of seeming so truly indebted that you came away as if it were *he* who had done the favour. Steve had grown thick and quiet. His maleness seemed to give a darkness to his flesh and a cast of heat to the whites of his eyes.

"What did you ask Steve for?" David said to his father. "There's you and I and Chris . . ."

Joseph never counted him, as he did Chris, when he figured the number required for a job like this. It always annoyed David. Yet, in a way, he was glad of it. The spectator sense had a special freedom when no *specific* niche in the job was assigned to you alone.

Everything was ready but the water. The big barn doors were open. Nails had been partly drawn in the boards of the manure shed, at the place where the carcase would be dragged out. The pole was placed across the big beams of the barn. It was ready for the hoisting rope that would be tossed over it, to ease the

pig up and down into the scalding barrel. The scalding barrel
had been chocked with boards nailed to the floor about its base,
so that it wouldn't tip. Joseph had sloshed lime about its sides
to staunch the cracks. The knives for scraping and the knife for
sticking had been brought to razor-edge by the spat-on whetstones. The men had tested them gingerly on the calloused balls
of their thumbs. They lay, by the whetstones, on the manger
ledge. The .22 lay ready on top of the feedbox. Its three shells
were placed carefully beside it.

Everything was ready but the water. The teakettle was
boiling, but the water in the double boiler and in the great
iron pot had only a wisp of steam over its surface.

The men waited. And the pig waited. It rooted its tough
snout furiously into the manure because it had been given no
breakfast. Its flaccid ears and jowls joggled peevishly. Its eyes
were as stupid-looking from their cautious, veering line of
vision as for their vacuity. It never lifted its head to glance at
anything directly.

This was the part that David always hated: that lull between
preparation and the shot. The pig was marked for slaughter,
but it was still alive.

The instant the pig responded to the bark of the gun with
collapse, the bottom would fall out of his tension, like a trap
door opening. Everyone moved at once then. They shouted
commands that were meaningless because each was already
executing them as prearranged: Ben and Steve rolling her over,
David and Chris grasping her hind legs, Joseph searching the
jugular. At the spurt of blood they all stepped back again, like
a kind of exhalation. They moved only when the automatic
buckling, flabbering convulsions of the pig flopped her near
their feet—while the trajectory of blood from the pimpled
mouth in her throat spent itself lower and slower. Then it was
all right.

Nor did he mind anything that came after. The manure on
his hands, the blood on his overalls, even if it soaked through
to his flesh; or the filthy toenails that must be shucked off
before they set. He didn't mind scraping the bristles from the
blow-puffed eyelids above the open gelid eyes; or basting the
bristles with water from the scalding barrel (roiled now with
blood, flakes of skin, and the faeces which always evacuated
itself automatically after death). Nor tying off the bladder
canal with a piece of string, after the pig had been hung and
its flesh had split back triangularly from the apex of Joseph's
knife as it pencilled down toward the navel.

It wasn't that he minded the pig being *killed*, either. It was just this horrible lull. Did the pig have ten minutes left, or fifteen?

There was no tension in the others. It might have been any other job. With one difference. With work at the barn every single remark seemed to be watched for the possibility of ringing a sexual twist on it. David's own ribaldry was not inhibited by his tension. The tension only sparked his ability to reshape and transcend their clumsy obscenities.

They leaned their elbows on the boards of the manure shed and surveyed the pig.

"What'll she go?" Ben said.

"Oh I dunno. Two twenty-five'll take every pound that's in her, won't it?" Joseph said. He underestimated her weight because she was his own.

"Look, Joe," Ben said, because it was *not* his pig and because he was Ben, "if that pig don't go two seventy-five, two ninety, I'm a fool."

"She ain't comin on, is she, Joe?" Steve said. "She looks kinda red back there."

"Steve shouldn't be looking at things like that," Ben said. "He's too young."

"Steve's been lookin so much at them things lately," David said, "he's sunburnt."

They laughed. Steve didn't say anything. A smirk shuffled around behind his eyes. It pleased him to let the inference stand, whether it was true or not.

"I'll see if the water's hot yet," David said. He ran to the house. The water hadn't come to a boil.

The men were in the barn floor when he got back.

"Well, sir," Ben was saying, "here she was with her dress caught up in the door latch and all you could see was these big letters on her drawers—SUPERTEST LAYING MASH."

It was one of his "stories." They'd heard it before, but they all laughed.

David's face was serious. "I don't know how true it is," he threw in, "but they said when she broke wind the first few days she had them drawers on you couldn't see her for dust."

"Ha, *haaaaaaa?*" Ben drew out the last 'haaaa' in a long inquisitive wail.

(Oh God, David thought, if that shot were only over . . .)

Steve looked up at the rafters. "You build this barn?" he said to Joseph.

"Well, it was Father's," Joseph said. "I made it over some. Or helped. Freem Lonas and Reuben, his brother Reuben, was the carpenters. They worked together."

"I guess they worked together more ways'n one," Ben said. "Half them kids o' Freem's was Reuben's."

"Did you hear about the time Freem caught Reuben warmin up the old woman on the kitchen lounge?" David said. (Would that damn water never boil!)

"No," Steve said, "What?"

"Well, Freem flew off the handle and Reuben said, 'Now, Freem, don't be so goddam touchy! We never meant nothin by it'."

"Ha, haaaaaa? Yes, sir, 'don't be so goddam *touchy*'!"

Ben mimicked Freem's voice. David had no gift of mimicry; but it was he who could twist Freem's phrasing to make a story out of a fact.

The pig fretted the trough with her teeth because there was no food in it. He had a sudden impulse to give her some last bite; but there was no way of sneaking it to her, and if he did it openly his act would be impossible to explain.

"Dave, take another look at that water," Joseph said.

He started to run, then stopped and walked. He always started to run when he was asked to look for something, and then stopped. The running made him feel like a child being sent on an errand.

The water was restless, but it wasn't really boiling.

When he came back this time, Ben was pretending to Chris that he saw a handkerchief of Charlotte's up in the haymow. Chris was grinning mildly, saying, "Oh, sure, sure . . ."

You couldn't tease Chris. A joke just eddied around him. And no one ever thought of teasing Joseph. Fun wasn't alien to him, obscenities came surely enough to his tongue in the composition of an oath. But he had no way of putting his shoulder to the wheel of a joke at all. His slow smile just followed around on the periphery.

The men sauntered about the barn. They examined a cow tie, or the hinge of a shutter, or the bent tine of a fork, with the spurious concentration of men waiting. David's tension kept him immobile. Ben tested his knife once more on the ball of his thumb. He made a mock swipe at David's crotch with it.

"Look out, look out . . ." he said.

"Go ahead," David said. "There's nothin there. Why don't you slash a piece off that old gut-ranger of yours . . . it's gonna slap your knee out one o' these days."

This routine of minimizing your own organs and positing enormity to someone else's—he knew it like the back of his hand.

"I oughta cut that thing o' yours off and send it down to Bess," Ben said.

"She wouldn't know what to do with it," David said. "She might use it to cork up her iodine bottle."

"She'd know what to do with it all right," Ben said. He turned to Chris. "D'ya think the old thing sneaks down there once in a while, Chris? I wouldn't put it past him."

Chris was sitting on a rung of the ladder to the hayloft.

"I wouldn't be surprised," he said sheepishly.

There was a curious embarrassment in Chris and David both. It was always like that when a group's general joking about women suddenly narrowed to the two of them. They never talked in front of each other about anything they did with girls. This odd constraint held, even more so, between David and his father. When *they* were alone (though it had nothing to do with modesty on either's part), they couldn't discuss even how the heifer made out with the bull. They couldn't urinate in each other's presence even, without embarrassment.

Steve picked up the ·22. He sighted around the barn with it. (Don't, Steve, for God's sake. Put it down, put it down . . .)

"Moses and Aaron, Joe," Ben said good-naturedly, "ain't that water hot yit? Bring it up here and I'll piss in it."

"I'll take it down and git Bess to piss in it," David said. "That oughta start the bristles on *any*thing."

"Ha, haaaaaaaa?"

He felt a stab of betrayal, the minute he spoke about Bess like that. Suddenly he despised Ben's sly smut. But he couldn't help saying what he did—not if it made them laugh. His heart beat fast as he walked to the house. Surely this time . . .

"The water's boiling," his mother said when he came through the door. (Ellen wasn't there. She always went down to the marsh the morning anything on the farm was killed.)

He lifted the cover off the double boiler. The water was turning itself inside out, as if with anger. He felt cold all over. He went to the door and beckoned for the men.

"Now dip some of that out before you lift it," Martha said as David grasped one of the handles. "If them handles give way it'd scald you to *death*."

"Ohhhhh, it's all right," David said.

"Well, take a holder," she said. "Them handles's hot."

"Take a holder, Dave," Ben said. He grasped the other handle. "I got me cap."

"It's all right," David said.

Now the water steamed in the scalding barrel, and Ben picked up the gun. He broke it down and slipped in a shell.

"*You* better shoot her," he said to Joseph.

"No, go ahead, you shoot her," Joseph said.

"Maybe I'll miss," Ben said, winking.

"No, you shoot her."

And now they were all standing by the boards outside the manure shed. This was the time that David could barely stand.

"Here, pig, pig, pig . . " Ben coaxed.

The pig stopped rooting. She glanced at him, obliquely, out of her stupid pig's eyes. He raised the gun and sighted along it to the spot just above the halfway point between her eyes. There was absolute stillness. David felt as if his own heart were contracting on the trigger.

(Pull, you damn fool, pull . . .)

But Ben waited too long to perfect his aim. The pig swung her head sidewise. He lowered the gun. "You gotta git em jist right, ya know," he said, "their brain ain't only that big." He made a little circle with his thumb and forefinger.

"Take yer time," Joseph said.

Ben raised the gun again. He followed the pig's movements with it. He kept the spot in her head covered, waiting for her to hold steady. Several times she was still for a second. David's tension would knot. Then just before the shot would have come, she'd move.

"She ain't facin me fair enough," Ben said.

Joseph got into the pen with her. He took hold of her tail. He slapped her rump and roused her around facing the boards.

"There . . ." Ben said, "that's good, that's good . . ." Joseph stood back.

Ben raised the gun. Again there was that second when the pig's head was still and the gun was still. David felt the tension would split him apart. But again she moved. She turned around and went toward a corner. Joseph tried to head her off, but she was completely stubborn.

"Don't git her runnin, Joe," Ben said. "Let *me* in there." He climbed into the pen. "Here, pig, pig, pig . . ."

And then the gun began again that awful circling. It would stop long enough for David's heart to contract on the trigger, then move again, because the pig's head moved a fraction of a second before her brain could be found surely. Circling and stopping, circling and stopping . . .

"Hell," Chris said, "let's throw her and stick her. There's enough of us here."

"Yes," David said, "let's." Anything but that goddam gun following her brain, circling and stopping . . .

"No . . . now jist take it easy," Ben said. "I'll git her . . . I'll git her . . ."

"Take yer time," Joseph said.

"There!" Ben exclaimed. "If she'd jist stay right there! Pig, pig, pig, pig . . ."

But she moved. She began to root peevishly.

"She won't raise her head enough," Ben said. "It's no good to shoot em low. She's lookin fer something to eat, y'see."

"I'll go get her an apple," David said eagerly. He'd walk slowly. He might hear the shot before he got to the house even.

Just as he turned, he heard Chris whisper to Steve, "Dave don't like to see anything killed."

It might have been Chris's hand across his face. It wouldn't have inflamed him so if Chris had said it in derision. It was that indulgence they always used. Their exposing a whim of his he'd thought secret left him as shameful for the whim's transparency as for the whim itself. Making a goddam fool of him. As if it was *killing* the goddam pig he minded. He'd have struck Chris right in the face, but it was the kind of anger that striking anyone wouldn't help.

"*Shut* your damn . . ."

He never knew if Chris heard his shout or not. Just then the gun barked and everything happened at once. The moment erupted into other shouts and movements. The swirl of his anger mixed everything up.

Chris grabbed up the hammer. David tore the boards off the opening without waiting for it, and leapt inside. He was first at the pig's hind legs. They were thick with dung at the feet, but he grasped them there. It was a gesture of derision at a daintiness in the others who even in their haste grasped a clean spot if possible. The pig began to buckle convulsively.

"Let *go* of em, let *go* of em," Chris shouted. "Grab her front legs." A pig's hind toenails could slash like a razor.

David held on. He felt blindingly strong.

Chris ran to the pig's head, still watching him. He and Steve rolled her over on her back. The point of Joseph's knife dented the tough throat skin. Then the "slshhhhhh" of bright blood crimsoned his knuckles and the back of his thumb, to the wrist.

They stood back. The pig flopped and bled, flopped and bled. Her body went limp and lolly. A fat smile fixed itself solidly on her caricature of a face. Joseph dug a clot of blood

183

from her throat. Ben had been pretending to look for a clean place to lay the gun down. He came over now. His finger sought out almost tenderly the tiny smudge so accurately between her eyes.

"Well, sir," he said, straightening. "I mind one time we killed a pig fer Cale . . ."

David started to drag the pig toward the opening. He felt so blindingly strong . . .

"Wait till I git the rope and the hook," Chris called. "No sense luggin yer guts out."

The rope was on the grass. The others all went for the hook, as if three of them could fetch it quicker than one.

David kept inching the pig forward even as Chris made the slip knot in the rope. Chris stooped to clinch it around the pig's foot. David knew their hands must touch. He flung the foot down. Chris gave him an odd glance.

"What's the matter with *you*?" he said.

"What's the matter . . .? What's the matter . . .?" He hadn't meant to speak at all. His anger spilled the words out—though it couldn't supply any that made sense. He could only parrot the sentence just spoken.

"I just said you didn't like to see anything killed," Chris said. "What was there about *that* to . . .?"

Oh, if the damn fools only had sense enough to let what they'd said lay. They kept dinging at it, making it worse. He wished he could get hold of Chris's *voice* somehow. He'd tear it to pieces.

The men strained on the rope. The grass was greased with light snow. They drew the pig's carcase over it, to the barn door.

As they tugged the pig up over the barn sill, David was crowded against the wall. The point of a nail ripped along the back of his hand.

"God!" he said, startled by the exclamation of the pain. But he didn't release his hold.

"What'd ya do?" Joseph said.

"Nothin, nothin."

"He tore his hand," Chris said. His own grip slackened.

"God!" the others said. They glanced at the blood. "Now! Everyone!" They kept lurching on the rope.

Inside the barn, the throb of his ignored hand seemed to synchronize his anger on a steady track. The calm, biting, beautiful part of it began.

Oh, it would be fine someday when they'd be yarding logs (and Chris, wanting to spare him, would try to reach the butt of each one before he did), to grasp the big butt of all and ask *Steve* to give him a lift on it . . . Or someday that had been tiresome at the Exhibition Chris would come to him and say, "Do you wanta go home now?" (when it was getting late anywhere, and people who'd had a better time than they were starting to leave, was one of the times being brothers became explicit), and he'd say, "No. But you take the horse and go if you like. I'll get a chance home . . ."

Now the pig was actually landed, the men asked about his hand.

"Don't it hurt?" Ben said.

"No."

"A nail, was it?" Steve said.

He kept his hand turned away from them, deliberately. He felt the stranger in them. They accepted so willingly, so without dispute, his answer that his wound was nothing.

Ben blew his nose, holding a finger against one nostril, then against the other. "I give one of *my* fingers . . . that one, no, that one . . . a hell of a clout with the hammer yistiddy," he said. They turned to the pig again.

Chris came over then. "Let's *see* your hand," he said. He took it in his own and turned it over. "You better git somethin *on* that," he said. He spoke loud, as if accusing the others somehow for accepting David's word.

For a second David felt a lurch in his anger, as if he'd glimpsed treachery in it. He could have let it go flaccid.

"Why don't you go to the house?" Joseph said. He was making cautious, expert slits in the pig's hocks to expose the gam strings.

"Oh, I won't go to the house!" David snatched his hand away from Chris's and reached for the gam stick.

He spread the pig's legs and fixed the notches under the gam strings. But when he let go, one point of the stick slipped free. It struck him sharply in the palm. His anger sparked again with the physical sting, focused again on Chris.

"Dave ain't used to spreadin gams," Ben laughed.

It was only the alternative routine joke: if you didn't exaggerate another's sex experience, you minimized it. But David chose to take it as a slight. He let it, also, grind his anger brighter.

"He's used to spreadin em with his knees," Chris said.

Again David felt the footing of his anger lurch. Chris never said anything like that. He was saying it now to save even a joke going against him. It was one of those times when Chris came out with that odd perceptiveness you'd never suspected

185

in him. You wondered suddenly how much he understood about everything else.

"Let's see, Dave," Joseph said.

He took the gam stick from David's hand. He fitted it so expertly that David's anger righted itself again. Goddam them *all* . . .

Joseph tied one end of the rope to the centre of the gam stick. He coiled the other end and threw it into the air. It went sailing above the pole that bridged the big beams, twenty feet up; but it didn't drop back on the other side. There was a rafter support running diagonally to the big beam. A spike was sticking out from it. The loop in the end of the rope hooked itself over the spike as neatly as a quoit.

"Well, I'll be damned!" Ben said. "I bet you couldn't do that agin, Joe."

"Now what?" Joseph said. He tried to shake the rope clear. It wouldn't let go. "Chris, go git the long ladder."

"We don't need no ladder," David said. "I can reach it. I'll go out on the big beam."

"Yes, and break yer neck," Joseph said.

"Oh, break your ass . . ."

He felt so blindingly sure . . .

Joseph said no more. He wasn't really worried: he'd have seen nothing extraordinary in walking the beam himself.

David glanced at Chris, waiting for him to say, "You know you git dizzy when you climb." He hated him for the words before they were spoken. But Chris didn't open his mouth. It was that assaulting perceptiveness again.

The others didn't protest his plan at all. And once again David felt the stranger in them. Not that it was a matter of indifference to them whether he fell or not, but because they denied him the danger. They assumed so unconcernedly (because it was no one close to them) that he would *not* fall—and coming back, not having fallen, where was the achievement in walking fifteen feet or so of beam?

He started up the ladder that went to the head scaffold. The ladder was tied securely, but Chris held it just the same. He ran across the scaffold and climbed up the short ladder nailed to the big beam. He stepped out onto the beam.

He stood on the beam. He glanced down. And suddenly where was the momentum of his anger?

He felt it gone, with the sudden hollowness you feel when you slip your hand into your pocket and your purse is not there. The barn floor looked stranger than distance alone could make it. It was only twenty feet away—no farther than the kitchen sink from the dining-room table. If he went down the ladders and stood on it, it would become as neutral again as the ground. But, glancing down, it had a yawning look. It was magnetic as an eye to anything loose above it. It had an impact of shock, of faint.

They were watching him. He had to move. His knees felt as if walking had been explained to them, but this were the first time they'd tried it.

Only fifteen feet to go, he told himself . . . five steps . . . no farther than from the pantry to the stove . . . on a beam twice as wide as the board we used to walk on when the path was muddy in the spring . . . only ten seconds . . . just ten seconds to keep steady . . . the time it took to lace a boot . . .

He made it. He clutched the support. Like a drowner.

They were watching him, but without anxiety. The barn floor was still sucking at his breath. He pulled in his breath with a great effort, got a hold on it. He unloosed the rope and tossed it across the pole.

It was half over. He turned and looked back at the scaffold. Ten seconds away. As close as that. Just ten seconds, not glancing down . . . He glanced down. The others had grasped the rope. They had hoisted the pig off the floor already.

Only Chris was looking up at him. He looked at Chris. He saw Chris looking up to the top of the hill, when they were all swimming. Someone was calling and they knew something had happened, though they couldn't make out which one of them it concerned, and it was one of the times when being brothers became explicit.

And then, with exactly the feeling he had often had in a dream of falling, he fell.

He knew nothing about Chris carrying him to the house and laying him on the dining-room table without taking off the cloth, though blood was streaming from the sickle-shaped gash where his cheek had struck the rim of the scalding barrel . . . or of the pig's flesh setting in wrinkles while the water grew cold . . . or of his father's cold rage when the doctor's horse came in sight, walking. Steve went back later to pick up his cap. He slipped the tablecloth from under David, with a sort of apology in him for being exempt from the unseemliness which these actions would hold if one of the family performed them. But David didn't know that. Nor did he see Ellen put her hand not to her head or her heart, when they told her, but to her mouth, as if it were her breath that was threatened.

He knew nothing, the next morning, of Anna rushing from Toby's car to Martha's arms, and they grasping each other as if it were one of *them* who had been hurt . . . or of Toby looking at him as if rupture of the body were something so baffling he refused to admit it. He didn't see Anna look at Toby when Toby made reference to the record speed of their trip; as if she felt like frowning, but as if, if she did frown, that would admit something about *him* which must be in-admissible.

He knew nothing until the next afternoon. He remembered opening his eyes. They were all standing there, dressed, in his room. He had the instant feeling that he'd overslept, so long that now he'd never catch up with them.

And he was always to remember Chris standing alone by his bed that night. Chris looked as if something he couldn't find words for hung heavily in his arms and legs. He looked as if he wanted to touch him. At last he said, "Was it what I said, Dave? I didn't mean . . ." He wanted to answer, "What . . .? Oh, *that* . . ." and smile. But he couldn't. He didn't smile. He said, "Would you ask someone to bring me a drink?"

He remembered the awful feeling when Chris turned and left the room. A feeling that the chance was gone to fix this thing up between them: that something was going to happen to Chris himself soon. If you try to resolve an old misunder-standing with someone back from being away, it's impossible: the meantime of absence, though over, makes the thing's im-mediacy irretrievable. This thing that was going to happen to Chris would separate them like that. This thing now must go forever unresolved.

CHAPTER XXVIII

MOST MORNINGS there was pain. It wasn't ex-clamatory, but a bleaching ache that whitened his senses like thumb pressure whitens flesh. For the first time he knew steady pain, not as something that grazed him in passing, but as a thing resident inside. Yet he didn't wrestle with it. When they asked him if his head hurt, he said no. He let the pattern of the pain imprint itself on him; as if by grudging a thing, whose nature it was to be fought against, and such reaction, he could deny it.

He personalized it: as if it were blows struck first in pardon-able anger but continued, through momentum, to unjust excess; and then, achieving no effect other than intensification of his privacy, became the weapon of their own defeat. He lay there, listening to it, hating it, but subtly possessing it.

But sometimes, in the afternoons, he would doze and awake and the pain would be gone. The thumb would be relaxed. The blood would course colourful through the vein again.

Then it would seem as if the pain had been something made real only by his attitude toward it, that it had tired itself out, vanished so completely there could be no seed of it left. If someone asked him then if his head hurt, he'd say, "No. But it hurt like hell this morning." They would seem to glow, for asking him about his head—now that the ache was gone.

There would be a quality quite wonderful in these afternoons then. Lying there, exempt from any possible task, listening to the others below go about *their* tasks (tasks with so much brighter faces on them, now that someone in the house had been grazed by death but miraculously not struck down), there would be a strange heightening of perception in him. There would be instants when the simplest things—a chance undulation of the curtain frill in the breeze, the sound of his mother's mixing spoon against the bowl—would be suddenly, sweepingly, shot with universality. As if he had happened on some shockingly bright phrase in the very language of meaning.

That afternoon there was the instant with the book.

It was a book Dr. Engles had sent him. It was different from any book he'd ever read. It was supposed to be a good book; but at first it seemed dusty, like something old.

And then his eyes fell on one sentence: "He turned back to the empty house and his heart bent forward against a wind." He caught his breath. That's exactly the way *he*'d felt when anyone had gone away.

Then there was: "A shaft of memory stabbed him like the slash of a branch against a window pane in the night . . . ," "the sound of crickets winding their watches . . . ," "Lint made a knitting pattern in the interstices of the screen," "It was that shocking cry of a child in extreme pain, which you mistake at first for laughing . . ." He had the flooding shock of hearing things stated exactly for the first time.

Suddenly he knew how to surmount everything. That loneliness he'd always had . . . it got forgotten, maybe, weeded over . . . but none of it had ever been conquered. (And all that time the key to freedom had been lying in these lines, this book.) There was only one way to possess anything: to *say* it exactly. Then it would be outside you, captured and conquered.

There was a scribbler by the bed. He reached for it and a pencil.

He wrote quickly, "Roger was angry with his brother." He hesitated. When he did, a listening seemed to spring up in everything around. It stiffened him. But he forced himself to go on. "He didn't want to climb the ladder, but something made him. His brother's face looked . . ." He thought: sad? . . . sober? . . . hurt? . . . *struck.* Yes, sure. "His brother's face looked struck."

He couldn't go any farther. The cleansing cathartic of the first accurate line (*there* was the thing itself, outside him, on the page) made him close his eyes. He felt as if he were going to cry.

His mother's voice brought him up short.

"Is that Rachel coming?" he heard her say to Chris. They were alone in the kitchen.

"Yeahhhhh," Chris said disgustedly, "that's *her.*"

"Is she past Ora's gate?"

"Yeahhh. She's comin here. What does *that* old bitch want?"

"Christopher!"

David slipped the scribbler under his pillow. Rachel might be coming to see *him.* He could just hear her. She'd whisper to his mother outside the door, "Well, that's fine . . . if Doctor Engles *knows.* He's made so many mistakes . . ." He could see her looking at him and saying, "Well, *Daaaaaavid . . .*" She'd draw out the syllables of his name as if she were comforting someone at a funeral.

And if the scribbler were in sight, she'd be sure to pick it up. She'd open it to that very page. She'd never come into the house that she hadn't brought up something that someone wanted to keep hidden. The thought of Rachel being the first one to look at these words he'd just written was awful.

He heard Chris go out. Then he heard the sound of the door again, as Rachel came in. He didn't hear her voice.

He heard his mother say, "Come *in,* Rachel. No, no, take the rocker." It was funny, he still didn't hear Rachel's voice.

He went to the head of the attic stairs.

"Don't look at this kitchen!" Martha said. "Things have been kind of upside down here lately, and . . ."

Then he heard Rachel speak.

"I don't know what I've done that this had to come to me," she said.

"Why, Rachel," Martha exclaimed. "What's wrong?"

"I've worked and I've slaved. I always tried to do what was right . . ."

190

"Of course you have, Rachel. But, tell me . . . What . . .?"

"I ain't got nothin agin *you*, Martha. Maybe you know nothin about it, I don't know. I *saw* him skin out."

"Who?" Martha said, completely perplexed. "You mean Chris? But what's Chris got to do with . . .?"

"Ask him," Rachel said. "Jist ask him."

"Of course," Martha said. "If Chris's done something to you, I'll call him." There was an edge on her voice.

"I musta bin blind," Rachel went on, "to ever allowed it. I don't know what I was thinkin about. But there, I thought I could trust him. I thought he was a good boy."

"Chris *is* a good boy," Martha said.

The edge in his mother's voice was sharper still. He knew she was fighting to control it, to avoid an overt scene. He could see her face. It would look as if it had been manoeuvred into a corner. It would be a little flushed, as if she'd been working over a hot stove."

"Call him," Rachel said. "*Call* him. I want you to hear everything that's said, Martha. I don't go behind anyone's back. When I have anything to say I say it right to their face."

The old bitch! He could see Rachel's face too. Her hair'd be drawn back tight from her forehead. Her eyes'd be feeding on this trumped-up drama. Her mouth'd be set in that line of uncompromising woe.

He heard his mother call Chris. Chris must have dodged out to the shop. He came in almost immediately.

"Hullo," he said grumpily. Rachel didn't answer.

"Chris," Martha said, "Rachel says you've done something to injure her. She wanted me to call you."

"Injure her?" Chris said. "What have *I* done?"

"No," Rachel said, "you haven't done anything. You stand there and . . ." Her voice went choppy. "She was all I had. I worked and I slaved . . . and now you've ruined her. You're as cruel as the grave."

Oh God, David thought. Charlotte. She's trapped him.

But it didn't seem as if either Chris or Charlotte was to blame. It was always like that with any bad news that Rachel brought. No matter how plain her own innocence, you still felt, if it hadn't been for *her*, the old . . . if she hadn't *attracted* it . . .

A chasm of silence split the afternoon.

He could see his mother's face: as if she had caught her breath just too late to fend off this blow on it. He could see Chris's: muddled with shame—not because of what he'd done, but because it must be discussed before his mother. He'd look like he did the time he'd had to ask her to make a bread poultice for a boil on his groin.

"Chris," Martha said at last, "is that true?"

"You needn't lie," Rachel put in, "you needn't lie . . ."

"Who the hell's going to lie?" Chris shouted.

"My children don't lie, Rachel," Martha said. "If Chris's got mixed up with your girl, he'll say so."

She didn't use Charlotte's name. She made it sound as if Charlotte were entirely to blame. If Rachel had come at it directly, in plain anger or plain grief . . . but she always premised beforehand that you'd be unreasonable or unfair, so that's the way you were.

Rachel paid no attention to anything they said.

"She told me it was you, and I know she was tellin the truth. She might get led astray, poor child, but I know she won't *lie*."

"Chris," Martha said, "did you know this?"

"No, I never. She never said nothin about . . ."

David heard the pump. Chris must be standing by the pump: In blind desperation for some kind, any kind, of action, he was ludicrously pumping himself a drink.

"I'll marry her," he kept repeating, "I'll marry her."

"I blame myself," Rachel intoned, ignoring him still. "I blame myself. I shoulda bin warned. His father before him . . ."

"Now, that's enough, Rachel," Martha said, "that's just enough . . ."

"Yes, shield him," Rachel said, "shield him. You've always shielded em all. I hate to say this, I know you got sickness in the house, Martha, but . . ."

"Oh, you stinkin old bitch!" David screamed.

Then he ran back into the room. He slammed the door, to shut it all out.

He didn't open the door again until Rachel was gone.

There was that stillness in the kitchen of an explosion over but the fragments still arcing back silently to the ground. He could see Chris's face: with no place to look. He could see his mother's: it would be the face of someone picking up the first bit of ravaged furniture from the steaming ashes of a fire, more in recognition than in salvage.

"Put a stick in," she said to Chris.

He heard the noise of the stove cover. Then the noise of the door as Chris went out.

Then Martha called to him. He'd never heard such weariness in a voice before.

"Dave, do you want anything?"

"No," he said, "I'm all right."

Chris was gone. They would still see him every day, but he had gone. It was too late now to show penitence for his own actions in the barn. You could only wash out a thing like that when the colours were fresh, when the hurt was still commensurate with the forgiveness. This new thing had revoked that hurt's immediacy. *That* Chris was gone now.

He caught a glimpse of his face in the mirror as he climbed into bed. It was pale and indeterminate. It looked as if it were waiting for some deposit of experience to focus it. The sickle-shaped scar caught up one corner of his mouth in a kind of weak smiling.

The situation between him and Chris suddenly shifted its perspective then. The things that happened to Chris had blood in them. They were newslike. They complicated him, changed him. People looked at him differently afterward. The things that happened to himself were pale, and narrative only. He stayed the same.

Suddenly, hurtingly, he was *glad* he had withheld annulment of this soreness between them. He was desperately glad that he *hadn't* thrown away his only equalizing weapon.

He took the scribbler from under the pillow and reread the lines he'd written. They had the same stupid fixity as the lines of cracked plaster in the ceiling. There was nothing in them, to come alive as often as they were seen. They were as empty as his name and address scribbled across the white spaces of the catalogue cover in a moment of boredom.

He took his pencil and blacked them out completely, obliterating even the loops of the letters.

And then, like the gradual stealth of a train's rumble in the distance so that you can't tell exactly which moment you hear it first, he felt the pain returning.

CHAPTER XXIX

IN THE spring there were two pigs: one to keep and one to sell. Joseph and Martha cut up the larger one for the barrel. David and Ellen took the other to town. It was wrapped in a sheet, its rigid hind legs sticking out beyond the back of the riding wagon.

"I think about three yards o' that curtain stuff," Martha said to Ellen. "Not too dear, y'know."

"Blue?" Ellen said.

"Yes," Martha said. "Like's in the paper."

"If *you* see anything you want, Dave," Joseph said, "a book er anything, why, take it outa the pig money."

"Yeah," David said. "Couldn't you cut that thing in two so it'd all shove in under the seat?"

"It can't git away," Joseph said.

That wasn't what bothered David. He was thinking of the drive through town. They'd attract a casual glance from the town people, then be dismissed as a young man and an old woman bringing a pig to market.

He despised most of the town people—especially its laughable bigwigs and those who paid them petty court.

They didn't seem like people it would be possible to know, or to be known by. They lacked the rich soil of his neighbours' original simplicity. They lacked too the rich soil of those people in the city who had gone beyond this artificial complexity of theirs to simplicity again. (He wouldn't have minded *them* seeing the pig at all. He had an affinity with them as inexplicable as the incidence of epidemic in a spot where no contagion could possibly have been carried.) The town people seemed to have only a thin personal topsoil. Nothing grew on it but a sparse crop of self-assurance. They were absolutely unresponsive to anything outside their own narrow communion.

He despised them, but he hated them too : they could make him feel so self-conscious.

He might despise the merchant who'd stop in the midst of counting out pay for the pig to wait on any well-dressed customer who came in. He'd think that if he and the town people were together with the originally simple of the country or the ultimately simple of the city, he could leave them as gawkingly on the fringe as if they were an audience at a party for the players themselves. But he'd feel awkward just the same. He'd despised the conversations he heard on the street. These interchanges were almost incestuous, so like their own average they were. He'd feel the vital variety of the people at home. But he'd know that if the home people were with him, he'd be in constant jeopardy lest they do or say something characteristic, to attract that inquisitive, then dismissing, glance.

He lacked his grandmother's quiet authority. She had no consciousness of it, or of any need to assert it. Hers might be the humble business of bartering a firkin of butter across the counter, but no one interrupted her. Or if one did, she had a way of glancing at him without interruption of her own speech. It was *she* who held the storekeeper's attention, and the other who backed up inside.

His headache was bad this morning. It was like a weather in his brain, dark and humid. He suspended thought.

But as they drove along, the pain lost out to the clamour of firstness in the air, as the sound of a train going the other way thins out until you can't be sure which minute you hear it last. A sense of earned lassitude followed. Then came the rush of communicativeness from everything he looked at, as if in congratulation. Then this new need to possess these things by describing them exactly in his mind. (The water trickled in the ruts like? ... like? ... anxiety. It was his, now.)

And then the whole multiplicity of them clamoured to be known exactly, and so possessed. The never-quite-exactness of the twinning of thing and word for it was so tantalizing he was glad when his grandmother spoke. It was like a hand on his shoulder bringing him back from an unmanageable dream.

"Don't forget the meat," Ellen said.

They came in sight of Rachel's house.

Joseph had thumbed out the long rope of tenderloin, intact, from its socket between the ribs and the lard. Half of it was for Chris and Charlotte.

"If *she* comes to the door," Martha had prompted David, "just ask for Chris and Charlotte and give it to one of them." Martha and Rachel weren't speaking.

They didn't go to the door. Chris was beside the road. He was opening a ditch the spring freshets had clogged.

He doesn't look as if he lived here, David thought. He looks as if he were working for them. Working and thinking. It gave him a sudden pang to see *Chris* thinking that way as he worked. It reminded him of someone who had never gone to school, trying to trace out the letters of his own name.

Chris was so preoccupied he didn't see them until David spoke.

"She plugged up?" David said.

He started. "Uh? Oh. Yeah. Hi, Dave, Gram. Goin to town?"

"Yes," Ellen said. "Where's that package, Dave? Martha sent along a fry of tenderloin."

"Well, thanks," Chris said. He hefted the package, smiling. "Did she send the whole pig?"

"No, hell, we got lots," David said.

"I planned to come over and help with the pigs," Chris

said. He discarded the smile. "But, well, Charlotte had kind of an upset . . ."

"That's all right," David said quickly.

Chris's glance wandered to the scar on David's face "How *ya feelin*, Dave?" he said.

"Me?" David said. "I'm all right, I guess."

"How's everybody else?"

"Oh, fine," Ellen said.

"Hear from Anna?" He seemed to be asking about people he *used* to know.

"We had a letter this week," Ellen said. "Thursday, wasn't it, Dave?"

"I guess," David said.

"She's fine," Ellen said. "You remember Toby—" (Do you remember the day we left you behind, hoeing? David thought.) "He was away for a long time, you know—but he's back in Halifax now. She sees *him* quite a bit. I think that's about all. How are you . . . and Charlotte?"

"Oh, I'm all right. Charlotte's none too good right now, but . . ."

"That's *too* bad," Ellen said.

There was an uncomfortable silence. Everyone was thinking about the baby.

"Well . . ." David said, "I guess by the time we get to town . . ." He gathered up the slack in the reins. Chris took his foot off the wheel hub.

"I planned to git over and help ya with the pigs," Chris said again, "but that was the day Charlotte . . ."

"That's all right," David said. "Want anything in town?"

"No, I can't think o' nothin. She . . . well . . . she lost the baby."

"Oh, Chris!" Ellen exclaimed.

"Yes." Chris nodded.

"I'm sorry," Ellen said. "I'm *sorry*."

"Yes." His face began to break up. "Tell Mother, will ya?" He turned toward the house.

David couldn't find a word to say. His only thought was: Chris, Chris, you needn't have married her at all. You could still be home.

He started the horse. Then he glanced back at Chris walking up the path to the house. He stopped the horse again.

"Sure there's nothing you want in town?" he called.

"No, I can't think o' nothin," Chris said.

But he didn't turn away at once, and David didn't start the horse.

There was a minute of silence. It seemed as if there was something more that must be said. Then when it couldn't be found, an acute self-consciousness made it impossible for either of them to summon the physical movement to break apart.

"Thank em fer the pork, won't you," Chris said at last.

"I will," David said.

He started the horse. Chris turned again toward the house.

"You wouldn't remember," Ellen said, "but I remember one day, you couldn't have been more than five years old, you cried to go for the cows with Chris. He felt so bad because they wouldn't let you that he went out and broke the handle of your cart . . . so you'd hate him so you wouldn't *want* to go with him."

"I remember," David said.

I I

Chris took the pork into the kitchen.

Rachel's kitchen was as bare as ever. The floor was clean, but without covering. The wooden lounge had a grey woods blanket spread over it, but no cushions. The chairs stood about the room, uncompromising as sentinels. The stove was like Martha's: a low square firebox, with the barrel-shaped oven rising on a long neck. But its animacy was annulled by the bleak square of zinc beneath it and the blindness of the front drafts. They were always closed so the wood wouldn't spend itself in excess. A slop pail held the dirty water. There was no sink. The clock stood nakedly on the mantelpiece. There were no envelopes tucked behind it. No basket of remnants (twists of yarn, short pencils, old buttons . . .) softened its relentless tick. It shared the shelf with a bottle of ink only. The bottle was still in its carton, a pen thrust rigidly upright beside it. There were no cupboards in the pantry. All the dishes could be seen from the kitchen, naked on the bare shelves.

The whole house was like that. The mechanics of living seemed exposed. It had the hollow echo of a house you are staying in for the night, after your things have been packed to move away.

Rachel sat by the front window, rocking. Charlotte stood before the mirror. She was rolling her long hair over one wrist, then twisting it into a knot like her mother's.

A subtle change had come over Charlotte's appearance since she married. The richness of her hair and her flesh seemed to have passed their ripeness. Now it was heavy and

197

musky. The small black hairs at the corners of her lips were more evident.

Chris put the pork on the pantry shelf.

"They sent us over a piece of tenderline," he said. (His family was never mentioned except as "they.")

"I wish they wouldn't *do* things like that," Rachel said. "They know we got no pig, to pay em back."

"They don't want nothin back," Chris said.

"Maybe not," Rachel said. "But I guess I'm funny. I hate to be beholden to anyone."

"Oh, Mother . . ." Charlotte said. She spoke as if she weren't quite sure whether it was impatience she felt or what.

"D'ya feel like fryin some fer dinner?" Chris said.

"I guess so," Charlotte said. "Would you like some fer dinner, Mother?"

"Don't cook any fer me," Rachel said. "I never slept a wink the *last* I et."

She was still rocking and staring out the window.

"They didn't grieve long fer *their* mother, did they?" she said abruptly.

"Who?" Charlotte said.

"The Bains. Ain't that Milledge Bain comin up the road?"

Charlotte glanced out the window. "It looks like him," she said.

"They said both of em was to the dance Friday night."

"Their mother's been dead a year," Chris said.

"Ten months," Rachel said. "*I* suppose it's all right fer them to dance, I don't know. They might as well dance as feel like it." She sighed. "Young people don't grieve very long nowadays. They're just waitin fer the old folks to go, so's they can git their hands on the property."

That's one for me, Chris thought, but he didn't say anything.

Charlotte opened the door and went out to the shop.

"Had I better take the paper off this meat?" Chris said to Rachel.

"Lottie'll see to it when she comes in," Rachel said. "It'll be all right fer a *minute* er so."

Charlotte came in with a few sticks of wood in her arm. She dropped them into the box by the stove.

"Lottie!" Rachel exclaimed. "What are you *doin*, draggin in wood!"

"I just got a few sticks, means I was out," Charlotte said.

"You know you shouldn't be draggin in wood, in your condition." She sighed. "I'd git it fer ya if I was able."

"You didn't say you wanted wood," Chris said. "I'd a gut it."

Rachel glanced meaningfully at the empty box.

"I know, Chris," Charlotte said. "I never asked you to."

She puckered her face at him, to let it slide. She brushed off the front of her dress and got the broom. A particle of bark wedged itself in a crack of the floor. She pried it out with a hairpin.

"We should git a piece o' oilcloth fer front a the stove there," Chris said.

"It'd be nice, all right," Charlotte said.

"I wonder how much it'd take," he said.

He spoke generally, but his glance addressed Rachel. He was opening the way for her to say, "Oh, it shouldn't take much," or "It'd save the floor," or something; to join them in a minor plan. She said nothing.

"Do you know how much it would take, Mother?" Charlotte said.

"I've no idea," Rachel said. "We always had enough ways fer our money to go without thinkin about oilcloth. It was all I could do to keep you clothed."

"Well, that's not now," Chris said heatedly.

"No." Rachel sighed. "You're right, that's not now. But, git it if you like," she added quickly. "It's up to you two. I got nothin to say about it one way er the other."

Charlotte turned suddenly away from Chris.

"I guess we should git you a new coat," she said, "if we think about gittin anything."

"No, dear," Rachel said. "I got lots a clothes to last me out, fer all I go. I won't be here too many more years."

Charlotte had just filled the stove, but Chris opened the cover and put in another stick. His hands shook on the holder.

Rachel got up. She took the floorcloth from its hook by the slop pail. She got laboriously down on her knees and began to wipe up the sickles of muddy water that had puddled from Chris's heels.

"Chris," Charlotte said wearily, "I wish you could remember to wipe off your boots outdoors. You know I don't feel much like scrubbin every day, and you know Mother ain't able."

"Don't . . ." Rachel whispered to her. "Don't . . ."

She looked up in a mime of supplication: Bear anything . . . bear anything . . . just so there's peace . . .

"Oh . . . Jesus!" Chris shouted.

"Chris," Charlotte said, "if you don't stop that swearin I don't know what I'll do. It goes all over me."

199

Chris started outdoors, but Rachel was in his path. He moved like someone dizzy. He turned to the cellar door and stumbled down the steps.

He circled around and around the cellar. He looked ludicrously into the potato bin and the vegetable bins. He aligned a stick of wood on the pile. Then he reached down into the apple barrel. The apple was wilty and half rotten, but he bit into it and chewed it the same propulsive ludicrous way.

CHAPTER XXX

"ABOUT here?" Joseph said. He nicked the pig's leg with the saw.

"No," Martha said. She drew her fingernail across the pig's leg, up nearer the body. "I think about there. I like the legs cut off as high as you can. So I can make stew pieces out of them."

Joseph sawed off the leg where she indicated, then sawed it twice again.

"How's that?" he said.

"That's fine," Martha said.

She put the pieces with the pile that was to go into the barrel last.

They took out the flap of spareribs next. She kept a steady tension on it while Joseph nicked it from the fat beneath. Then she indicated the contour of the ham with a quick circle of her finger. Joseph followed the circle exactly with his knife. He separated the ham from the body precisely at the glistening hip socket.

He set the ham aside. She picked up the bloody trimmings and scrap-shaped pieces and put them in the pan with the head. They'd be soaked out for head cheese. She put the backbone in the pan with the ribs, to be kept fresh.

"What about the shoulders?" she said. "Will we cut them up or leave them as they are?"

"Whatever ya say," he said.

"Did we cut them up last year?"

"I think we did."

"Well then," she said, "I guess . . . or what do you think?"

"I like em pickled and smoked, myself," he said, "but *I* don't care."

"The only thing," she said, "*pieces* come in so handy for a boiled dinner."

"Well, how about cuttin *one* up then, and leavin the other one whole?"

"Yes," she said. "Why didn't I think of that? That's what we'll do."

It was a trifling agreement to reach, but somehow it gave her an odd glow.

Cutting up the pig with Joseph, she didn't know why, was one of the mutual undertakings that seemed to give them a curious closeness. One of the times when the husband-and-wife feeling became explicit.

He didn't know exactly how she wanted it done until she told him; but after she'd told him, he did it more exactly that way than she could have done it herself. She knew just the smooth boundary she wanted on the ham, but if she had taken the knife herself it would have come out haggled and botched.

"I hope Dave don't forget about Chris's tenderloin," she said.

"He won't," Joseph said. He paused.

"You shoulda put in the toenails," he said, "fer Rachel to scratch her old ass with."

"Joseph!" A clap of uncontrollable laughter struck Martha.

It was one of those outrageous things Joseph came out with sometimes in a moment of savagery—not trying to be funny at all. They'd strike her so funny she'd laugh until she was weak. She'd had hysterics once. He'd been chasing a frolicking heifer and come back into the house, shouting, "Git her, no! I wish the hell I had a hot poker to stick up her . . ." and when she looked at him he had had David's cap perched on the top of his head instead of his own.

She forced herself into abrupt seriousness, trying to sober up.

"I wonder if Anna's tenderloin went all right," she said.

"I imagine," Joseph said. "Is this all right fer the strips of bacon?" He scored off the belly pieces with his knife.

"Yes, I think that's about . . ." She went off into laughter again.

Joseph glanced up. "What are you gittin into such a gale over?" he said.

He pretended ignorance, but he was half smiling. He'd recognized his own joke now and was a little amused with it himself.

She shook her head. "Keep quiet, Joseph," she said, "or I'll get foolish . . ."

The package of tenderloin had been waiting for Anna when she got home from the office last night. She knew what it was. A spot of grease from the butter it was fried in had struck through the package. She didn't open it then. She was late, and Toby was taking her to a party.

Anna's face still held the prettiness of a softly brown-haired, softly brown-eyed child. She talked and acted like the city people now; but there was a little wistfulness about her eyes as if she might be someone going without her glasses. Her face seemed always to be in a precarious balance. If the balance were broken it wouldn't shatter, but go small—like the face of a disappointed child who doesn't cry. But sometimes some special thought would illuminate it. Then it would slip right past the other faces that were almost exactly like it in physical detail, and become really beautiful.

It became like that now, with the thought of Toby.

His face struck her with such clarity it was like a blow. His eyes were so clear a blue they seemed exposed, like a nerve. He had a tic of good nature at the corners of his mouth. Recklessness and shyness and quickness to be crestfallen were all mixed up in it together.

The good part of it was, he was like his face. He never dissembled about anything. When he liked being with her better than anything else he could think of at the moment, she knew it for sure.

It was the bad part of it too, later, at the party.

He danced every chance he got with Faye Maclean. That wouldn't be dissembling either. She began to talk faster and laugh harder with her own partners.

And then she saw Faye leave him abruptly. Some outlandishly frank remark of his, she supposed. She watched what happened. Whenever he'd move toward Faye after that, to ask for another dance, Faye would include his movement in her general glance until he was almost up to her; then casually turn her head the other way.

He sat by himself then. He didn't try to look as if he weren't lonely, the way anyone else tries to cover loneliness up. He looked like a boy who has the feeling of being snubbed, without recognizing it or realizing that any of it may be showing on his face.

He was watching *her* now. She danced past, laughing with Jack Newlin. She avoided his eye deliberately. Suddenly it was a wonderful party. For some crazy reason (David could have told her why, or Martha) she loved him harder than ever before because Faye—how could she?—would rather dance with someone else.

The first minute she was alone, he came over and sat beside her.

"Having a good time?" he said.

"Mmmmm," she said. "It's a good party, isn't it?"

"I've seen better," he said. (Oh Toby, you crazy . . . nobody lets *on*, if they're not having as good a time as everyone else.)

"Aren't you enjoying yourself?" she said.

"No," he said. "Let's beat it."

She laughed, helpless. How could you pay anyone back for making you jealous, if, when you came up to their defences, their defences were all unashamedly down? He didn't do anything according to the rules.

"But, Toby, we couldn't leave so early," she said. "What would we say to Faye? It's her party."

He smiled then, the good quick way. "No kidding," he said, "would you go? I'll fix it up with Faye."

He would, she thought. He'd probably just tell her he wasn't having a good time, because that happened to be the truth. She doesn't mean a thing to him. He'd rather be with me.

"All right," she said. "I'll go. But you better let *me* explain to Faye."

Out in the street it was wonderful. It was the first time she knew he really loved her, better than he'd ever love anyone else. He doesn't know it, she thought, but I do.

Some of the stores were still open. Every so often when they'd come into the shine of a lighted window he'd squeeze her shoulder a little. He'd give her a clear kidding smile, with just enough shyness in it to make it absolutely theirs.

None of the party was left in his head now at all. But something else was, she could tell.

"Toby," she said, "what's on your mind? You're up to something."

"Wouldn't you like to know?" he said.

"Is it about me?"

"Sure it's about you! What do you think?"

"Is it something nice?"

"Pretty nice," he said. The crazy artless way he smiled was like a touch.

"Tell me," she said.

He made like a frown. "Oh, I couldn't do *that*."

He's going to buy me something, she thought. He always

bought her something when he felt good like this. So that he could stand back, unabashedly, and watch her pleasure at it. It wouldn't be anything thoughtful, anything he'd remembered her wanting. It would be a *present*. An extravagant child-present.

"Hmmmm," he said. "Let's see what they have in here."

They went inside. They were at the counter before it dawned on her what was really in his mind.

It was a jewellery shop. He pointed to a tray of diamonds beneath the glass.

"Could we have a look at those?" he said to the man. A sudden self-consciousness was mixed up with the kidding now.

The man placed the tray on the counter.

"Toby," Anna whispered, "what are you *doing*?"

"What's it look like?" he said. "We've been working up to this, what's the sense of fooling around?"

"But Toby . . ."

She felt half hysterical. The man was watching them. She just stood there and looked at the tray.

"Unh, unh!" Toby said. He held his hand over the row of large diamonds at the top. "Don't get any ideas now."

She laughed, helplessly. (And why was it, right then, looking at Toby's face completely fulfilled with the present moment, that it was David's inconsummate face she thought of? What about David, now . . .?)

"Toby," she began, not knowing what to say, "how do you know I . . .? Maybe I don't *want* to . . ."

"You better."

He spoke with mock sternness. But his eyes were happy, delighted at her confusion. It was exactly the way he'd watched her confusion when he looked her up the first day he'd been stationed in Halifax again. He was a sailor now. She'd seen him almost every day when she first came here. Then the Navy had stationed him in other ports, until last month. He'd assumed that they'd start in again right where they'd left off .   . as if it had been overnight he'd been away, instead of all that time without a single letter.

She gave his shin a little push with the toe of her shoe: it was no use . . .

"All right," she said. "That one then."

His face really sobered. "Oh now, I was only kidding," he said. "I guess I can stand you a better one than that."

Anna knew that was all the lover's speech there'd ever be. But something about it reminded her of that crazy kind of tenderness of his that wasn't like anyone else's at all. She had a little trouble to talk.

"No," she said. "I like that one, honest. I love it."

Out in the street, he studied her again. He was pretty happy with himself and the whole thing.

"Well . . . ?" he said.

She looked at him, to reply. All at once his close unwithholding face struck her so hard she had to turn her face away.

"What's this? What's this?" he said. But she knew he was pleased that she was almost crying.

"Nothing," she said. She pounded his arm gently, helplessly, with her small fist. "Nothing . . ."

She was to feel like crying again that night—when she opened the package of tenderloin. She saw how patiently each slice had been wrapped in waxed paper from the cornflake boxes. She pictured all the talk that would have gone on while they were preparing it. She knew how they had covertly warmed themselves at the thought of her pleasure in this remembrance of her.

And then she felt like crying because she'd been so long away she wasn't as touched as they'd believe. She felt like crying as for a kind of guilt: that she had an evening dress, but didn't think of it as a "good" dress now; that she said "the show," instead of "the moving pictures"; that the sight of strangers no longer sealed her into the family unit, as it used to do when they'd be having an ice cream in the restaurant in town. Tenderloin used to be so special a treat for them that it made the night they had it for supper almost like Christmas. She felt like crying, because, when she tasted a slice of it now, it didn't taste much different from the pork she could order any day here.

They'd thought the night this arrived it would be the big thing of that evening; and this was the night Toby had asked her to marry him. If Toby should ask her what was in the package, she was afraid, not wanting him to laugh, that she would lie . . .

CHAPTER XXXI

THE WORK of the knife and saw was done now. Martha was selecting the pieces to be given away.

"Will that be all right for Ora?" She held up a piece of shoulder, patting its edges into firmer shape. She scraped the bone dust from the saw off it with the knife. "Or had I better put a little piece of rib with it? She always sends a good piece."

"Suit yourself," Joseph said.

She tried a section of rib with the piece of shoulder. "What do you think?" she said.

"There's lots a rib in the *pan* there fer us," he said.

"Yes," she said. Again she felt the unaccountable surge of warmth at this small concurrence. "That looks better. I hate to send anyone a mean-looking piece."

"How about Bess?" Joseph said. "Gut anything looked out fer her?"

"No."

Joseph took it as an answer to his question. It was not. It was the automatic syllable of negation. No! Not when the morning was so perfect.

Sometimes, most times, Bess's name would fall from Joseph's lips as harmlessly as any other. She never knew when or why these spells would strike her. She was never prepared for them. But now Bess's name was like a rock thrown into the morning's surface.

Her mind ceased to work sensibly before she could examine the cause and discard it. She felt the instant sense of isolation, forsakeness. Her perceptions converged inwards. The fascination of speechlessness settled on her like a weight. Her own hands, the overall jumper of Joseph's she was wearing, his clumsy rubbers on her feet, were like things seen on another woman—someone outside herself.

Joseph was poking about amongst the pieces.

"That one'll do, won't it?" he said.

"Yes."

She spoke as if her voice wouldn't carry to him at all. Single words she could still find, but the swift-flaking silence was covering the sentences.

Joseph began to pluck out some bristles that had been missed.

She glanced out the door, as if for escape. It was as if she were in dusk while the others were in daylight. The soaking fields seemed grimy in their own rags of mist. The branches of the apple trees were praying fingers stony with lost hope. The pieces of pork looked raw and bloody.

"His father before him . . ."

She had never believed a word of Rachel's insinuation. But the thought of Joseph being a man flashed into her mind. He'd be helpless not to feel, when he took the pork to Bess's door, the thing of Bess being a woman (a thing which she, another woman, could never feel). That was suddenly more isolating than any thought of him forsaking her deliberately.

Joseph glanced out the door to see what was holding her gaze.

"Hey . . . *Milledge*," he shouted abruptly. Milledge Bain was just disappearing into the stretch of road the house hid.

"Hey . . . Milledge," he called again. "Do you wanta take a look at that heifer now? I gut her in the barn."

He didn't *place* the piece of pork anywhere. He just dropped it. He ran toward the road, without glancing back.

Martha put Bess's piece of pork alongside the others that were to be given away. She put the hams into the dishpan. She carried them, one at a time, to the cellar, and laid them in the bottom of the barrel. The weight of them made her arms tremble. Then she carried panfuls of smaller pieces.

She fitted them around the sides of the barrel as expertly as she'd ever done. But her hands moved with the information of habit only. She had no thoughts, only the scars of thoughts, in her brain. The disc of her sentience moved faster and faster, until all the separate impressions on it became a steady blur of white.

She saw the men come back from the barn. Joseph chatted leisurely with Milledge in the road, as if his work and hers had been forgotten. His back was turned to her. *Everything* seemed to turn the other way then. Finally.

When Joseph did come back to the shop something in his face told her that, for the moment, the thing of the pork was superseded. She knew he was waiting for her to ask if Milledge had bought the heifer. She couldn't.

"Where's the hams?" he said at last.

"In the barrel," she said.

She had, somehow, to answer a direct question. If she shrank from reply, she shrank worse still from anything that would make the situation overt.

"Milledge took the heifer," Joseph said.

She felt like running, because she couldn't speak. She could, must, answer questions; but she couldn't volunteer anything. She kept piling the pieces of pork into the pan.

"Did ya take the bacon pieces too?" Joseph said.

"Yes."

"I was comin in a minute."

She started with the pan to the door.

"He give me forty dollars," Joseph said.

She hesitated in the doorway. His words stopped her physically. For a second her mind almost came clear again. She very nearly spoke. (This was what had superseded the pork. He was always like that when he'd got a good price for anything He'd bring the news to her almost sheepishly, like a present to be searched for in a pocket. He'd maintain his quiet, as if he didn't understand her glad exclamations, though the funny slow smile on his face belied that.)

The moment for reply slipped away. And once it had passed it seemed to rush so fast and far away she couldn't reclaim it. She felt desperately like running again. She went through the door.

Joseph glanced at her face. He focused it, for the first time that morning, out of his general glance. He knew from the look on her face, as if it were cold, that somehow the morning had gone off the track. He put the good news about the heifer back into his mind again, a little sullenly with unadmitted hurt. He put it back like a present that has been refused.

"*I'll* take that pan," he said. His voice had a touch of impatience.

Martha relinquished it to him, helplessly.

Down cellar, they packed the last pieces of pork into the barrel.

Joseph was silent now too. Martha was his weather. Her moods settled into the very grain of him. Their sense of being at once so cripplingly close together and so strainingly far apart seemed to make the cellar too cramped to hold them both. Sometimes their hands touched. Martha's hair brushed his face as they lifted the pieces from the pan. Then, it seemed as if the cord on which their awareness of each other was hung must snap. Visibly or audibly.

The pan was almost empty. Martha took a potato from the bin and went upstairs. She dropped it into the pot of pickle on the stove. It sank. The pickle wasn't strong enough. She added salt, and stirred, until the potato floated. She rinsed the potato off and put it on the pantry shelf, to be cooked with the others at noon. Then she carried the great pot of pickle downstairs.

Joseph looked up. "What are you luggin that pickle for?" he said. "I'd a got it in a minute." She didn't answer.

She lifted the pickle to pour it over the meat.

"Here," he said. He grasped the handle himself. "Can't you wait a second?"

"I can do it," she said.

"Well, do it then!" he shouted.

The moment he heard his own words, his breath lurched, as if to suck them back. But it was too late. Now the gap was acknowledged, it split wide open. He felt a helpless tumbling, as if off a ladder after the first lost step. There was nothing to do now but act according to his words.

He rushed out of the cellar. Martha . . . Martha . . . Martha . . . His thoughts were every one of her. They swirled upward like a flock of small birds rising from a bush . . . rising in a cloud and flying in a cloud, darting around and past each other. The outline of the cloud shifts from instant to instant, but never strands or breaks apart.

Martha's thoughts were different. At the sound of Joseph's voice—Joseph the first, with his own mouth, to make the situation overt—they clustered tight. Birds *settle* on a bush that way.

In the shop again, Joseph began to skin the meat from the pig's skull.

His thoughts shook. Now what got into her *today* . . .? Just because he wasn't right there to carry the meat down cellar . . . When any other time . . .

She never wanted him to wait on her. Why, he'd *seen* her . . . she'd work so uncomplainingly in the hay field or helping him unload wood that he'd forget that she had only a woman's strength until he'd catch her taking advantage of his trip to the pump to lie down flat in the racks; or until he'd pause to straighten a stick that had landed crooked on the pile, and notice her sink down for a minute on the sled bench. She wouldn't tell him she was going to wash quilts the day he went to the Exhibition. When he'd ask her why she didn't get him to carry the water before he left, she'd say, "Oh, I didn't want you to miss the ox pull. I didn't mind." Or days when he'd be burning brush or at some other job he couldn't leave till dark, coming across the pasture he'd think of having to fumble around with a lantern doing the chores . . . and then when he went into the kitchen she'd never say a word about waiting supper and she'd have milked, herself, and got in the wood and water. If he said, "Why didn't you make the children carry in the wood?" she'd smile and say, "Oh, they was busy," or something.

She was always making excuses like that, for other people . . . she was *more* than fair. She'd give in too, lots of times when he'd be too proud-spirited himself to do it. Yes, and most times she didn't get worked up over trifles as much as *he* did. She'd say, " 'Where's that hammer? Where's that hammer?' Fwaa . . da . . da . . da . . da . ."; mocking his everlasting seriousness, but laughing, and after a minute he'd be laughing too.

Then why today . . . over a little thing like . . .? What came over her when she had these spells?

"It's her," or "It's him." These words he'd heard others use, about two people who had quarrelled, came into his mind. It can't be her, he thought. It must be me. His temper ran out suddenly; as the half faith in one of the two possible decisions does when the other has been finally reached.

And suddenly he had a glimpse of Martha as startlingly clear as if it were the only snapshot of her that had ever been taken and kept. He saw her watching by the pasture bars (with an old jumper of his held over her shoulders) when it was past the time for him to come home from chopping, just before she turned and saw him coming home another way. He saw her hands, memoried with work, lying outside the patchwork quilt some morning he had awakened first.

The head was done. He thrust a wire through the fleshy part of a rib flap. They always hung the ribs up in the shop, to keep them cool. He hesitated. This would be an excuse to speak to her.

He put the rib down and went back to the cellar. Martha was putting a last sprinkling of coarse salt on the pickle.

"Will I hang up the ribs in the shop?" he said.

"You always do."

Her voice sounded crippled. The bafflement struck again. It flinted the temper afresh.

It was always like that.

Outside, work would draw out the anger, as the heat of the oven door drew out frost in the axe bitt. It would be easy to go inside and make it up with her. But inside again, her silence seemed to give a shrillness to the rattle of the dishes or the stove brush or anything she handled. And words seemed to come out in the same shrivelling pitch. They struck about the

210

room and left the silence afterward still warier and more huddled.

He couldn't do it *without* words, either.

He couldn't dig a trench for her sweet peas as an overture. It would be as if he were taking advantage of someone sick—someone who must watch, but was powerless to correct any line of it that went intolerably in the wrong direction. Or if he let his resentment take itself out against some other object—in a curse at the stove cover that dropped on his toe or a rough shove at the cat that kept whining to be let out—it would seem as if he had struck her. She'd make him think of one time he'd given a cow he'd been chasing one final blow with the switch, after she was tied up. When he went to milk that night she was crouching in the stall.

He could no nothing. The silence would tick so against his nerves that he'd leave the house.

He left the cellar now and went back to the shop. He sighed, as he sighed sometimes when his hay was all in cock and an unrelenting spell of wet weather set in.

He began to clean up the shop. His thoughts smouldered now. They could find no air for their combustion.

The pictures of other times like this came and went in his mind like photographs dropped one by one into a flame. The face still smiles fixedly, even as the flame licks it.

Once she'd been struck with that sudden pain she had sometimes. He'd held a dipper of water to her lips, and as soon as she could speak she'd said, "You spilled it on your coat."

Another time, the timber company's representative had stopped for him to go in town and help him look up some deeds (they'd have dinner at the restaurant). She'd brought out his good coat and his good cap and whispered, "There's money in *my* purse." And another time he'd crushed his fingernail beneath a rock. He'd bored a hole in the nail with the point of his jack-knife to let the black blood out, but it had still throbbed at night so he couldn't sleep. She'd got up and made a bread poultice and she'd said, "Is that too hot? You got to have it as hot as you can bear it . . ."

What made her speak, those times? Why was it that when the spell was broken they seemed closer than ever? They never mentioned what had gone before. Not a dreg of spite or clumsiness or shame was left.

He thought: We might have gone back to cut the keel this morning . . . I was waiting till some time we could go together. I know she wants to go when I go. . .

He thought, if the flue should burn out and catch on the dry shingles . . . or if the horse should kick me . . .

And then suddenly his thought sounded to him as it would if another man were hearing him speak it. A new kind of anger struck him, for harbouring such womanish softness. Of all the goddam . . . Letting a woman make a goddam sawney out of me . . .

He'd go back alone and cut the keel. Maybe she wanted to go, maybe she didn't. He didn't *give* a damn. He'd just go. He didn't have to tell any damned women everywhere he went. He didn't have to ask any damn woman everything he did. If he was late for dinner, he didn't care. Yes, he'd take the oxen too, and snig it out to the road after he'd cut it. He didn't care if it was five o'clock in the afternoon before he got home.

And she'd speak first, by God, if he had to keep quiet the rest of his life.

Martha watched him yoke the oxen. Her gaze was as incurious as an invalid's staring at his own pale hands. Silence seemed to puff out from the separateness, the singleness, of everything she looked at. It settled inside her. Her own speechlessness leeched at her brain.

The sudden, single sunburst of pain gave no warning.

It bolted through her chest and down her arm—red, swift, shining. Each of its sharp knives cut at anything that clung. It melted the thick flakes of silence instantly. It forced her lips, before anything else could stay them, to cry out.

She gripped the window sash. And then like a light flaming intensely bright the second before it goes out, the pain flamed bright and then it was dark.

When Martha opened her eyes, she was lying on the lounge.

She didn't remember sinking there. I must have fainted, she thought. I'm glad none of the others were here: they worry so. I suppose I should have kept on with that liniment. But it didn't seem to do much good, and there were so many other things . . .

She sat there, crying a little, she didn't know why. The silence inside her was gone. She felt weak, but whole. The kitchen things looked friendly again, manipulatable to her touch.

She stood up and looked toward the barn. Why, it must have been only a second—Joseph was still yoking the oxen.

She saw him yank upward on the yoke, as if in petulance, when the oxen bent their heads to the sprigs of new grass. Afterwards, when the straps were finally tight, he patted the oxen momentarily at the crown of curly hair between their

212

eyes. Again she had the feeling of husband-and-wife as a thing explicit.

She didn't know why. It always came at such odd times. When they were ready for bed and he'd turn to her and say, "All right?" just before he bent over to puff out the lamp . . . or when David used to come home with a prize for arithmetic and Joseph would look at *her*, as if it were she who had won it . . . or when the crowd would be thinning out at a pie social. She'd cease listening for a minute to what some other woman was saying and look at him, and he'd have ceased listening to what some man was saying to him, and they'd both know at the same moment that it was time to go.

She felt like speaking. She went to the door and called to him, "Joseph, will you be late?"

But he didn't hear her. The wind was blowing away from him. He turned the oxen back the log road.

The touch of sun at the hollow of his throat made Joseph's heavy jacket for the first time this year a winter thing. For the first time the soft wind in the stirring trees was close and of this place alone.

Now another year was beginning for him and Martha, a kind of repeated lifetime. He adjusted his step to the measured pace of the oxen . . . on this earth that was his in the same way that he and Martha belonged to each other. His temper was drawn out again like liquid that loses its strength if left uncovered in the open air.

The soreness between him and Martha still weighted him, but it was encysted. His sentience was still leashed to it, but the leash became more and more elastic.

His thoughts—or less like thoughts than like exhalations of shifting pictures which his mind didn't quite call up in outline —slipped ahead. His feeling borrowed ahead from times when somehow (somehow, as always) this thing now would be resolved and past. The both-tired closeness nights after the sap gathering, when they wouldn't light the lamp before bedtime; and the feeling, after they'd both laid their clothing across the same chair, of the sweet clean bed . . . The box he'd place in a sunny spot for Martha to sit on the day she cut the seed potatoes for him to drop, slicing them gravely and surely, so that each piece had two eyes . . . The touch on his hands of the dry mittens which she'd warmed on the oven door and brought to him when he came into the yard with the second load of wood; when the pair he'd started with were clammy and cold . . .

He thought, explicitly, of his plan to snig out the keel and keep her waiting all afternoon. He didn't see how it had ever sounded right to him. How could it ever have been *his*? He had a clear picture of the day in town when the thought had come to him for the first time: she hadn't had a new hat for three years.

He wished he hadn't brought the oxen. He began to hurry. He thought of turning back. Then he thought: I'll just *cut* the keel, I won't even limb it out. I'll come straight back.

CHAPTER XXXII

MARTHA FRIED some tenderloin until it was almost brittle. That was how Joseph liked it. Then she took the meat from the pan and made his favourite flour gravy. She got the single bottle of quince she'd been saving for company, from the cellar. That was his favourite preserve. Then she got out the tablecloth (which she could no more omit, even if she were eating alone, than she could sit through a Sunday afternoon without changing her dress) and set the table.

It was almost noon.

She sat down to wait for him, with her darning. She always had the same feeling when she darned a hole in Joseph's socks or mended a tear in his coat: as if she might be bandaging a patient child's small wound. As her fingers moved, each of her sensations was like a messenger of good news. She had the feeling which comes so seldom, consciously, that you wouldn't want to be anyone else in the whole world.

It was half past twelve, and still Joseph hadn't come.

"I'll go and meet him," she thought, "he can't be far. He's never late if he can help it."

She put the meat and gravy on the back of the stove. Then she closed the drafts and left the house.

(She didn't know that Joseph was dead.

"With the keel money and the pig money and the money for the heifer, I'll buy her a piano." That was the thought he'd been so busy with. He didn't notice how the keel-piece was swaying in the breeze as his axe clove deeper and deeper into its butt. The tree had no obedience in its heart, except to physics. It fell exactly when it must. His thoughts and his breath, strong as they were in their own way, were insubstantial, and powerless against it. One great branch pinned him to the ground, and its physics satisfied, itself lay still. The oxen glanced up, then began to browse again.

There wasn't an instant of pain. There was only a second of upward-darting alarm, like the instant of almost-flight in a bird before the shot strikes. But Martha would never know that. There was no break in his flesh, but the blood gathered cold and blue beneath the skin. And wherever his thoughts had gone now—wherever the knowledge of just how to locate the ham joint exactly, or the core of loneliness in him that no face and no words but hers could quite reach—she would never be able to find them.)

When Martha got to the foot of the mountain, the sun was so warm she took off the jumper of Joseph's she'd slipped over her shoulders, and lay it on the pole bridge. She spread it out flat, not to miss it on the way back. What is he doing? she thought. The dinner will be cold. She tried to remember whether or not she had filled the stove before she left.

"Joseph," she called.

There was no answer. There was only that odd hollowness about the silence when you call to someone in the woods and there is no reply.

She felt no anxiety; but with her voice dropping down into the woods alone, the urgency to meet him began to have a little clamour about it. She followed his tracks up the mountain, walking faster now. She walked faster at each bend in the road, thinking surely she would see him when she turned it,

Now and then she called. Sometimes she stopped and held her breath, to catch the sound of the oxen's tinklers. But there was only the soughing of the breeze in the trees, stiller than silence.

The sun slid way past noon, way past dinner time. An irrevocable lateness seemed to quicken in the air.

Then she was running, and calling at the same time. Her breath clucked in her throat. Joseph's not-answering made the remoteness in everything about her suddenly inimical. It struck like bells. It struck for some awful extra moment of time she'd stepped into, inextricably—one that everyone else-was ignorant of and safe from.

And then, when she was almost to the top of the mountain, she heard the tinklers. She sat down on a stone, weak with relief. Tears started suddenly for love of their familiar sound.

Joseph would be walking in front of the oxen, coming down the mountain. She listened for him to give them a command. She listened for the sound of the bells to grow. There . . . that one was nearer, and that one, and . . . that one *seemed* fainter but it couldn't be. Sometimes the cow bells would sound fainter and fainter though they were coming toward you, right up until you saw them. Yes, listen, *that* one was nearer . . .

"Joseph," she called, "Joseph . . ."

But the breeze was against her. And now when she listened she couldn't hear the bells at all. The silence sounded *its* bell once more, like the bell for recess over. She felt the cramp of fear returning.

She began to run again. And then she saw the oxen. They glanced up at her, but their eyes didn't change. She looked at their big, warm, friendly bulks. She smiled.

"Joseph," she called, not very loud this time. He must be right there.

And then she screamed.

She screamed, and then she stopped screaming. She moved toward him, and then stopped moving. She sobbed, and stopped sobbing. She shivered, and stopped shivering. She said, "Joseph, Joseph . . .," and then she stopped saying "Joseph, Joseph . . ."

And then, with Joseph lying there as if all the deafness in the world were smiling out at her from him, the quick-flaking silence began to close in on her, and the forsakenness.

She put her apron over her face. She whispered, "Joseph, you forsook me . . . you forsook me . . ."

II

David and Ellen came in sight of the house.

"You put in the curtain stuff, didn't you, Dave?" Ellen said.

"Yes," David said. "It's under the seat."

"I think it's just what she wanted," Ellen said. "It's got all the colours of the paper in it. You didn't lose the pig money?"

"No."

He felt the thick, exciting roll of money in his inside pocket. He thought of counting it out into his father's hand, down to the exact penny. His father would truly wish that he'd spent some of it for himself, but wouldn't be surprised that he hadn't. He'd ask him to take five dollars (the present-like amount) now . . . two dollars then, *any*way. Somehow this offer to share, from whichever of them happened to have money, and the go-on-with-you protests against it, always made them all feel like crying.

"*When* did Joseph take the sods away from the house?" Ellen asked.

"This morning," he said. "Early."

"*I* didn't notice," she said. "The house always looks kind of bare after the banking is taken away, doesn't it?"

"Yes," he said.

"I remember one year the sods froze up early and he had to bank it with brush. We all went with him to get the spruces. He stuck whole trees all along the house, and the rest of us piled branches in behind them. They caught the snow. I think it was the warmest winter we ever had."

"*I* remember," David said.

They drove into the yard. No one came to the door.

When David glanced at the door-shut, fire-out, banking-bare, blind-eyed house, he had one of those odd feelings that struck him sometimes, he never knew why. Suddenly whatever he looked at would have the air about it of a November dusk, the night before the first snow. It would seem as if everything had gone by while he slept, down the road, and now he'd never catch up with it. He had, for a moment, a feeling as if he and his grandmother were the only things animate in the whole world.

Ellen stepped onto the footrest of the wagon.

"Just steady me a little," she said.

David put his hand under her elbow.

"All right," he said. "I've got you."

CHAPTER XXXIII

"HAVE YOU gathered all the vegetables?" Ellen said.

"All but the cabbage," David said.

"You better get in the cabbage," she said. "This is Hallowe'en."

"I'm getting them now."

"Put on your mittens."

"Ohhhh . . . mittens . . ."

"It's cold," Ellen said.

"I don't need any mittens," David said. Gentler, the second time.

"No, I suppose you're young . . ."

Her mind stayed clear, except for asking things over. But, late years, she felt the cold.

David always keeps a nice warm fire though, she thought. David is a good boy. It's a quiet life for him here with me, alone; but he never complains. He's like his father that way. His back bears whatever settles on it. He doesn't try to shrug it off. Yet I can see Martha in him too . . . when he's lonesome or hurt, when he doesn't know that his face is giving him away. Yes, and sometimes Christopher, and sometimes Anna. He's like them all. Sometimes, she thought, I couldn't say how, he reminds me of that boy in the hayloft. For a second she felt an inner warmth. I wish, she almost thought, it could *be* . . .

Then she glanced across the bare, stretching, October fields. Rain-sodden leaves from the bare trees clung in the aftergrass. Only the blackened heaps of potato tops remained in the garden rows. She felt colder again.

"Is everything locked up?" she said. "This is Hallowe'en."

"They never bother *us*," David said. He put on his cap and jumper and went to the field.

Ellen moved the mat frames closer to the stove. More than ever, lately, her hooking had become a kind of visiting. Memory could bring back the image of the others, but not the tune of them. These pieces of cloth which had lain sometime against their flesh could bring them right into the room.

That was the lining of the coat Joseph had worn the day he got their last Christmas tree. She had washed it and brushed the lint from the seams, but a spot of dried balsam still clung. There weren't many things of his left now, they were almost all used up. Could it be five years ago? Could it be almost five years for Martha too? Not many things of hers were left now either.

That was her apron. An apron had always seemed like one of her features. The doctor said her heart must have been bad for a long time . . . but what did he know about the kind of heart sickness that left her housecleaning untouched, and the same dress on her in the afternoon as in the morning, and her dahlia bulbs in the earth, that fall, to freeze? What did he know about that look her clothes had, like the coat of a sick animal . . . and that look on her face all the time, as if she had to translate everything that was said to her? as if verbs had lost their meaning, because the only language that beat in her was description (of one thing), spoken in the heartless key of the wind? What did the doctor know, for all his instruments and learning, about that look on her face as if there were no place in the world for a look like that?

She sighed and turned to the newer garments.

Brown. That was a shirt of Christopher's. It came from the big bundle he'd brought over the day before he went away to war. Charlotte could hook, but Rachel wouldn't allow a mat in the house. She said they were too dusty. Chris in England . . . Who'd have thought that *he*'d be the one, the only one, of them to see her homeland? She glanced at his letter on the windowsill. The big letters of the address were childish looking, and the short stubby sentences inside were helpless to communicate anything.

There seemed to be something Christopher and David wanted to say to each other that day. She'd felt it, when Chris suggested suddenly that they go look at the cattle. But she knew they hadn't been able to say it even when they were alone in the barn; for when they came back Chris had suggested they go look at the pigs. She knew they hadn't said it there either, or at all: she'd seen the way David touched Christopher's clumsy bundle of clothing afterward, when he thought her eyes were turned away.

David took a bath the next morning and went to town himself. She knew he'd tried to enlist too. She knew he had lied about his health. Futilely. Because she had seen him kneeling before the basket of drop apples he was cutting up for the cows that night. Suddenly he'd thrown two or three of the apples fiercely against the shop wall . . .

White. That was the blouse Anna had worn the day she and Toby were married. The day before Toby's destroyer took him to the Channel. That was the one time David had gone to the city. He'd given Anna away. She could never find out how he'd liked it there. He'd never discuss it at all.

And white again. An old suit of Toby's tropical whites. Anna had sent it home. She thought David might get some wear out of it. And strangely enough, he had. He never *would* wear anyone else's clothes. But he had worn that.

Beneath it was a bright check. How had that got in with *this* bundle? Those were David's first pair of long pants. He'd bought them with the prize money for that essay. No one had even known he'd sent it in . . .

She paused and looked toward the field.

How strange it is, she thought, that David, of all of them, is left here. Whether, as it sometimes seemed, he had a love of this place as binding as blood, or as it sometimes seemed, a hatred of it so dark and stubborn as to fascinate him beyond the fascination of any possible kind of love, she didn't know.

If it hadn't been for me, she thought . . . if it hadn't been for his health . . . would he have gone away? He can learn to do anything. Even farming, which comes most unnatural to him, he can now do well. If he'd gone some place where he might have found the thing that was *meant* for him . . . I wonder if my sisters ever had any grandsons, she thought . . . and what they are doing in England.

She watched David's movements in the field. He moves like someone who never thinks that anyone else thinks about him, she thought. David is a good boy . . .

She drew the frame a little closer still to the fire. At the touch of extra warmth, she felt content. She always felt content when the crop was gathered and the day growing cold, but the fire burning brightly in the kitchen stove.

David moved rhythmically in the field, pulling one cabbage after another. He clove off the tortuous root cluster with a single slice of the knife, discarded the saucer-shaped outer leaves crisped at the rim or stencilled by the summer's bugs, and placed the tight heads in piles.

His face and clothes seemed pinched, as if in reflection of the day. A pinched November blueness was in the air. The shabby air hung motionless from the stripped trees and skeletons of caraway. Rain-dark clouds clung, motionless and curled at the edges, to the rim of the bare mountain. The buildings looked dark and closed in on themselves. There seemed to be a near-sightedness about everything. David's thoughts clung low to his brain, like the clouds that curled above the mountain.

He'd never rebelled at being left here to take care of Ellen. He'd taken up that future the same way he accepted any circumstance. He'd go on wearing his thin clothing long into the winter, though he *had* woollen clothing in the closet. He'd continue work in his bare head in the sickening heat, though the other men went to the house for their straw hats. He'd climb, a thousand times, two steps in one over the broken ladder rung (until one day he'd fix the rung, and then go on, in a kind of panic, to fix the button on the barn door, the loose shingles on the shop . . . until everything on the place was mended).

It didn't seem like five years that he'd been alone here.

It didn't seem like any time at all. These years were like a kind of suspension, before time became really, movingly now again. Though never consciously called up, an absolute conviction was always there; sometime, somewhere, just as surely as ever, everything was still waiting.

But that sometime was never today. Each day's routine immobilized him by its very immediacy. It had to be cleared away, extinguished, before the real nowness began. Each tomorrow (never doubted, in prospect, as a break in the repetion of today), itself becoming today, was repetitive nevertheless.

He bore the constant pain in his head the same way. He had never sought any cure. He merely accommodated his day *to* it, as a stream little by little comes into a new course around a boulder in its middle.

There had been no conscious moment when the pain ceased to be a contrasted thing, had become a feature. But now it was there, unquestioned, like the climate of his mind. It damped his thoughts so that no one of them ignited brightly or singly. They writhed in a cluster, like the clump of worms you turn out of a can when the day's fishing is over. The matching of physical effort to the day's tasks (almost, but with stubbornness never quite, beyond it) became a kind of isolate career.

There were moments when he'd feel a flick of dismay. He'd glance at the bruised-looking winter horizon, coming from the well at dusk, and he didn't know why, a sigh would catch in his throat. He'd be fleetingly appalled when the year of some event that seemed like yesterday was discovered, on subtraction, to be seven or eight years gone from this one now . . . or when he'd seen a face of his own age he hadn't seen for some time, and notice its flexibility gone, the certain promise in it now of what it would someday be, irrevocably . . .

But the dismay was transient. He wasn't unhappy.

His loneliness was absolute, but it wasn't intolerable for being something foreign.

The seed of it had always been there, even when he was at the hub of fellowship with others. (There was never one of them he could really talk to, though they never doubted that they were talking to *him*.) He withdrew from them in bitterness because he was no longer whole. It was self-willed. Because he was lonely, there was a self-biting satisfaction in deliberately making himself lonelier still. There was a satisfaction in their puzzlement that when he *was* with them, in any occasion he couldn't avoid, the old wit, the old humour, the absence in him of any isolating mark of the solitary, were still there. And when he withdrew to himself, it wasn't to a strange place (as *they* would find, forced to their own company). It was the most familiar ground he knew.

At first the neighbours couldn't believe that he *preferred* to be alone. They still dropped in to spend an evening. Their spastic conversation was embroidered only with staples of comment. ("We better git the snow now than later," "If we just had what one o' them fuhllas makes in *one day* . . . ," "I tell ya, ya never know from one minute to the next . . .") These were as satisfying a coin of intercourse to them as if they were brand new. It never occurred to them that they weren't equally satisfying to him. David stepped up the tempo of the talk as surely, as neighbourlily, as ever. They never suspected the curious sense of abeyance their presence provoked in him.

But finally they stopped calling. Because David never came into their houses at all.

(Now he sat in the kitchen, evenings, reading from dark to bed—or until the silence, which made a pleasant lapping sound while his grandmother was busy with her rags or her knitting, took on a desperate insistence when she put her work away. She sat, then, her gaze far away, tapping with the very tips of her fingernails . . . tap, tap, tap . . . on the nickel clothes bar that ran along the side of the stove. She called it "condoling," and it besieged his mood almost intolerably.)

And now, working in the fields, the obbligato of ache in his head chimed with the quiet feeding orbits of his thoughts (each one branching immediately, then the branch branching, until he was totally encased in their comfortable delta). It isolated and crystallized him into a kind of absolute self-sufficiency.

If a neighbour approached him there, a sense of bareness

would come over him when he looked up. The strange presence precipitated a sudden definition of his own body in his consciousness: the scar, the tentative expression, the inapposite work clothes ... The others would seem so solid and opaque, and he'd seem absolutely transparent. He'd talk more animatedly than they (safe in their opacity, they need make no such effort), and they'd notice nothing. But not until after they'd gone would the chime of the ache and the feeding thoughts creep back. They'd congregate, one by one, like animals that have been scattered by a strange footfall; to knit themselves together again and re-establish his completeness.

His neighbours had changed, as the village had changed. The road was paved now. There were cars and radios. A bus line passed the door. There was a railway line along the river. With this grafting from the outside world, the place itself seemed older; as the old who are not remembered are old.

And the people lost their wholeness, the valid stamp of the indigenous. Their clothes were so accentuate a copy of the clothes outside they proclaimed themselves as copy, except to the wearers. In their speech (freckled with current phrases of jocularity copied from the radio), and finally in themselves, they became dilute. They were not transmuted from the imperfect thing into the real, but veined with the shaly amalgam of replica.

It wasn't so with David.

Part of his loneliness had always been that he could tell the coin from the replica. Just as part of it now was that even in his isolation he was not islanded from the true spirit of the changing times. It was as if a kind of extra sense kept him parallel with it, without dependence upon participation. He had been born with a condition for universality within him. In whatever place or at whatever time or with whatever person he found himself, his first response was not adaption but recognition. He could be old with the old, or young with the young.

That was the part which most made his loneliness absolute. There was no single place he fitted in.

Yet when loneliness is as absolute as that, it can be sustaining.

It builds satisfactions and shields out of countless small things. The comfort of the pillow at night ... the successful manoeuvring of an impossibly crooked stick into the firebox ... the turnip tops filling exactly the number of bags gauged for them ... the two apples eaten at eight o'clock each night ... the left index finger held, in a mannerism, against the nose ... the alternate day's shave falling, this week, on Sunday ...

Except when, as time went on, glimpses through the blind faith that someday he'd be as young and plastic as ever again, came oftener. They were more defined and shattering than the sigh at the well.

One day he was straightening the perimeter of the woodpile. He did this each day, though he'd be disturbing the pile again the next morning. Steve was passing down the road. He shouted, "Dy'a do it with yer eye, Dave, or dy'a use a compass?"

For a second his fussiness was revealed to him as the most intolerable stigma of all, the stigma of the solitary. And all the rest of that day he did everything carelessly, approximately. (Though the next day the tidiness returned—not by conscious acceptance but by grooving in again of its own persuasion.)

One day a young boy and a young girl dawdled up the road. He'd seen this couple clowning together countless times before, and felt nothing. But now the work he was at parched in his hand. The very vacuousness of their antics (isolable as they were of everything else in the world) seemed like the only real thing there was. He stood there like the uninvited child.

He'd had no part of girls for a long time. They might only glance at the scar on his face, but he'd be conscious of it all the time. And Bess had married again. He was so convinced that sometime he'd have all the girls he wanted that he hadn't felt any loss. But now the girls of "sometime" seemed like a trick. He felt an awful reorientation. He had a desperate urge to leap back through the years, physically . . . to make it himself in that boy's place.

That night he went to the dance in the schoolhouse.

He danced with the youngest girls there. He was a better dancer than the boys they'd come with, and he kept them giggling almost constantly. But somehow in the little slacks between laughter, in the moments when the music had stopped and they stood, before it began again, with their hands fallen apart, there would be an awkwardness in the girls. It wasn't of shyness but of perplexity. They seemed more content sitting on the benches with the boys who'd brought them. They'd sit with these boys, not laughing at all; they'd be stiff with shyness. But the engagement of each others' presences was without interruption.

The ache in his head heightened glaringly. It seemed like a normal feature become in the presence of others insistently protrusive. He left early.

He lay awake a long time that night. He felt the desperate blight of one who, used always to having everything at the party gravitate toward him, for the first time feels what he has

224

only observed, unfeelingly, in *others* before; the getting back only of such response as they'd striven for, their departure unremarked and unprotested.

(But the next morning his headache was worse still, his work that much harder to accomplish. The chime of the extra ache and the extra victory of effort re-established his sufficiency again. The girls of "sometime" were realer than ever.)

Or one night, reading, some passage might ring suddenly like a bell: the portrait of some desire he had never consciously realized, some thrust of identification. He'd slip away, rushingly, transcendently, into the person described or the place . . . and then settle back again into his chair and this room, crushed almost physically. (But intenser still, then: tomorrow, tomorrow . . .)

Or again, one day he'd *feel* better. The cast which health puts on things (as impossible to imagine or to believe in, when one is ill, as it is impossible to imagine or to believe in the cast which illness puts on things, when one is well) would be like a clamp taken off his circulation. Then he'd have a stricken glimpse of the years gone by as of an utter emptiness. Their victories over handicap would seem entirely negative. (Until the ache grained back with such subtle gradualness that its reversing persuasion was unnoticed until it was complete.)

Another afternoon he was raking scatterings of timothy the horse rake couldn't reach in a rocky corner. A long sleek tourist car stopped at the gate. The man asked if they might get a drink of well water from the pump.

At first only the man spoke. The others in the car continued their private conversation. The way the man worked the handle only a dribble came. He said to the man, "Perhaps *I*'d better . . .It has a physics all its own." The man laughed. The girl, the daughter, with the smooth simple clothes, smiled at him suddenly. The boy, the son, his own age, said, "Temperamental, eh?" as to a friend.

When they drove off, he knew they'd been curiously taken with him. When they went out of sight, he felt like running. He left the tiny windrow unraked, a few goddam wisps of hay . . . (But that night when the chores were done, he closed the windrow and carried the hay in his arms to the nearest accessible pile.)

Or whenever he'd see the way a wife and husband stood together at a grave . . . or the way they stood together after one of their children had almost (until he threw up) choked on a chicken bone . . . or the way a man fastened the safety pin that held his child's mitten to the sleeve: clumsily, almost without distraction from his conversation with another man, but gentler than his large hands did anything else . . .

Worst of all was the day he had the accident in town.

A car, turning out from the curb, crumpled the hind wheel of his wagon. It bent the seat irons into a senseless pattern and tumbled his load of vegetables onto the street. They lay crushed and split.

The driver tried to cover up his own guilt with a false belligerence. But David himself wasn't angry. It was raining, his feet were wet, his head throbbed . . . He felt only dismay at being plunged into the leading role of a tumultuous situation which depended for its resolution on the manipulation of bluff. Bluff was something he had no talent for, no rehearsal in. He despised it. He wanted just to be out of here, not to have had it happen at all.

He watched the other's belligerence himself, stolidly and fearlessly. But he had no talent for gauging when a show of reasonableness would work best, or when insistence on *more* than his rights would be the only means of insuring his rights at least. He wanted his rights, no more, no less. He'd *have* them . . . but he didn't know what to do.

A crowd had gathered. He looked at them. He'd never felt the stranger in people so strongly before. A sort of evil seemed to possess their faces: a sly rapturous feeding on the spectacle of other people in an uncertain mess, a gloating in their own uninvolvement.

Then he saw a face among them he knew. Ben Fancy's. A face from home. He walked over to him in a kind of release.

"He turned out without looking, smack into me," he said. The desolate collision sound was still in his ears. The desolate collision twistedness was before his eyes.

"I didn't see it," Ben said (though he had). He lowered his voice. "But you want to make him pay ya, Dave."

He looked at Ben's face again, and he saw what had come of keeping to himself too long. This was no longer a face from home. There was no family feeling in it. There was the same stranger in that face as in the others. He caught his breath. Oh, Father . . . Mother . . . Chris . . . Anna . . .

Or worst in a way all their own were the glimpses provoked by the trick of a cloud pattern . . . or the blue dusklight seeming to come upward from the snow . . . or by any thing, face, thought, or feeling, which he seemed to see exactly, in an ephemeral instant.

226

There would be an awful challenge about each of these things, to name it. An accusing: as if it had been put there for him, and him alone, to see exactly and to record. As if in having neglected to perceive *every*thing exactly he had been guilty of making the object, as well as himself, incomplete.

Sometimes then he would get out the scribbler. He might put down, "The trickle of water corkscrewed its way down the ditch," or "He looked as if he had taken his good face for everyday" . . .

If that seemed perfectly right, conviction would flood him: If he wanted to, he could do as much for everything in the world. Yet with it there was dismay at his neglect of all the things gone by. There was the thought of all the things he would never *see*, to know exactly. There'd be such a terror of failing in even one particular, that he couldn't bear to tempt performance further.

Or maybe the only words that would come (though the perception was still there, exactly enough) were inapproximate as a pattern built with crooked sticks. He'd feel a tension nearer than anything he'd ever known to the limit of what can be borne without madness. He'd have to get up and dissipate it, sickly, guiltily, in movement.

Yet even *these* things left no impression that was permanent.

He brought the cabbage over now, on the wheelbarrow. He carried them, an armful at a time, down cellar. He came up into the kitchen and washed the earth from his hands.

"When are you going to get the cabbage in?" Ellen said.

"I got them in," he said.

"That's good," she said. "This is Hallowe'en."

"They never bother us," he said.

Suddenly he had a picture of Old Herb Hennessey. He heard himself, as a child, saying, "Aw, let's not bother Old Herb . . . he's no fun." They'd always called him Old Herb. Not because he was really old, but because he lived to himself.

For a second he felt a sudden panic. It reminded him of once the day had seemed to grow late while he was working, though his watch said only three o'clock. Then when he looked at his watch later, it still said three o'clock. He saw, with a start, that it had been stopped.

But that too was transient. The texture of youth was still intact in him. No blow or defect or unhappiness is ever accepted as truth, so long as time can always be made to begin at the beginning again.

I must write to Anna tonight, he thought, and ask her why she can't come home for a little visit. He had only to summon the thought of Anna, at any time, to feel warm and vital and safe again.

CHAPTER XXXIV

ANNA SAT alone in the apartment. Toby had left her.

She might have known that if she started to hurt him . . . Anything that hurt him just turned strange. He just stepped over it, to where the going was smooth. If he hurt me like David used to sometimes, she thought: *knowing* that he did it, and exactly *how*, but with the same sore spot in his heart afterward as I had in mine. The bond that she and David had, that helplessness not to inspect their feelings, separated them from the others but gave them a feeling of home in each other.

She stared at these small cramped rooms: the only quarters they could get in wartime Halifax.

They had never belonged to her except as they belonged to him and her together. She had always lived in a *house*: one her own father's hands had built. And now Toby was gone, these rooms seemed to disown her; as if in vengeance for the strangeness she had dealt out to them.

She had tried to brighten their dinginess with needle and cloth. But she sewed clumsily. There was an odd pitifulness about the effect, as about a child's bouquet.

The transformations she wrought pleased Toby, though (when she had drawn his attention to them), as much as if they had been done expertly. He had only a nomad's interest in his surroundings, they had no claim on him. Only what happened while he was there mattered.

And after a while she began to imitate him in his carelessness of them, as she imitated him in everything else.

But, beneath her thought, the disregard bit her, even as she practised it. It grated against a hidden softness which, try as she might, she couldn't quite deny: the sisterly custody of household things, things hard-won and valued, which she had learned in the house where she was born.

And now that Toby was gone, the unbelonging of these rooms struck at her through all the cloth she had patched over their surfaces to give them a face, with the bareness of bone. Relentlessly. It brought back the bareness of other features of life here which had assaulted her before now only fleetingly. The row of ashcans in the rain. The impersonal clink of milk bottles in the delivery boy's basket. Hands held out, with the glance elsewhere (though she held out her own hand now as ritually as they), for the change from a clerk or the streetcar conductor. A foul word of adult knowingness from the mouth of a child in a narrow street. The laugh of a friend at some joke which had only a mechanical catchphrase humour in it. A little whirlwind drawing up the chewing-gum wrappers and scraps of newspaper from the sidewalk. The unembarrassed silence of the woman next door as they hung out their clothes from adjoining balconies. Some face which for an instant was all the faces about her—because of its absorption (without respect for them) in things alone, with never a trace of wistfulness on it . . .

He was gone.

But I don't care, she thought defiantly . . . ("I don't care . . . I don't care . . ." she'd said to David the night they asked him on the sleighing party, but not her.) Your face won't hit me any more. I can step over things too. ("I don't want to go anyway," she'd said to David, "I got lots of other things to do . . .")

And then (as sometimes when the rush of Christmas shoppers in the store would bleaken the cosiness of her own list and later, with strangers jostling her on the cobbled hill from the ferry where a dingy harbour breeze fingered the discarded wrappings of food and the rags of beer cartons and someone's heavy foot scraped the patent leather off her new slipper so she swore aloud, but after that, when she was alone, thought, surgingly, Mother, Father, Chris, David . . . or as when David had said, "It's not much fun, Anna. It's not for girls"), then the first tearing tears came.

She let them come, as they would, for a few minutes. Then she dried her eyes. She sat staring at her feet, as a child does who arrests his crying in one great effort when someone comes into the room. She had that look on her face of the child; which, if there is anyone who loves him there to see it, gives to the toes of the shoes he stares at, or to any other part of his clothing that is anywhere worn, the most assaulting forlornness there is.

It had been perfect just before.

It was the day the first warning of autumn had struck in the air. Even in the city she could feel it. It always made her happiness sharper, if she were already happy. If she weren't, her heart would feel away from home.

She had erased away the long morning with work, waiting for his convoy to come in. It must have come in while she dozed, in the afternoon. She went to the window the minute she awoke; and there he was. Walking up the sharp cobbled hill. The first sight of him on any day still jolted her breath.

He had something under his arm. When he came nearer, she saw what it was: an enormous French doll. He had carried it home to her, all the way from Newfoundland, not even wrapped. She didn't know why, but *because* it wasn't wrapped she felt like crying.

She hoped suddenly that no one had giggled at him. It would never occur to him that there was anything odd about carrying a thing like that under his arm along the street; but if anyone giggled, that instant crestfallen shadow would go over his face.

He had a bottle in his greatcoat pocket, and they each had a drink. A drink with him always gave her a smooth, ringing feeling . . . a nice soft sense of gaining speed . . . a spreading Christmas Eve happiness. She couldn't drink with anyone else at all. Drinking didn't affect *him* in any way; except to make him more than ever as he really was.

"What do you want to do," she said after supper, "go to a show?"

"No?" He gave it the inflection of a query.

"For a walk?"

"No?"

"Uhhhhh . . I know. Whist?" She tried to imitate the tack of his mood with a teasing in her own voice.

He shrugged his shoulders elaborately unattracted to whist.

He wasn't silly when he clowned, he could really do it. She wanted to tell him that, but she couldn't. He wouldn't understand what she was getting at and the thing would be spoiled.

The restraint made a little stiffness in her. She was afraid he'd mistake it for withholding. She felt like someone who joins the dance of glee at another's good news. After a while the other may notice that each manoeuvre he instigates is being followed all right, but in imitation, not spontaneity. Toby had a child's illogic in argument, but a child's instinct for spotting the deviation of any mood from his own. And he wanted her to share any mood of his completely. He could never understand why anyone shouldn't feel exactly the same way about anything as he did.

"Well, what *do* you want to do?" she said.

"Just sit here with you? What's wrong with that?"

There wasn't a thing wrong with that. It was wonderful.

He hadn't asked her what *she* wanted to do, but she didn't mind. Just so he didn't want to *go* anywhere. She knew she absorbed him completely then, because he always said what he meant.

They sat there with something like the conspiratorial amusement of children between them—almost as if there were a joke about being grown-up and acting that way, seriously, that the other grown-ups didn't know about at all. It didn't seem possible that he could leave their way together sometimes as suddenly and completely as the shift in a dream.

But she was *conscious* of her happiness: he wasn't.

And after a while she couldn't help watching it, guarding it. Please don't go away. Please don't say something about someone else or some other time. She kept gauging the interplay of question and answer three or four speeches ahead; trying to keep them both on subjects that were safe, to pilot the conversation away from any dangerous tangents.

She said the wrong thing almost immediately.

"You crazy . . ." she said, smiling at him indulgently, "toting that doll to me all the way from Newfoundland!"

Suddenly he sat upright and began to chuckle. The way he chuckled ("ha, *ha*") at some really wild hash of common sense in a movie comedy, or at any story he might be repeating which contained words like "rassle" or "ka*lonk*."

"That was quite a night," he said. "They had this punch board there, and I guess I'd have been poking away at it yet to get that darn doll if this dame hadn't made me let *her* try for me. . . High as a kite . . . and, what do you know, she got it the first punch!"

She tried to think of something to deflect him; but panic was racing through her like a flame.

"Where was that?" she said.

He didn't notice anything in her voice.

"I don't know," he said, "some joint about six miles out of St. John's . . . Some place Slim knew. We had Slim up leading the orchestra, and . . ."

While I was lying awake, she thought, thinking how cold the water would be. She felt suddenly like someone who has come to a party, glowing with the feel of her good dress, and all at once, inside the door, her dress turns shoddy and homemade.

He never thinks of the water . . . he's perfect for a war, she thought. He was really innocent of any belief in danger, but

231

the danger-brightness lit up everything for him just the same. It made the strange faces as absorbing as the familiar, as if there were a drink in everyone and everything all the time: reflecting on *him* and lighting him too, though he knew nothing about that at all. He was exactly like the heroes in the silly magazine stories that no one really believed in—not a bit of the danger he passed through rubbed off on him. She couldn't bear to read those stories, because the *girls* in them were never like herself. He's perfect for a war, she thought; and I'm no good for a war at all.

He was chuckling. "You should have seen us coming back to ship. Five o'clock . . . high as kites . . . lugging this great big doll . . ." He wouldn't know why that shouldn't amuse her too.

"What about the dame?" she said.

"Oh, hell, we ditched them!"

Them? It was a party, then. If he were only *trying* to make me jealous, she thought . . . I wouldn't care about the girls, if you'd hide it; if I couldn't just *see* you there, the way you're telling it, so completely with them.

"What happened?" she said. "Did you get too fresh with them or something?"

He looked surprised. "Naah," he said. "You know me."

That's it, she thought desperately. I don't know you at all. I think I know you inside out, and then you're a total stranger. You're not like anyone else. When I'm not right there, I'm not with you at all.

"Was she a good dancer?" she said.

"Who? Oh. I dunno, I guess so. When did you get *that* outfit?" He glanced at her new clothes as if they were some new delightful feature he was just discovering in her.

He'd forgotten the other completely. But she couldn't. His face came before her: some future day, with not even a shadow of her left in it, all in the present with someone absolutely new. He wouldn't take a bit of her with him; he wouldn't leave a bit of himself behind, any bit he'd miss.

Oh no, she thought foolishly, no . . . you won't leave me first. I'll leave you.

She got up and lit a cigarette. She riffled through the pages of a magazine on the ash stand, and put it down again.

"What time is it, dear?" she said, turning his wrist over so she could see his watch.

"Seven," he said. "Right on the dot."

"Is that all?" she said.

She turned the end of a yawn into a little smile. She picked up the magazine again.

The quiet between them sounded now. He knows it has changed between us, she thought . . . with that instinct of his . . . but he doesn't know why.

"What's the matter?" he said. "Don't you like the doll?"

She saw him glance at her. He reminded her of a boy watching to see how he's making out in an effort to win back someone's pleasure.

"Why, certainly," she said; but she yawned again, this time without smiling.

He looked baffled. And then she felt the hurting power she too had. She didn't feel any more like the smile-when-they-smile-at-you girl at the party, with the home look clinging to her as plain as a garment.

"I ran into Jack Newlin yesterday," she said. "What do you suppose he was doing? Getting a Christmas present for Sophie! Already, mind you. He made me try out all these fancy lipsticks and stuff. We had a barrel of fun. I wish you could have seen the make-up kit he got for her."

"I bet it was a honey," he said. He wanted to go along with her, but his false eagerness dried up abruptly into a funny little doldrum.

"Maybe we could ask Jack and Sophie over for some bridge tonight," she said. "Jack's such good fun. You don't like bridge much though, do you?"

"Not much," he said.

He was pacing about the room now. All the smiling had gone out of his face.

"I don't know what Jack sees in Sophie, do you?" she said. "There's so much to Jack."

"I never thought Jack was anything wonderful," he said. There was a touch of irritation in his voice.

"I know," she said earnestly. "Nobody does, if they don't really know him."

She had met Jack through a girl at the office. It was everyone's knowledge that he was crazy over her. It was chiefly from Jack that she'd picked up the city way of talking: the way she tried not to talk when she went home.

They were quiet again. Then she said, "Didn't you want to go to a show, really?"

"No." The syllable was quite flat this time.

"There's a Spike Jones show at the Capitol," she said, as if she were teasing him.

"I don't want to go to the Capitol," he said. "What's wrong with staying home once in a while?"

"Nothing," she said. "Only it seems kind of silly just sitting here and looking at each other."

He gave his head a sudden impatient shake.

"What's wrong with you, Anna?" he said. "Half the time lately . . . every time I . . . I don't know . . ."

"I'm afraid I don't either," she said. "I'm sorry."

"Maybe I'd better go live on ship," he said. "Then you wouldn't have to look at me at all."

He glanced at her, waiting for her to kid him. He doesn't mean a word of that, she thought. He'd forget in a minute, if you kidded him. But the taste of her own hurting power was in her like a drunkenness.

"That's up to you," she said.

"All right," he said, suddenly really angry. "All right . . . I will . . ."

Don't, she thought, don't let him go . . .

"All right," she said. "All *right*."

He was gone all right. The room cried it: that still accusing cry of table and chair and curtain and door and bed when someone goes and someone stays. His face struck her. She turned away a little, physically, but it followed her. She closed her eyes, but it struck her again, three or four times.

You won't strike *me* like that, she thought. ("They don't have to ask me if they don't want to," she'd said to David. "I don't care, I don't care . . .") She went to the mirror, trying to block out his face with the sight of her own.

And then that part of it went, while she was standing there; like drinks taken to defocus and astigmatize unhappiness wearing suddenly thin, and the peaks of this unhappiness showing with more intolerable clarity than ever through the lifting fog. The party was over. When the party was over you went around and cleaned the dregs out of the glasses and put them away. It was morning, they'd gone home, and it was too late for any but that grey daytime sleep.

You'd start with his clothes first. He hadn't taken anything but the uniform he was wearing. Maybe he'd come back for the others. Maybe he'd just get new ones. You could start with that shirt on the chair.

Her hand touched his shirt, and his face struck her from every direction. She pressed both hands against her face and began to cry. (She'd known it *would*, but, but . . . the sleigh had really gone without her. David . . . David . . .)

That was Tuesday. The worst thing about Wednesday was

the silly tunes on the radio he was always humming. Thursday it was better. But Friday night she dreamed of the day they had taken the car up the mountain road. His face was nearer in the dream than it had been that day in the flesh. She awoke before it was quite light. She was afraid of staying awake, and afraid of going back to sleep.

That night she called Jack Newlin.

"Jack," she said, "I have news for you. 'My husband has left my bed and board and I will be no longer responsible for any debts contracted by him in my name.' " It was an old expression she remembered from the Newbridge weekly paper.

She felt a burning gaiety. But she wasn't really talking to Jack. It was for Toby's benefit. ("I couldn't have gone on their old sleighing party anyway. Hi, Freda? Oh, Freda—let's do that tonight: *You* know, what we *said*.")

Jack suggested that they go dancing somewhere and talk it over. Sophie wouldn't mind. Hell, what if she did?

In the car Anna talked with the hectic brightness of a recording with its revolutions speeded up almost to racing.

"Where'll it be?" Jack said.

"How about the Grotto?"

That's where Toby always went dancing. He might be there himself. (Just once to let him see her free of him . . .) Toby *would* be there. There was that constant obbligato of his face, watching and listening. It was easy to laugh, really laugh. ("What are you laughing at, Anna?" Freda said when the sleigh passed them. "I didn't say anything funny.")

But Toby wasn't there. And after a while the face was turned away and she thought: he isn't coming at all. Her laughter echoed like laughter in an unfurnished room.

"Do you want to dance this one?" Jack asked.

"No, thanks, Jack," she said. "But you go get someone else . . . go on. I don't mind."

"Oh, *I* don't care whether I dance or not."

Why couldn't it have been Jack? she thought for a second. I wouldn't dare sit here with Toby like this, with my face giving me away . . .

"Jack," she began, "you're the best darn—"

But she never finished, because just then Toby actually came through the door.

He was with a good-looking girl she didn't know. He looked awkward with her. That wonderful unconscious awkwardness of his was the first thing that struck her, and then the look on his face. He didn't look as if he were having a good time.

(Cover it up, for heaven's sake, if you're not having a good time, you crazy . . .)

"All right, Jack," she said quickly, "let's dance."

She glanced at Toby and the girl dancing. They're just dancing around together, she thought. They're not laughing and talking like Jack and me, and the dancing following along beside it. He can't do it my way at all.

The very first time Jack left her she looked up and saw Toby coming towards their table. She felt her sureness panic. (Toby, don't you know you can't come right *over* here and . . .?)

"Hello," he said.

His eyes were throwing out feelers for fun, but the rest of his face held back a little to see how it was going to go.

"Hello," she said.

"How about a dance?"

"Well, I don't know," she said, "Jack . . . Oh, I guess it's all right."

She smiled. She noticed a tiny crestfallen tic in his face when he saw that her smile had no negotiation in it.

They danced silently for a minute. He's a crazy dancer, she thought. He's not quite on the tune, ever. He bumps into half the people in the room and he thinks they're bumping into him. He's the most wonderful crazy darn dancer . . . The silly dance tune seemed to flood her like some really important articulation. She felt the way she'd seen David *look* sometimes, when the essence of any small thing would strike him exactly, if it were only that of a smooth stone.

"You seem to be having a good time," Toby said.

(Oh, Toby! Don't you know you're not supposed to let on you think I'm having a good time?)

"I *am*," she said. "Aren't you?"

"Oh, I guess," he said.

"Who's the handsome girl?" she said.

"Aw, you wouldn't know if I told you," he said. "She's kind of a dope."

(But you're supposed to say she's wonderful, you crazy . . . Her mind threw up its hands.)

All of a sudden she felt hurtingly ashamed of what she'd been trying to do. It was like the time she'd tried to make Effie feel it didn't make any difference to *her* if Effie left her birthday party before the presents were opened . . . and then she'd found Effie's present for her tucked away on the clothes rack, because it didn't have any tissue paper on it like the others.

236

For suddenly she knew the truth: She was the only bright thing in his life that was *steady*. She was the one he'd always want to go home with, if the party was slow, or when the party was over. That was enough.

She smiled at him then, really smiled. The sort of smile that passes between two people in a railway coach when something happens which only they two, of all the others, see to have been funny in exactly the way it was. The unwithholding look came back into his face instantly.

"Do you want to go home?" he said.

"Now?"

"Sure. Why not?"

"Toby," she said, "you're crazy. What about the girl?"

"Oh, I can get someone to take *her* home," he said. "She won't mind."

"But Jack . . ." she said. "All right . . . after this dance."

"You're not sore, are you?" he said. That was something that had to be asked sooner or later—so just say "no" quickly, and have it over with.

"No," she said. "Oh Toby, you're so darn . . ."

"What?" he said. "What are you trying to get through you?"

"You wouldn't know," she said, "you wouldn't have the least idea." She beat his arm with one small fist, with laughter and tears about equally close. ("Didn't you have a good time, Dave, honest? Did you sit by yourself half the time? Oh, Dave, Dave . . .")

"All set?" Toby said.

"Just wait till I get my things," she said.

She turned away from him, to go across the dance floor to get her coat and to tell Jack. Quickly, almost running, before he might say something about some other place or some other time.

It was three years before Anna went home to Entremont again. Even when Toby's ship was away for months, she wouldn't leave Halifax for a day, lest that should be the day he came back into port.

CHAPTER XXXV

DAVID WAS counting on two whole weeks to himself. It was the morning Ellen went to Annapolis for her annual visit with Mrs. Burchell. Their husbands had made the first trip out from England together.

"You'll be careful with the fires, now won't you, Dave?" she said.

"Yes."

"And now don't forget and leave the cover off the bread box."

"No . . . No . . ." And then more gently, "Sure you got lots of money?"

It wasn't exactly that he was glad to see her go. When the bus went out of sight, he wondered, angrily, if the woman in the seat with her would glance smugly at the old-fashioned clasp on her purse, and when she opened it to get out her handkerchief, at the few bills folded carefully inside. He was suddenly assaulted by the thought of all the things she did for him beyond her strength. Now she was gone, they put her in a minor light.

But he felt a heightened identity, an expansive relaxation, in being absolutely alone. He thought of all the things he *could* do (whether he did do them or not, actually, didn't matter) without explanation to a single soul.

Maybe it would rain. He'd take the new book up to the attic and read it there.

Years ago, unknown to anyone, he'd traced some relatives of theirs in England from the signature and postmark on an old letter of grandmother's. Now, one of them sent him these books regularly. He was a don at Oxford, about David's own age.

At first he hadn't liked the books. They had more to do with the shadow of thought and feeling which actions cast than with the actions themselves. They seemed blurry. Reading them was like study. But now he found them more rapturously adventurous than any odyssey of action. This one was a novel by someone called Forster. It gave him such a lyric feeling to recognize the absolute truth of what the author said about whatever people he dealt with (though he himself had never known anyone like them, actually) that sometimes he'd have to look away from the page.

He'd put the light out in the kitchen, so there would be no one to bother him. It gave him a curious satisfaction to think of hearing them try the door and then go away. He'd read in the attic, with the rain against the roof and the windows. He'd feel himself radiate into and possess every corner of the empty house.

There were no friends at all now. The leitmotiv of the headache had become constant; and the hearts of those who are young and free and those who are young and not free never quite touch. But a limiting illness, if chronic, brings its own anaesthesia : simply because the single day's freedom from it which would be enough to invalidate utterly the dull cumulative lustre of resignation never comes.

The loneliness had become an unattended tune in his bloodstream and his mind-stream. It touched him only whitely, stilly, like an impression of the weather. Its wick was turned up only when the days would first begin to lengthen and the winter dusk would come down blue and distant on the white frozen fields, or when the trunks of the grey birches would darken just before it rained, or when he'd waken from a dream wherein the quality of some time gone by and of faces forgotten had been intimate beyond any power of the mind's deliberate remembering, or when he'd stand by the window and watch the headlights of the Saturday night cars increasing up the road to his house and then shining dimmer on their way to town without stopping.

But even then it was only the loneliness of a child for whom there's an instant unpondered pulse skip in the beat of the day. It wasn't what bends the hearts of people who have had something and now it is gone. It wasn't unpleasant *at all* now. Hewing his life to fit his condition had come to have the tidy thrill of fitting together a small puzzle. It was like steady conversation with a partner inside himself, silent, but faithful beyond question.

It was only when he stepped off his own place that he'd feel really alone. Then a fluoroscopic bareness would denude him, as when a moving picture is stripped of all but its pale bones if the theatre doors are thrown open and the daylight let in. The loneliness would seem exposed. It would be somehow shameful in the presence of others who had company.

He stood by the mailbox now, with Anna's letter open in his hand. She said that she and Toby were coming down to the farm for Toby's leave. He felt for an instant as if the ground he stood on had threatened to give way.

For a moment, before he was glad, he felt a lost feeling, a regret at this sudden fracture of his mood of the morning. For a moment he wondered how he would be able to manage the noonday nap he counted on to make the rest of the day tolerable. For a moment the good way it had been yesterday flashed into his mind. He'd listened to the war news while he pulped the turnips for the cows, comfortable equally in the subconsciousness that his health exempted him from any decision whether or not to take active part in these far-off battles, and in the fact that he could listen to news of them without taking time out from his work.

The war had gone around David. It was like all the rest of the things that happened to the others.

He *had* tried to enlist. But the flush of will which had seemed to confute his physical limitations, on the way to town, had crumpled before them as soon as he was stripped in the examining room.

The busy-eyed young doctors glanced at the naked men as if they were an irritating accumulation of data to be sorted and filed. The other two men made clumsy jokes between themselves about their nakedness—for the doctors' benefit. They tried to establish some sort of contact with the doctors on the basis of masculine humour. The doctors joked with each *other*; the men's jokes they might not have heard.

One man glanced down at himself.

"I wonder," he said, "if they could give a fuhlla anything to make this thing grow."

"I wish they could," David said. "In cold weather mine shrinks so I'm always getting it caught in the buttonhole of my drawers."

In the laughter that followed he *joined* the other men. Even a doctor conceded him a millimetre of grin. But when his turn came to stand before the doctor, though the doctor was of slighter build than he, his assurance left him as if it were there in the corner with his clothes.

"How did you get that scar on your head?" the doctor asked.

David told him.

"Ever had any trouble with it since?"

"No," David lied.

The doctor sounded his chest. "Ever have any trouble with your heart?"

"No."

"Well, you better go see your own doctor about it when you go home . . . and forget about this," the doctor said, half-concernedly. He was turning even as he spoke and pointing to one of the other men: "Williams? Are you Williams?"

He wondered now, if Anna had explained to Toby why he wasn't in the war.

Sometimes on the bus he'd felt that the servicemen were looking at him and wondering why he wasn't in uniform. He'd wish he had some gross external disfigurement as explanation. He wondered if he'd feel like that all the time with Toby. He wondered what conversation would be possible between them. Toby had been in the thick of the invasion, right there in the Channel the day of the big morning. Toby was free. Other people were free. When they were with you the routine you'd worked out alone seemed suddenly skimpy. You had to keep justifying it, or poking fun at it. They felt no such necessity to comment on *their* way at all.

II

Anna had said they'd arrive on Friday, but they came a day ahead.

David didn't hear the bus stop. He had just finished his lunch at the corner of the table. He was putting away the mug and the spoon and the egg cup. He wasn't thinking about them at all, when they eased the door open. They were both laughing; still tiptoeing in a mock-cautious way, to continue the spirit of the surprise.

If he'd been sitting watching for them, he couldn't have helped the initial reaction of the one who stays to the one who comes. He'd have felt a sudden emergent loyalty to his own circumstances, like a kind of fence. But caught unawares by the good sight of Anna's face, he was taken up instantly into *their* mood.

Anna hugged him and kissed him. The sudden scent of woman's garments and face powder and soft young hair thawed any restraint. She glanced about the kitchen.

"Why, Dave," she exclaimed, "you're clean as wax! Isn't he, Toby? *Where's* Gram?"

"She's in Annapolis," David said.

"Oh, is she? Well! With Mrs. Burchell? How *are* you, you old . . .?"

Toby too had started to speak; but he seemed to lose control of the greeting, with David and Anna isolated in each other. He just stood there, smiling nervously. He didn't know whether to keep his hand held out or to withdraw it.

241

David thought: I'd forgotten he wasn't one of the sure ones.

He hoped all of a sudden that Anna *hadn't* told Toby about his illness. He knew it would never occur to Toby to wonder why anyone else wasn't in the war. He wanted to have it the same with all three of them, with nothing about him they'd have to keep taking into account, that would put him outside. He didn't feel any of the defensiveness he'd always felt with Toby before. Only that odd little constraint, as if each were waiting for the other. He never thought of the scar.

"Hi, Toby," he said, taking his hand.

"Hi, Dave. How are you?"

"Fine. How are you?"

"Fine. How . . .?" In his fluster, Toby almost forgot he'd said that already.

"How long have you got?" David said, turning to Anna.

"Ten days." They both answered together. "Starting tomorrow." Toby put his arm around Anna. They said it as if ten days were the same as thirty days or a year or forever, because it didn't start till tomorrow.

There was a small silence. Toby looked as if he were embarrassed for having hugged his wife.

"Say," he said quickly, "how about a little drink?"

Anna made a mock frown. "Before dinner, darling?"

"Sure," Toby said. "This is an occasion or something, isn't it?"

"All right then," Anna said, "a little one."

She went into the pantry and brought two tumblers out to the kitchen table. She waited for Toby to open the suitcases. "Is this new paper?" she said, looking about the room. "That's a new couch cover too, isn't it? What did you ever do with that old whatnot that used to be in there by the hall door, Dave?"

"It's out in the shop somewhere," David said.

Toby looked up from the suitcase. "Where's the other glass?" he said. He was tumbling the clothes out every which way, searching for the bottle. "Dave'll have a little drink with us, won't you, Dave?"

"Darling," Anna said, "Dave . . ." She puckered her lips and just barely shook her head at Toby.

"Sure," David said quickly, "I'll have one."

He looked at Anna. She remembered how that same expression used to come over his face when he'd be going swimming with the other boys and his mother would say, before them, "Now you be careful, David, you know you're not strong enough to swim in deep water."

She brought out another tumbler and poured out for them

all. She put the glasses side by side and added a little to this one, then to that one, so that they all had exactly the same.

After they'd eaten, Anna said to David, "Don't you always have a nap after dinner, Dave?"

"No," he said, "no." (Please, Anna.)

"But Toby wouldn't mind, would you, Toby?"

"No," Toby said, "I wouldn't mind. Go right ahead." He wouldn't mind, but he wouldn't understand either. (Oh please, Anna.)

"I'm okay," David said.

She began to ply him with questions then. One came so fast on the heels of the other that he had scarcely time for reply.

Was Steve married? Yes. Was Ben Fancy still alive? No. Did so-and-so still live in such-and-such a place? No, they'd moved to town. Did they still have salutings? Hardly ever. Who was *that* coming up the road? Keith Wallace, they were new people. Did Old Herb Hennessey still live there by himself? Yes. Did he remember the Hallowe'en they . . .? Yes, he remembered.

And every so often she'd break into her own questions with, "How *are* you, anyway?"—as if she couldn't get over the wonder of them all being there together.

"All right," he'd answer; closing up a little, even with her, when the question concerned himself. Keeping secret, even from her, what the doctor had hinted about his heart.

"What do you hear from Chris?"

It was a question she'd put off asking. Now she couldn't bring it out easily.

"He's all right," David said. "It was only a foot wound. He's somewhere out West, working in a factory. He only stayed here a week after they sent him home."

"I don't wonder—with those two."

That was all they said. But he knew what they were both thinking. They were thinking about the scar on his face, and about Chris, of all people, being cooped up in a factory. They were thinking about the Christmas Chris had got them imaginative gifts they'd never dreamed of expecting from *him*.

Toby had got up and begun to prowl about the house.

He lifted up this thing or that and set it down again: the little knickknacks on the mantel beside the eight-day clock; the carved wooden bowl that held the curled-up snapshots . . . He twirled the big wheel of the spinning wheel in the back room . . . He lifted the cheesecloth from the butter tray that lay on the ledge of the stone fireplace and traced the clover leaf pattern of the butter mould with his finger . . . He walked to one window and looked across the pasture of the dark spruce mountain, and then to another and looked beyond the ploughed land to the orchard and the marshes in the long cut of the valley and farther off, till it was only a silver thread, the winding river. Curiously, intently, as a child explores new surroundings.

"Toby!" Anna called. "Are you *ranging* again? Dave'll think you're rude, dear"

She was only joking, but he came back into the kitchen, completely reduced. He would never get used to people saying something they didn't mean, even in a joke.

"Go to it," David laughed. "For heaven's sake, Anna, I don't care."

Toby was as instantly reassured. He wrinkled his nose at Anna and went straight back.

"Say," he called suddenly from the parlour, "Dave's got an organ."

Anna made a little gesture of helplessness. "He's happy now, he's found an *organ*."

Toby raced back to the kitchen. "Anna," he said again, "there's an organ in there!" It was Anna he addressed, but David wasn't excluded. It was the way they always spoke to each other : through her.

"I know," Anna said. "Dave can *play* it too," she added with mock slyness.

"Can you play it, Dave?" Toby said. "No kidding?"

That he could play the organ was one of the things David had always felt silly about with strangers. Somehow he didn't mind admitting it to Toby now.

"Oh, I . . . I mean . . ." he said.

"Bup, bup, bup . . . now don't mutter," Anna said. "You know darn well you can."

"Then what are we waiting for?" Toby thrust his palms out flat. Then he grasped Anna and David each by an arm and hustled them into the parlour.

"If I play, you'll have to sing," David said.

"Don't worry," Anna said, laughing. "He's dying to sing, aren't you, dear? The minute he gets a drink he's got to sing. And any other time I could coax him till . . ."

"Aw, Anna . . ." Toby said. He was completely reduced again.

"I *like* an organ," he said to David quickly, earnestly; as if David might think he was just singing to show off. "I like to sing with an organ better than anything. It wouldn't hurt to have a little tune, *would* it, Dave?"

"Sure," David said.

He meant no, but it didn't matter. The drinks were in them

dissolvingly, joiningly, now: the smooth way it is when no one seems to notice if the answer fits the question only approximately. Even if you don't answer at all it's not like silence. The thoughts of the others are all swimming along, close against your own, behind the silence. The pain in his head was like a far-off tune hummed by someone else.

But it was when Toby actually began to sing that the drink, or whatever it was, really lifted in him.

The organ was old, but its tone was good and true; and suddenly Toby's strong clean voice was singing with the organ, the same good clear way the organ sang. It was so really ringing and pure when the note went high that David felt a little chill trellis up his spine as if he'd struck his elbow.

He was sitting erect on the swivel stool. At first he felt stiff and silly. He could see his own face directly before him in the organ's circular mirror. It demarcated him, abrogated the pleasant dissolution of the drink. But when Toby began to sing, the drink began to lift in him more dissolvingly than ever. He pressed out the volume flaps with both knees, held the keys down hard. It seemed as if he himself were singing, in the organ.

And then Toby nudged him to sing too. He nudged Anna, who was holding up the coupler key that stuck from disuse, to sing. Then they were all singing together. His voice and Anna's were reedy and thin; but singing with Toby, it was as if the good clean lighthearted way Toby sang were in their voices too.

He looked at his face in the mirror. It looked filled out now and all the waiting gone from it, as a face smooths out before the fire, after it has been old looking and pinched about the mouth with sharp cold.

And singing there, all together, with the true climbing tone of the organ and the drink absolutely solvent in him now, it was a new kind of moment altogether.

They sang a few songs. Then Toby popped out and brought them in another drink. It was mid-afternoon before they went back to the kitchen.

As they passed through the narrow hallway, Anna's arm brushed Toby's hat off the the clothes rack.

David picked it up. He held it in his hand a minute, examining the gold braid on the anchor.

"Try it on, Dave," Anna said.

David put the hat on. It fitted, but the stiff weight of it felt strange. He thought how odd it must look with his faded overalls.

"No," Anna laughed, "not *straight* like that." She reached up and tilted it to one side. "There!"

David tried to strike a comic pose to cover his embarrassment.

"Say," Toby said, "that looks all *right*."

"Do you know something?" Anna exclaimed. "You two look alike. With that hat on, you look alike. Stand over there alongside each other, till I see."

Toby and David seemed to feel a sudden awkwardness then. David just smiled and hung the hat on the hook again.

When it was time for the chores, Toby went to the barn with him. But the ease of the afternoon wasn't there somehow, when they were alone with each other. They fell apart, single and separate, as two magnetized particles do when the medium which conducts the current between them is removed.

Each of them seemed to be watching a little. Toby was as intent in exploration of the barn as he'd been in exploration of the house. (How did the grab fork *reach* the hay? Did the calves have names? I guess the old cows really go for that cornmeal, eh?) But their conversation was only question and answer. It seemed tied to sober fact. Because of his best uniform Toby had to watch where he stepped; and one of them seemed always to be ducking aside to let the other pass. And when David poured out what water the calf didn't drink, into another pail (so that after three or four days the leftovers would fill it), he did it stealthily, when Toby wasn't looking. If Toby asked about it, how could he explain that, no, there was lots of water, it was just a little habit of squaring things off?

He'd been so long with only his thoughts to talk to. In the company of a second person (with no third person there also, to take away the directness between him and the other) these disengaged thoughts listened so loudly they headed off his tongue.

The mist of the drinks was thinning now. The pain pushed back through. It had an added insistence, as if he'd been disloyal to it. Going back to the house he fell in behind Toby. It seemed as if the pain were showing through the back of his head; if Toby came behind *him*, he'd feel that awful transparency.

But it was as easy as ever again that evening.

They couldn't decide what to do. Finally each wrote out a suggestion. They dropped them into Toby's hat. Toby drew one out.

"Do jigsaws!" he announced triumphantly.

"Jigsaws?" Anna said. "Toby, *you* put that crazy suggestion in there."

"*I* know," he said. "There's a whole flock of jigsaws in the closet. Swell ones."

"Toby, you *weren't* snooping in the closet!" She looked at him as if it were this constant little exasperation with him, more than anything, that made her love him so fiercely.

They cleared off the table and did jigsaws. They were all together in one thing again. There was that curious gaiety about it of adults playing at a child's pastime. Toby hummed as he scrutinized the pieces from every angle, trying, rejecting, exclaiming softly when one slipped into place. They passed pieces (not for my section but possibly for yours) back and forth, silently. Their attention was all focused outward on the puzzle. It left everything else free to flow together. None of the awkwardness of having to fit speech together or to match each other's moods was there at all.

David lingered downstairs after Toby and Anna had gone to bed.

He waited until he heard their door close. Then he tiptoed into the hall. He took down Toby's hat. He put in on his head and looked in the mirror. Then he tilted the hat to one side and assumed a gay careless smile. He thought of the free way Toby had, and of the far places. The hat doesn't look funny on me, he thought. We do look alike. It could be me . . .

"Dave," Anna called, "will you look in the big suitcase and see if I brought my face cream?"

He put the hat back on the hook as if he had been stung. She couldn't see him, but he felt as if he had been surprised in an act of indescribable foolishness.

CHAPTER XXXVI

THE next afternoon they went hunting in the old orchards.

A big American company had bought these farms solely for their timber. The company had no interest in the houses or the fields. The people had moved to town. The houses just stood there. Their doors were open and their windows broken out by hunters. The walls were still upright; but the kitchen floors sagged toward the cellar, the plaster had warped and crumbled.

They came to the old Delacey house first.

"Let's go through it," Toby said. He was excited as a child.

They went through the house. Their voices echoed hollowly

in the empty rooms. It gave Anna a funny feeling to look at the wallpaper: the pattern of roses which it had taken Mrs. Delacey so many evenings to decide on and then to hang with flour paste. It still brightened the walls, though there was no eye now to see.

Toby poked about eagerly in the closets. He popped back to show them whatever object he happened to find.

He found the lace insert from a shirtwaist front, discarded after the buttons had been cut off. ("Now who do you suppose wore that?") A yellowed letter. ("I. Was. So. Sad. To—something or other—That. Clara. Is—something—oh, yes—Gone. How. You. Must. Miss. Her. Only. Time. Will . . ."). A snowshoe. ("Look, Dave, couldn't you take that home and make a mate for it?" But he laid it down and promptly forgot it.)

"Don't look," he called once, like a child. Then he came out of a bedroom with a braided oat-straw hat, bobbing with artificial cherries, on his head. He had an old maribou stole around his neck. They laughed until Anna got hysterical.

He even found a jar of preserves. The Delaceys must have missed it when they cleaned out the pantry. "Shall we break it open," he said, "and see if they're still good?"

"No," Anna said, "let's not."

No, David thought, let's not. He didn't know why.

They went out again into the still fall sunshine.

It was a perfect afternoon, intimately warm and absolutely quiet. The sunshine plated the dry leaves on the apple trees. It poured, like rain, through their branches. It was like a fruit missed when the others were picked: now the essence of absolute ripeness, just before it drops of itself.

Nothing visited these orchards but the timid partridges, to bud in the apple trees, at dusk; and the soft-eyed deer. They had such a trigger-ready shyness in them that their eyes seemed scarcely to rest on anything for two consecutive instants or their feet to rest, quite, on the ground. There was a funny atmosphere about these abandoned fields when you came there on an afternoon like this. It was as if you had stumbled, like children in a fairy tale, on some niche that time itself had wondrously missed.

There were no partridges in the trees about the house.

"There's a back orchard," David said. "Do you want to try that?"

"You go," Anna said, "you and Toby. I'll wait here." She sat down on a sun-warmed rock in the field.

"Okay," Toby said. "Let's go, eh, Dave?"

"Okay," David said.

But he felt the constraint again. Hunting there alone, falls before, his thoughts had woven quietly in and through each other like the interstitial weavings of a puff of smoke. They'd been the perfect company. He shrank from walking back there now with someone else. These thoughts would be like a third person the other couldn't see. The obligation to talk would make an awkwardness between them.

He glanced back at Anna. She was sitting absolutely still on the rock, looking straight ahead. Her chin was cupped in one palm. He knew what she was trying to do. She was letting her mind float. She was trying to melt into the very texture of the afternoon . . . to know it completely, and so hold onto it forever.

Toby stopped to urinate as soon as Anna was out of sight. "God, it's swell back here," he said. "So darned quiet." They both stood urinating pensively. Then he added, a little self-consciously, as adult men do when they first joke together about women, "Fair place to bring a girl, eh?"

A grin came bold out of lurking, into David's eyes. He nodded. "Yeh. Wouldn't do her a helluva lot of good to yell for mother back here, would it?"

They both laughed then.

It was the way two boys laugh who have both been uncomfortable in someone's parlour, though neither's fidget is realized by the other until they are outside and one of them grimaces back at the house and exhales a prodigiously drawn-out fart. The awkwardness disappeared as suddenly as that. When two men have laughed together as they did over a joke about women they are never strangers again.

"I guess you bring all your girls back here, eh, Dave?" Toby said.

"No," David said, "I never had many girls." He didn't boast. He didn't mind admitting to Toby now that he hadn't had an awful lot to do with women. "I guess it's when you *sailors* are around that the girls have to stitch up their gussets."

"I dunno," Toby said. "Some of the boys maybe. I never broke my neck over em myself."

He said it as if women were fine and natural all right, but, hell, that wasn't the only thing there was—he couldn't be bothered chasing his legs off after it. That was the way it struck David now too. He had the good feeling then that he'd had when he tried on Toby's hat and they'd looked alike and he'd thought, it might be me.

They came to the edge of the back orchard.

"You remember Effie?" David began. "Well . . ."

But Toby grasped his arm suddenly and pointed to the partridge. It didn't matter about girls now.

The partridge trotted across the ground, darting its neck out nervously, folding and unfolding its tail. It flew before they could get a shot. They stood perfectly still, cocking their guns, their eyes on the tree. The flock in the tree began its warning twitter. They were hidden by the leaves. They twittered and then whirred all at once into flight.

Both men shot at once, and the headlong motion of two birds crumpled suddenly in midair.

David and Toby ran under the tree and picked them up. Their warm bodies huddled bonelessly, a drop of blood at the point of each beak. The men stroked the soft feathers that covered the wildness, the nervousness, they had tamed with death. They stroked them with that curious tenderness a hunter feels for the thing he kills.

And walking back to the old house again with this other who was like him, David felt the man-fibre they both shared, even with his pain, and the man-togetherness. Having spoken of and felt the same way about the thing that *made* them men, the way a man feels about a woman, there was less loneliness in him than at any other time he had walked here before. There was less loneliness, in a way, than if he were walking here with a woman; for though a woman you might love, your love was only possible because she was different. The only people who can take loneliness away are the people who are the same.

For the first time there was less awkwardness between him and Toby *without* Anna there. Nothing remained of the awkwardness except the conscience that it had all gone.

Toby held his partridge up for Anna to see, when they came in sight of her. David did the same. Anna too touched the birds tenderly; but her tenderness was of a different sort. She touched the shred of leaf still clamped in one of their beaks.

"Aw," she said, "it seems kind of a shame, doesn't it?"

There was only the newspaper in the mailbox that night. Times before when the mailman had left the paper only, David would feel the day go suddenly remote. It didn't matter tonight.

They didn't open the paper until they'd kindled the fire for supper. Then Anna spread it out on the table.

"Toby!" she exclaimed. "Here's a big picture of the *Apache!*"

"Where?" he said. He moved over to the table.

"Oh, Lord!" Anna said. "She's been sunk."

She said "sunk" as if it were a heavy word, swallowed rather than uttered; as if it turned her half sick.

"*She* has?" Toby said. His voice went casual all at once, as if Anna's discovery had turned out to be no more than an ordinary bit of news.

"Here's a picture of Rod Martin," Anna went on quickly. "Toby, isn't Rod the kid that had dinner with us last Christmas?"

"Yeh," Toby said. "Missing?" But he didn't lean over and look at the picture himself.

"Yes," Anna said. She sat down in the chair by the table. One arm was still in a sleeve of the jacket she had started to slip off. "He told me he broke that little piece off his front tooth acting smart on a bicycle," she said. "He helped me dry the dishes . . ." It might be true about the others, but there must be some mistake about Rod.

"I saw him down at the canteen a coupla nights before we left," Toby said.

Anna looked at him suddenly, as if she had a desperate need to touch him.

But he fished the back part of the paper, the part with the funnies in it, and took it over to the couch. He read it idly. It might have been a magazine he'd seen so often that now he followed the lines of the advertisements too.

David said nothing at all. He had a sense of being outside this. He felt that he shouldn't look at the paper at all.

"I'll help you get supper, Dave," Anna said, ". . . in a minute."

After supper Toby took the front part of the paper and sat in by the radio, alone. His face was no soberer than usual, but he was reading with a funny sort of brightness. He didn't get up and go to the barn with David when David went to do the chores. David had a feeling that even Anna was outside now, that there'd been nothing real about any of the afternoon before.

But no one spoke of it again, and then it was over; and the next day David and Toby went to town for the beer. That was the best day of all.

David was topping turnips on the sidehill when Toby came over after dinner.

"Dave," he said, "do you realize we're all out of beer?"

"No," David said. "Now that's bad!"

"Suppose," Toby said, "if I gave you a hand with the turnips, we could hop the bus and . . .?"

"I guess so," David said. "Sure, I guess so." For an instant he thought: I could just about finish this job by supper. He hesitated. "Unless," he said, "you hop the bus, just *you* go . . ."

"Aw, you might as well come along too," Toby said. "I'll help you finish the turnips."

So Toby got another knife, and they worked up the rows together.

He didn't have David's practiced knack. David slashed off the root tendrils, then switched the turnip end for end and severed the neck of leaves at the top with a single blow. Toby wasn't fussy about clipping the root tendrils clean. Sometimes he cut into the turnip itself. He didn't pile the tops, as David did. He just left them wherever they fell in the row. I'll have to go over his work again tomorrow, David thought.

But he slowed his own pace to match Toby's, so they could keep close enough together to talk. It made him think of times when you were a child and there was somewhere to go, but you had work; then another child pitched in and helped you so you could both go, and the simplest remarks you made to each other had a ring of exciting conspiracy. The pain was like a far-off tune again.

There wasn't much time before the bus was due. They dressed in a rush, with Anna speeding them on their way. It was like the times when he'd decide he didn't want to go to the fair in town. Then when it was too late to speak a chance with the mailman he'd want to go desperately. His mother would bustle about, like Anna did now. She'd speak a chance for him with someone else. She'd liberate him from the sulkiness with himself for having let the first chance slip by.

They called back and forth from bedroom to bedroom about what kind of beer they'd get (though there was plenty of time for that decision, on the bus), and Toby borrowed one of David's shirts. ("Sure you won't mind, Dave?" "Hell, no . . ." "You're sure?" "Sure . . .") They were like boys: making the glow of doing each other small favours and of receiving them from each other, more emphatic still, by mock remonstrance.

When they got on the bus David tried to head Toby off, buying the tickets. But Toby thrust an elbow into his ribs, grimacing with the corner of his mouth. There was a slight scuffle, and Toby paid for both.

It wasn't like getting on the bus alone.

The people in the bus all seemed friendly today. When you got on the bus alone, all the faces seemed ready to be against you. You were sitting in the bus with someone else today. You watched lazily out of the window, speaking once in a while, and clowning a little. You looked, containedly, at the strange people who got on: the way the others who had been on the bus together looked at you when *you* got on alone.

A girl two seats ahead reached down and straightened the seam in her stocking. Toby clucked his tongue softly against the roof of his mouth. David winked. They grinned at each other knowingly, both feeling the same thing about a woman's leg. The bus slid along past a man fall-ploughing on a hillside. David looked at him, not with condescension exactly, but without curiosity or identification: the way the others looked at you when they went by in the bus and *you* were ploughing alongside the road.

On the way back, each had a carton of beer under his arm. There was another scuffle for the tickets. This time David won. And all the way home, all through the bus, they were the focus of that unreasonable little sense of amusement which the sight of two people bringing home something to drink always provokes.

It was nothing more than that. And afterward David wondered what had been so special about it.

Until it came to him all at once: there hadn't been any *thinking* about it. He hadn't thought about the way it was, at all, all the time. Even the thinking that the awkwardness had all gone was gone too.

It must be like that with all the people who had friends. It must be like that with all the people who didn't get on the bus alone. Everything in his life had been black and white before. Now, for the first time, there was colour.

CHAPTER XXXVII

ONE day toward the end of Toby's leave, he and Anna went in to see Ellen, between buses.

They hadn't sent word that they were here: that would bring her straight home. They had all agreed it'd be a shame to break up her vacation (and, though the motive was not consciously admitted, their unit of just three). "But we couldn't go back without seeing her," Anna said. "If anything should happen . . ." To her . . . or to Toby? It was a sentence that she never finished, even in her mind.

When they asked David to go too, he made an excuse that the butcher might come to look at his fat steer. He wanted to be alone today. Alone the *good* way: cosily, protectedly, with the thought of the others coming back at night. Something formless was swarming in his mind. He must be delivered of it—by seeing its shape projected onto the scribbler page.

Every so often he must milk his mind like this. If he didn't, it felt fetid with the decay of infant ideas, born with all their features but never freed to breath . . . or else dry and rattling with their bones, like the skeletons of beetles cocooned in the corner of the window sash.

He watched the bus go out of sight. Then he brought his scribbler and pencil out to the kitchen table.

He knew, without seeking, what his subject would be today.

This would be a boy who knew what everything was like. Who knew exactly about . . . well, for instance, war. He'd never seen a war, but that didn't matter. He knew whenever he saw two soldiers walk down the street how it was with them : Some quickness kept flowing—no, *running*—from their uniforms into their faces.

He made a note : "a quickness kept running into their faces."

And immediately the first was released, other facets of that picture came tumbling on its heels : "Danger joined them like an extra kind of health." "The distance from them to the other people in the street was greater than the step between . . ."

He felt the excitement he always felt when the crust of an idea was first broken, when the first sentence lay outside him. But, as always, one sentence accomplished didn't leave that much less to be told. The idea fronded suddenly like a million-capillaried chart of the bloodstream. He felt the panic of having to encompass every bit of it.

How could he do it, to get it all in?

Could this boy be telling, maybe, what he saw when he looked at the pictures of war?

Or wait, no. Why couldn't you make it sound as if it were this boy's *own* face in all the pictures?

It wouldn't be credible, but he was telling it that way because (this wouldn't come out till the end—yes, *yes*, that was the way to do it) he was . . . sick; he'd never been *any*where, but he had to make them believe it was his face in all the pictures, so he could have the war over with. He couldn't have it over with, like the others who'd been there and returned got it over with, unless they believed he knew how every bit of it was. You could put in somewhere, "Are you listening?" Yes, that'd be the title : "Thanks for Listening."

A whole line came to him, out of nowhere. He didn't know where it would fit, but he wrote it down. "Maybe you didn't recognize me sometimes because a face looks different with the blood on the outside . . ."

You'd start out with going away: One time the picture showed him with his girl, and one time with his wife. It was easier somehow to leave the wife than the girl, because when it was the wife the other things were all in *her* somehow, and when he remembered her that took care of everything at once. How desperately hard they tried that last minute to ... to ... "to drain the whole draught of the her-and-me."

He said the phrase out loud. It was true. It was his. He felt like crying. Oh, it was wonderful, to be able to do a thing like this ...

Then the great flurry of how it was with *everything* blizzarded inside his head, the things that *always* came to him after the first line: How you could love the land's face and the day's face, but how they never loved you back; the sun would come out brighter than usual the day your father died, and the wind would cut, as blind and relentless as ever, the night your brother was lost in the woods ... How a man could be trapped by his own nature ... How, though you cut open his flesh you still couldn't penetrate the skin of separateness each man walked around in ... How this place had aged, with change ... How the knitted warmth between its people had ravelled, until each was almost as alone in his own distraction now as the city people were ...

He shook his head, as if to scatter a swarm of gnats. He came back to the single thing he'd chosen to say today. He put together the lines of it in his head. He saw the very script of them there. He added there, erased there, got them almost as they must stay, before he wrote them down on the paper.

(If I tell you about the time I saved a battle, don't think I'm trying to sound brave. I'm just trying to tell it truly. I *was* brave that day, though. I needn't have crept up to throw the grenades into their ammunition pile. I was alone. No one would have known I'd seen that chance. I could have crept the other way. I thought of that. No matter where you are there's nothing like staying alive. But I didn't. And after they gave me the medal in the picture I'd make wisecracks about it with the other guys, but sometimes I'd touch the ribbon in the dark, like the first prize I won at school ...

And do you remember the quiet picture on deck that morning of the invasion, the morning we had the bread and wine before the battle? The very-white of the padre's garments and the bare cross against the sun on the sea looked sort of beautiful, didn't they? Well, that was a true picture. We'd been cursing before, and we'd be cursing after, but I think we were glad to

255

do this thing together. I think our rough feet knew enough to tread gently then . . .)

Or would that make him sound like he was a soft guy? He wasn't a soft guy, that had to be plain.

(One night we were talking about what we wanted most when we came back. When it came *my* turn I said what I wanted most was to jump square-footed into one of those goddammed apple pies we were all over here fighting for. They laughed a new way then, and I knew I was all right with them. It was the best feeling in the world to know that it wouldn't do for any *outside* guy to kid me for being small.

And there were the girls. Sometimes there'd be two or three of us, and two or three girls, and it wasn't any tea party. We were young and no one was going to keep anything away from us we felt like; and we did it because it was the one thing we were all alike in and doing together in a strange land where one of us would have been lost by himself . . .)

He had never felt as fluent as today. He felt complex, manifold, *furnished.* It was just the opposite to what he felt when others were there : so much simpler and less intricate than they.

He tightened for a minute when he came to the part where this boy's friend was killed beside him, and the part where his friend saw *him* die. But then it came right out, quickly and whole. So much smoother than the rest that what had gone before seemed all elbows, yoked down with the wrong words like a clumsy translation.

(We were always together, Tony and I. The sea was in us both, like a song we knew the tune of, but never the words. The land was fine. You looked ahead to it. But when you got there it was always a little like coming home and finding the others gone. If the sea is in both of you like that, you stick together like the only two people who speak the same tongue in a strange country.

There was no picture the morning Tony died. I don't think there was anything a picture would have shown. We were there alone and Tony's breath was tracing a tune, when the bullet came. I saw all the hearing and the seeing and the touching go out of him like a breeze. All at once the breath with the soft tune on it went I don't know where. I saw the strange whisper of death on his face even before his body fell to the deck.

I said, "Tony!" but I knew. And then after I knew, I put my arm beneath his shoulder before I called the others, and I said "Tony" again.

And I suppose when I said "Tony" the second time I meant all the bright times we'd had because we were young together in a place where death was jealous of our breath. I suppose I meant the first moment of never-again dark on the day. I suppose I meant the wonder that his flesh was no lighter for all that had gone from it. I suppose I meant that he was dead, but that somehow I'd save his part of the pain and the laughing in the world for him always, fiercely somewhere, where it could never be lost . . . I don't think we were fighting for liberty or justice or any fancy things like that in this war. I think we were fighting for the guy next us . . .

And I remember the morning it came to me. I had more time than Tony. There had been pain, and now there was no pain, so I knew. But Tony was such a good guy to have with you then that there was hardly any thinking at all.

For Tony had done all the things, even the ones you'd missed. He'd been in all the places—even this one, so it couldn't be a strange place for the young. And so there was no evening part to it, and you didn't think of the springs that would come again, for someone else. Because it was the first time you had ever seen Tony quiet like this. You knew it was the same way with him now that it was with you that other day, when it was your arm and his breath. And in a minute like that when it's clear how another can have for you the things you might have had for yourself, the meaning of everything else is clear too. That's why the day didn't seem dark or too soon . . .)

It was getting late. He forgot that it was time for the bus. He tore the pages out of the scribbler and read them over. He sat there, with the luxurious feeling of being spent with accomplished expression.

He didn't hear the bus stop. He didn't see Toby and Anna until they came in the door. He felt that instant denuding when he saw them. The mirror of his consciousness was stripped of everything but the reflection of his own face: pale, tentative, and struck with the long burning scar.

He tried to scrabble the pages together and get them out of sight before Toby reached the table. But one fluttered to the floor. Toby picked it up.

"What are you writing, Dave?" he said, laughing. "Love letters or your will?" He began to read aloud. " 'When they write the story of this war, no one will mention me. No one guessed that any of those faces was mine . . .' What the . . .?"

David grabbed the sheet from his hand almost savagely. If Toby read what he'd written, he thought he'd die. The whole thing seemed unutterably shameful. How could he have put down anything so damned sickly and foolish? War was about as much like that as . . . He opened the stove and thrust the papers into the flames.

"What *were* you writing, Dave?" Toby pressed him, half amused, half baffled, "a story or something?"

David saw Anna shake her head.

"Nothing," he said. He turned quickly to Anna. "How was Grandmother?"

"Fine," Anna said. "Bless her, she was so glad to see us."

"She was swell," Toby said.

"She kept saying Toby reminded her of someone. She couldn't seem to drop it," Anna said. She hesitated. "Dave, she looks well, but, I mean . . . do you think her mind, a little . . . ?"

"No," David said. "Only she forgets."

"Ahhhhhh," Toby groaned pleasurably. "How about a beer?"

"Okay," David said. "Sure."

They had a beer. And a second. And a third. And along about the fourth beer, with Toby and Anna there, David reread the story off his mind. The validity crept back into it all over again.

CHAPTER XXXVIII

THAT was Tuesday, and this was Thursday. Today Toby and Anna were walking up the winding road that went to the top of the mountain.

David had wanted to go too; but he had known, even as they coaxed him to come, that it was a day when the man-and-wife feeling between them was a thing explicit. It was a day for *them* to be alone. He said he had to stay home and bank the pigpen and the stable—an early snow might come any time.

They were walking up the winding road that went to the top of the mountain. Leaving the fields behind, and the houses and the people in the valley and the restless river that moved in and out with the tide. There were only three days left before Toby went back to his ship, but the shadow of his going away wasn't heavy on the days yet. They didn't speak about his going away at all.

The first grey days of November were past, when the earth lay defeated and colourless and old; and today it was suddenly warm again. Not the sad October warmth, the pale gold hanging in the air of the gently dying afternoons, but like the hopeful spring warmth again. It was Indian Summer.

Pools of dead leaves lay ankle deep in the log road, rusty and dry. The sun was all over in the bright blue sky. It smiled on the needles of the spruces and slid down the pale silver poplars. It settled warm and steady on the dry leaves and the grey rocks. There was a strange sound of stillness about it all. As if the pine needles and the dead leaves and the grey rocks and the clean-smelling brook with the pole bridge they passed over were all singing together a quiet song, like the drowsy hum of wires or of bees. It was as if all the things of the earth were meeting together in reprieve, before each of them died its own separate way.

At the foot of the mountain they began to walk through the spruces. The spruces had a thick safe smell. They were like a cushion between them and the valley where the people talked and moved and the nervous river ran. They soaked in the sunshine and the stillness and kept it close. And through the spruces Anna could see nothing.

She could see nothing but Toby's face. His dark skin, darkly pale with health beneath the moist-looking hair, and a good look in his eyes when he laughed. She knew it was the one face for her among all the others. She had never been so sure of that as she was today. It had been wonderful since they were home here. They had sloughed off the city way. He hadn't left her once. She hadn't had to watch at all.

And now in the centre of the safe woods-stillness, shut out from everything but the road that wound up to the top of the mountain, she didn't think about his going away. That didn't seem real. This seemed like the shut-in time of a dream. It didn't seem real that in three days someone would be trying to kill him.

They stopped for a cigarette, sitting close together on a flat stone. I could reach out and touch his face, she thought. Flesh, she thought, there's nothing quite like it. There's nothing quite like Toby's strong young flesh to have near me in the quiet woods.

They didn't talk much. Their thoughts had an almost antiphonal, churchy sound in their heads, with the spell of the day. Ordinary words didn't quite fit them. They were silent as children are, in a place so enchanting that they don't trust themselves to speak about it, because it is splendid beyond anything they've been used to at home.

They looked at their cigarettes soberly; blowing out pale funnels of smoke and watching them spread and melt away in the calm air. One dwarf maple in the clearing still clung stubbornly to its topknot of flame. The leaves swayed a little, absently, but there was no breeze you could feel.

"It's perfect here, isn't it?" Anna said at last.

"It sure is," Toby said.

"It *is* perfect, though, isn't it?" she said. "You couldn't want it any better than this."

"We should have brought the gun along," he said. "There might be a deer."

"No," she said. " I wouldn't want to shoot a deer today, Toby."

Hunting had been fine yesterday. She hadn't thought of weariness, tramping after the wounded buck and looking for traces of blood on the leaves, and somehow you didn't think of the buck, sick and puzzled and bleeding in the dark. But she didn't like to think of blood on the leaves today.

"This is Thursday," he said, "isn't it? Thursday . . . Friday . . . Sat—"

"This is Thursday," she said quickly, "all day." Friday and Saturday couldn't get at this afternoon yet. Nothing could get at it through the dark quiet spruces. She looked at the road, winding up and out of sight to the top of the mountain.

There was no sound but their quiet breathing. The woods didn't seem to be breathing this afternoon, but she supposed it must be going on, very softly. It was funny about breathing, she thought. It went on steadily, keeping you alive, but you weren't conscious of it at all. It was like being with Toby. Just being together with him made all the difference in the world, even if neither of you said a word, and you didn't have to think about it at all. But when you did stop to think of being alive with Toby, it was sort of wonderful.

"You know something?" she said. "I'm absolutely sure I love you."

"Well?" he said.

"Nothing. I just wanted to say it."

He looked at her and laughed, completely puzzled.

"I could kiss you if I wanted to, couldn't I?" she said.

"I don't see why not," he said. "Say, what is this?"

"Oh, don't look so scared," she said. "I'm not going to. But I *could*. That's all I was thinking about."

She looked at him, with the smile—incredulous, enveloping, and somehow idolatrous—that she always had for him whenever she pointed out some vagary of his that he couldn't be made to see was anything out of the ordinary. As if these vagaries centred him in a kind of light, that she stood at the edges of and absorbed a funny kind of warmth from.

"Last night when we were doing that crossword puzzle, you

said a seven letter word for 'opulence' was 'wealthy'! You
tried it: w-e-a-l-."

"What if I did?" he said.

"Nothing," she said. "But you did."

"It could have been," he said.

"No, it couldn't have been," she laughed. " 'Wealthy' is the
adjective."

"I know," he said. "But some of those things are cock-eyed."

He didn't see. He was never right about little things like that.
He had the same artless way about these puzzles that he had
about everything. They'd had a lot of silly fun over these
puzzles they'd never think of bothering with in the city. They
had a lot of silly fun together that other people never had at all.
I love him, she thought, and I could touch him. The dry leaves
swayed quietly on the branch, as if they were remembering a
breeze, faintly.

They threw their cigarettes away and went along the road
that wound up to the top of the mountain.

Now it was steeper, and they were leaving the spruces behind. There was nothing but hardwood when they came nearer
the top. The bare hardwood gave a light-spreading feel of
space. The straight pillars of birch and the great worn maples
locked their branches as they reached into the sky, their quiet
shadows laced together on the ground. There was age and
strength in the hardwood, with the still spaces among the bare
limbs clean as shavings. She could see a long way through the
bare limbs, but not beyond them. And through the hardwood
with the clean warm-grey limbs was the winding path their
feet would take to the top of the mountain.

As they left the valley farther and farther behind, the valley
didn't seem real. The spruces were between them and the
valley, keeping the time safe. And now, with the climbing
steeper, a lightness lifted in her heart. It was like the swimming
peace of wine.

"Do you want to go to the top?" he said.

"Oh yes," she said. "Let's go right to the top. You can look
down over the whole valley."

She could feel the muscle of his arm, hard and warm through
the sleeve of his jacket, as he held it lightly.

He was thinking. They didn't know he ever stopped to think,
but he did. It's nice up here, he was thinking. There's a sort of
haze about it. It's almost like dreaming. It must be very still
here when there's no one on the road. It wouldn't be any fun to
walk up here alone. Her face is small and happy. Her face is
soft and gets broken so easily There's a soft smell to her hair,

like a child's hair. She has kind of a dreamy way to her thinking, I guess that's the woman's way. She lives a lot of ways a man doesn't even know about, like a child. A man has to keep a woman safe, like he would a child. A woman is always like a child. I won't like her eyes when I go away, like the whole world was a wind or something blowing against her face. I'm only a man. I have only one way of thinking and I can't do anything to help her. They'll be like a child's eyes outside the window. Her face is small and happy now, though. We've been together, and now the man's way or the woman's way alone isn't enough for either of us. It's a funny thing you can't think through, the way it is with a man and a woman. A man has no way of thinking it out. A man doesn't have to think about it at all. But this is nice, he thought . . . touching her arm, and the child's smell of her hair, and the bare maples happening here along the road that goes to the top of the mountain . . . Indian Summer is the nicest time of all.

They were coming near the top now, bending more as the climbing became steeper still.

"Sometimes it's nice and quiet like this when we're out at sea," he said.

"No, Toby, it can't be. I don't like the sea."

The sun was overhead and the stillness was loud and moist-smelling and clean. The trees were thinning now but, looking back, they covered the side of the mountain like a great blanket; and you couldn't see where the road wound up and through them. It was as if the road had escaped at last out of the valley, up and through the trees, and found the safe quiet place it was looking for.

Anna felt a strange excitement, as if she too were coming to the peak of the day. It was like the Christmas so long ago when David gave her the little ring with the bright red stone. (What ever became of it? she thought. I should have kept it as long as I lived.) The tree was in and the room trimmed and the nuts and candy in the bowls; and there was an hour left before supper for her and David to talk, hushed with the smell of the tree, about something each knew the other was getting, but refusing to disclose what it was. An hour when everything was ready for Christmas, but before time had begun to eat into Christmas Eve itself.

Then they were really at the top of the mountain, standing close together in the flat clearing beneath the single great pine, looking down over the whole valley. Down over the hardwood and the dark back of the spruces, over the patches of pasture and field, and so far-off and soundlessly the houses and the dark thread of the road, and further still the silver-twisting thread of the river. It was like the intactile landscape of a dream. Tiny specks of cars moved in and out of sight along the thread of road, but not hearing them, it didn't seem as if they were real.

And standing alongside her own husband's flesh beneath the single cool pine at the top of the mountain, looking down through the Indian Summer air over the long steep wall of trees to the sun-soaked valley where the houses looked like houses in a stereoscope and the people made no sound, the life they'd left in the valley seemed like a dream. It seemed as if this minute on the top of the mountain they'd been climbing to was the peak of her whole life.

She drew a quick breath and her heart lifted inside her.

It lasted, and she couldn't speak. And Toby didn't speak. It lasted for one long minute.

Then for the first time she felt a small breeze starting, against her cheek; and the fear came. The fear came all at once. As it used to do when she was a child and had been too happy. She saw the look on her own face, small and pale, as if she had glimpsed it suddenly, passing a mirror.

She knew that Toby was going away.

She stood perfectly still until he spoke. It seemed a long time before he spoke.

"Well," he said, "shall we start down again? Or do you want to rest a while?"

"No," she said, "we might as well go now."

And then they were going down the mountain and it began to turn cold and she knew that Toby would be leaving tomorrow. They would never have the other two days together at all. The time began to go. This would be the last day; and the day before the going is shadowed with the going, so that there is no free time left.

It was different, going down the mountain.

The sun began to move strange down the sky. The sky changed, as if all the summer life had gone out of it. It was blue and strange, like the sea. The sea would be in Toby's mouth, when he could swim no longer. She hated the sea. The sky was cold and lonely and had no breath in its blue lips, and the broken fingers of the trees couldn't reach up to touch it. The sun crept cold into the cores of the trees. The whole afternoon seemed full of all the things that lived without feeling or breath: the mateless sun and the memoryless trees and the tired road and the bruised sky and the chill breeze that was the breath of all the dead things in the world, moving bare as a ghost among the withered leaves.

"It's turning cold, don't you think?" Toby said. "Do you feel it?"

"Yes," she said, "there's a cold breeze."

She drew her jacket tighter about her. It was a jacket of Toby's, with the cuffs rolled up. She had on a pair of David's work gloves, that her hands were lost in. The happiness in her face had given a comical air to the clothes, coming up. But now these clothes gave their definition to her. She looked small inside them. As a child looks small who has no *other* clothes but the discards, always cruelly too large, of someone else.

"And it was so *darned* nice a little while ago," Toby said. "Indian Summer. It's treacherous."

They came to the hardwood again, going down. The trees were weary and separate now. They were memoryless and old. The pale sunlight falling through their grey branches was like the gaunt hiding place of death. She shivered, although the air wasn't cold enough to make her shiver.

"Tired?" he said.

"No," she said, "I'm not tired."

She didn't want to talk. Her voice had an empty sound to her, and it was hard to find any words at all.

"It won't take long to go back," he said. "We can walk faster, and it always seems to be shorter going back, did you ever notice that?"

The time was going fast now, and there was no way to stop it. It was going so fast she couldn't think.

Then they were at the stone again where they had sat and smoked. She saw the crumpled ends of their cigarettes. She picked up the dead cigarettes and put them into her pocket. He laughed at her. It was really cold now.

"What was *that* for?" he said.

"Those were the cigarettes we smoked, going up," she said.

"I know *that*," he said; but she couldn't explain.

"Look," he laughed, "the breeze has taken off those last three leaves. Don't you want them too?"

"Will you wait?" she said. "You wait, won't you? Don't walk ahead."

"Of course I won't silly. Don't look so scared."

"No," she said, "never mind. I couldn't find the right ones. I don't want them." She took the crumpled cigarette ends out of her pocket again, and dropped them in the road.

They were coming into the valley now, and as they came nearer and nearer the end of the road, the time went faster and faster . . . the little time of the last day. There was nothing you could do to stop it, and she was frightened.

"You're shivering," he said. "Are you cold?"

"No," she said, "I'm not cold. Are you cold?" The short useful sentences were the only ones she could find. A great cold stone was rolled in the path of her thinking.

The time was going now and there was no safe day left between tonight and tomorrow.

"Anna," he said, "is something wrong? You're so . . . I don't know what. What's wrong?"

"It was just Indian Summer," she said.

"What?" he said. "*What* was just Indian Summer?"

"There's nothing wrong, Toby," she lied. "Really there isn't."

He doesn't know, she thought. He doesn't know at all, and I can't tell him. It's too late now to say anything. You can't remember how to say anything at the last but the short wooden sentences. The city talk is gone altogether. If there's anything that should be said, it's too late to say it now, because the numbness is there like the winter in the hardwood with the darkness coming to it now, unspeaking. You can only try to keep your eyes off his face.

They came to the spruces again, going down. In the spruces it was really dark. It was hard to see the road. She stumbled. The great ashen darkness seemed to puff out of the spruces like smoke; and if you stepped off the road into them you'd be lost at once and they woudn't hear your cries. She thought of the buck they had wounded yesterday, sick and puzzled and bleeding in the dark.

They came nearer and nearer the valley, passing the brook that separated the valley from the mountain. Thin splinters of ice needled out from the sides of the brook, and under the pole bridge it made a shivering night sound as it ran.

Then they had left the road altogether and were out in the level fields.

It was lighter in the fields, but looking back, the mountain was a single great cloud of night, and the road they had travelled was all swallowed up. She wondered how they had found they way down it at all.

She could see the house now, waiting for them. And walking toward it, she dreaded it, like some dumb hostile thing. She hated the way their footsteps kept shortening the distance from it, steadily.

It was like the time David was delirious with fever when he was a child and she would play outside as long as she could possibly see, trying to forget a little as she played the coal at her heart. Trying to make herself believe that nothing could happen to him as long as she kept the sun and the fields and the mountain in sight *for* him. But when it came dark she could think of nothing else but going back into the house, where the silence was that would mean he was no better; and as she'd come nearer and nearer the door, it was like it was now.

David was in the stable. The mailman had brought a registered letter for Toby. He had signed for it and propped it up against the dipper, in the centre of the kitchen table.

Toby guessed what the message in the official envelope would be before he opened it, and when he read it the few words were perfectly clear. But he read them over and over. He didn't like to take his eyes from them, to tell her.

"I've got to go back, Anna," he said at last. "Tomorrow."

"I know," she said. "I knew it."

"But how could you know?"

She didn't answer. But she put her hands on his face and her mouth hurt, because she knew that after tomorrow she would never see his face again.

"You'll have to catch the *morning* bus," she said.

CHAPTER XXXIX

TOBY took the morning bus to town. The train would bring him back past the farm, but there was no station here. Anna didn't go to Halifax with him. It would be easier to go back alone to their rooms in Halifax from here, than from the waterfront.

The bus was due at eleven-thirty.

Breakfast talk started out the same as always; but as the morning wore on, it slackened. It became two hours and then one hour before the bus was due. Then the conversation seemed to run down entirely. It seemed as if Toby and Anna had used up all the last-minute things too soon. Now there was nothing to do but watch the clock and the road.

They had an early dinner. As soon as the dishes were cleared away, David invented chores for himself outdoors. He felt the spectator's subtle banishment and guilt. Though when he did come into the house there didn't seem to be anything private going on between Toby and Anna: no kissing or confidences.

They just kept moving about, from room to room. They glanced at each other awkwardly, as if they didn't want to let each other out of sight, but as if there was no way they could and close enough together to stop the bus from coming.

The packing was finished. Anna had folded Toby's clothes

in the suitcase as soberly as if she were composing someone's limbs. The suitcase stood, accusing, in the centre of the kitchen floor; as if *it* were what had betrayed them.

The clock struck eleven. Toby put on his greatcoat and picked up his hat. They both looked at each other as if, if they'd only realised *before* that soberness was a more binding thing than smiling . . .

"Have you got your scarf?" Anna said, though his scarf was in plain sight about his neck.

"Yes," Toby said.

Then after a little she said, "You're sure you've got your pen?"

She'd asked him that, but he put his hand to his inside pocket once more.

The unfinished jigsaw puzzle had been transferred from the kitchen table to the centre table in the front room. One of them would pick up a piece of the jigsaw now and then, in passing, and try to fit it in somewhere; but the piece was never the right one. Then one would move to the sink, taking a sip of water from the dipper; or to the fireplace, lifting up an object from the mantelpiece; or to the window, looking down the road; and after a minute the other would move alongside. But they wouldn't stand in any one place long. There was no place in the house they could find to stand that would stop the bus from coming.

David carried the suitcase to the road. He watched for the bus there, by himself.

When the bus shot into sight, coming fast around the far corner, he ran in and tapped on the window. Toby signalled okay to him, but he didn't come out at once. The bus was rushing closer. David tapped again. Toby came to the door, then turned. David saw his arms reach out. The bus was almost opposite the house. Toby dashed out then. He gave David a glancing handshake as he ran to the road. "Good luck," David said, and Toby called back, "Okay, boy, thanks for everything."

The bus slowed down and Toby got on. Its motor idled a minute while Toby bought his ticket. Then it picked up volume, and the bus began to creep away. And then, gathering speed all at once, the bus went faster and faster around the corner out of sight.

Anna was still standing at the window when David went into the house. She didn't turn. She just said, "Was the bus crowded?"

"No," David said, "not bad."

He went to the shop and picked up his hack and went over to the field next the railway cut.

The train would pass this field. Toby will be looking toward the house, he thought. He'll see me. We'll wave to each other, and I can tell Anna that Toby waved to us.

He was at the top of a row when he heard the noise of the train. He ran down to the bottom, close to the tracks.

But when the great nose of the train came in sight, thundering nearer and nearer the cut, the old awkwardness came back. He dropped down on one knee, pretending to tie his bootlace. When Toby sees me, he thought, he'll wave. Then I'll look up, as if I just *happened* to be here, and wave back.

Toby wasn't in the first car, but he saw him in the second, clearly. He was walking ahead through the train with another sailor. As the train came opposite the field, he turned to the other sailor and said something. Both of them appeared to laugh. He doesn't have to wait with them, like he does with others, David thought.

He stood up straight then, and waved.

But Toby didn't glance once, not once, toward the house or the field. The train went by.

David stood rooted in the row. He leaned on the hack he'd brought with him to dig out the stubborn parsnips. He followed the train with his eyes. The train wound quickly through the cut. The grey cloud of its smoke thinned and settled over the trees. The clucking of its rails became a far-off clatter. And then the whistle of the train blew ever so distantly for the next station, and the whole train had disappeared from the day.

A hollowness sucked suddenly against his breath. Toby's knife still lay there, abandoned beside the carelessly topped turnips . . . and Toby had gone away in the train. All the thinking came back in a rush.

But the panic wasn't only that the one friend he'd ever had had gone away. It was more than that. *It was always someone else* that things happened to, that was the panic of it . . .

He looked at the apple trees he had pruned to such perfect shape, and so proudly, in the spring that was gone. A baring and frightening light shone suddenly on his own life. It was like a strip of daybreak striking down a long naked corridor.

This was the toppling moment of clarity which comes once to everyone, when he sees the face of his whole life in every detail. He saw then that the unquestioned premise all his calculations had been built on was false. He realized for the first time that his feet must go on in their present path, because all the crossroad junctions had been left irretrievably far behind.

Anything your own hands had built, he had always thought, your own hands could destroy. You could build a wall about yourself, for safety's sake, but whenever you chose you could level it. That wasn't true, he saw now. After a while you could beat against the wall all you liked, but it was indestructible. The cast of loneliness became pitted in your flesh. It was as plain for others to see and shy away from as the slouch of a convict.

I will always be a stranger to everybody, he thought—the others know that I don't know what any of their things is like. My own life brimmed and emptied so soon, and I could never fill it again.

A montage of all the things he had never done with someone else flashed on the screen of his brain. Then they fragmented into pictures. Each one was realized completely and simultaneously in a single instant, as a whole day's happenings may pass in the elastic time of a moment's dream. The tidy little pleasures he'd had by himself—the pleasures that had tricked him—shrivelled like dried peas.

He had never gone on a fishing trip with them, sitting sidewise in the front seat so he could clown with the ones in back, leaning over to cramp their knee tendons with his grip, when they pretended they were going to stop the car and open his fly the next girl they came to . . . No man had ever shouted, in a mock argument when everyone was drinking, "Where's Dave? Where's Dave?" and then come over and put an arm over his shoulder and said, confidentially, "Dave . . . listen . . . now tell us the truth. Did you ever know me to . . . ?"

No woman had ever been watching for him when he was late for a meal or late from town or late from anything else —scaring herself deliberately (so she could flush the consciousness of what their belonging to each other really meant to her) with the thought, what if anything has happened to him? . . . He would never, never now, sit with a wife and child at the school closing, with the child's gamin face lit up and the water glistening on his subdued hair but his eyes flagging a little when he wasn't called up for any prize . . . or, for some reason, put his arm about this woman when they'd come across a wilted thistle (not a bunch of daisies or a sheaf of goldenrod, but a thistle) that the child had toted around through the whole day's trip, in a broken preserve bottle. . . .

No, nor never stand, never now, and watch a child watch the train of the circus they couldn't afford to go see in town pass through the cut, with the child's face hurting him more than anything he had ever felt, and yet everything else in the world suddenly devaluated beside the exaltation of the child's belonging to him . . . He would never keep repeating, "Did you see it plain?" after the deer ran across the clearing, so that each time the child answered "Oh yes!" the child could have the excitement all over again . . .

He stood there immobile.

There had been a war, but he hadn't been in it. There had been these things while he was alive and young, but they'd all been for other men. The trains had all gone by. The grey smoke settled on the fields and he was standing there alone, with a hack.

They went away to war and maybe they'd never come back. There was always that maybe-the-last-time brightness rushing along with them in the trains. It bonded them together. They went with the trains, laughing and thoughtless. They took with them all the life from the valleys they left, but they didn't see that. They never stayed at the station to see the grey smoke settling on the faces of the people turning home, settling on the bare fields.

And what if Rod *is* dead today? You had a drink with him last night. And the sadness isn't the same when you drink again tonight as though you'd known each other some other way. This drink tonight has a funny brightness, because the one you're drinking with knew Rod too. The little badge of maybe-the-last-time that neither of you can see except on the other burns brighter still. They forget Rod, he thought. They remember their wives and their friends. But it's the funny way they remember Rod all the time, even when he's out of mind, that's real. The way their wives cry and their friends miss them has no part in it like that at all.

He thought of Toby at the pulse of all this, with a fierce jealousy. It had *always* been like that for Toby. They went away together in the trains, but it wasn't like the way they rode with you in the bus. They sang the sailor's hymn on the deck, that day of the big morning, but it wasn't like the singing in the parlour that day. There was incongruous brightness about it being a hymn (like "Aged 17" on the tombstone that day) and about Rod not being there now who had had a drink with you when death was at his elbow. The little things of the farm had been fun for Toby, but they were things for a leave only. Now they were nothing to him. Toby had never talked to him about the day of the big morning. He was outside . . .

A hard ball of new misery came at him (as if he were a figure shot at in the booth of a fair, one with sentience no one knew about). It struck him and set his lips working: he had been Toby's friend *here*, but that would mean nothing to Toby now.

He'd never had that little badge, he'd never had a drink with any of the Rods . . .

He fought back with desperate, foolish plans.

When Toby comes back, he thought, I'll do something to put *him* outside, something *he*'ll be jealous of . . . But then he knew that nothing he could ever do would put Toby outside as *he* was outside this. He knew that even if Toby was killed—more than ever, if Toby should be killed—he was beaten.

He heard Toby's voice, as clearly as if he were there, singing the sailor's hymn that morning clear and strong above all the others voices. A blind hatred of Toby went through him. It seemed as if that were a part of his own life he was seeing—his life stolen before his eyes, and drawn away just fast enough that he was always a step behind when he gave chase. It wasn't fair. His face was like Toby's . . . the hat didn't look funny on him . . .

A wild longing possessed him. He *had* to be inside, singing on the deck that day of the big morning, with the little badge that was invisible except to the others on him too . . . He *had* to be inside and, cruelly as they and as thoughtlessly, put everyone else outside . . . leave even wives to cry, with that beautiful thoughtless cruelty. They walked ahead in the trains, together. They didn't do some chore, carefully, at dusk, with no one there.

He looked about the field. The afternoon was grey and still with the train gone. He looked about like someone looking for a place to run, the blind way people run out of doors when their clothes are on fire.

The thought of the night chores came to him: filling the coffee tin to the second nail scratch with middlings because the calf was now two months old; dipping the cracked corn for the hens from the wooden box he'd built to hold just enough from one feed delivery day to the next; straining the milk into the creamer if the mess seemed smaller than usual, as if by straining it slowly he could make it rise higher; wondering if it would rise high enough to surface exactly level with the glass gauge on the side . . . And, later, the book he'd be reading. The damned, airless, tricking book . . . They walked ahead in the trains—there was always that company, that maybe-the-last-time brightness—and the smoke of the train settled behind them and the train of your own life went by and left you standing there in the field.

A sudden gust of tears surged against his breath. It broke with a little cluck. He caught his lower lip hard between his teeth.

His face puckered as if all its nerves had been struck at once. The scar burned white as moonlight in the chill afternoon.

"Damn you," he shouted to Toby, "I'm not crying for you ..."

And then he raised the hack high above his head, till the pain of his head ran freely down his arm and down his whole side. He moved for the first time. Quickly, almost running, he rushed up the row with a wild comical stagger. He slashed at the pulpy flesh of the parsnips blindly, wherever the hack fell, the whole length of the long even row.

And then the hack was still in his hands again, and in his mind there was only a stillness like the stillness of snow sifting through the spokes of the wagon wheels or the moonlight on the frozen road or the dark brook at night when the children have all taken their laughing home ...

It was dusk when Anna called him to supper.

He was on his knees, patting the torn flesh of the parsnips back into shape as best he could. Maybe if he put sods around them in the cellar, they wouldn't spoil. There was no trace of thinking on his face now. Nothing but the crusted smudge of a tear track he had wiped at with his dusty hand.

He glanced at Anna's face when he came into the kitchen. She didn't look as if she had cried at all.

"Weren't you cold, Dave," she said, "with just that thin jacket on?"

"No," he said, "I didn't mind it."

They didn't mention Toby. They moved about as if each were clumsy with some secret guilt.

They sat down to the table and Anna picked up her fork.

And then—what was there about starting to eat the first meal alone?—she dropped the fork and began to sob. Totally, collapsing, like a child you can do nothing to distract.

"Don't cry, Anna," David said softly. "He'll be all right." He hesitated. "He waved to us," he said.

Anna's disordered face shifted back into shape again with a single movement. She gathered up her breath. She brushed away the betraying tears with one hand. Her face composed itself into such quiet it had a blunted look.

"Did the potatoes get done?" she said. She drew in her breath quickly whenever the words threatened to break. "I don't know, I don't seem to have much *for* your supper tonight, Dave."

"This is fine," David said.

Anna, Anna, Anna ... Her name sang in his head.

Now, even with Anna . . . even with Anna now . . . he was outside.

He was measuring out the middlings for the calf when the bus came. It stopped and Ellen got out. She started toward the house with her suitcase.

"Leave it there," David called to her from the shop door. "I'll get it."

"Well, don't run, child," she called back. "Now don't run."

"Child"!

This day . . . this day . . .

The pail of skim milk was almost more than his left arm could support on the way to the barn, but he didn't shift it to the right or set it down, halfway, and rest. Something unplastic, unbent, unshuffling in him, still drove straight ahead. His father, Joseph, would keep chopping as long as he could see, though his axe was dull and his feet were cold and the rest of the crew had given in to the blizzard hours ago.

CHAPTER XL

DAVID stood at the window now, watching the highway.

An ache fountained somewhere above the scar. It never rose to actual pain, but it seeped through his whole head. Rain had taken the first snow on the fields and then the sudden cold had come. Detail came clearly enough to his sight, but it was as if another glass, beyond the glass of the window pane, covered everything, made touch between any two things impossible.

He stood absolutely still.

"What are you doing, David?" Ellen turned from the rug.

He didn't reply.

"What are you looking at, child?" she asked again.

"Nothing," he said.

She turned back to the rug.

"Have you fed the hens, David?" she said.

"It's only two o'clock," he said.

"It will soon be dark . . ."

"It's not dark yet."

She filled the spaces between two circles with strips of the tablecloth. Blue . . . she searched for a strip of blue.

"Have you fed the hens, David?" she said.

He turned then, suddenly. In a single movement he took his cap from the row of hooks beside the window and put in on his head. He took his jacket from the next hook.

Ellen turned. "Where are you going, child, at this time of day?"

"Not very far," he said.

"Will you be warm enough? You're not half clad."

"Yes, yes, I'll be warm enough."

"Don't fall."

He put on his jacket and filled up the stove again. He hesitated. "The stove's all right till I get back," he said.

Blue . . . blue . . .

Yes, that was blue. That was David's. That was a blanket. That was the blanket they'd wrapped David and Anna in the night they were born. They were twins. But David was not a baby. How . . . ?

She turned. "David," she began, "how . . .?"

There was no one in the room. *David* was here. Where was David?

David walked down the path to the gate. The wind had turned the mailbox at right angles to the road: the mailman would think there were letters to go tomorrow. He straightened it automatically. He stepped into the road without looking.

A car swerved and its horn blew. He started. The sound of the horn gave him that instant sense of exposure. The woman in front looked at him idly, without break in her conversation with the driver. His glance didn't follow the car when it had passed.

He went across the road slowly, his eyes on the ground, then past the barn and over the bars between the cow yard and the pasture. In the pasture his step quickened. He hurried across the cradle hills and around the bunches of juniper and alders, to the road that went to the top of the mountain.

His mind was still. The headache and the beating of his heart and flesh were suspended, with a downward tension, from his brain. They were in his head like a sound. His flesh had weight without solidity. His thoughts clung tight to his brain, like a fog that hugs the fields. There was no beat in the day. Time was not a movement, but a *feature* of the frozen fields.

It was not the mood of defeat. Defeat pushes the inside back a little, but the inside and the outside remain distinct. Nor of despair, when the gap widens further still: there is still the bridge of conscious loneliness. Nor of apathy, when the inside is routed completely and the outside moves in to fill the vacuum.

Though the will remained unbroken, it was the mood *after* all these. The movement was reversed. Even the sensations of his own flesh had become outside. The inside was nothing but one great white naked eye of self-consciousness, with only its own looking to look at. The frozen landscape made no echo inside him. There was no tendril of interaction.

And then (in the reverse of what happens when you stare at a pattern of lines until suddenly the pattern moves off the page and cleaves to your retina), as he looked at the frozen landscape it was as if the outline of the frozen landscape *became* his consciousness: that inside and outside were not two things, but one—the bare shape of what his eyes saw.

His legs moved automatically. He spread the wires of the fence apart and bent to pass through them. A barb caught in his pants. A little gust of irritation bifurcated the inside from the

275

outside again. He extricated the barb from the cloth and let the wires fall back into place.

As he straightened, a dizziness whorled in his head like the sinuousness of the medicine he'd taken as a child, when it was poured into water. He waited for the darkness to thin away.

He walked quickly down the sidehill of the pasture, and there was the log road before him, shining and straight. Sled loads of wood had compressed it hard and smooth. Until you were close enough to see the yellow urine-holes of the men and horses, and the manure and hubble-peak ground brown into the whiteness, the runner tracks shone like isinglass.

He stepped out onto the smooth road. All at once walking became almost effortless, as if his flesh had levitated.

The road crossed the swamp, dotted with alders and clumps of reed, before it disappeared into the dark shelf of spruces at the foot of the mountain. A team of horses was coming across the swamp toward him. Grey moustaches of frost ringed their nervous nostrils. They lifted their sharp-shod feet daintily. Their necks arched nervously sidewise as if a play of heat lightning were never still in their muscles. Their flesh shuddered with it as when, in the summertime, they tried to dislodge a fly.

It was Steve's team, David saw, as they came closer.

Steve sat on a bag of hay at the front of the load. He held the reins tightly in one hand, and in the other a long peeled switch. Now and then he'd flick a shred of bark or lichen off the wood with it, or let the frayed tip of it drag alongside the sled. He watched intently the little wake of granulate snow that followed the runner as the runner sheared through the crust.

His mind was still too. But not in the way that David's was.

No thought shaped itself into the boundaries of singleness or clarity; but the ingredients of thoughts slid and mixed together in his head softly. They rose and fell smoothly in the bright hard day, the way the sled runners rode up against rocks by the side of the road now and then, and then slipped smoothly back into the track. Health was in him like a cadence. It was memoried only with the bright day-memory of food or heat or cold, or the shivering night-memory of softer flesh against his own. He wasn't conscious of his body at all. It was neither inside nor outside.

Steve's half-thoughts made a cadence only slightly louder than the unattended cadence of his flesh. They drifted upward from his mind, then thinned away, like a column of smoke flattening out and dissolving in a lazy air.

He had a half-plan forward (to dig a well?) . . . a half-reflection backward (the log *leaning* right, but the wind wrong) . . .

a half-picture of some face in another time (with maybe a wisp of half-sadness), or of some word that had been spoken or would be spoken (not heard now as from a tongue but like a word read). The smile or the frown appropriate to it came through partly to his lips. He had a half-shimmer of a touch (another child maybe . . . his son's face seemed like the only possible way a son of his *could* look, but what might a girl look like?) . . . a half-recognizance of now (the sled runners worn thin—then the smell of the coal in the forge and the sound of the bright hammer-clink on the bright-hot steel) . . .

He had lived as many years as David, but time itself was a thing he would never hear or see. There was inside and outside for him too, but he would never look at the eye of his own watching. He saw the trees and the fields. Yet in a way he didn't see them at all. A tree was a tree, a thing for the axe. A field was a field. You hauled across it when it was frozen, ploughed it when it was soft. That's all there was to it.

Steve came close. The image of the fields was replaced in David's consciousness by the image of his own face, obtrusive and transparent at the same time.

He and Steve kept their glances awkwardly apart. They gave no indication they had seen each other until the distance between them was just right for the first words of recognition. But as soon as they had spoken, the awkwardness disappeared. David's mind deliberately suspended its own nature. It assumed the cast of Steve's. He could synchronize his behaviour with any of theirs now. He could put their thoughts into words; and hearing them spoken, they'd be as pleased as if they'd been able to find the words themselves.

Steve would expect some congratulatory remark about his new team, then some reference to the body. The body was Steve's one steady joke.

David glanced along the load. "Cord or better?" he said.

"Yeah. Little better'n a cord, I think . . . Nine, ten feet."

Steve stretched out one leg and drew a packet of makings from his overall pocket. He rolled a cigarette. David straightened the nigh horse's breeching.

"Nice little team. Twelve hundred?"

"The mare's around twelve. Horse's a little heavier."

"A little quick, ain't they? But I'd rather have em that way . . . and willin."

"They're willin all right. I musta had thirteen feet on em yistiddy . . . green wood. Look, them things jist rabbit-jumped that raise be the house there." He ran the switch over the washboard of wrinkles in his high leather boots.

"How's the goin?" David said.

"Beautiful. She's a little scratchy on the pavement, but the mountain's beautiful. Hell, I had to bridle the front sled too. Goin choppin?"

"No, I guess it's too late today. Just takin a little cruise around."

"I see a nice pocket a second growth up there on you when I was huntin this fall. I don't believe it's had an axe in it since yer grandfather cut there."

"No, I guess it ain't. I'll have to strike that some day soon."

There was a moment's silence. Steve put the reins under his rump. He flailed his arms a couple of times around his chest.

"Sharp, today, what?" he said.

"Yeah," David said. "Should have a mitten for the old thing today."

"Yeah," Steve said. A little smile lit in his eyes, as if some secret place had been tickled behind the slow dark face.

"I guess you'll pull something up over it tonight, eh?" David said.

"You're damn right," Steve said.

He laughed out loud. David laughed too and moved off.

Steve started the horses. A minute or so later he reined them up again.

"That's what *you* wanta git, Dave," he called, "a little thing to pull over it these cold nights."

"That's what I got to do," David called back. "Save on wood, eh?" But he was far enough away that Steve couldn't see his face clearly. It wasn't necessary to fabricate a smile this time.

Steve moved on. His thoughts were defined, now.

Tonight. Yes, sir, boy. The little smile nestled through all his flesh. He glanced at David. Comical duck. Make a dog laugh. Queer bugger. Choppin! Hell, he just goes up there and roams around. I see him roamin around up there last week. Funny bugger. Not much like old Joe. Kee-roust, *that* man could chop. Dave ain't strong, though, I guess. ("Not strong" was like the name of some place in his son's geography, where people with strange customs lived.) Wonder how his heart is these days. No good to ask him. Can't git nothin outa him. Queer bugger. Good bugger, though. Never see him flustered. Never see him mad but that once—the night Chris picked out the smallest pack of moosemeat fer him to carry. Never know them two was brothers. Smart bugger. Smart as hell. God, that thing could spell in school . . . And figures . . . And books . . . Funny it never got him nowheres. Nothin stuck up about him, though. Wonder if he ever gut around that Bess Delahunt after she married agin . . . er that girl a hers . . . what was her name—Effie? Plan he did. Never find out from *him*, though. Close. ("Git over there, Molly! Where the hell d'ya think ye're . . .?") Roamin up there all be himself and it cold enough to . . . Comical duck. What was that he said, now? . . . *oh*, yes. The secret little smile came back. You're darned right he'd pull it up over tonight . . . (How did that new song on the radio go—"You're my filligiducha, shinimarucha . . ."? He hummed it, amused.)

He glanced back once, at the bend of the road. David had gone out of sight. He shook his head. Comical duck . . .

David moved along the road. His mind was still again. The scrub spruce became thicker nearer the end of the pasture, but he could still glimpse the bare fields through them. Even the ghosts of whatever things had happened here seemed to have fled. A no-memory was in the trees bleaker than the cold.

He came to the pole bridge at the foot of the mountain.

The brook was frozen inward from the rocky banks, hard and colourless. Only at small open spaces near the centre could the water be seen. It hung in drops from the scalloped lips of the ice and flowed coldly over the drowned reeds beneath.

He stopped at the bridge. He stared at the pads of a rabbit track. They were stalked like mushrooms by the snow thawing beneath them, then freezing again. His gaze was like a child's at print he can't read. The cold air's circle of contact with his head defined his head's heaviness.

Then he began to feel the air like a hand at his temples. It sent a little of its coolness inside, drew a little of the heaviness out. It made a little shrug in the stillness like the first deep breath after a long quiet hour in a closed room.

And then a little blood began to steal back into the day's flesh. A little pulse crept back into the road and the trees, like flesh made face by the information of invisible thoughts behind it. A living movement began to come into the insensible movement of the brook, as a trouble melts and moves as it begins to be told. Everything he looked at was refocused (though not quite instantly: the voice that breaks into sleep is woven into the dream for a second, before the second of waking).

His mind had a new stillness now. When a quarrel's heat is past, and then the friend's devaluation is past too, there is only overture necessary for reconciliation. Just before the inundation of peace made again, there is that sort of stillness then. Tendrils of thought began to curl outward. The way his grandmother and the fields had seemed to him struck him with a kind of penitence; as if they had been docile before some wounding on his part. Even his illness seemed like some guilt of his own.

He took a long deep breath. And then he began to climb the mountain.

II

The mountain rose with immediate sharpness from the beach of the pasture. The spruces at its base were impenetrable to the eye. There was no breeze, but a sigh hung in their branches all the time.

David walked along the road through the spruces. He bent forward to the incline. The beating of his heart brought a kind of lightness to his body now. The cold air and the rush of his blood thinned the ache and the emptiness, distributed it more tolerably throughout all his flesh. A brightness played over his thoughts, like the quickening of fever.

He stopped a minute at a spot where the road levelled off. He noticed two cigarette butts on a bare patch by the flat rock. He lit a cigarette, himself, and looked around. He could see nothing but the spruces, from turn to turn, and the smooth white lane between them. The sight of the houses and the bare fields (stripping as the first cast of dawn that sentences the wakeful's last hope of sleep) could not reach him at all. He was alone. Now he was absolutely alone.

He said, "It's perfect here." Involuntarily. Aloud.

With the use of his tongue, the sound of it suddenly in the stillness broke the grip on his thinking as the first halting words of forgiveness do. The face came back to everything.

Shape and colour reached out to him like voices. The black-green sweep of the spruces' lower limbs like an inhalation sustained immobile in the chest of the tree . . . the yellow-green of the hemlock branches, twig-laced in a snow crystal pattern, like a breath outward . . . the lemon-green murmurous-needled pine overturned by the wind, its ragged anchor of roots and earth like the shape of the thunder of its own falling . . . And, beneath the trees, was the other, inch-boundaried, earth-clinging forest : the brown-green moss and the mayflower runners and botany-book topknots; the grey-green, antlered lichens. And here was a stump that had once been green, but now was white as bone; and there was a grey rock, heavy with its own un-shapeliness. It had never had any touch of green at all, nor ever would . . .

He thought of the fields. Unseen, they no longer seemed bare. He thought of the people in the valley. Now they were out of sight, his own face moved kindredly among them. They were pliant in his mind's eye to whatever aspect he cast them in. His thought didn't fall back before them, as it did before the shrivelling light of their physical presence. (Angry words you have ready dissolve if the other is unexpectedly smiling; the joke dissolves if he is sullen.)

He could think of anything now. Everything seemed to be an aspect of something else. There seemed to be a thread of similarity running through the whole world. A shape could be like a sound; a feeling like a shape; a smell the shadow of a touch ... His senses seemed to run together.

He looked at the high blue sky and he heard again the first sound of his father's sleighbells coming home from town (holding his breath at the corner of the house, to make the listening more intense). He felt again the touch of the ground under his feet as he ran inside to tell Chris and Anna and to wonder together what his father had brought them. He tasted again the water that ran cool and clean even in the dusty summer beneath the scooped-out banks where the ferns grew. He smelled the thick safe smell of the spruces and he felt again the touch of Anna's hand the day she'd left her play to pick blueberries to buy herself the silk dress on the catalogue cover. It had come dark and she hadn't come home and he, of them all, had been the one to find her. She had been lost and crying, and he had cried too—because he had found her, and somehow too because she had only a few berries in her dipper and those were full of green ones and leaves ...

He felt the touch of the log road under his feet and he smelled the incarnate oranges on the Christmas tree. He tasted again the incredibly translucent saluting "wine." You barely sipped it at first so it would never end, then more fearfully still when it did lower in the cup; but it was sweeter somehow when it was almost all gone ...

He saw the grey rocks and he felt again the great ashen bolt of sickness that came out of the barn floor into his stomach the second before unconsciousness, and saw the shadow of the mailbox on the road the day he'd opened Anna's letter and the word "telegram" struck at his eyes ... He heard a jay cry, and he saw the light strike through the branches again after his first blindness in the daytime, that first time with Effie ...

It was as if time were not a movement now, but flat. Like space. Things past or future were not downstream or upstream on a one-way river, but in rooms. They were all on the same level. You could walk from room to room and look at them, without ascent or descent. It was as if the slope of time had levelled off at this moment. It didn't go by while you were reaching out to touch it. It was waiting for you. It waited for you to straighten things out, before it moved on.

He moved on. The brook crossed the road higher up. He lay flat and drank. His face was mirrored in the brook. It was parched looking as with sleeplessness. The blood of his thoughts made no fulness in his cheeks or eyes. Strands of hair escaped raggedly under his dislocated cap. He didn't remark his face in the brook; or how, when his lips touched the water, its image wobbled and disintegrated.

When he rose, the blackness swam in his head again. He stood and waited for it to clear.

I'm tired, he thought, I should go back. But it wasn't like the tired when you had to lift not only the dreaded log but your muscles too. It was like after that, a long time after that. Then any of the logs was possible to lift, because your muscles were bottomless.

He walked on.

And now he was halfway up the mountain, where the leafless hardwood began. Past the branch road where he and Chris had built the lean-to and believed that made them feel like men for the first time; past the branch road where he had done the thing with Effie that he'd thought was the miraculous short cut to manhood, but hadn't really changed anything; past the highest point of the brook that had held all their images at some time or other as they knelt to drink, and now fell downward behind him.

The road elbowed here. It cut perfectly flat across the mountain, then turned sharply upward again.

The hardwood, unlike the spruces, stood singly and separate: the gaunt grey-bare maples with half shells of fungus along their sides; the slim white-bare birches with kidney-shaped dappling of brown on their curling yellow-lined bark; the shining-bare silver poplars; and the heavy-bare lizard-barked beeches. The cold yellow sun and the thin cold air hung and breathed in the spaces between them, like a great centrifugal eddy of lightness. Their limbless trunks broke into a twist of searching branches as they reached higher against the sky. They were as still as their own laced shadows in the soundless air. There was no green here at all. Last summer's leaves lay on the ground, carpeted tight with the cold. Their membraneous yellow was diamonded with white pinpoints of frost.

There was a clearing on the left. Here switches of maple sprouted from the stumps. They had the pink blush of blood.

And along the road here, there was the pink blood too.

David remembered the shots he'd heard yesterday as he watered the cows. A tiny trail showed on the runner tracks, where the blood had stained brightly at first, then fainter as it honeycombed into the icy crust. It had gathered and dropped steadily from the loose body of a rabbit in some hunter's hand.

He stopped again, to rest.

And, turning, suddenly across the clearing and swiftly downward over the dark shoulder of the spruces, in the swimming mist of lightness like a breath caught in falling, he saw far-off and beneath him and in every sharp detail the whole stretch of the soundless valley. This stretch of the road was on his own woodlot. He was alone. The safe wall of spruces was protectedly between him and the valley. And far below him he could see his own house and his own fields.

A cloud skimmed the sun. With it, a wide skirt of shadow slid swiftly along the road, then disappeared. He had seen a momentary undulation ribbon through the oatfield like that on a still summer's afternoon.

And suddenly a breaker of exaltation rushed through him in just such way.

It was the thing that comes only once or twice ever, without hint or warning. It was the complete translation to another time. There is no other shock so sweet, no transfiguration so utter.

It is not a *memory* of that time: there is no echo quality to it. It is something that deliberate memory (with the changed perspective of the years between changing the very object it lights) cannot achieve at all. It is not a returning: you are there for the first time, immediately. No one has been away, nothing has changed—the time or the place or the faces. The years between have been shed. There is an original glow on the faces like on the objects of home. It is like a flash of immortality: nothing behind you is sealed, you can live it again. You can begin again . . .

A spring of tears caught in David's flesh. He wasn't standing on the road at all.

He was waking that clean April morning and touching Chris's face to wake him too and tell him that the very day was here at last—the day they were going back to the camp on the mountain. And he saw how wonderful his father's face was for *not* knowing (as he himself did) what a splendid thing he was doing as he adjusted the strap lengths of his pack . . . and his mother's for not knowing what mystery she dealt in as she packed the food . . . and his grandmother's for not knowing his legs could never get tired . . . and Chris's for not knowing how wonderful he was because he was going too . . . and Anna's because (all at once he thought he was going to cry) she had to stay home. And because they didn't know (as he did) that the road of all the days ahead would be long and wonderful because they walked together . . .

And then, again and again, like the mounting of music that keeps passing the melody from one instrument to another, he was translated to other moments . . .

He was lying in bed after the dance, wider awake than he could ever be in the daylight. The swirl of the dancers he'd watched from a corner, the eddies of laughter, and the heart-swinging fiddle music moved livelier than ever in his brain. but there was a kind of hunger following along behind it all, and reaching for it.

And then, all at once, the answer to it came. A quiet spread out over all the loose ends of excitement. It gathered them up into a swimming peace. It was so beautifully simple: When he grew up he'd be the best fiddle player in the whole world . . .

(They were dancing past now, his music springing in their movements. They were smiling at him. And then they stopped dancing and came and stood beside him, quietly. They looked at him with a shining in their eyes, as if they couldn't understand how it was *possible* for anyone to play like that. And he was so proud and humble both. And he loved them, he loved *everything*, when he heard his own music and saw the way they looked at him. It was so wonderful and easy and he had *found* this thing he could do.)

And then he was sitting in the schoolroom . . .

The afternoon sun dozed on the jack-knife designs cut into his desk and on the Map of the World and the Globe and the softwood floor. A bee was buzzing against the bottles of molasses lined up along the windowsill. The room was like an island of hush inside the great whispering *out*side of the ripe fruit on the huckleberry bushes and the ball waiting to be thrown and the long steep hill. And he tried the arithmetic problem that was three grades ahead of him. He tried it several ways, and then he saw that the number he was dividing with this time was the same odd one (139) as the denominator in the fractional part of the answer at the back of the book. Everything inside his mind was gathered up in one great shiver of unity. He knew he'd be the most famous mathematician there ever was . . .

He was in the kitchen, *again*, that day they were talking about the drive . . . and suddenly he rushed out and broke the jam. He could hear the great shout from the bank, as he leapt from log to log, because no one had believed it could be done . . .

And then he was in town. In the tent at the fair. The strangers were crowding about him, and his father's hand had never seemed such a good thing to have in his. Then the man and girl with the bright scarlet shirts came out on the platform and danced. They were so wonderful you couldn't imagine what sort of thing they could be saying to each other when they stepped back inside the curtain. And then he was driving home after dark and sleep was so near that if you closed your eyes the wagon seemed to be going backwards . . . and suddenly he knew he'd be the most wonderful dancer that people had ever seen . . .

And then he picked up the magazine that blustery afternoon. He saw the pictures of sailors leaning over the rail of a ship, and he knew he'd be the only man who ever went every single place in the world and did everything in the whole world there was to do . . .

And then, abruptly, he was standing on the road again. The trees were back in their places. The moment of translation had passed as quickly as it had come.

He lit another cigarette and went on. The road climbed sharply now, and straight, to the top of the mountain.

His heart was beating fast. And now the voices of the things he saw had an edge of insistence. A sharper, drawing, eating challenge. They began to swarm. They asked, and then listened, to be heard exactly. He had felt this insistence of theirs before, but never as now. Never so bold and relentless, giving him no quarter whatever.

His mind was not confused: that was the exquisite tantalization. If he took the voices one at a time, his listening could trace sharp and clear every vein of their story.

And yet some unquenchable leaven in the mind's thirst kept sending it back for the taste of complete realization it just missed. Even if you listened thoroughly, they seemed to wait, with that awful, chiding stillness, for something more. The mere *presence* of the objects about him was like a kind of accusation. It was as if you'd been given eyes for the first time; your first sight was met by the teeming insatiable hunger to be seen, of everything there was. The swarming multitude of all the voices it was physically impossible to attend to gave him a sense of exquisite guilt.

The fact of that maple growing exactly that way; that beech; that pine . . . That little cloud that way and no other; that little cloud I didn't see, exactly the way *it* was . . . The road running that way; and all the runner tracks laced over it exactly as they are . . . The number of the leaves; the exact number of all the leaves . . . That birch; the trees behind that birch . . . The sun; exactly the way that shadow is under that poplar; exactly the way the shadow was there yesterday . . . That cradle hill; exactly the number of all the cradle hills; the shape exactly of all the cradle hills I do not see . . . That limb twisted that way and exactly that shade of grey . . . yes, the twigs on that limb; exactly the way each twig is bent; yes, yes, the *leaf* on that twig; exactly the way the veins are in that leaf and no other way; exactly the way the sap is inside each vein I cannot see . . . The number of needles on all the spruces; exactly the way each one is bent; and the way the one I didn't see moved in the wind yesterday; the way the cells inside that one needle were; yes, exactly the way the sun made a shadow on that needle in the smaller-than-a-second of that morning a year and twenty-two days ago . . . The exact way the log chain spun itself a little channel in the snow on the road; yes, exactly the way that one lump of snow spun that day; the way the one crystal and the smaller-than-crystal of that lump of snow spun that day; exactly *what* it was; and the motion of it, and the colour of it; and the shadow of it; in that very place, unlike any other . . . And exactly the number of crystals of the snow in other places and other times that I didn't see . . .

The voices became suddenly infinite. Each one fanned at the touch of thought into another infinite divisibility.

They sounded and rushed in his head until it seemed as if he must go out *into* these things. He must *be* a tree and a stone and a shadow and a crystal of snow and a thread of moss and the veining of a leaf. He must be exactly as each of them was, everywhere and in all times; or the guilt, the exquisite parching for the taste of completion, would never be allayed at all.

The road rose sharper still toward the top of the mountain.

Now the hardwood was greater. The limbs began higher up on the trunk, and the breath of the cold sunlight in the spaces between them lifted lighter and lighter.

Time was moving again, faster than ever now. Each moment just escaped the reach of the moment before it.

And David's legs began to move faster. Without direction from his mind. They moved now like the limbs of one who has run until he can run no longer, yet runs on because the voice of his frightened child is still calling. His heart was beating faster too. He didn't hear it at all.

And now the fact of exactly the way that *faces* happened to be—exactly that way because of exactly all the *feelings* behind them—added its cry to the voices of the objects about him. It was a more exquisite accusing still.

. . . the face of my father nights in the kitchen listening to Anna hear my spellings, hearing a son of his own flesh spell correctly words he himself didn't even know the meaning of . . . His face the day the hay was perfect to haul in and then the wagon wheel struck a rock and broke. When he unhooked the horses from the wagon the nigh one tangled in the traces and sprained her hip so she could barely put her foot to the ground. Then suddenly the wind came and flattened the corn, but the rain didn't come; and then we got out the single wagon after the wind died down and put the single horse between the shafts and Father smiled at me and said, "We'll lick her yet, son" : and then, right then, the first great drops of rain came . . . And his face the night the day's work was all done and the lonesome-shadowing sun sank red in the windows of the church and the barn and in the needled-over puddles by the woodpile and Mother came in from the line with the chilled clothes in her arms, still silent, and the long silent evening and the long silent night were ahead.

. . . yes, and my *mother's* face that night . . . And the next night when Father looked at the flowered wallpaper she'd put on alone and silently all through the day and said, "That's the prettiest paper we ever had" . . . Her face that day in town she had on her best voile dress and the town woman came into the store clothed in silk beneath her fur coat and with shining black gloves. His mother had held the flaps of her coat tight together over her own dress with her bare hands and he'd wished suddenly that he could kiss her . . . And her face that day she'd come from behind them when they carried his father to the house, holding her apron down tight against the wind with both hands . . .

He was almost running now, as if in escape. But the faces pursued him, with the relentless challenge of exactly how each one was.

. . . his grandmother's face sometimes when she was busy and they'd mention England or the sea and she'd look out the window for a minute and her hands would lie still in her lap . . . And her face (and the town woman's face) when the town woman said to her, "We're collecting all around for the novelty sale, Mrs Canaan—but of course we don't expect you to spare anything you need," and she answered, "I have a cup of my grandmother's that Queen Anne drank from once . . . but I don't suppose any of *you* women would have occasion to use that here, would you?"

. . . and Chris's face nights when he'd come in from the plough and Charlotte would say, "Chris! Look at your feet! Do you think I *like* to scrub?" He'd go back and wipe his feet on the grass and stand a minute in the yard and then walk slowly to the barn, though there was nothing in the barn to be done . . . And his face the day he came back, after the lay-off at the factory, and Charlotte hadn't gone to meet him at the station . . . And the day a month ago when he said, "She's left me. They've rented the place to me and gone to live with the old bitch's mother in Beaverbrook" . . . And every night now when he drops in to see how we're getting along but I never say, "Why don't you come home with us?" . . . And his face the day I showed him Toby's wrist watch and he said, "Could I wear it fer an hour er so?" and I said, "No. You might break it."

. . . yes, and Toby's face (why was the challenge just to listen to it exactly, so much sharper than the old challenge to make his own like it?) the night they'd been playing that foolish game of Telegrams. Toby said, "*I* know. D-A-V-I-D. 'Dave's Arotic. Very. Interested. Dames.' " and Anna said, "But it's 'e,' dear. *E*-rotic," and I said, "How about, 'David's Appendage Very Interested Dames'?", and we all laughed . . . And Anna's face a minute after, when Toby said, "Dave, you oughta see some of those dames in Naples" . . . And her face the day—he looked about him as if for some place to run, the way he'd looked about the field that afternoon three years ago when Toby went away for the last time—the day she was playing blindman's buff with the other children. When it was her turn to hide her eyes the other children giggled together and then ran home and left her standing there and I went out and said, "Anna, I know where there's a robin's nest" . . . And her face a week ago when he'd said, "Why don't you *stay* home, Anna?" He knew from the look on it that, now, she'd be less lonely working in the city.

. . . yes, and his own that day too, feeling the most awful blankness he'd felt yet, for knowing that he didn't really mind that Anna didn't want to stay . . . And the face of Chris and of Anna and his own face, if he could have seen it, that day they got turned around on the mountain. They thought they must be almost in sight of the fields, and then they came again to the same tree they'd left an hour ago . . .

He brushed at his forehead, as if he'd run into a cluster of floating cobwebs.

But there was Rachel's face at the window when Bess would go down by and she'd say, "It's no wonder Effie's no better'n she oughta be" . . . And the faces of the men at the frolic when Bess would go down by and they'd wink at each other and make indecent motions with their hips.

. . . and Bess's own face the morning of the Christmas tree at school when the rest of them stopped for Effie, with their teacher's presents of handkerchiefs or cakes of Baby's Own Soap wrapped in tissue paper in their hands. The women who collected for the treat hadn't called for Bess's fudge that she'd put the extra nuts and raisins in, and she had no present for Effie to take at all. Then, desperately, she took the new feed calendar off the wall and wrapped it up in a cylinder of brown paper and all the children snickered because anyone could tell it was only an old calendar . . . And her face the day I was working alongside the road and she went by blindly with her apron on in the middle of the afternoon, choking out to herself, "Fred, I never . . . I never, since I married you . . . You had to listen to Rachel. God *knows* I never, not once . . ." And Fred's face (and theirs) that same night when the brook-smell was cool on the Baptizing bank and he knelt and put his hand on her wet clinging hair. He looked at the others as if he'd strike them when they tried to help him carry her home and he carried her away all alone.

. . . and Effie's face too, that day of her sickness, the first time I'd ever seen her in bed; looking in Bess's clean soft bed as if that were the only place she'd ever belonged, and forgiving me without understanding for the tear the bushes had made in her skirt and for the stain of kerosene on it.

. . . yes, and Steve's face when he'd pick up a magazine off the lounge and make out he was reading the lines but his eyes would be slinking sidewise to any pictures of girls on the opposite page . . . And Jud's, setting off the day the rate collector caught him in the barn and just as the rate collector went behind the brindle heifer she coughed and her bowels moved at the same time . . .

He smiled at that. For a couple of minutes the listening lulled and slackened altogether.

Then as the climbing became sharper still and the sunlight still brighter in the cold spaces between the larger trees, the accusing quickened again. It was like the woodsaw gaining such speed that the teeth disappeared.

All the faces there were everywhere else in the world, at every time, waited for him to give the thought to exactly how each of them was. (What about the Englishman or the Frenchman or the Micmac who might have stood on this very spot exactly how long ago?) There was the listening fact of the presence outside him of every eye, every lash, every smile-wrinkle of every cheek that had ever been; possible to be known, but unattended, because he had never seen them . . . And the frightening clarity . . . *I could realize the whole content of everything there is,* he thought, *if they didn't swarm so.*

He came to the spot in the road where he could see the keel-piece. They had never limbed it out. They had let it lay there when they cut and hauled the rest of the wood around it. He looked at it.

I can think of my father sinking his axe again and again into the keel, he thought, *and then the wind coming and the tree falling, and the single thought seems to contain it all. But just as I move on to something else the thought breaks down like a stream forking in the sand. Then the forks fork. Then the forks' forks fork, like the chicken-wire pattern of atoms . . .*

There is the branch of the tree growing exactly that way because it has stood there exactly that number of seconds and because its roots broke and wandered exactly as they did under the earth (and under that map-shaped patch of shell ice with the algebraic equations—what is my calculus book?—for its million kidney-shaped markings and parabolas and "Nude Descending a Staircase" patterns—what is the mind of a man who would draw like that?—exactly as they are), and because the sun shone on it that particular way in some second gone by. The blood in my father's body ran exactly that way because the elbow moved exactly so and because he glanced up at the sky so that the skin puckered beneath one eye exactly as it did. The foot, standing where it was (If we hadn't taken the car that first day!) when the tree fell, contained the implication of everything that bent it to this spot exactly that way and then. The hands' muscles moved as they did because the chemistry of food into tissue was exactly so . . . And exactly what was his hand, with the chemistry of the hair on the back of it exactly so, and there then, partly because of exactly all the things it had touched: my mother's face, and Anna's and Chris's, and mine . . . ? And "hand" is a word, and what is a word? . . . And "n" is a letter in the word, shaped exactly that way, and sounded by exactly that movement of the tongue, and in exactly how many other words? And behind the tiniest delta in the tiniest line in my father's cheek, and behind the smallest of the smallest arcs of movement of his arms, were implicit exactly all the thoughts that led him here . . . exactly here . . . exactly then . . .

All the thoughts there were, at every time!

A new panic struck him. *All the thoughts behind every face,*

at every time . . . They had a *double* accusing, because of themselves *and* of the things they mirrored. They were shapeless
and infiltrate through each other. Their fluctuate form was not
traceable in space or boundable by time. It was broader than
space, and faster than time, and not containable by definite
quantity in either. But each one was exactly as it was, just the
same . . .

He halted suddenly.

"Stop!" he cried. Aloud.

But the voices didn't stop.

They added a new voice to their frenzied forking, to the
bright singing stinging scream of clarity in the accusation of
the unattended. Exactly how did the voice *itself* fluctuate,
according to the exact inexactness of the listener's listening?

He thought: Myself amongst them, *thinking* of myself
amongst them . . .

He screamed "Stop!" again.

But as if in answer, yet another still-quicker multiplying
multitude was added. (As if, though the first charge was un-
answerable, yet if it were somehow answered, he would be
free . . . and then a sudden overwhelming accusation was seen
beyond that one.) Suddenly there were all the voices of all things
everywhere at all times as they *might* have been. If the wind
had been exactly that infinitesimal way different sometime . . .
If somewhere some face had smiled a hair's breadth differently
. . . If only one thought had shaped itself exactly that little way
other than the way it did . . . Then all the rest of it . . . He heard
the crushing screaming challenge of the infinite permutations of
the possible . . . the billion raised to the billionth power . . .

He screamed, "Stop, stop . . ."

Then he thought: Myself screaming "Stop." Then he
thought: Myself thinking of myself screaming "Stop," thinking of myself thinking of myself thinking of . . .

And then he put his arms about the great pine and thrust his
forehead against its hard body. He screamed, "Stop . . . Stop . . .
Stop . . . STOP . . ."

And then he raised his head and he saw that he was at the
very top of the mountain.

He had been within sight of this great solitary pine before,
but he had never stood beneath it. It was beyond the last ridge
of the great hardwood. Beyond it the lane of the road levelled
off between low-clinging scrub, and then fell.

He looked down at the valley and the river and the road
beside his house.

His own house was tiny and far-off but clear in every detail, like a model of itself. He looked over the hardwood and the spruces and the patchwork of choppings and the whole stretch of the log road, twisting and turning through the trees and then rising sharp and straight to the top of the mountain. Everything was beneath him now. The breath of falling caught in the distance and the clear sharp air.

Sometimes after a long stretch of freezing the wires sing with the cold. The ice is bound and shining with it. The ground and the trees are locked with the bearing of it. All things have hidden their blood away from it, but their voices and features are sharper still. Then the air that has been taut with the stillness of it relaxes at one definite instant.

As then, the air softened now, all at once, as he stood there.

And, without warning, suddenly again, the translation came.

All the voices were soaked up at once. Not in a vanishing, but as the piercing clamour of nerves in fever is soaked up in sleep. Sleep is the answer. At the moment of waking again their voices are still there, but the finding of the answer goes out over them, smoothening and softening and absorbent as firelight. There is no accusing in them now. They are like the challenging strangeness of a figure walking back-to along the road. As you come closer it turns and discloses the face of a friend.

He stood there, looking down over the mountain and the valley, and it was as if the sun-shadow passed swiftly over all the voices as the sun-shadow had swept across the road.

I will *tell* it, he thought rushingly : that is the answer.

I know how it is with everything. I will put it down and they will see that I know.

(Once, while he was still in school, he had composed a petition from all the men in the village, asking the government for a daily mail. When he read it back to them they heard the voice of their own reason speaking exactly in his. Their warm wonder at his little miracle of finding the words for it that they themselves couldn't find, or recognize for the words of their own thoughts until they heard him speak them, made him and them so fluid together that it worked in him like a kind of tears.)

As he thought of telling these things exactly, all the voices came close about him. They weren't swarming now. He went out into them until there was no inside left. He saw at last how you could *become* the thing you told.

It wouldn't be necessary to take them one by one. That's where he'd been wrong. All he'd have to do . . . oh, it was so gloriously simple . . . was to find their single core of meaning.

It was manifest not differently but only in different aspects, in them all. That would be enough. A single beam of light is enough to light all the shadows, by turning it from one to another.

He didn't consider *how* he would find it. (The words he'd put in the scribbler before now had never fallen smooth over the shape of the remembrance, or enclosed it all. But the minute he put the scribbler away the perfect ones seemed surely possible to be found the next time.) Nor how long it might take. (If you took a hundred years, then—though neither this thought was explicit nor reason's denial of it, for the swelling moment to transcend—he would live a hundred years.) He knew only that he would do it . . . It would make him the greatest writer in the whole world.

The sun-shadow passed swiftly through his mind. The translation was utter. It lasted and spread in him like the swimming exaltation of wine. (They had all read his book now. He felt that wave of pride and humbleness both, as they looked at him and thought: he understands everything . . .)

And looking down over the whole mountain in the softening air to the valley beneath, it was as when the last load of wood had left the log road for the smooth fields and you looked back and saw the stumps where the chain had caught, and the rock that had smashed the runner the noon when the going was best, and the place where the skid had broken and upset the sled . . . but this was the last load. There was nothing left on the road to go back for now. The sweating and straining and fearful caution as you eased the patched-up runner over the cradle hills, and the sharp watch on the sun that threatened to take all the snow, were all of yesterday: made now a comradely kind of song.

He saw his own house in the valley, and tiny and far-off his grandmother come out on the porch.

She is old, he thought, and *she* sees everything so dimly. He had a sudden pang of guilt; because of that, and because of his sharp reply to her about his clothing.

I will ask her if she's warm enough, he thought, the first thing when I go through the door. Then I'll go over and tell her that's the prettiest rug yet.

Everyone seemed suddenly radiate with a neglected warmth, which waited only for his overture, to be released and glow.

I'll go over and help Steve unload his wood, he thought. He's as good a fellow as I know, Steve is . . . I'll make the light shine kindly on him in the book. On all of them. I will

293

tell them just as they are, but people will see that there is more to them than the side that shows. They're rough in their speech and in their bodies, but when they're sober they're never thinking sly thoughts. They curse and they bla'guard, but it's not really cursing and bla'guarding at all, it's so thoughtless—there's never any cast of chill or connivance about anything like that they do. None of it sticks to them. And when they do stop to think of anything they've done and are penitent, they're hurt more keenly and inexpressibly in the penitence than the offended ever was by the deed. When each of their days is over, all its roughness is rubbed out when they quiet down to sleep, like the innocent erasure of a child's sleep. They're intricate as anyone else, but there's no hardness about it. They're the best people in the whole world.

He caught his breath. He felt like the warm crying of acquittal again. Even my mother and my father and all the others who are gone will know somehow, somewhere, that I have given an absolving voice to all the hurts they gave themselves or each other—hurts that were caused only by the misreading of what they couldn't express. They will see that anyone who must have loved them so well, to have known them so thoroughly, could never have denied them once, as sometimes they may have thought I did . . .

I will ask Chris to come live with us, and he'll know that I forgave him long long ago. And Anna. How could I have ever thought that Anna and I could grow away from each other? (The morning of my first trip to the mountain, the Christmas tree, the blindman's buff . . .) How proud she will be when she sees what I have done. (The skates . . .)

He could hear his voice saying to her on the phone, "What do you think, Anna—my book won the prize!" Then the line would be still, because they'd both be crying; then they'd both be laughing at each other crying . . . Oh, Anna, Anna . . .

And then he felt the beating of his heart.

And then the blackness swam in his head again. He waited for it to clear.

And then the blackness turned to grey and then to white: an absolute white, made of all the other colours but of no colour itself at all.

And then the snow began to fall.

Ellen's rug was down to its last two concentric circles. She selected the rags for these very carefully. Scarlet. That was scarlet. That was the cloak David had worn the night someone laughed at his piece in the school play. She hooked in a rag of that.

Only one tiny circle remained. White. White . . . She picked up the scrap of fine white lace and made of it the last circle. She smiled.

"David," she called, "the rug is done. Come see."

He didn't answer. She turned, but he wasn't in the kitchen. Then she went to the door and called. There was no answer. She could see him nowhere.

"Where *is* that child?" she said. "You never know where that child is."

The snow began falling all at once, but without hurry. Gathering dreamily and thick, high up; thickening until the sun was gone, and then drifting slowly downward, each of the great flakes moving soundlessly in all directions, even upward again sometimes as if in memory of a breeze, and then, finally, levelling off and finding the road or a tree or some part of the valley to lie on. Near at hand they fell lingeringly and separate, like tiny white feathers from a broken wing; but farther off they made a grey cohesive curtain in the air itself; and far far off downward, over the spruces and the valley, they made a solid sheet like the greyness of twilight, that thickened denser still until the valley was completely gone.

At first they lay detached, each of them as nothing on the trees and the road; and then they began to aggregate soundlessly, but like a sound gathering, until the spruces had warm white epaulettes, and beneath the great maples the ground was all white, and on the trackless road there were no tracks but now a white track could be made.

A train whistled beyond the valley. Then it thundered along the rails and was gone. Its smoke hung behind it and settled in the valley, and then slowly it disappeared too.

The snowflakes fell on David's face and caught in his eyelashes and melted. They caught in the strands of hair that escaped beneath his thrown-back cap and melted. They melted in the corners of his mouth. They clung to the wool of his jacket and the wool of his mittens without melting.

And then they clung, without melting, to his eyelashes and his hair. And then they did not melt on his eyelids or on his cheeks or in the corners of his mouth or anywhere on his face at all. And then they grew smoothly and exactly over him and over the fallen log that lay beside him until the two outlines were as one.

A partridge rose in the grey-laden air. Its heavy body moved straight upward for a minute, exactly. But David did not see that.

And then its grey body fell swiftly in one straight movement, as if burdened with the weight of its own flight : down, between the trees, down, swoopingly, directly, intensely, exactly down over the far side of the mountain.

Afterword

BY ROBERT GIBBS

The way in to *The Mountain and the Valley* is, of course, through the Prologue – through those first sentences that compress and foreshadow so much. The opening sentence spans the whole of David Canaan's life, "all his thirty years" spent in Entremont. The second introduces "the log road that went to the top of the mountain," the way that David will take on this, the last day of his life. Following paragraphs design the setting for us: North and South Mountain, the river, the highway, the valley, wide but "shut . . . in completely." The seventh paragraph begins the process of representing the present hour, detail by detail, establishing a rhythm that, page by page, will cumulatively turn the narrative into a prose poem, musical in its large design and in its parts.

The Prologue's title, "The Rug," draws attention to a feature both of the large narrative design and of the local music. And in the Prologue, Ellen the rugmaker, as keeper of the family's memories, as designer, assumes her roles. The narrator tells us what she sees, looking at her work, her history: "The pattern of the rug was not intricate. It had a wide dark border, then a target pattern of circles radiating from the centre of the canvas." Ellen will complete her rug in the Epilogue, not at the border, but at the "radiating" white centre, which is there already in the design and from which the outer circles take their form and place as much as from "the dark border" where she began. She will complete the rug at the moment when David will reach the top of the mountain, when his consciousness transcends its limits as the totality of human experience appears to break in upon it. In his illumination, and in hers, is all the completion that Buckler's narrative seems to expect of art – and of life.

Though the simple lines and taut frames suggest a rigidity in the large design, Ellen and her rug music will return again and again in the novel as a kind of release. In the Prologue, the rug music asserts its character: "Red ... Red ... Yes, that was red. That was a tablecloth. The neighbours had given it to Joseph and Martha ... " Ellen's scraps and the memories they evoke here stand for the lives of the characters and for crucial events in those lives, which will be fully lived out in the chapters to follow. The broken lines of Ellen's thoughts contrast with the closed lines of her rug. They represent the rich, resonating details that will play throughout the novel against its analytical bent, its linearity, its formal symmetry – its dark border.

The progress of David Canaan's life will appear by the end of the Epilogue to be as inevitable as is the progress of Ellen's rug, but the substance of his and his family's lives will be as variegated as Ellen's rags. So what may seem at first to be an arbitrary and obvious formalism lodged in a single large metaphor turns out to be more organically musical in the way Buckler works it out.

One may ask, given the novel's richness of imagery and closeness of engagement, why Buckler felt any need for a large enclosing design. One could argue from its very pervasiveness that the design must have grown with the quotidian details rather than constitute an imposition upon them. Formal containment within the surrounding frame perhaps mirrors a view of life as appearing free when it is experienced moment by moment but, seen as a whole, evidently circumscribed. In other words, Buckler designs paradox into his novel, a paradox that is most apparent in the climactic mountaintop scene – the implosion that occurs in David's consciousness when the lid is about to shut on it and on the novel.

One may also want to link the formal design to the period when the novel was written. The years after World War II, the late 1940s and early 1950s, brought to some writers – a whole generation of British and American poets, for instance – a need to forsake free and open forms for tighter, more traditional ones. The need may have been partly a response to the unsettling effects of the War; it may have reflected a distrust of revolutions and brave new experiments. For some of these writers, tighter forms meant closer irony, reflecting moods of sadness, emptiness, and bitterness following on the strident slogans and unspeakable horrors. For other writers, as they looked back, the pre-War period began to be seen as a relatively innocent and stable time, for which formal order seems an appropriate counterpart. And in still other instances, as in the poems of Dylan Thomas, formal designs acted as "containers" in both senses of the word, of impulses, dark and light, that could scarcely be contained. Buckler's very use of strict formal design, therefore, invites the reader to appreciate the tensions of a whole historical moment as well as of one individual's life.

In a poem-novel, care in shaping individual sentences, paragraphs, and chapters inevitably extends to care for the total design. I think it significant, however, that for his third book, *Ox Bells and Fireflies*, written in the 1960s, Buckler found an open form, totally unlike the design of *The Mountain and the Valley*, even though he drew his matter and imagery from the same sources and used them again to suggest how rootlessness and isolation had displaced connectedness to family and community, and to the earth itself.

An important means of ordering any narrative is the voice. Buckler uses a narrator whose omniscience, in the sense of his knowing things that his characters do not know, at times becomes explicit, though he never presides with the overt cosmic irony of a Hardy narrator. Illusions of distance between narrative voice and the consciousness being depicted vary constantly. For instance, at times an analytical voice predominates, often attempting close definitions of indefinable relationships. Here it describes David's role among his peers: "It wasn't brotherly liking, but a kind of narcissism. He seemed forever, by the twist of essentiality he gave to whatever they said or did, to be disclosing and illuminating a part of themselves they'd never recognized before."

Another voice not attached to a particular character depicts diurnal and seasonal events in passages (and sometimes whole chapters) that compose short prose poems within the larger structure. Such is Chapter VII, which begins, "In the country the day is the determinant. The work, the thoughts, the feelings, to match it, follow." The impersonal voice often modulates to one more involved with a particular character's responses. One mark of this modulation is a shift to second person – "You awoke again, all at once. The instant thought that another day had something ready for you made a really physical ticking in your heart." The shift impersonalizes and generalizes, while at the same time it draws the reader in to a close complicity with the presiding voice and so with the consciousness being depicted.

In the second part of Chapter VII, David's thoughts filter seasonal events as he ceaselessly rehearses his lines for the school play: "He thought of them when Chris was dropping seed potatoes, aligning the odd one that tumbled out of place, with his foot; pressing it into the soft brooch-coils of manure automatically." The play of "the words" against physical phenomena builds through the rest of the chapter. Between it and the climax and anti-climax, which occur in Chapter X, the pure idyll of the Christmas chapters suspends yet sustains the excitement. David's apotheosis, the height toward which these chapters and Part One as a whole have been building, comes during the play:

> None of all this was consecutive and time-taking like thought.
> It was glimpsed instantaneously, like the figures of space.
> And orchestrated in the subliminal key of memory: cold
> water reaching to the roots of his tongue when thirst in the
> haymow was like meal in his mouth . . . the touch of the
> crisp dollar bill he had changed his dented pennies for. . . .

Here the analytical voice gives way abruptly to a discontinuous series of sensations, which reiterate the music of Ellen's rugmaking and forecast the greater apotheosis of the Epilogue.

These chapters, VII to X, are among the most lyrical and free-seeming of the novel. Yet they complete the large outer circle of the design. Even into the idyllic interlude of Christmas, dramatic irony inserts itself with the recurrence of David's dream:

> David slept and he dreamed that they were all walking back
> the road that led to the top of the mountain. All the trees
> along the road were Christmas trees. They were shining with
> presents, but as he reached for something (for himself or for
> Anna) the thing would disappear, and Herb Hennessey
> would be there, cutting down the tree.

Looking back from the end, one can see how this dream, a version of which appears in Chapter I, represents the pattern, repeated in large and small events, and highlights its symbols: the road to the top of the mountain, the evanescent Christmas shine. Herb Hennessey, the solitary, representing an antithesis to the Canaan family, makes ominous appearances that foreshadow David's state of isolation at the end – or the state he might have reached if the end had not come.

The Mountain and the Valley is not a romance. David, unlike Anne of Green Gables, does not rise from his mistakes and disappointments unscarred, nor does Chris, Toby, Anne, Joseph or Martha. Momentary lapses and chance interruptions – the word spoken out of season or not spoken when called for – have lasting consequences. What occurs in the Canaan family over two generations and through the War mirrors the larger world in its movement from stability to restlessness, connectedness to rootlessness.

There is, though, for all the irony in its design, a kind of transcendence at the end of the novel. The central consciousness depicted retains at the moment of dissolution its will to affirm: "I'll make the light shine kindly on him in the book. On all of them." And serenity remains in the completed pattern, in the figure of Ellen the survivor as we last see her: "Only one tiny circle remained. White. White . . . She picked up the scrap of fine white lace and made of it the last circle. She smiled." Following this, the narrator puts in place his own last piece, beginning quietly – "The snow began falling all at once, but without hurry." – but ending dynamically with the flight of the partridge "down between the trees, down, swoopingly, directly, intensely, exactly down over the far side of the mountain." David's soul flying out of its valley? Natural life going on, patterned but not confined? Whatever it is, it leaves this well-closed book, in a way, unclosed.